DESTINY'S BOOT

The Barsian Job: Part One

FJ Mitchell

Cover art and illustrations by Nataly Zhuk

ISBN 978-1-9160626-0-3
Printed and bound in Great Britain
by Clays Ltd, Elcograf S.p.A

FJ Mitchell can be found on her website:
www.fjmitchell.co.uk
and
www.authorsreach.co.uk

To Dozer.
he stole our toast
and our hearts

and our sandwiches
half a boot
the last piece of cake
the middle of the cake
and the box the cake came in

he's in the book
for when we need to find him
and feel his nose on our knee
his tail in our eye socket
and his love

and to my mother who would be horrified
at taking second place to a dog
but even more horrified not to be mentioned at all

Contents

LEVENBRANDT

WYRDFRITH
FOREST

BAY OF
PINES

PINE HARBOUR

No

ORE

WESTERN
OCEAN

THE SCAR

GREATMOUTH

SUREN
FOREST

FULLPORT

THEOGENES

AZURE STRAITS

High Haven

THE BA
YEAR 2

Prelude

THE WATER WAS red and churning for a few moments. Then came the noises – shredding, tearing and slurping. When all was finally silent the voices began to argue.

"You said he was strong enough."

"He was!"

"Not looking like it from here. He'll barely even give that thing heartburn."

"It was just bad luck."

"So what now? Who's next on the list for the interview?"

A piece of paper fluttered to just above the surface of the water and hung there. It was a long list of names, but every single one had been crossed out.

"There's no one else?"

New names suddenly appeared at the end of the list.

"You kept THAT quiet."

Reflected in the reddened water was a sudden flurry of activity from high up in the air. A large ship at full speed, fighting off three smaller ones. Bodies launched off the sides of the attacking vessels plummeted to the water below. Two of the marauders started to burn and the third suddenly exploded, scattering flaming debris across the sky.

"They seem efficient."

There was a brief cough of laughter from one of the commentators which was quickly smothered as a new and more commanding voice made her opinion known.

"We have tried all your other candidates. They failed. We move forwards with these, and we do it now. There isn't much time left."

"They'll still have to survive the interview."

"My dear, the interview will have to survive them."

Chapter One
Viva High Haven

THE SKY CITY of High Haven hovered at permanent anchor on the border between two ancient empires. Independent to its very core, the floating island was home to the dispossessed, the entrepreneurs, the criminals – society's misfits, free thinkers, and those with a flexible moral code. Carefully positioned at the nexus of several trade winds, free enterprise was the city's lifeblood: there was nothing that couldn't be sourced if you had the coin and nothing that couldn't be sold if you had the balls.

The majority of High Haven's residents had fled there from the Barsian Empire, which loomed just out of telescope range to the north. Barsia had once been all powerful, its gleaming and prosperous capital the envy of the world, but much like the white marbled buildings of its grandest city, its influence was now no more than

3

memories and dust. It was an empire without an Autarch and in that vacuum, the Barsian High Council's focus was survival, not glory. As a result of their desperate need to hold the fading nation together, all of Barsia, from Soleya in the south-east corner, to the northern bastion city of Levenbrandt, had been made to adopt a deeply conservative constitution. There were garrisons in every town, businesses were heavily regulated, and the use of magic was fiercely controlled.

In deliberate comparison, the flying city luxuriated in its independence. There was no central authority, no taxes and no laws against mages. In fact, there were no laws at all. The signs that stated: *'High Haven, even if you get brutally murdered here, you'll die free'*, were both warning and promise. Savage honesty was the city's best policy and its streets were always bustling with people who appreciated the liberties that were utterly unavailable to them in Barsia.

As the sun shone down on High Haven's busy port one glorious morning, it highlighted the diverse array of ships bobbing gently at their moorings and the vibrancy of the multi-coloured buildings behind them – everything looked exactly like a holiday brochure. The beautiful scene was undeniably the best view of High Haven, for once you walked into its streets, the reality of so many people living on a chunk of floating rock was a visual you wouldn't want on any postcard. The buildings and their occupants were all pushed together like the vegetables in a fridge drawer – colourful and fresh on top, dank, desperate and sweaty beneath. It wasn't a city for delicate constitutions or anxious dispositions, but it was a perfect place for pirates.

On board the *Warrior*, one of the sleekest vessels in the sky harbour, Captain Philip Kennedy Junior sat in his cabin and slung another cup of black coffee to the back of his throat. He was still tired after spending the previous day trying to create the perfect job advertisement for new crew members. Things had been bloodier than usual in the last few months, as it seemed there were more aspiring sky pirates than ever before, and many of them coveted not only the *Warrior's* success, but also her rakish looks and powerful aetheric crystal engine. Originally, Kennedy had appreciated their good taste, but when ragged schooner after ragged schooner tried to attack them, it became boring as well as bloody.

As the clock chimed the hour, Kennedy got to his feet, briefly checking his appearance in the mirror before heading out on deck. To his immense satisfaction, at least thirty applicants were clustered amidships under the watchful eye of the *Warrior's* existing crew. He was just about to call for the first candidate when he noticed his half-brother, Sparkz, heading towards him.

Kennedy had never known he had a sibling, so the day Sparkz had stepped aboard the *Warrior* had been one of the most exciting of his life. At first the conversation had been somewhat downbeat as Kennedy learned that his brother's life had been drastically different to his own. Sparkz hadn't had a supportive family, in fact he'd been alone since he was a teenager. He'd worked a hard apprenticeship before living hand to mouth as an engineer on any ship that would take him. After several minutes feeling decidedly uncomfortable about his own privileges, Kennedy had assured his brother that his life was now transformed. The *Warrior* had been without an engineer for a few weeks – did Sparkz have any experience of aetheric crystals? For example, did he know that prolonged exposure to an unshielded one was the quickest way to melt an actual brain? Of course, that was a completely random question and nothing whatsoever to do with the current vacancy.

Kennedy's memory of the day he'd gained both a sibling and an engineer so intelligent that the *Warrior* not only flew faster but had aetheric-powered indoor plumbing never failed to make him smile. Having water pressure so fierce that he'd had to commission metal toilets from the local foundry always gave him full bragging rights at any pirate bar.

As he waited for Sparkz to join him, Kennedy stood proudly in the doorway of his cabin. He'd made a point to dress up for the interviews, so he was wearing his best tie – the one without any rips or stains – and he'd even secured his man bun with two bootlaces instead of one. Brushing imaginary crumbs off his long coat, he beamed at his brother as he walked over and leant casually against the cabin wall.

"We're matching, bro!"

"Yes, we're both wearing a black coat. You know I don't own any others." Sparkz shrugged indifferently. "Remember? Lonely, abandoned boy roams the sky routes with only what he can beg, borrow, or steal."

"And I am so sorry. I wish our mother had told me – I would never have stopped looking for you."

"Would have been a lot easier than tattooing her family crest on us when we were born," Sparkz muttered, shoving his hands in his pockets.

Granted, that overly personal moment of truth when

they'd both revealed their well-hidden tattoos had been awkward, but after Kennedy pointed out that they were just two grown men alone in a room, with their trousers around their ankles, comparing body art, it had become a lot more awkward.

Not wishing to dwell on that memory for long, Kennedy cleared his throat in what he hoped was a deep and commanding manner before mentally preparing himself for the long morning of interviews.

As he and Sparkz stood together, shoulder to shoulder, no-one would pick them for relatives. Kennedy was the boy whose pirate parents had owned their own ship and instilled him with confidence and self-belief. When he was old enough, they'd set him up as the captain and disappeared, leaving no forwarding address. He was a muscular unit of a man, easily standing a head and a half above his brother. His wavy blond hair gave him an angelic air which was perfectly matched by a dazzling smile that could light up a room.

Sparkz, in comparison, had a smile which could light up a small room with lots of windows as long as it was noon on a cloudless summer day in the tropics. His hair and eyes were dark brown, his gaze rarely still. Where Kennedy was open, Sparkz was guarded and where Kennedy had an unrequited yearning for one member of the crew, Sparkz had been requiting her regularly.

"You said no one in their right mind would want the job; but look at them all!" Kennedy gestured triumphantly to the mass of applicants assembled on the main deck.

Sparkz flicked a derisive glance in their direction. "I have. And I stand by my previous comment, brother.

Not a decent pirate among them. They're all either decrepit, addicts, sob stories, idiots, or poxed. That guy – look at him – even his pox has pox." He pointed at an orc who looked like his eyes were about to drip out, slide down the crack in his bulbous, greasy nose and dribble over his inflamed lips. "You're being naïve, Kennedy, most of them just want to rob us."

"Don't be so judgemental!" Kennedy looked over at his brother with a challenge in his eyes. "Prove it."

"Simple." Sparkz raised his voice to address the crowd. "If anyone's here to kill us and steal our shit, just crack on already."

A good two-thirds of them immediately surged forwards, pulling weapons free from their belts as they moved. Kennedy's eyes widened in shock, and he grabbed for his swords. Just as his palms closed around their hilts, the charge suddenly halted, the would-be attackers in front being slammed into by the ones behind until there was an untidy dump of bodies in the middle of the deck. All of them were staring, their horrified eyes fixed on a spot above Kennedy – the roof of his cabin. Then, as if driven by a single thought, almost every hopeful withdrew their applications, turned, and ran. They streamed away across the deck and even fought each other to get to the gangplanks. Some shouted, some screamed, some even cried, but in under a minute, the hostile takeover had been reduced to a pity party.

"She's doing it again, isn't she?" Kennedy asked his brother as they both stared rigidly ahead.

"The Misspelt one?"

"Don't start this again." Kennedy hissed. "She's literally right above us. I can see her shadow."

Sparkz's lips twitched into a grin at his brother's discomfort. "I know."

"So stop!"

"Stop what?" Sparkz's voice was the epitome of innocence.

"The name thing! You wind her up and walk away while the rest of us have to deal with the results."

"A-r-k-e spells Ark. If she wants to be called '*Arka*' then she should spell it properly."

Kennedy rolled his eyes. "It's a name! You use a Z instead of an S at the end of yours."

"Still sounds the same."

Their whispered discussion was interrupted as a woman's voice, dripping with droll amusement, called down from the cabin roof.

"This is *not* a care home for the terminally useless. Kennedy, you suck at recruitment."

Without another word, Arke landed neatly beside them. Even if the horrifying illusion of a king cobra wreathing her head and neck hadn't been present, her entire look should have been a warning to the unwary. Shirt, trousers, boots, glances – all dark, all day, every day. To anyone bold enough to remark on her unchanging wardrobe, Arke's answer, if she was in the mood to provide one, was always the same. Firstly, she hated shopping; secondly, black showed less blood; and thirdly, it was her way of limiting collateral damage. Sensible people who just wanted to live sensible lives would think twice about bothering someone who was permanently funeral-ready.

As the ship's deck emptied of the would-be attackers, Arke cancelled her illusion, the snake ebbing away into puffs of blue smoke which dissipated in the sunshine. Everyone who knew her was well aware of the fact that she *could* charm the birds from the trees, but they also knew that she was far more comfortable making them so terrified they just flew away. The giant snake effect was excellent crowd control, as the magic that created it also made every single viewer believe its dark eyes were looking right into their own and its spectral fangs were ready to bite only them. Arke shook her head wryly as she looked over at the *Warrior's* crew who were sheathing their weapons with obvious relief.

"This *should not* be a care home for the terminally useless."

Kennedy tried not to look directly at his crewmate when she became the monster who ate the monster that lived under the bed. He enjoyed the effect an application of pure terror had on their enemies, but the sight of her in that monstrous form was enough to make him rush to the little captain's room. It didn't matter that she'd been his mother's best friend and present for his entire life; what made Arke herself was also what set her apart from everyone else.

Arke was a Soulbound; simply put, she'd signed away her soul to a demon in exchange for the use of their magic. Doing so had changed her body as well as her life: she no longer aged normally, she could absorb more damage than was natural, her short hair was so brightly silver it shone like a beacon, and her eyes were pits of darkness in her always pale face.

"None of them died. I must be losing my touch." She shook her head slowly as the last of the rabble scrambled away from the ship.

Kennedy glanced at her, relaxing as he saw that her essence of snake had completely disappeared. "There's still two honest, brave and worthy applicants left!" He looked back at the deck with an almost child-like delight. "Look, there's a salty old pirate, he looks wise, and strong and…"

His words were cut off by a loud thud as the wise, strong looking, old pirate fell to the deck, quite dead.

"Annnd he's just really tired?" Kennedy continued hopefully. "Ellie, could you render the gentleman some assistance please?"

He watched Ellie, the only halfling on the crew, scuttle across to the body, check for a pulse, and then look up at him with a shake of her head. As Kennedy flicked a meaningful glance from her to the gangplank, she grabbed the body by the boots and started to drag it away while frantically puffing into her straggling fringe to keep it from obscuring her vision completely.

"Dead. Tired," Sparkz remarked acidly.

Kennedy squared his shoulders resolutely. He absolutely refused to let another minor setback diminish his positive mood. "There's one more applicant and they're an Ornithol! I don't think I've ever seen one so tall. Their beak looks razor sharp, and they have their own wings. Just think of the possibilities!"

He bounded over to greet the rainbow-coloured applicant like an overexcited Labrador. "I'm Captain Kennedy – thank you SO much for coming to see us today. Here on the *Warrior* we can offer you all the excitement and adventure you ever wanted. In the interests of full disclosure – there's also the occasional moment of danger, but we always face it together.

Teamwork makes the dreamwork!"

The Ornithol tilted their head this way and that as they listened to Kennedy's effusive speech, possibly unsure whether they'd found a job opportunity or the High Haven Insane Asylum. They might have jumped to an interesting conclusion if they'd turned around, as the old man's corpse, now wreathed with magical crackles of energy, had begun to rise unnaturally from the deck. Kennedy was perfectly placed to witness the incident and quickly tried to rescue the situation while Ellie grimly hung onto the body, sputtering a mouthful of curses as she fought to pull it back down. He knew there was only one person on board who was both willing and able to create such a scene.

"Arke, *thank* you for trying to *help*, but I'm sure Ellie is more than capable of conveying him to the dockyard chapel of rest." Kennedy kept his voice warm, even though he was silently and fervently wishing that the Soulbound would take a day off from her pathological 'get the dead off the ship before they're cold' policy. However, his forced positivity winced as much as he did when he remembered Arke's penchant for malicious compliance and the body suddenly thudded down on top of the halfling, pinning her to the deck.

"Blessings on his return to the perpetual rainbow. My name is Ruby. Is there an application form to fill in? I brought my own pen." Introduction complete, the Ornithol plucked a blue feather from her wing with the nervous nod of someone who'd been practicing her ice breaker since seeing the job posted on the noticeboard.

"I see what you did there! Amazing!" Kennedy beamed. "And ALL the blessings! Blessings on blessings for that old gentleman's tragic, untimely, sudden, unfortunate… condition." Kennedy tried to keep Ruby's interest on him, so it did not wander to where Ellie was clambering out from under the corpse and flinging her very wide repertoire of X-rated gestures in Arke's direction. "I have so many blessings on board. And no need for forms; none at all. We don't care about your past unless you want to tell us; all we need to know is whether you'll work hard and be loyal to the ship and her crew."

"Does it matter that I haven't sailed before? Or that I've only just left school?" Ruby asked, somewhat anxiously.

"A graduate, eh? That's excellent." Kennedy knew that new hires were so much easier when they didn't have preconceived ideas about how things were done. "Don't worry about a thing, we provide full on-the-job training!"

As he shook hands with Ruby to seal the deal, he spotted the Soulbound stalking directly towards Ellie and the corpse. Knowing her as he did, he did not believe that Arke intended to defuse the situation in any way.

"Ellie!" Kennedy called hurriedly. "Come and meet Ruby!"

The halfling quickly sidestepped the Soulbound's ominous approach and scurried over. As Ellie started to talk to the Ornithol, Kennedy took a moment to observe his new hire with warm interest. Being a giant, brightly coloured bird who sported a pair of humanoid arms as well as wings was a thing that few individuals could pull off without looking like they came straight out of the pages of a comic book. However, Ruby managed it effortlessly, her windswept rainbow chic rubbing shoulders with a childlike sense of innocence and that distinctly unchildlike razor-sharp beak.

Kennedy was thrilled to have even one fresh crew member on board, as he'd have been the first to admit that recently the *Warrior's* roster had rivalled the obituary column in the High Haven Gazette. At least they'd signed on before dying though, unlike the old seadog flying through the air towards the side of the ship. Suddenly realising what he was seeing, Kennedy looked up at Ruby, fervently hoping she hadn't noticed.

Unfortunately, for all his efforts to pretend the *Warrior* was a professional and disciplined ship, Ruby, with her incredibly keen Ornithol eyesight, was already watching as the ex-pirate soared limply over the side of the ship; her head swivelling to follow his trajectory as her beak opened in shock.

Thankfully for Kennedy's increasingly stressed state, Sparkz had been paying close attention to the on-board entertainment from a position near the gunwales. Noting the young Ornithol's growing consternation, he activated a red and blue sigil tattoo on his left index finger and pointed at the freefalling corpse, his magic instantly covering the old pirate's body in a pyrotechnic display which probably left it close to medium rare.

Tapping two fingers to his forehead, Sparkz turned to his brother with as serious a look as he could muster. "Blessings applied."

"Oh, that must be a traditional sky pirate burial!" Ruby exclaimed. "I'm so excited to learn your customs!"

Behind her, Kennedy flashed an overly enthusiastic thumbs-up at his brother. "We are more than happy to teach you; have a starter's bonus." He quickly pressed a ten florin coin into her grasp and shook her hand again, so deliriously joyful that he prolonged the handshake until Ellie hauled on the back of his coat, making him step away.

"Let's get you settled in the crew cabin," the halfling grinned up at her new crewmate. "You'll just have to remember to mind your head on the low beams. Captain never does, might explain a lot."

⚔ ⚔ ⚔

ARKE CLIMBED BACK up the ladder to the cabin roof and clicked her fingers with a burst of bright blue magic. In an instant, a furry monstrosity appeared in front of her, springing into the goofiest play bow that a slab of bones and tissue which had been infernally moulded into a Rottweiler could manage. She ignored the dog's effusive greeting and sat down, having to defend herself from his curly tail before it whipped her across the face as he leapt in circles trying to grab it. Dozer was clearly in an excellent mood and when he finally threw himself down beside her with a happy sigh, his mistress's hand automatically started to stroke his velvety fur.

Arke hadn't been a Soulbound for long when she'd suggested to her demon that a non-mortal pet might be good company, so it wasn't a surprise that she'd been a little naïve with her specifications. She'd simply said that she wanted a loyal companion that wouldn't die if it fell off a building, bounced on a series of awnings and landed in a magically derived pit of acid. Lucky had not been well named.

In retrospect, letting her demon choose a dog had not been one of her smartest moves. However, he'd sworn there had been no choice to be made as the only other canine available had been the most evil-natured creature to walk between the planes – a chihuahua called Mr Stumpy with three legs, two teeth and chronic hellitosis. That was a lot like halitosis, but his breath actually melted your face if you got too close.

Despite his many less than ideal attributes and an intelligence that rivalled that of a brick, Arke's bad good boy had always provided the companionship she needed. He'd also never been late for a single bedtime and even though she no longer needed him constantly at her side, Dozer was still the best hellhound she knew. Of course, he was the only one, but she didn't mention that as he tended to get a nervous stomach when he was upset. White lies were better than rancid Rottweiler farts or being woken by that ominous gulping that always heralded a sticky mess of whatever it was that infernal monstrosities ate when they were in their home plane.

Arke was enjoying her sunny moment of peace until it was interrupted by a heavily accented male voice. As ever, her demon's words were contained entirely within her own head and the sound as familiar to her as her own internal monologue. "Now that all the excitement is over, I could not help but notice that you are feeling devilish today. Maybe you are in the mood for a song?"

"Start warbling and you're spending the rest of the day in my wardrobe."

"One moment amicable, the next, scorched earth, when all I was doing was making a suggestion to pass the time more companionably." A dramatic sigh reverberated through Arke's skull before the speaker brightened again. "Perhaps we should warm up for the induction of the new crew member?"

"Doubt we'll be needed, rainbow bird doesn't look much like a troublemaker." Arke made herself comfortable, shutting her eyes with pleasure as the sun warmed the cabin roof beneath her.

"Compared to you, no-one does. Would it hurt to add a little colour now and again? Start small, maybe a grey shirt rather than black? A belt with a silver buckle?" The voice's tone changed as it became apparent that Arke had completely checked out of the conversation. "A purple feather boa, sequined leotard, patent leather high heels, fishnet stockings, fake eyelashes and a tramp stamp that says 'Bitch'?"

Most demons took little to no notice of their pledges, but Arke's was different – he believed in a far more personal approach. Not only did he give her his powers but also his sole attention, taking up residence in her body from the moment she'd signed the contract. However, that wasn't the only thing that set him apart from other soul-sniping denizens of another plane. Granted, he did appreciate a little light anarchy followed by a touch of chaos and finished off with some gory mayhem; but there was so much more to him than that. Even the crew, some of whom had been around since the first *Warrior* had been christened, had a deep, albeit wary, respect for him, since he fulfilled more than one vital role on board.

With Kennedy's proficiency in hiring the wrong person for the job, it wasn't a terribly rare occurrence that a new recruit managed to sour relationships on board to such an extent that not even a light stabbing would fix the problem. Although he vetoed actual murder among his crew, Kennedy wasn't averse to using Arke and her demon as the most hostile HR department in existence. When he became aware that a situation below decks was untenable, troublemaking newcomers were ordered to shadow the Soulbound for the day. The longest any of them had ever lasted was two hours.

It was never the dodgy dog, Arke's less than adorable nature, or the terrifying experience of her lesson in piratical swordsmanship that did it. Of course, those things didn't help, but in the end, it was always the introduction to her demon that broke the spirit of anyone arrogant enough to think they could throw their weight around on the crew deck. During the weapon drill, the Soulbound always made sure to have a one-sided conversation with her blade. The bout always ended in the same way, with some variant of the question: 'Why are you talking to a sword?' None of the troublemakers were ever the same after Arke's dark and mesmerising eyes clung to theirs while she explained that she talked to it because it was the physical embodiment of the demon who owned her soul.

"I can hear him all the time in my head, but when he is my blade it feels like more of a conversation." Her tone would be conspiratorial, her face an expressionless mask as she leant forwards and placed the hilt of the sword in their hand. "He wants to say hello."

"Greetings to you, my name is Stabbington Bear. I apologise for my strong accent – I am not from around here. Also, it makes me sound exotic and interesting."

On the rare occasions that they were stupid enough not to react to that introduction, the demon usually finished them off with an effervescent display of heavy-duty yodelling. Sometimes they would even pass out from pure terror, and he was always incredibly smug for days after that sort of over-achievement.

Sure, Stabbington was technically a demon, but he was also warmly encouraging, deliciously hilarious, and excellent company. His friendship with the young Philip Jr was the reason why Joy Kennedy had often tried to frighten her son with bedtime stories about demons that tortured people for eternity. However, in the 'do as I say, not as I do' manner of mothers in any plane, Stabbington was still her preferred babysitter. Nothing said perfect pirate parenting more than an unsupervised toddler dragging a demon blade around the deck of a flying ship.

While the demon and Kennedy were old friends, Stabbington's relationship with Arke was way more complicated. He'd been privy to everything, her thoughts, her dreams, every experience, for every moment they'd been together. And after forty-three years, that could be both comfortable and incredibly irritating.

Arke blinked, tuning back into Stabbington's lengthy soliloquy on ridiculous outfits and scowling in response.

"If I wanted a partner who never shut up, I'd have married one. At least there would've been some practical benefits."

"If I were your husband, I would need so much therapy we would be penniless."

"Don't worry, if you were my husband, I'd have killed you after a week."

"A week? Imaginary human me must be seriously hot."

Stabbington's tone was so satisfied that Arke wondered if his next request would be for a cigarette.

"You know what looks great at this time of year? The inside of my wardrobe," she snarled.

"You are VERY disagreeable today, so maybe I would like some quiet time, completely alone in the darkness, without any sound but the soft sobbing of a lonely, broken-hearted demon."

Arke was perfectly unmoved by Stabbington's descent into melodrama. "I'll leave Dozer on the bed. Your imaginary tears will be drowned out by his snores."

The voice in Arke's head was suddenly silent. Granted, it was the silence created by a sulking demon, but she was fine with that. He could never be quiet for long.

Chapter Two
On the Town

DARKNESS WAS FALLING when Kennedy finally finished his inventory and decided it was time to have some fun. The Pirate Festival of *Stealorama* was in full swing and doubtless there were already several bodies bleeding out in the gutters. To be honest, it was just another night in High Haven, except at *Stealorama*, churros were king. Kennedy was a complete sucker for sweet pastry treats, especially ones dipped in chocolate.

He marched out on deck, shouted, "Churros are on me!" and by the time he reached the end of the gangplank most of the crew were at his heels. It was a great feeling. He high-fived Ruby who was similarly excited and coincidentally the only sober one there since the others always pre-gamed. "This is how the *Warrior* rocks!" He had to repeat himself twice before his pirate posse could be persuaded to give the Official *Warrior* Return Cheer™ of 'This is how the *Warrior* rolls'.

Their performance was a little disappointing, but at least none of them deliberately fluffed the line this time. Kennedy beamed with pride and strode out, truly believing he was at the head of his loyal crew as they owned the streets, right up till he turned to remark on an interesting looking stall and found that they'd all vanished.

"Fine, pay for your own churros then." He licked his

21

lips in eager anticipation as he headed for the nearest vendor, more than ready to satisfy the craving that had been building all day.

After the third serving of the sweetest, fluffiest treats he'd had since he'd dreamt about eating his teddy bear, Kennedy licked his sugary fingers clean and wondered about undoing his belt a notch or two. It was time to head to the next location of his gastro-centric tour of *Stealorama's* delights. He was strolling down a quieter street towards the main market area when he suddenly felt a hand relieving him of his coin purse.

Knowing he was too full of decadent deliciousness to give chase in comfort, Kennedy closed his eyes in concentration for the briefest moment and brought his alter self, an ethereal representation of his own form, into existence. Like his father before him, Philip Kennedy had a single, but exceptionally useful, magical ability: he could split a section of his ego off to work independently of his main body. He knew Sparkz was more traditionally talented, the master of many spells, but to Kennedy's mind nothing bettered making a duplicate of yourself who could act independently, wield weapons, and always beat you at chess.

"Find the thief," he instructed and the alter shot off at a run. "The *other* way!" It chose the right direction on the second attempt and caught up to the miscreant in mere seconds.

So it was that Grimlet, a scrawny, scruffy, little orc who was just congratulating himself on the score of a lifetime, was swept up into the air by his collar. Part of Kennedy's ability to project his ego was the power to instantly re-fuse his corporeal body with his more ethereal one, even over considerable distances. As soon as his alter caught up to the young orc boy, Kennedy's physical self merged with it to apprehend the thief personally.

"Don't kill me, don't kill me! Please! I got to get money, I'm so hungry!" Grimlet croaked, struggling to pull the collar away from his throat.

"There's always another way," Kennedy replied, grabbing the coin purse from the orc's hand and placing it safely back inside his jacket. "Maybe we could sell bits of you for parts? There's always a market for those – which hand do you write with?"

"Neither!" the would-be thief replied hoarsely. "I don't go to school! Let me go, mister, please."

"Is this where you tell me you have eighteen brothers and sisters who will all come after me if I hurt you?" Kennedy lowered his prisoner to the ground, looking him up and down critically.

"No. I'm on my own. I promise if you let me go, you'll never see me again."

Kennedy grinned wolfishly and leant down towards the orc, his voice no more than a whisper. "No-one will miss you then."

Eyes widening in fear, Grimlet threw a wild punch at his captor who blocked it easily and suddenly burst out laughing, his expression changing instantly from menacing to warmly amused.

"Steady slugger, you could pull something swinging like that. I was just trying to teach you a lesson about what trouble you could get into if you don't work on your pickpocketing game. But on reflection, you look like you need a good feed and some clothes that don't stink like a sewer." He released the terrible thief with a smile. "My name's Kennedy. What do you want? There's a good sausage stall up ahead, too cheap to be real pork but it tastes enough like it."

"Folks call me Grimlet." The young orc hesitated for about as long as it took him to hear his stomach's next angry grumble. "You paying?"

⚔ ⚔ ⚔

ON THE OTHER side of the market, Ruby was following her nose. She was furiously hungry after spending the day learning all about life on her new ship and worrying that the sin of omission was still a sin. On her journey to High Haven from the convent of the Sisters of No Mercy, it had quickly become obvious to her that letting people know she'd been an acolyte of the god Chromatia was not her wisest move. Everyone she'd met had been friendly right up until she mentioned her background, after which they'd just made everything super weird. Either they'd almost demanded her blessings and prayers or left abruptly while making excuses so terrible even she realised they were lies.

As a result, Ruby had made an executive decision not to tell anyone at the interview, hoping that if she got the job she could prove herself to her new crewmates before coming clean about where she'd spent her childhood. However, that had made her conscience distinctly uneasy, and it had taken most of the day to convince herself that, since Captain Kennedy had told her he didn't need to know about her past, she'd done nothing wrong. With the release of the guilt inherent in her system, Ruby was finally able to contemplate food.

Walking past an alleyway, the most delicious scent

she'd ever experienced thrilled her senses and her empty stomach let it draw her along to its source. Just as she stepped out into a brightly lit courtyard filled with a small array of stalls, sideshows, and other diversions, she noticed the body of an ogre collapsed on a nearby bench, covered in what was left of a giant bag of the most amazing smelling food. Her genuinely kind nature and religious training overrode her need to eat, and she knelt beside him, praying. The whole worshipping thing had never been her strongest skill as she always forgot the words to the hymn or sang in the wrong key. Back at the convent, she'd quickly learnt to pretend to be doing what the others were and not to meet anyone's eye.

"I call on the blessings of Chromatia to aid you in your safe passage."

In the absence of remembering any more official verses, Ruby figured that this was the most appropriate (and easy) thing to repeat. So she just kept saying it, right up until the ogre moved, making the entire bench wobble as he sat up. He had a huge mop of dark brown hair, which looked not so much in need of a wash as a strong-armed man with a scythe, and his bloodshot eyes paid homage to the amount of liquor he'd already imbibed as he blinked at what was possibly the strangest hallucination he'd ever had.

"What do you want?"

His voice was hoarse, and Ruby inched away, realising that his breath didn't so much smell of alcohol as taste of it.

"Oh! You're alive!"

"Yeah?"

"I thought you were dead!" she blurted out, rather

panicked, as he leant forwards to stare balefully at her. "I prayed for you!"

"Uh?" The ogre frowned in a baffled manner and smeared a sleeve across his nose in a vague attempt to clean it. "Prayed? For Krugg?"

"Yes, I thought you were ill or you know…" Ruby mimed 'dead', head on one side, eyes crossed, tongue out.

With a chuckle at her play-acting, the ogre pointed a meaty finger at her. "Funny bird. Maybe we be friends."

"Yes!" The Ornithol was quick to agree, as she'd always regarded strangers as friends she had yet to introduce herself to. "My name is Ruby."

The unlikely pair beamed at each other, a bond of friendship instantly springing to life.

"So what does Ruby friend want to do?" Krugg asked uncertainly.

"Eat. What are those?" She pointed at the messy remnants of the ogre's snack which were strewn liberally over his person.

"These?" Krugg dragged a very limp, very squashed, very moist looking morsel out from his armpit and ate it with relish. "Chips."

"*Chips*." Ruby spoke the word slowly and deliberately, giving it a passion that had never existed in the world before.

"From over there – Maisie Oil's stall."

The Ornithol moved with pace and Krugg was left behind as she strode towards the vendor.

"I would like one '*Chips*' please."

A deeply unamused gnome with livid burn marks on one of her cheeks, looked her strange customer up and down judgementally. "What size?"

Ruby held up her hand, making an approximation of the size of an average chip with her thumb and forefinger. "About this?"

The scoop that was brutally slammed to the counter gave both Ruby and everyone in the vicinity fair warning that she was about to receive a deeply personal retort from the stall holder. Thankfully, the timely arrival of Krugg saved the situation.

"No need to get ratty, was just a joke. She'll 'ave a big bag with everything."

Together, Ruby and Krugg had more fun than an ogre and Ornithol had ever had. They ate a great many bags of chips, played Whack-a-Troll and even went splashing in the fountain until the rainbow-coloured bird learnt about the way *all* the public water in High Haven was recycled. However, not even that could lower her spirits, for she'd landed an actual job on a sky ship, made new friends and discovered the delicious glory of oily fried potatoes. This day had been one of her best days ever.

ẋ ẋ ẋ

ARKE'S EVENING WAS proving much less entertaining. As usual, when they were ashore, she'd been on Kennedy duty. Years ago she'd had promised his mother, that she would always watch over him and that was an agreement the Soulbound would never break. Granted, he was a grown man now and more than capable of looking after himself, but he was also equally and sometimes surprisingly capable of finding trouble. Normally ever vigilant, she'd inexplicably lost focus for a few moments while trailing him through the market, and ended up heading down some dark side-streets.

Her location didn't worry her, as she knew that there weren't many potentially murder-ridden alleys that didn't improve with the application of a few well-timed spells and a razor-sharp blade. Stabbington himself was still sulking, but this also relaxed her, for if there was trouble afoot, she knew he would tell her in an instant. So she let whatever muse was calling her do so in peace, and after a strange circuitous tour through the creepiest parts of town, she ended up in front of a dilapidated building. She regarded it with vague interest for a long moment. It looked like an old hotel that had been closed to guests for years; the front door hung part off its hinges and swung limply as if there were a breeze; from inside there came a faint light and some vague sense of music. If there was ever a scene from a horror story where the hero should never venture inside – this was it. Thankfully for her curiosity, Arke was not a hero, so she walked right in and found her way to the source of the light, a room which looked to have once been the hotel's parlour.

Ahead of her was a little round table covered with a frayed tablecloth, yellowed with what she hoped was just age. Two frail and ancient chairs, their fabric seats scoured and withered by the years, leant at jaunty angles. One was empty and the other was host to a what looked like a goblin, if goblins were ever victims of bad taxidermists. She could hear the music more clearly here, a gentle, plinking tune more reminiscent of a dentist's waiting room than a decaying, musty salon. The place had 'Murder Scene' all over it – the only thing that would make it more obvious was if someone had drawn a dead body silhouette on the floor next to a copy of the

Coffins 4 U catalogue.

"Welcome. Sit down." The goblin moved, its skin almost creaking with age as the body came to life inside. It smiled with all two of its teeth and as it breathed, Arke could almost see the ancient dust being propelled out of its lungs.

Arke's life experiences had been such that she was not in the least bit alarmed or surprised at the sudden reinvigoration of what, on closer inspection, looked to be a woman. There seemed to be no reason not to do as she was asked, so she perched gingerly on the other precarious chair which shifted in indignation under her. The goblin lady's paper-thin eyelids scraped rhythmically over her shrunken eyes as she surveyed the Soulbound intensely, all the while muttering some muffled words. At length she nodded, glancing to the side of the room briefly before pulling a battered pack of tarot cards from her sleeve and shuffling them with incredibly ponderous movements.

"Interesting scent you have. A touch of demon here, a whiff of something else there."

"Well I could've stepped in something on the way in." Arke's patience was usually rated in negative numbers and although the ancient goblin had piqued her interest, that was quickly waning. "If you're going to do something, get on with it before your body remembers it's been dead for years."

The wizened, trembling hands spread the cards on the table in a wide arc. "Pick three and only three."

Although Arke was vaguely disappointed not to be able to hear Stabbington's no doubt colourful descriptions of this strange experience, she remained unworried by his refusal to speak to her. She knew that the wardrobe was genuinely his worst nightmare and the last time she'd lost her temper enough to put him there, he hadn't talked to her for a week.

"Do I look that that much of a mug? What's the bet that these are all dire warnings of doom so it doesn't matter which I choose?" Arke asked, eyeing the cards.

"Three you shall pick," the goblin intoned, her expression unchanged.

With a shrug, Arke tapped on three random cards, suddenly tiring of whatever this was. Her guess was some sort of shakedown or robbery, but she wished whoever was plotting would cease the theatrics and get down to business. A good fight would liven up her evening, but parlour tricks designed to intimidate or unnerve were really not her jam.

A chalice. A hanged man. A tombstone.

"This is my surprised face. You'll notice it looks no different to my normal expression. I'm not paying for this, by the way."

Arke barely listened as the goblin woman made the expected dire prognostications from the cards. Her attention had shifted away from the crone to the empty bit of room that the goblin's eyes kept shifting to as she spoke. They were not alone, and she felt her adrenalin spike in response to that realisation. Now that the overture was over, surely it was time for the show?

"Very enlightening." Her tone made it clear that she thought nothing of the sort. "Do I get a drink after all that?"

With halting, skeletal articulation, the ancient goblin unfolded out of her seat and left the room. Arke tensed, fully expecting this to be the moment the hammer would drop, but nothing happened except the crone eventually delivered what might have been tea eighty years ago. Now it was congealed and vaguely sizzling. It looked too obviously poisoned to actually be poison and although the power move would have been to down the entire cup, Arke's flexes had never been beverage related.

Nothing about this place made any sense and as the goblin woman sank dryly back into her chair, Arke gave up waiting for anything more interesting to happen. With a blank expression, she stood up and carefully poured her drink all over the cards, making sure to douse every single one. When nothing happened, she shook her head slowly and left the building, dismissing the whole bizarre event from her memory.

⚹ ⚹ ⚹

BACK IN THE main streets, *Stealorama* was going swimmingly. There were book burnings at every street corner and children dancing amid the embers of ancient writings. Sparkz emerged from the largest casino in High Haven and leant tiredly against a wall, beer in hand. He'd headed off the ship straight after the morning's amusement and spent the day with the Wizard. That wasn't his real name, of course, but 'Tattooed by Wesley' didn't have the same ring to it. Working for his brother had been profitable and Sparkz had quickly been able to increase his skin art until all the spells he'd mastered were now represented on his body. His busy mind had always struggled when forced to concentrate on a single thing, so his discovery of the eye-wateringly expensive magical ink had been a revelation for him. It was worth every penny to simply be able to think of a spell and have it activate automatically rather than have to silence the forty-nine other things swirling around his head and commit to just one.

From the tattoo parlour, he'd set off to the casinos, pockets all but empty and skin tingling with the new magical ink he'd acquired. Not unexpectedly, but definitely to his immense satisfaction, he'd had excellent luck with the cards, winning both a pleasing amount of money as well as a curiously magical ring. It was too big for him and certainly not his style, but the power humming inside the decorative stone meant it was far too interesting to sell, at least until he worked out what it did.

Sparkz was both an astute gambler and a bad patient, so the moment a headache started to throb behind his eyes, he'd left the tables in search of some fresh air. He was sipping his beer and examining the magical ring when his peace was disturbed by a gaggle of noisy, drunken pirates chasing a pig up the street. He was aware that this wasn't a surprising turn of events on any given day in High Haven, but he was tired, and his tolerance level was on the marker labelled 'Boom'. Tucking his new ring away in an inside pocket, Sparkz pointed at the oncoming pig and watched as a tattoo on the back of one knuckle lit up, illuminating the glyph of an oil can. Instantaneously, the creature became covered in lard, stopping in confusion at the sensation, which allowed the pirates time to leap on it, their gleeful cries filling the street. However, just as quickly as they'd slid onto the pig's back, they slid right off again, starting up a full hunting cry as their slippery prey squeaked free and began to run again.

Sighing, Sparkz muttered about his need for peace and quiet and how the pirates were disturbing it. The pig and the pirates. He levelled another finger at the unfortunate creature, not even bothering to look at his hand as a different tattoo lit up. A bolt of pure energy arced towards the animal, striking deep into the porcine body. In an instantaneous fountain of body parts, the pursuers, the street, and a number of surprised seagulls overhead, were doused liberally with essence of pork. The pirates wiped gore from their faces and looked at a suddenly smiling Sparkz, whose headache had instantly cleared in the face of such a gloriously satisfying ending to the chase. Unsurprisingly, the group of mince-splattered men didn't seem as happy as he was and started towards him.

"Hey, that was OUR pig!"

Shrugging with broad indifference, Sparkz stirred the pot just a little more. "Now it's a pig jigsaw – a pigsaw, if you will."

That was enough for the pirates to lose their tempers. The air became thick with deeply ungrammatical threats and insults as the group stalked menacingly towards him, encouraging each other into a righteous fury about the forced abandonment of their hog roast plans.

With a surge of displeasure, Sparkz realised their shouting was already part way to bringing his headache back. It was time to clear the area. He cracked his knuckles before pointing a finger at one, then another and another, harmlessly causing the first to glow blue, the next red, yellow, green…

"This little piggy went to market… this little piggy

should've stayed at home… this little piggy became roast beef, and this little piggy became bone… and THIS little piggy went…"

The offal covered mob had stopped their cocky walk as the rhyme began and looked from one to the other as they became human fairy lights, clearly unsure about what to do next.

The first one to back up, muttering "This guy blew up a pig, I'm outta here", started a riot of standard face-saving calls of "He's not worth it".

The men scattered, running away down the street, and diving gratefully, if not gracefully, behind random passers-by for cover, just in case.

Sparkz waved sardonically and leant back against the wall. He was enjoying another swig from his bottle of beer when he spotted his brother walking up the road accompanied by what appeared to be a scrawny orc wearing clothes he'd stolen from the local drag venue. He raised his eyebrows for a moment before remembering his brother had a penchant for rescuing waifs and strays. Sparkz had only been on board the *Warrior* a month, but he knew the score. The ones he'd met had already ended up dead, but Kennedy's heart was in the right place. Unlike Cuthbert's. And Roger's. One month, two street kids. This was number three. Child safety was tricky on board a sky pirate ship and in Sparkz's opinion, this one would make an excellent target with a shirt that sparkled like a disco ball and flares so huge you could hide a pair of geese under them.

He was about to go and tell the kid his days were numbered when he saw Kennedy accidentally bump shoulders with an even more sartorially unhinged local.

Taking a moment to fully assess the scene, Sparkz couldn't help but note that if it wasn't the season for ruffles in High Haven, the self-styled gentleman was determined to make it so. He was wearing absolutely every ruched ripple that money could buy.

The collision itself had been nothing, but he watched with interest as the would-be fashionista postured wildly at the alleged affront. The woman on his arm, dressed in a manner that promised everything but revealed nothing, quickly stepped away as the drama unfolded.

Sparkz raised an amused eyebrow as the ruffles quivered with indignation in Kennedy's general direction. "Are you seeking an appointment with my fist, sir?"

This was fine entertainment and he dropped his empty bottle in the nearest rubbish bin as the indulgently clad young man affected a boxing stance, performing what he must have thought were perfectly executed jabs in his opponent's direction. Flicking a curious glance towards the woman, Sparkz chuckled as he saw the pained expression on her face and guessed that she was starting to regret offering the girlfriend experience. Someone was *not* getting lucky this evening.

"It was just an accident."

Sparkz heard Kennedy's brisk rebuff and saw his brother start to walk away when the other man's perfectly manicured hand grabbed his arm.

"It was not. You assaulted me!"

Sparkz's smile grew wider as the situation escalated and he watched Kennedy pluck the man's hand from his sleeve before stepping away.

"I'm sorry you think that. Have a nice evening."

Although Kennedy had shown no indication that he was paying much attention to the beruffled man's blustering, Sparkz knew his brother was never unprepared. As Kennedy moved to disengage from the situation completely, the man-about-town swung a punch at him. With the swiftest of countermoves, the incoming fist suddenly became Kennedy's stress ball. As the bone-crushing pressure on the man's hand drove his opponent to his knees, Sparkz watched his brother look down with an icy expression that wordlessly promised intimate knowledge of the afterlife.

"Either you lie down, or I will put you down."

In a sad end to Sparkz's floor show, the whimpering gentleman finally recognised his tactical error and nodded quickly as Kennedy's resolute grasp manoeuvred him around to face the darkest puddle on the street. Neither participant mentioned that it was probably only around fifty percent rainwater as the defeated challenger prostrated himself, ruffles bobbing on the ripples of shame.

Sparkz pushed off the wall and sauntered towards his brother with a thin smile. Kennedy nodded politely at the very disappointed, probably very ex-girlfriend, before addressing the garishly dressed orc in a fatherly tone.

"His choices led him to that puddle. There is always another way."

No-one spouted crap as eloquently as Kennedy and Sparkz was opening his mouth to remark on that fact when he heard his brother's tell-tale snort of amusement as well as his far less fatherly comment.

"Plus I've only just had my coat dry cleaned. Blood's

an absolute bitch to get out of the stitching."

Heading down the street in his brother's wake, Sparkz was perfectly placed to enjoy the sight of the soaking wet gentleman on his knees, trying to recover some dignity and wiping his now furious face clear of murky water. His appreciation of the scene only rose as he looked up and realised he was in the right position to see the finale of the performance. Stepping from the shadows, an expressionless Arke strode directly over to the scowling fashionista. Sparkz knew that the Soulbound was never one to leave a beaten opponent capable of retribution, so he was not surprised when, without breaking stride, Arke's knee hit the ruffled man square in the face, landing him in the filthy puddle once more. The man reacted with some deeply irritating high-pitched mewing noises, but thankfully these were silenced as Arke's next step brought a foot down heavily onto his face with such an audible crunching of bone that several plastic surgeons in the town were woken from their slumbers.

Catching the Soulbound's eye as she strode away from the puddle, Sparkz raised a hand in wry salutation and continued walking, catching up to his brother just before Ruby and Krugg emerged from a side street ahead. After greeting them enthusiastically, Kennedy launched into a far too animated infomercial about the most incredible stockist of diamante flares he'd found in the market. It was when the words 'crew uniform' flew excitedly from his mouth that a horrified Sparkz had to step in, quickly suggesting the location of the best churros in town. That tantalising prospect stopped his brother before he started expounding the merits of dungarees over trousers and ended up with an extremely localised mutiny. In fact, Sparkz had barely finished his sentence before Kennedy had forgotten about clothes and had them all hurrying towards the delights at The Sugar Daddy.

Chapter Three
All Fight on the Night

"CAPTAIN!"

Hearing the broadly booming tones of a familiar voice, Arke turned to see the *Warrior's* giant first mate running up the street as fast as someone that large could run while trying not to knock people over or win himself a coronary. Paltos, one of the longest serving crew aboard the *Warrior*, was massively tall and possessed muscles that were bigger than whatever Kennedy had called the scrawny orc boy's whole body. The first mate was unique, proof that not all giants were granite faced, hairy monstrosities. He was also one of the few people that the Soulbound had never wanted to punch repeatedly in the face. Her restraint had not been down to lack of provocation; Paltos loved to talk but had no brain to mouth filter and a complete disregard for any of her warning glares. There was just something so eminently likeable about him, that not even years of his twinkly eyed teasing, monologues on skin care regimes, or expositions on the intricacies that kept his immaculate goatee perfectly trimmed had stopped Paltos being one of the few people Arke actually considered a friend.

"What's happened?" Kennedy sprang forwards to meet the giant.

"Ellie... bar fight... this way!" Paltos panted, his face red with exertion and his bald head glistening with sweat.

Surprised as she absolutely wasn't by this news, Arke gestured for the others to join Kennedy, knowing there was little time to waste. High Haven bar fights were rarely innocuous affairs and Ellie was only known for her ability to get into trouble, not out of it. The redhead and alcohol had a simple relationship: she drank it, and it made her angry. The moment she was even half-cut, she had a fuse even shorter than her halfling self, and Arke could well believe the rumour that she'd once castrated a man with her teeth for asking her to show him her freckles.

The crew sprinted through the streets into a seedier district where every shack was a tavern and every cardboard box a brothel. Finally arriving in front of the cheapest, and thus the busiest, pub in High Haven, Paltos pointed breathlessly at the building. His direction was unnecessary, for the place was wicked with drunken brawlers being thrown out of windows, scrapping in the gutters, or bashing each other's heads on the walls. There was nowhere else Ellie would be.

Watching from the doorway, Arke sighed as she spotted Ellie perched up on the piano at the far end of the tavern, fending off attackers and cursing fit to explode. She sighed again as Kennedy marched headlong into the maelstrom, clearly ready to do some serious redhead rescuing. Or some serious bruise collecting. The Soulbound suppressed a wince as a folding chair was slammed into his face by a tall woman dressed in the crew shirt of the *Tempestuous Affair*. Arke knew it would take more than that to make a dent in Kennedy's thick skull, but she narrowed her eyes in brief confusion as he stopped walking and held up a commanding hand to stay the next attack before counting out some florins from his coin pouch.

"Good to see you, Catriona." Kennedy's outside voice boomed across the room. "While I've got you here, can you give these to Captain Bruce with a thank you from the *Warrior*? His information was spot on."

Arke looked on as the completely unapologetic woman put the chair down and pocketed the money while Kennedy's smile never wavered. It remained on his face when Catriona looked back up and he swung a punch so perfectly weighted that the *Tempestuous Affair's* second mate, her pocket now full of coins, was unconscious before she hit the floor. Arke nodded with deep satisfaction as Kennedy pushed on through the chaos. That feeling quickly dissipated as she watched him tackle the room like an especially talented damage sponge. It was obvious to her that his determination to get to Ellie made him an easy target for what seemed like every single piece of furniture in the tavern. Stools, chairs and tables as well as the only pinball machine in High Haven broke themselves on his broad shoulders.

Finding her temper distinctly triggered by Kennedy's ridiculous singlemindedness, Arke's blood pressure was grateful for the feathery distraction that came in the form of Ruby. The Ornithol headed to the left, vaulting over some tumbled tables and spinning like a rainbow-coloured tornado towards two unpleasant looking individuals who were terrifying her fellow Ornithol, the *Warrior's* parrot shaped chef, Porro. Normally, the Soulbound would have been keen to assist him in his defence, but the memory of the tapioca, fennel and halibut pizza he'd served for lunch was far too fresh in her mind. Ruby had clearly forgiven him for that culinary abomination, so Arke decided to hang back and see how things went before intervening.

In a blur of colours, Ruby spun out of her personal whirlwind and into an aerial scissor kick with an impressive crack of her wings. One of Porro's attackers, a woman who had been trying to punch him in the midriff, was launched backwards, her eyes registering nothing but rainbows. Her companion, a man clutching a broken bottle, quickly dropped it in favour of a chair which deflected Ruby's flying foot at the last moment.

Watching the Ornithol's first strike with a wry smile on her face, Arke remarked to a still stubbornly silent Stabbington that it was a decent enough rescue, for at least Ruby reached her destination without imprinting her face on a selection of furniture along the way. The quickly suppressed snort of amusement from her demon made the Soulbound's grin a little wider. It didn't feel right being in a fight without his usual wicked commentary and that brief reaction to her words told her that his sulk was coming to an end.

She didn't have time to make another comment as, with an excited shout, the ogre that had joined their party simply ploughed through the brawlers towards the Ornithols. Arke had barely paid attention when Ruby had introduced him so had no idea what his name was, but the moment she heard his battle cry, she realised that her previous inattention no longer mattered.

"KRUGG, KRUGG, KRUGG!"

Arke nodded with approval as the ogre's bulldozing skills showed scant regard for the health or safety of anyone in his way. She flicked a glance towards Kennedy's struggles with several furniture wielding assailants and wished he was paying attention to the masterclass, before turning back to see Krugg dangling the man who had deflected Ruby's kick in front of the Ornithol and pointing at him with a meaty finger.

"Go again, Chip Bird!"

As Arke watched Ruby trying to find the words to decline the ogre's odd kindness, the man drew the tiniest dagger she'd ever seen and stabbed it into Krugg's hand. As a direct result of his actions, the last thing to go through his mind was the ogrous shout of "Yeet!" and then the wall of the tavern.

Inside Arke's head, Stabbington finally snapped out of his sulk to roar with laughter as the Ornithol comically peered through the roughly humanoid shaped hole in the wall and into the darkness of the street outside.

"Do you think she is asking if he is OK? This must be her first bar fight. Ah, Ruby, look out." The demon sighed sympathetically as the Ornithol was body slammed by a trio of vaguely brick shaped dwarves. "Lesson one – never turn your back on a brawl."

"Let me go! I want to help Kennedy!" squealed Grimlet.

"And do what? You couldn't hit water if you fell in a river."

Recognising Sparkz's voice, Arke turned to see the engineer on the other side of the doorway. He was holding the young orc by the diamante studded collar with the wary expression of someone who had firm beliefs about the venomous nature of children.

"Just let him go," the Soulbound suggested as she flicked a glance to where Kennedy was thoroughly failing to dodge the impact of a piano stool.

"Doesn't look like my brother needs any help breaking furniture with his face!" Sparkz shouted, yanking Grimlet backwards as if he were a dog on a lead. "Or are you volunteering to listen to his lecture about being responsible adults when this idiot gets pummelled into pâté?"

"That may come sooner than you think." Arke nodded pointedly at a hulking figure hauling itself up off the floor behind Sparkz. She wasn't sure exactly what he was, but she could see that every inch of his skin was covered in a myriad of piercings, including what was probably a new one – a plank with a protruding nail that was stuck in the side of his head. "Meaty Mountain just erupted and is looking right at you."

Sparkz sighed theatrically. "Do you think that tiny thing on his shoulders is the control mechanism? I've seen matches with bigger heads."

"Maybe he just wants a snack." Arke pointed meaningfully at Grimlet who panicked, tore himself free of Sparkz's grasp and dived under the nearest table.

"The average size of a brain is two clenched fists; I doubt his head could accommodate even one," Sparkz commented. "He's similar in stature to an ogre but the cranial dimensions are all wrong. Maybe a sub species? If I were to estimate the approximate size of his forehead from the likely lens size of its glasses and then cross reference that measurement with Ruby's friend who just used her as a bowling ball…" The engineer moved towards Arke as he spoke, deliberately ignoring the looming hulk that was mere feet away from him.

The Soulbound glanced over her shoulder to where

Krugg was celebrating a strike and the Ornithol was picking herself out of a heap of brawlers, before turning back to Sparkz. "You'd still have to fight the meaty one because he's not stopped looking at you like you ate his pet wildebeest. Nice try though."

"There's no fight about it. There's gold in that there mountain." Smiling with dark amusement as the shadow of his would-be assailant fell over him, Sparkz looked down at his wrist where his newest tattoo, that of a technically perfect thermometer, was starting to glow.

Arke watched dispassionately as the Meaty Mountain's approach halted abruptly and he screamed in pain, clutching at himself desperately as every piece of metal on his person became red hot in an instant. He staggered backwards and toppled down the steps into the street, leaving Sparkz looking exceptionally smug.

"That was either an extreme overreaction or his piercings weren't just facial ones."

Before the Soulbound could blink away that unpleasant mental image, a meaty arm hooked around Sparkz's neck and he was yanked backwards out of the door with enough force that the soles of his boots briefly appeared level with her elbow as she stood leaning on the doorframe.

"Seriously?" She sighed, increasingly exasperated.

"Very seriously, I would say." Stabbington's heavily accented voice sounded in her head. "This fight is not going well for us; Kennedy apparently thinks with something that is not his brain so is getting splinters in his pretty little face from all the furniture he is eating, while Sparkz is in the arms of the meaty boy and Paltos is still outside trying to get his breath back. Tonight, it

45

appears as if a handful of toddlers with heavy duty teething rings could do embarrassing amounts of damage to us."

The demon wasn't wrong. Arke refocused her gaze on Kennedy as he ducked, dived and was thwacked in the face with monotonous regularity. With an even deeper and more irritated sigh, she decided that it was time to step in before he managed to get seriously hurt.

At first her intention was simply to use a little magic to make him lighter than air. Out of reach, out of bludgeoning distance. But then two extremely large orcish hands groped her from behind and a voice demanded she perform a service that she was definitely not in the market to provide.

Stabbington immediately launched into a tirade of extremely offensive curses and Arke took a moment to appreciate the way his accent made the words sound poetic. Then she grabbed a finger from each of the offending hands and drove them back towards her assailant's wrists in one smoothly brutal move. Bellowing in pain, the orc staggered backwards, straight into the path of a broken bottle that someone else was waving around. She didn't even turn to look when his shouts became screams behind her. She was done with him, just as she was about to be done with all of them.

Normally, Arke was an equal opportunity purveyor of chaos and destruction, but after her close orc-counter, she deliberately targeted the burly idiots who were trying to stab, punch and grab Ellie off the top of the bar. Flexing her fingers, she called up her demon's magic, launching some equally burly blasts of pure energy at the heads of her crewmate's attackers. She watched with grim satisfaction as they flew backwards and splatted against the wall.

"Ah, very nice use of colour. That panelling needed a little something to make it stand out." Stabbington was always appreciative of her interior decoration skills.

"Who's next?" Her tone was as dark as her eyes as they scanned the room in search of her next victims.

Stabbington's suggestion was both practical and diabolical. "Anyone who has hurt your people, for that cannot stand."

Narrowing her eyes in concentration, Arke created a giant ghostly hand in the air above her before sending it flying towards the group of men who had landed the heaviest blows on Kennedy. Fingers closing to a fist, the magical hand slammed into the luckless brawlers, crushing them all to the floor in a textbook example of overkill. "And now *they* cannot stand."

"All that and some wordplay too; I have never been so proud," Stabbington chuckled.

As the entire tavern stilled into shocked silence, a goblin popped up behind the bar. He quickly started to polish any glasses that were still intact, using spit and his entirely unconvincing attempt at a beard. After a moment of bristly saliva smearing, he swept his gaze over the carnage before turning his attention to Arke.

"There's rules for bar fights, you know! Anything up to and including permanent physical disability is acceptable."

"I'm no expert but that all looks pretty permanent to me." Sparkz walked unsteadily towards the bar, blood welling from a cut on his eyebrow. Ignoring the detritus on the countertop, he grabbed the first bottle he could reach and downed it in one.

Without even appearing to have heard the goblin's complaint, Arke moved to stand by the pool table and picked up a cue, expertly sharpening the end to a spike with three strokes of her dagger. Then she glared at the rest of the brawlers, all of whom were looking at her with wide eyes, having halted mid-punch the moment her spell had hit their unlucky fellows. The wispy bearded bartender looked between her and Sparkz with a frown.

"No need to kill paying customers. Hey, is she on the rag or something?"

Everyone expects their last words to exude a little pathos, but as the goblin's head exploded with the sound of an overripe watermelon being crushed in the tusks of a hippopotamus, it was too late for him to change them.

"Couldn't tell you, she's always like that." Sparkz dumped some coin on the counter and grabbed another drink, never wanting to leave a question unanswered, even if his words were falling on extremely dead ears.

Joining his brother at the bar, Kennedy glanced down at the goblin's body as he grabbed a beer.

"Read the room, my dude – can't say she didn't show you what she could do."

While all the ex-combatants started righting furniture, clearly deciding it was eminently more sensible to sit down and shut up, Ellie crossed the room and handed Arke a brimming glass of clear liquor.

"You never said you could explode goblins."

"Only their heads." The Soulbound shrugged, downing the dubious looking liquor in one.

Ellie snorted with laughter. "That's kinda enough

though. Wish you could teach me how."

"Probably best I can't."

"Maybe you're right." The halfling took a swig from the bottle in her hand before pouring Arke another glassful. "I'd miss killing them the old-fashioned way."

With a clink, the pair toasted that thought before heading over to the bar where a strangely identical barman had appeared and was busy serving the *Warrior* crew as if nothing had happened. Behind them, bodies were being hauled away by gnomes in hi-vis jackets which bore the logo of the High Haven Sausage Company.

As Arke and Ellie joined the others, the tavern started to fill up again. Not a single patron seemed to notice or care about the random blood splatters and drag marks on the floor. Grimlet ducked out from under his table, leapt up on the bar and mimed exuberant finger guns at them all.

"You guys are the shit! Can I have a beer?"

"Language, Grimlet." Kennedy's expression was briefly disapproving, before he shrugged and slid a bottle towards the young orc. "Just the one."

⚔ ⚔ ⚔

THE *WARRIOR* WAS peaceful the next morning, as most of the crew, bar those unlucky enough to be on duty, were lying very still in their beds and wishing they'd never been born. Every creak of the ship at anchor was like a pistol shot in their sore heads and even the simplest act of movement was agony. Last night's new friends had made themselves at home – Krugg the ogre had slept out on the deck with a tarpaulin for a blanket and Grimlet had immediately been taken care of by Urzish, the

Warrior's helmswoman and a fellow orc. She'd scolded Kennedy for letting him get near a tavern, get inside a tavern and get close to danger, but strangely said nothing about the determined minesweeping that the boy had done after the fight.

Down in the galley, a very worse for wear Porro dragged himself to work and started making pancakes with every type of hangover reducing ingredient he could find while groaning to himself about his meagre willpower when it came to alcohol. When Ruby suddenly breezed in with a hearty welcome, the parrot flung a dramatic wing to his forehead and begged for some silence on this cruel morning. With whispered apologies, Ruby tiptoed across the galley, carefully turned the chef back towards the crew quarters and gave him a gentle shove. She was apparently no stranger to pancake making even if her style of cooking was best described as alarming. She dashed and spun from one surface to the next, flipping here, mixing there, serving with a flick of the wrist from about five feet away. The results were surprisingly tasty and unlike Porro, she even served breakfast in bed to those who just couldn't make the trip to the mess.

"Where am I?" Krugg sucked in about fifty pancakes that Ruby handed him before realising he was on a strange vessel.

"The *Warrior*. Do you remember me?"

"Chip Bird. Yes." The ogre nodded and then belched an impressive sirocco of pancake flavoured air. "Ruby! Friends!"

"Yes, friends. And do you remember Captain Kennedy? The *Warrior* is his ship." Ruby beckoned to her captain who was having a coffee out on the deck, feeling much more the thing after a hearty breakfast.

"Kennedy!" Krugg mimed being hit in the face repeatedly.

The captain cringed a little but kept his smile. "Thanks for the memory. Krugg, isn't it? You were very jolly last night!"

"Krugg always jolly."

When you've seen a hungover, snaggle-toothed ogre force a smile then you've experienced sudden gripping nausea. Kennedy looked away briefly. The pancakes had been great the first time but knew he wouldn't like to experience them again. He gazed into the clear blue sky, taking a deep cleansing breath before turning back with his usual happy expression.

"That's the spirit! Would you like to join the crew?"

"Krugg has job, forty florins a month. How much you offer?"

"Ten florins a *week!*" Kennedy beamed persuasively and offered a hand to shake.

The ogre considered a moment, his brow furrowing as he counted laboriously on his fingers. "I choose this ship with friend Ruby."

Kennedy wished he'd thought about the technicalities of shaking hands with an over enthusiastic ogre, but thankfully for his delicate human fingers, Krugg's bone-crushing vigour was interrupted by Paltos who came to inform him that there was a port official at the gangplank demanding their berth fee.

"Didn't you pay us up yesterday?" Kennedy queried with a frown.

"Yup, went to the office myself. Forgot to say there's

a new harbourmaster, busy looking fellow with shifty eyes. Guess Petra got retired… one way or another. The new guy said he'd like to have a chat when you had time." Paltos gestured to the rows of shacks in front of the warehouses.

"Get Arke to come…" As Kennedy spoke, he saw the first mate's eyes flick meaningfully to a point on the deck just behind him. "Again?"

"Always."

The Soulbound's ability to appear when there was even the slightest hint of trouble was unparalleled. As she stood next to her captain with the hint of a smile on her lips, Kennedy shook his head slowly.

"How do you do it?"

"A lady has to have her secrets."

"But what's your excuse?"

Sparkz sauntered over, not even bothering to hide a smirk behind his mug of coffee as the Soulbound spun on her heel with an expectant nod to Ruby and headed towards the gangplank, Ornithol obediently in her wake. Kennedy pointed a finger at Sparkz's coffee and then nodded over to the clipboard carrying gentleman on the quayside.

"Drink up while I catch a rat, then we'll go meet the new boss on the block."

Without any further explanation, Kennedy pasted on a smile and headed down the gangplank to meet the official, offering a hand to shake in a friendly manner. What wasn't quite so affable was the way he used the greeting as an opportunity to twist the man's arm up behind him before starting to frog-march him towards the offices. The prisoner's complaints and cries for help were rapidly reaching an irritating crescendo when Sparkz caught up with them. In a brisk, business-like manner, the *Warrior's* engineer shoved what could have been a rag, a sock or someone's lightly stained stocking into the man's wildly flapping jaw before basking in the enforced silence.

High Haven being the pirate city that it was, the only reaction the entire interaction received was an expletive-ridden shout from the orcish captain of the ship moored next to them. Apparently, the official's pathetic whining had woken him up after a particularly energetic night so if the boys wanted any help disposing of their prisoner, his larder was always open.

As the *Warrior* party headed down towards the administration buildings, most of them quickly regretted their recent life choices. Any busy harbour on a bright sunny day was a full body experience at the best of times and even with pancakes and coffee fighting their hangovers, the short journey proved to be somewhere between taxing and hellish. They felt nothing but relief at finally reaching the freshly painted office with its new sign announcing ALOYSIUS GORKI – *Harbourmaster – High Haven Harbour (now under better management)*.

Kennedy reached to open the door and, with that one innocuous act, unwittingly launched the entire crew of the *Warrior* straight into the path of Destiny's boot.

Chapter Four
Destiny's Boot

I AM SO SORRY about this, Captain. He will absolutely be punished for trying to cheat you. Sometimes the help is... *unreliable*... I am the new harbourmaster, Aloysius Gorki, a friend to every vessel that docks here. Whatever you need, I am your one-stop shop: information, advice, a little of this, a lot of that. I have a long and shining history of running smooth and honest ports to their absolute recommended maximum turnover and profit. I work hard so you don't have to."

The little man's broadly smiling but strangely wink-ridden performance was unusually polished for a harbourmaster, the majority of whom had hands like hams and accents so thick you could use them to cover roads. Kennedy kept his smile fixed in place to counterbalance any hint of the little frown that usually gathered between his brows when he was thinking. It was odd that he'd never heard Gorki's name before, considering the *Warrior* had docked at almost every port in Barsia, but he equally knew it wasn't beyond the realms of possibility that the halfling had been working in Nidea or further afield. Paranoia aside, Kennedy realised that it didn't really matter to him anyway. High Haven was just another port and once they'd established a working relationship, he doubted he'd ever need to see its harbourmaster again.

On reflection, Kennedy realised he'd rather like that,

since he was already picking up troubling vibes from Arke. While he was willing to give Gorki the benefit of the doubt, he didn't have to look at the Soulbound to be uncomfortably aware that she was deeply suspicious of the man. He'd long ago realised that when the hairs on the back of his neck stood on end, it meant her magic, as well as her unpredictable temper, were on the rise. It was time for Kennedy's preferred extraction protocol – smile, shake and scarper, before Arke's suspicion turned to outright hostility. Granted, her instincts were usually right, but he was still too hungover to want a fight, and too fond of High Haven to get blackballed.

"This one's a player," Sparkz hissed in Kennedy's ear. He leant on the wall to his brother's left, his hand resting on the pommel of the whip that was clipped to his belt, its leather coils laced with well-worn metal.

Sparkz's wry tone was testament to the fact that he hadn't been even slightly deceived by the wordiest over-acting since Lesley Henderson, the Butcher of Rhymes, had conducted her own defence using only iambic pentameter, a string quartet and prolonged eye contact with every member of the jury. Gorki had the same swagger to him alongside an unwavering belief in his superior status which had clearly originated from doting parents and inhaling books about how to be an alpha male.

To give credit where it was due, those books must have been incredible to overcome the natural challenges the harbourmaster must face every time he looked in a mirror. He was an odd-looking chap with an almost entirely bald head which was mocked unmercifully by his astonishingly hairy ears. His face could best be described as lumpy and his monobrow was a thing of wonder. Even for a halfling, Gorki was tiny and had to sit on four cushions just to see over his nose as well as the lip of his desk. In short, which he was, it looked like he'd bounced off every limb of his family tree on the way down.

While the harbourmaster was loudly and theatrically commanding his cowering employee to stand outside and wait for punishment, a tall red-headed henchwoman with elven ears and a nasty looking spear walked in past the *Warrior* crew, brushing muscular shoulders with Arke as she went. The newcomer reeked of magic and a perfume so strong that it made Kennedy sneeze. He turned his head slightly to throw a warning glance at the Soulbound whose posture had reached DEFCON 3 the moment she'd been bumped.

"This is my assistant, Kayla. She doesn't just do the accounts, if you know what I mean," Gorki chuckled in a greasily confidential manner as she positioned herself on one side of his desk and leant her spear against the wall, her face a mask.

"Great to meet you both." Kennedy's smile was so well practiced it could effortlessly cover far worse lies than that. "So, can you drop the receipt over later? I expect you're busy." The looks being exchanged between Arke and the red-headed assistant were making Kennedy increasingly nervous; in fact he could almost taste the magical energy hanging in the air as the two women stared each other down.

Kayla, the bodyguard, was textbook beautiful, as long as the textbook was *Stunningly Terrifying Elves You Should Avoid at All Costs*. Kennedy was one hundred percent certain that if he'd ever seen her before he'd have instantly remembered something pressing to do in the opposite direction. With another furtive glance at Arke's fixed expression, he also felt sure that the Soulbound didn't know Kayla either, for if she did, they'd already be in the middle of a battlefield. They needed to leave before things got out of control as it was entirely on brand for Arke to act on her instincts without waiting for a suitable time or even a pause in conversation. Kennedy was well aware that her fuse had been lit when the henchwoman's deliberate shoulder bump had issued its silent challenge, so it was only a matter of time before everything went spectacularly sideways.

"Yes, of course we can do that," Gorki answered Kennedy's question with a greasily obsequious smile. "Kayla will bring it over." He motioned to his assistant who paid him no attention, her unblinking gaze still battling with Arke's steadfast death stare. "The *Warrior*, yes?"

"Thank you; yes." Kennedy turned as if to try and usher his crew out of the office.

"While I have you here, Captain, I've heard you run as competent a ship as can be had around here. I'm hiring a team for a special piece of work which carries with it a very attractive remuneration package."

Kennedy turned back slowly, eyebrows raised in question. He noticed Sparkz was paying more attention to the harbourmaster now that money had been mentioned but Ruby was looking out through a high window and Arke was still locked in a silent stare-off with the red-headed elf. Desperately hoping she didn't start a war until they could find out what '*very attractive*' meant in actual florins, Kennedy looked the harbourmaster directly in his tiny little eyes.

"Feel free to elaborate."

"This job," Gorki was suddenly all business, his rounded fingers gripping the arms of his chair as he leant forwards, "is classified. The payout is more than generous, but in the customary manner of these 'sensitive' contracts, I will expect a signed agreement before I give you the details."

"Sounds lucrative." Sparkz looked at his brother with a wry smile.

"Sounds deadly," Kennedy replied. "Who turned it down and suggested us instead?"

"It has been more difficult to find someone due to my recent relocation to this beautiful city; however, I'd be a very poor sort of harbourmaster if I couldn't make subtle enquiries about suitable candidates. Those enquiries were often answered with your names, and so here we are." Gorki's smile widened and he gestured to the *Warrior* crew with what was clearly exaggerated deference.

"Let's see this contract then."

The halfling reached into a drawer and slid a file over towards Kennedy. The room was expectantly silent as he read the document, his expression unchanging as he checked the small print carefully and then turned to tap the file on Arke's shoulder. That action broke her concentration on the '*if looks could kill*' contest with Kayla and she took even less time than Kennedy to read the agreement, her eyes rapidly scanning each line right down to the last tiny sentence. Then she looked up, fastened her dark gaze on the harbourmaster, took two abrupt strides up to his desk and used the file to swipe everything on it to the floor in one brusque movement.

"For someone so *short* you seem to expect *long* terms."

"It's a standard contract!" Gorki protested.

"Maybe that's true under the rock you crawled out from." As she spoke, Arke stalked around the desk until she was standing beside Gorki's chair. "Claiming our SHIP if we don't finish the job to your SATISFACTION is not a *standard* anything!"

In one smooth move, Arke lifted the chair along with its halfling owner and placed it on the top of the desk so that Gorki's head was only a few feet away from the ceiling. Kayla was so tense she looked like she was about to have an aneurysm, but did not move to stop the Soulbound, who radiated triumph as she eyed the bodyguard's strained expression.

Kennedy was in the grip of pure, thundering anxiety as he watched Arke lean against the side wall from where she could watch both the harbourmaster and his assistant. He felt as if he'd aged years in mere seconds and he could hear a voice in his head that was probably his own, praying to any god listening that neither woman would start a fight which would probably blow half the docks into oblivion.

"I apologise unreservedly for the fact that my contract has underperformed in the face of your expectations." Gorki's precarious position apparently did not prevent effortless obfuscations slithering from his mouth even though they were clearly in direct opposition to the bubbling tension behind his expression.

Sparkz moved to stand beside Kennedy, his crooked

smile making his amusement with the floor show more than obvious. "You must *really* want us to do this job, Mr Harbourmaster. So do we have to speak to your boss or are you *high* enough up the food chain that you can change the contract?"

"If only it was that simple." Gorki was still digging his metaphorical heels in. Obviously not his real ones as they were free swinging off the chair which was perched on the desk.

"It is if you want us that badly," Sparkz remarked, his voice and posture that of pure, calculated indifference. "Last chance."

The harbourmaster's irritation was clearly beginning to border on anger as he locked his glittering eyes on Sparkz. However, Kennedy was more than happy to let his brother negotiate while he continued to watch the more potent threat in the room. He noted with some relief that the elf's attention had now switched from Arke to Sparkz, her gaze flicking over his brother as coldly as if she was sizing up how many of his body parts she could sell on the black market.

"Time to go," Sparkz tapped Kennedy on the shoulder and nodded towards the door. "We don't need his bullshit job."

Gorki cleared his throat decisively. "How about we make this a gentlemen's agreement instead? I trust you, you trust me."

"No contract?" Kennedy checked, knowing he had absolutely no trust in the man whatsoever.

"Verbal agreement and a handshake to seal the deal." The harbourmaster beamed disingenuously, spreading his hands wide. "I *much* prefer doing things the old fashioned way."

Kennedy dragged his eyes away from Kayla and looked questioningly at Arke who shrugged with her perfectly normal lack of enthusiasm. She was in. He nodded at his brother, the gesture a go ahead to continue the negotiations.

"We'll need a down payment for our working expenses." Sparkz loved nothing more than the dirtiest end of dirty deals, and Kennedy knew he'd wring every last florin from it.

"Of course." Gorki nodded to Kayla who dumped a pouch of gold coins onto the desk with a dismissive scowl.

Approving the quantity with a single glance, Sparkz moved his gaze up to the harbourmaster's face. "Then tell us about the job…"

The *Warrior's* crew watched impassively as the red-headed elf lifted her employer and his chair off their perch, smoothly setting them down behind the desk. She slid a challenging glance towards the Soulbound before positioning herself with one hand resting on the chair back and an icily serene look on her face. Seemingly oblivious to his assistant's attitude, Gorki unlocked one of his desk drawers and brought out a chart which he unrolled across his desk as he talked, his composure returned to its customary smug equilibrium.

"As well as being a harbourmaster, I'm also an entrepreneur. Having plenty of strings to my bow keeps the old brainbox busy. Fingers in pies, toes in the water, a little dip here, a little deal there. Anyway, the long and short of it is – one of my ships is missing; it was a prototype, the fastest thing in the air, and since I've a lot of money invested in the thing, I want it back if it's at all salvageable. I have a rough location for the search after a survivor was picked up." Gorki tapped a finger on the chart, then drew a wide circle and finally just gestured vaguely in the air over that area of the map.

"The Greyspines?" Kennedy looked from the chart to Gorki and back again. "Did you fall and hit your head? Whatever would possess you to send a prototype over there?"

"Just seeing how she'd do in a bit of weather."

"A BIT of weather? Those mountains invented so many ways to die that there aren't even names for them all!" Kennedy couldn't fathom why anyone would send any ship, least of all an untried and clearly expensive one, to take on the worst storms over the worst terrain in the entire Barsian Empire.

While any salvage job was a challenge, one in the Greyspines was going to be ridiculously difficult. However, the Kennedys had always enjoyed beating the odds. He looked back down at the chart, eyes narrowed as he assessed potential routes to the red X that Gorki had indicated. "And how accurate is your information? What's the status of the ship? The last thing we want to be doing is hanging around the mountains waiting for the native tribes to use our bones as toothpicks. I've heard they don't tend to ask first."

"We're pretty convinced it's good intel." The harbourmaster sat back in his chair, exuding slimy confidence like bad cologne.

"Still, I'd like to speak to your guy."

"I'm afraid that's not possible; he's still recovering from his ordeal."

The problem with a non-pirate trying to blag their way past a group of pirates was that the buccaneers were entirely more proficient in bullshit. They bathed in it, they revelled in it, they loved it, and they could absolutely smell it on Gorki's breath.

"Right." Kennedy shrugged. "Well, I think we're done here. I'm not risking my ship on the basis of a red cross on a map. If your 'sailor' recovers enough to talk to us, you know where we are for the next few days."

The *Warrior* crew took their captain's cue and turned away, all except Arke who'd been watching the harbourmaster's body language with evident interest from her position to the side of his desk. There was something about the way his gaze had briefly flitted towards the dark doorway in the corner of his office that had caught her attention.

"Wait, please. I'm sure we can work something out." Gorki almost threw himself off his chair and hurried after Kennedy, with Kayla striding alongside.

The moment her way was clear, and without hesitation, the Soulbound pushed off the wall and went straight to the shadowed door, trying the handle only to find that it was locked.

"I might be a fool but I'm not suicidal." Kennedy's voice was firm as he kept walking towards the exit. "Without meeting your man…"

Their conversation was cut short by a crash from the other end of the office as the Soulbound kicked the locked door so hard it nearly fell off its hinges. In less time than it took to blink, the red-headed bodyguard materialised in the doorway in front of her nemesis, her hand snapping out and fastening tightly around Arke's throat, lifting her easily off her feet.

"KAYLA!" Gorki's shout went unheeded as his assistant choke-slammed the Soulbound down on the desk.

"DON'T!" Kennedy spotted Stabbington's blade suddenly materialise in Arke's hand, the tip of the rapier instantly drawing blood from her assailant's neck.

The air was almost humming with the magic potential crackling between the women as they stared daggers at each other, blood flowing more freely from Kayla's throat even as her fingers squeezed harder on Arke's. It would be dangerous to try and split them up directly, so Kennedy cast a frantic glance around the room for something to divert their attention.

His immediate instinct was to throw the harbourmaster out of a window to distract Kayla, but as the office suddenly illuminated with all the colours of the rainbow, Kennedy realised that he didn't need to exert himself. Behind him, Ruby began chanting some oddly musical words and as she did so, a dark cloud appeared, hovering over the desk. He'd been utterly unaware that the Ornithol possessed any magic, but her reveal was as timely as it was decisive. Kennedy beamed with appreciation as a sudden torrent of freezing rain threw itself over both Kayla and Arke, instantly interrupting their dangerously intimate moment.

"Nice one, big bird," Sparkz remarked with a wry smile, "though we could've sold a lot of tickets if you'd let them get going properly."

"KAYLA, STEP AWAY!" Gorki ordered, his expression darkly furious.

Without a word, the elf let go of Arke and backed up

into the doorway, arms folded, frown at maximum. The Soulbound peeled herself off the desk and looked at Ruby, her expression disgusted as she wiped the water from her face with a sleeve.

"Divine magic? Are you shitting me?"

"We can talk later," Kennedy interceded quickly. "The room?"

Arke nodded and stalked after Kayla, looking up into her face with an expression that was a pure and perfect challenge.

"What's in there, Gorki?" Kennedy asked.

"Files. Boring files."

If the harbourmaster was discomfited when some very odd guttural noises started to come from the room in question, he didn't show it and continued his sentence with poise. "And the sailor. We may as well let them see him, Kayla."

"Absolutely." Arke's face broke into a bright and wicked smile directed entirely at her nemesis. As the bodyguard moved reluctantly to one side, the Soulbound executed the mother of all patronising winks at her before walking in.

After spending less than a minute in the room, watching a filth-smeared young man drawing one identical map after the other while keening to himself in a strange rasping tone, the Soulbound headed back out. As she stepped clear of the door, she handed the least disgusting drawing to Kennedy before turning to Gorki and dropping the bombshell with a tone so smooth it could have buttered toast.

"So, you didn't want us to meet him because we'd know instantly that the poor bastard has had his mind wrecked by some heavy-duty possession event."

"Sounds like you need to start talking, Mr Harbourmaster." Sparkz looked in the little room and then back at Gorki. "Have you even bothered to take him to hospital?"

Without even a flicker of emotion at what Kennedy guessed was the rapid unravelling of his entire gambit, Gorki spoke in a completely normal manner, as if to give the impression that he had always intended to reveal the truth.

"Of course I did. They couldn't do anything. Apparently he's been like this since he was picked up; I don't know what else to do but keep him comfortable."

"One – don't pretend you care; and two – how about you find someone who knows a lot of languages?" Arke suggested.

"Languages?" Gorki and Kayla spoke almost as one, their voices as perfectly matched as porridge and oysters.

Arke rolled her eyes. "Aren't you *super talented* detectives? If you actually listened to him, you'd know that he's repeating the same few words over and over and they're not Barsian."

"He is?"

Kennedy couldn't make up his mind whether Gorki was genuinely surprised or just playing his part. Either way, he was more interested in the two red marks that the unfortunate sailor had drawn onto the map Arke had given him. One was definitely a ship. He peered more closely at the other, trying to figure out what it represented.

Kayla slipped into the storeroom, bashing shoulders with the Soulbound again as she brushed past before listening to the young man for a few moments. "Pretty sure he's saying one word in different languages." Her voice was as sharp as her glares, her accent so middle of the road she could have been from any city in Barsia. "I can pick out a couple I know but I've never heard the others. He's saying 'Treasure'."

"Is he?" Gorki smiled toothily. "Well I never."

Kennedy almost slapped the harbourmaster in the face with the hand-drawn map that he'd been holding, and Gorki quickly recoiled from the anticipated blow. However, Kennedy had only been thinking about violence, rather than pursuing it, and simply held the second of the two red marks so close to Gorki's face that his nose could identify the origin of every stain on the paper.

"I couldn't think of any obvious reason that your average shipwrecked sailor would be possessed," Arke remarked, scrutinising the map as she stood behind Gorki. "And I've never heard of any resident of the Greyspines being interested in anything other than murder and fresh meat, not necessarily in that order." She pointed at the second mark which Kennedy, with a little context, had worked out was a very basic drawing of a treasure chest and piles of coins. "But if this is right and he's happened upon some ancient hoard and its guardian – well then, this mind-mushing stuff all starts to make much more sense."

"I would say he was lucky to get away in one piece, but I don't think he did." Sparkz shook his head with something that was almost sympathy.

"That X wasn't on your map. You didn't want us to know about the possession or the treasure." Kennedy yanked the parchment away from Gorki's face and gave the little man the hardest of hard stares. "What's the bet that you were hoping we'd fall foul of whatever monster was guarding its hoard, kill it because you've heard we're good at that and then have a few ships waiting to 'relieve' us of the good stuff on the way back?"

"There's no need to jump to conclusions." The harbourmaster smiled in what he probably hoped was a winning manner, but just made Kennedy want to punch him hard in the face. "I heard you were the best crew in the area when it came to dealing with mystical beasts or arcane energies and having seen you in action I'm more than confident in your abilities – look how easily you discovered the truth! So let's make our agreement – I want my ship back and if there is treasure, I'll take fifty percent." He held out a hand expectantly.

The butt of Sparkz's whip firmly pushed Gorki's tiny fingers away from any possible handshake. "Five."

The counteroffer was as hard as Sparkz's face as he continued the process of trying to rip as much value from the deal as possible.

As the crew walked back to the *Warrior*, every single person who had been in the office knew that this was absolutely and completely a terrible, terrible job. It smelt so rotten that not even Krugg would eat it and tasted so bad not even Porro could have cooked it. Huge mountains, notoriously deadly weather, dangerous natives, possession, lies, indeed the entire index page from *How To Get Dead* balanced against a boatload of money and that oh-so-seductive frisson that came with the chance to lick risk right in the eyeball.

Kennedy and Sparkz walked to the captain's cabin

and poured their much-improved down payment, now a huge pouch of gems, onto the table. Sparkz picked up a big handful of the jewels and let them run through his fingers, listening to the tiny musical clinks as they dropped. He started to tally up their value while his brother pored over charts, marking waypoints and calculating distances. Finally, Kennedy loaded a careful selection of gems into the case containing his magically enhanced pistols. They were expensive to run but their added extras had saved his life more than once.

"When do we go?" Sparkz said at last, putting the remaining jewels back into their velvet pouch and tossing it to his brother.

"Tomorrow?"

"Good. I've got a date with Fate, Hop and Clarity tonight."

"Sisters?" Kennedy rolled his eyes with weary expectation.

"Well, I'm hoping they'll show me heaven."

"I'll pray for you."

Sparkz winked and headed out, leaving Kennedy standing in the middle of the room, shaking his head and wondering how two brothers could be so different. He was pretty sure he didn't want to flit from bloom to bloom like a butterfly, but it would be nice, once in a while, to be able to cuddle something other than his pillow. With a slow sigh, Kennedy pushed those thoughts away, grabbed his writing set and started carefully listing things that needed to be checked before the *Warrior* left harbour.

Chapter Five
Could it Be Magic?

THE FIRST PART of the journey was strangely peaceful and borderline enjoyable. The sun was shining, the skies were clear of other pirates, the winds were light. The crew relaxed, running drills and getting down to all the maintenance that was needed after the brutal last few weeks. Porro was even happy to be on deck playing his precious accordion without constantly whining about it being damaged. His huge repertoire of songs kept everyone entertained and the only member of the crew who might have deconstructed his instrument to stop the sing-alongs abruptly disappeared into her cabin whenever she saw the parrot emerging on deck.

Sparkz spent a lot of time shirtless in the sunshine while he and Zeke, the engineering assistant, tried to make a prototype flamethrower. Zeke was a Bior, one of a small group of magically constructed metal servants who appeared to have been given sentience by the Night of Terrors. That one, terrible event over two hundred years ago, had changed Barsia forever. A massive explosion had razed its capital to the ground and released a tidal wave of raw magic which had surged across thousands of miles with all the attention to detail of an emotional toddler. The Empire had reeled from the body-blow, barely surviving the loss of its capital and its leader, the Autarch, as well as so many of its people. The only even slightly positive thing that had come from the event had been entire races of new citizens such as the Bior and the Ornithols – as the magical shockwave that rolled across the land had apparently created just as randomly as it had destroyed.

The flamethrower plan was an attempt to shore up the *Warrior's* deck defences which weren't so much slightly lacking as completely absent. The ship had an enormously powerful aetheric lance mounted in the bow but that was absolutely useless if they were boarded. Having been offered a choice between fiery death machines and grapeshot firing cannon, no-one aboard even hesitated to select the hotter option. After all, the weather was warm, spirits were high and normal guns just didn't have the *also can be used as a barbeque* zing to them. After hearing the crew's decision, Sparkz had made a point of remarking to whoever would listen that if any of the idiots on board accidentally stood at the wrong end of one, Porro would need plenty of butter to make the meat tasty.

Meanwhile, Kennedy was busy running drills, teaching line dancing, and arbitrating between Sparkz and Paltos after an unfortunate deck fire. But he needed to do more – it kept his mind off what might lie ahead. However, as he hung off the side of the ship on a series of ropes, he wondered why he'd thought cleaning the hull while in flight was even a slightly good idea. Laboriously chiselling sky snails and other unpaid passengers off the timbers with nothing between him and the ground while the wind buffeted him mercilessly was far more terrifying than he'd anticipated, but he was a Kennedy, and he wasn't going to give up until the job was done. It took four days, six pairs of pants and several fingernails before he was satisfied with his work. Although he was extremely gratified to note that the *Warrior* was faster and far more aerodynamic after his hard work, he promised himself that he'd never do it again.

As is sometimes the way, the random trolling of existence hit high gear a few days later, almost as if it wanted to give Kennedy cause to fully appreciate his hours of perilous toil. The morning had started out with an al fresco breakfast of flame grilled sausages and freshly ground coffee, but the crew's plan of spicy chicken and vegetable kebabs for lunch was cancelled by the sight of a merchant ship limping northwards. It was obviously trying to hide in what little cloud cover there was, but the winds were blowing all its visual protection away and as Kennedy handed his telescope to Ruby's keener eye, he looked over at the avaricious face of his brother with a raised eyebrow.

"Check all around for other vessels please, Ruby. Don't grin like that, Sparkz, yes, it's a big merchant ship flying a dangerous cargo flag, but don't get excited just yet."

"Going north on this route — someone's been shopping for Nidea's finest magical goodies." Sparkz smiled wolfishly. "It's not really going to take us *that* far off course, is it?"

"Depends where the rest of the convoy is; I have no desperate urges to die today. That size merchant doesn't leave port without heavy escorts."

"But the payout…" Sparkz's rapt expression made it obvious that he was already working out how he'd spend his share.

Kennedy folded his arms stubbornly and waited as Ruby scanned the horizon until the clouds to the south parted and she was able to see her first airship combat.

"Two merchants like that one and some smaller ones. There's a lot of smoke, I can't quite see."

"Someone else attacking the convoy; good news for us." Kennedy's face broke into a wide grin. "We can be on and off before they even notice." He looked up to the helm. "Ellie, steer for the merchantman, all speed. Ruby, do you want to go and knock on Arke's door, tell her to get her shit together for boarding...?"

"She already has."

The Soulbound's voice came from right behind him and Kennedy looked heavenward with a small sigh before turning slowly to face her. He wasn't at all surprised to see that she was fully battle ready, her reinforced leather jacket fastened right to its topmost button and its high collar flipped up to protect her neck.

"You know I hate it when you do that."

She ignored his comment and pulled out her telescope, surveying their target with a well-practiced eye. "Magic cargo for the Barsian Empire's hands only, I can almost smell it from here. Looks like they've been through a storm and taken some damage. I hope you're not planning to steal the entire ship as we won't be making a quick getaway in that thing."

"No, not at all. We'll go in, take the premium items and scram. You know Crimbles always pays well for potions and raw goods."

Snapping her glass shut, Arke looked up at Kennedy warningly. "Don't get over-excited this time. Stay on the

Warrior till I let you know things are under control."

"Does he really get that excited?" Ruby headed to the helm in the Soulbound's wake. Behind them, Sparkz began mercilessly teasing his brother about her comment.

Completely ignoring the Ornithol's question, Arke reached into the communication box by the wheel and rang three bells in quick succession before handing Ruby her telescope and pointing towards the battle. "The smaller vessels are Barsian escorts, do not take your eyes off them. They start moving towards us, you shout it out. Clear?"

As the *Warrior* rapidly closed in on the merchant ship, the Soulbound's boarding party assembled on deck and Kennedy, now loaded for bear, monster or anything in between, took the helm. Sparkz was in position in the engine room and Zeke, with his Bior strength and endless endurance, stood ready on the main deck to help move boxes of stolen reassigned goods. Aboard their target, the crew could be seen massing on the main deck, muskets at the ready.

"They don't look very friendly," Paltos remarked with a casual grin as he stood with the boarding party on the far side of the cabins. A familiar whirring noise was building in the centre of the *Warrior*, the planks below the crew's feet vibrating as the ship's main weapon charged.

"Hey captain, have you dated any of those people? They look angry enough to see you," Urzish called, looking up at the helm as she leant on the cabin next to Paltos, calmly sharpening her axe. Even though her posture was incredibly relaxed, the orc's eyes gleamed brightly, for a little light pillaging was always a welcome

FJ Mitchell

way to relieve the boredom of long journeys.

"It was ONE time," Kennedy shouted back with a grin. A musket fired, the ball whizzing high overhead. He looked over at the merchantman, shielding his eyes as if to see better. "Jenny? Is that you?"

"Which one was Jenny?" Paltos asked. "The tall one with the limp plaits? No, I remember now, wasn't she the barmaid who let you sniff her apron?"

As the crew continued with their teasing back and forth about the entirely mythical Jenny, Arke climbed up on top of the cabins and stood looking down at the merchantman with narrowed eyes. Various musket balls whistled in her general direction, but she ignored them, taking her time to familiarise herself with the target's layout.

"Ready to fire, captain," Ellie called from the targeting booth just below the helm.

"One across her bows, if you please," Kennedy replied, undoing his top button as he began to feel a familiar excitement burning through him. He summoned his alter, who would go aboard the merchantman with Arke, and grinned confidently at Grimlet, who was looking nervous as he stood holding the grappling irons which would be used to pull the two ships together.

The deck vibrations reached their zenith and then went silent before the unmistakeable sound of their aetheric weapon firing crackled around the *Warrior*. Ellie's marksmanship was perfection itself, the bright beam of light ripping through the air just ahead of the merchant ship.

Right on cue, Paltos stepped out into the open and took a deep breath before bellowing his words across the narrowing distance. "Live or die, it's up to you. Weapons overboard. You have ten seconds."

The rest of the boarding party formed up at the rail as the magically powered lance began recharging and the merchant sailors quickly started to throw all their guns and swords overboard.

⚔ ⚔ ⚔

ARKE NOTED THE filthy expression of the officer at the wheel as he saw his men raise their hands in surrender as the *Warrior* approached at the perfect angle, causing only the slightest jolt as the two ships bumped together.

"Urgh. This vessel has magic suppression devices," Stabbington complained as Arke vaulted the *Warrior's* railings and landed on board the merchantman. "They give me a headache."

"You don't have a head. They give ME a headache," she muttered under her breath as she strode over to the sailors, gesturing for the officer at the wheel to join his men in the middle of the deck. He dawdled over with exceptionally bad grace and the narrowed eyes of someone who was busy making plans, so she didn't waste any time intercepting him as her crew quickly searched the other captives.

"You're an edgy little thing, aren't you?" The man looked Arke up and down with open derision, his voice laced with an accent so upper class it probably had its own entry in *The Who's Who of Barsia*. "I saw you watching me, pretending you weren't afraid of musket fire. I'm the captain of this vessel, in case you were in any doubt."

The entire ship heard the man's words and all heads turned with interest to the upcoming collision of egos.

Arke's lips twisted in a sardonic smile as she held the merchant captain's gaze while summoning Stabbington's blade to her hand. With an upwards flick of her wrist, she cut straight through the man's belts, dropping his swords, pistols and trousers to the deck in an instant. Her sword hand did not stop there but kept moving upwards, ripping through the man's shirt and waistcoat before halting just as the tip of her blade touched his throat.

The merchantman's captain was immediately suffused with embarrassed and incandescent rage as even his own crew started to laugh at his predicament. "You dirty wh…"

"I would be *very* careful what you say," Kennedy interrupted before the man gave Arke a reason to kill him. He always kept his alter close to the Soulbound when she was heading a boarding party and had quickly merged with it as the confrontation began. Having moved directly behind the captain while his attention was on Arke, the barrel of Kennedy's pistol now nestled unmistakeably in the small of the man's back. "Ask yourself, is it necessary? If it's necessary, is it kind? And if it's not kind, is it going to end up with you dead?"

With an exaggerated sigh, Arke looked at Kennedy. "New pick-up line? What was wrong with 'Would you like to see my sword collection?'"

"No-one ever said yes."

Behind them, Paltos was getting the merchant crew to open the main hatch and prepare a chain of hands to move goods over to the *Warrior*. The giant first mate had been part of the crew for almost as long as Kennedy had been alive and had an uncanny instinct for locating premium products, no matter how well hidden. If it wasn't nailed down, then it was fair game. Once they'd even stolen a solid gold throne so heavy that even a much younger Paltos had struggled to carry the monstrosity out of the palace they'd liberated it from.

"The Sky Guard are going to splatter you thieving bastards across the sky." The captain of the merchant, even while bodily exposed to the elements, clearly enjoyed the sound of his own voice far too much to be sensible and Arke silently increased the pressure of her sword against his throat.

"Respect the surrender," Kennedy remarked calmly.

"I haven't…" The merchantman's captain began but Kennedy shoved the pistol harder into his back as Arke stepped reluctantly away and sheathed her blade.

"It's the ONLY thing keeping you alive right now. Now shuffle over to the others."

As the man awkwardly tried to pull up his trousers while he walked to join his crew, Kennedy put his pistol back into its holster and grinned at Arke, eyes twinkling, clearly unable to suppress the perfect comment that had sprung into his head the moment he'd seen her embarrass the merchant.

"He's that hot you needed to undress him in public?"

In Arke's head, Stabbington started roaring with laughter, but the Soulbound just looked at Kennedy, eyebrows raised in dark exasperation before pointing to a cabin door at the stern of the ship. Then she crouched, grabbed the enemy captain's weapons and launched them over the side.

Obviously deeply amused by his own line, Kennedy checked the main hatch, noting with satisfaction that their new prisoners were diligently piling up boxes of goods as quickly as they were brought out of the cargo hold. The merchant's captain was watching them too, scowling as he tied a length of rope around his trousers to hold them up. Once Kennedy had finished a quick assessment of their initial profits he moved past the officer, heading to the cabin Arke had indicated, but as he did the captain launched towards him, a long-bladed knife dropping from his sleeve into his hand.

With perfectly honed reactions Kennedy sidestepped, slipping his hand around the hilt of one of his swords and drawing the blade with a menacing hiss. As the other captain swung wildly with the knife, Kennedy punched him hard in the face with the weapon's guard and continued walking, smoothly sheathing his blade again.

"Leave him. He's not worth killing."

Arke took a deep breath and released her white-knuckled hold on Stabbington's hilt before grabbing the merchant captain's knife and hurling it over the side. Silencing arrogant and irritating individuals was one of her favourite pastimes, but Kennedy had given her a direct order in front of two crews and she wouldn't undermine him.

"He's bound to have some valuable trinkets in his cabin. Whatever we don't want, you can throw overboard." Kennedy grinned and she looked up at him with a wicked sparkle in her eyes – petty revenge was still revenge after all.

⚔ ⚔ ⚔

OVER ON THE *Warrior*, Ruby stood at the stern, telescope to her eye as she dutifully observed the battle to their south. The clouds were clearing, and she could see that the two other merchant ships were manoeuvring smartly to keep away from the trio of pirate ships even as they tried to use their targets as shields against the Barsian escorts. The Ornithol had already seen enough to understand why Kennedy had been exceptionally reluctant to tangle with the convoy defences. Although the Empire's cutters were small, they roamed in packs, seemed able to turn in their own length and fire some seriously punishing volleys from their deck guns. The first pirate ship was already aflame by the time she could see it properly and she watched some of the escorts cluster around the stricken vessel, firing mercilessly until it broke into three parts before plummeting to the ground, wreathed in smoke.

"Why don't they run?" Ruby took a brief break from the telescope to send blessings to all the souls who were about be freed from their bodies. Then she turned to look at Ellie who was standing nearby, also watching the battle while heaping curses on the convoy escorts.

"The Barsian Empire hates magic and it hates lawbreakers," the halfling replied, mockingly rolling the R in Barsian. "They would exterminate every pirate if they could. And lots of pirates have magic engines."

"Instead of?"

"The glorious Empire has mechanised. Cogs and pistons and smoke and steam."

Grimlet wandered over to listen and wrinkled his nose with disgust. "That stuff stinks. The Barsians don't use magic at all?"

"All the time – for them and only them. Everything we're stealing from that ship is magical; and ALL for the

Empire's use." With a hollow laugh Ellie pointed over to the distant vessels. "Like there. Each of those Barsian cutters has a pair of bow chasers that we call Cataclysmic Convertors – long range, super accurate and oh yeah – they fire enchanted projectiles. The whole Barsian lawbook that says '*Magic is bad*' goes out of the window when it suits them." She spat on the deck in disgust. "If they hit the *Warrior's* exhaust with one of those things, we'd be shards of nothing in an instant. Their magic bullets and our aetheric crystal make beautiful explosive babies – BOOM. The end."

Ruby had been taught Barsian history and laws for as long as she could remember but had never had cause to question them. She frowned, thinking out loud. "They must have needed to find something that was super effective to keep their shipping safe."

Ellie stuck out a foot and kicked her in the leg. "Those Barsian pigs spend their lives arresting mages, punishing them for just existing; but THEY can use magic and that's just fine! Tell me how that's fair?"

"Well, the Empire was almost destroyed by magic – they probably want to keep it controlled in case it happens again."

Ruby looked down at Ellie who shrugged, clearly having only heard vaguely about things that happened over two hundred years in the past, so she continued.

"We learnt about it all, the capital just exploded and there were no survivors. All that's left is a massive, irradiated wasteland. It changed everything for a long time and for some of us, forever. Where do you think my people came from?"

Ellie shrugged. Like most pirates she never seemed

to care what her crew mates looked like or what rock they crawled out from, as long as they adhered to the code. "No way that locking up kids who can make the wind blow or talk to animals would stop that happening again. I'm not buying it." She sighed with obvious frustration and looked at Ruby, then over the deck of the *Warrior*, her voice hardening as she spoke. "I never went to school and all I know is what I see. The normal people get used and trodden on by the rich pricks up top and if you're unlucky enough to have some magic you're even more screwed. I'd rather die than go back to being a sheep."

There seemed to be nothing else to say, so both went back to looking through their telescopes, watching the distant battle until there was an almighty explosion and both merchantmen just seemed to disintegrate in a giant multi-coloured cloud. One of the pirate ships was badly damaged in the explosion but the other, a little further away, immediately lurched to full speed, putting its nose down and diving away amid the smoke and debris.

While Ruby called down more blessings on their souls, Ellie shouted encouragement to the fleeing ship as half of the escorts dove to follow it. No-one on the *Warrior* was paying any attention to the merchantman's captain who had slipped away from his men and sneaked onto the pirate vessel, disappearing down a rear hatch without being noticed.

"What happened?" Grimlet squinted towards the smoke curiously, trying to see the details of the battle.

"Magic stuff goes bang if you're not careful; that red pennant means dangerous cargo. Don't ever forget that." Ellie gestured vaguely to the flag flying from the merchant they were lashed to.

"Don't worry." Ruby reassured the young orc quickly as his eyes widened in horror. "It won't just up and explode." She took a breath and looked over at the halfling, suddenly doubting herself. "I don't think?"

"We'll be fine as long as no-one breathes too hard on the thousands of bottles of boom juice down in her hold." Ellie grinned at Grimlet whose expression did not hide the fact that he was absolutely not reassured by her words.

"It can't be THAT dangerous?" Ruby said uncertainly, pulling the telescope away from her eye in respect to the helpless pirate vessel which was being systematically dismembered by the cannons on the Barsian ships.

"Magic suppression devices are stupid money and there'll be at least two on a merchant this size to stop anything that escapes making sweet, explosive love. Shipping any sort of magic is high risk, high reward."

Ellie turned away from the scene and kicked at a coil of rope with visible frustration. The other pirates should have known better than to get caught by the escorts, but it didn't stop her heaping vitriolic curses on the Barsians.

No-one aboard the *Warrior* wanted to watch as the stricken pirate ship desperately tried to defend itself, as they knew it had absolutely no chance against the three escorts who circled it like terriers, mercilessly harrying the vessel until it simply blew up.

At the sound of the inevitable explosion Ellie's shoulders slumped and she turned back, removing an imaginary hat in respect. "There goes the *Whistling Pig*. RIP you glorious bastards." With a curt nod of farewell, her face returned to its usual scowling expression. "I'll tell Kennedy we need to go. Maybe they're damaged and won't come for us, but we don't take chances."

Chapter Six

Imperfectly Executed

DOWN IN THE *Warrior's* engine room, Sparkz was busy investigating a coolant leak in one of the conduits leading away from the central basin where the aetheric crystal was held. The hum that suffused the room was constant but muted as their power source was only being required to provide enough energy to keep the *Warrior* hovering. He chatted away to himself, and maybe just a little to the giant purple crystal, as he traced the leak back up the morass of pipes, fully engrossed in his work. It was rare to get a stationary moment out of port to perform essential repairs and he was taking full advantage of the boarding to fix a few loose connections that had come to light since they'd left High Haven.

He'd just found the problem and turned to climb back out of the pipework to fetch a new washer, when something smashed heavily into the side of his head. Sparkz became Sparko instantly, slumping into an awkward position while still lodged in the pipes.

The merchantman's captain hefted the large wrench in his hand with satisfaction before locking the engine room doors from the inside. As the bolts slid home with a heavy clunk, he headed for the control panel, stopping briefly to address Sparkz's limp body.

"Your filthy rabble of a crew were too busy stealing my cargo to notice me sneaking on board. So now I just need to hold things up until the Sky Guard get here. Then I'll have the deep and abiding pleasure of watching your executions."

✗ ✗ ✗

"WHAT WE HAVEN'T got, we don't need! MOVE IT!" Kennedy shouted across the deck as he ran back towards his ship in response to Ellie's warning. The two crews were busy moving the boxes of contraband down into the *Warrior's* hold as he jumped over the railings and landed on her deck. Striding quickly towards the stern, Kennedy pulled out his telescope, focusing its lens on the three escorts who were heading at full speed in their direction.

"There's more chasing the last pirate, sir," Ruby warned, pointing into the low cloud below them.

"How many?"

"Four."

Kennedy swore heavily. "OK, first let's get the merchant between us and them. Ellie, spin the engines up and turn us to starboard. Let's get the last few boxes stowed, double time!"

"Captain! I can't get the engines to answer!" Ellie shouted from the helm where she was wrestling with the control levers.

Trying to pretend he hadn't noticed every single person aboard stop working and gaze at him with mounting horror, Kennedy kept his voice calm. "Go to neutral, then into reverse, and then forwards again."

"I HAVE! It's NOT working. Any of it!"

Keeping a confident pose under the pressure of that sort of doom-laden news was tough, but Kennedy just about managed to stride rather than scramble across the deck and up the ladder to the helm. There had to be an explanation for the *Warrior's* lack of propulsion, and though he knew that Ellie was more than capable of flying the ship, he still hoped that she'd completely and inexplicably forgotten how to do so. The alternative was much worse, and as the control levers flicked limply in his hands, Kennedy finally had to face the deeply unpleasant truth – they were sitting ducks.

"Ellie, get to the engine room and find out what's going on. If the problem's there, get me a fix time; if the problem's with the helm, just get us moving and we'll work out steering after."

The halfling scooted off, brushing past Arke who was standing at the foot of the ladder, lips pursed as she watched the approach of the Sky Guard cutters. Kennedy leapt down beside her, his tone sharper than he'd have liked it to be.

"We need to buy some time; I'll turn the merchant to shield us."

"I'll find the magic suppression generators." Arke vaulted back over onto the merchantman's deck and headed towards the open hatch. "We could use a big fiery distraction."

"As long as it can wait till the *Warrior's* clear. You think it'll take them long to get her moving again?" Kennedy sprinted to the merchant ship's wheel, casting a worried glance at the three enemy vessels as they approached at full speed.

"How lucky do you feel?"

"Right now? Not at all."

"Well I'm going to jump down here – it's dark and I can't see a landing spot. If I break my leg I'll admit our luck has turned." Arke flashed Kennedy a grin, but that only made him feel worse. The Soulbound always engaged peak charm when things were bleak. "Tough crowd." She jumped and Kennedy heard her cry out as if in pain.

"If you were really hurt you wouldn't have made a sound!"

"Get your game face on and buy us some time – no one Kennedys like Kennedy." Her voice faded as she headed deeper into the ship.

Kennedy knew exactly what she meant and forced a smile to his face as he ran his hands over the wheel, that familiar action soothing his nerves as he took charge of his thoughts. He needed to tackle the basics. Firstly, keep the merchantman between the cutters and his ship. He reached for the engine control lever and brought up the power until he had enough to manoeuvre with. Secondly, create a human shield. He glanced over at the *Warrior's* deck where Paltos was massing the merchant sailors directly above the engine's exhaust. It was unlikely that the Barsians would want to murder their own citizens, so it never hurt to use prisoners as protection.

Spotting his captain looking in his direction, the first mate flicked a thumbs up and Kennedy returned it, forcing a bit of swagger to the gesture. His crew knew the score and that gave him purpose. He always struggled with the responsibility he felt for his people, a few of whom had been with him since he was a child. However, the best way to protect them was to play to his strengths and Arke was right, no-one Kennedy'd like Kennedy. As the escorts grew closer, he leant on the wheel, whistling softly to himself as he prepared to perform.

He watched as the three escorts displayed their sailing prowess, charging at the merchant before turning sharply when they were within hailing distance.

"Ahoy, pirate captain!"

A sharp voice shouted from the closest cutter and Kennedy raised a casual hand in greeting to the uniformed officer at its bow.

"Ahoy, Barsian Sky Guards. Do you require assistance?" His voice was warm and friendly, his trademark happy expression in perfect position.

There was a brief pause. Clearly that wasn't the answer they were expecting.

"Release your prisoners and surrender!"

"Release *us* and surrender!" Kennedy replied affably, still with the biggest smile he could muster.

"No?" The Barsian commander's voice seemed a little more confused.

"How can you expect *us* to let *them* go if *you* won't let *us* go?"

Silence hung in the air for a long moment, only broken by a hammering noise from below decks and a muffled curse from Arke. Kennedy started talking quickly to mask any further disturbances, guessing she was busy trying to suppress the suppressor.

"Barsian Legal Code, Statute 1143.1b. Or maybe it's 1143.1c. Anyone over there have the ledger? No? OK, so it states that in the event of a complete breakdown of communication in a hostage situation, adequate measures should be taken to balance the expectations of both hostage takers, hostages, and the hostage negotiators. That can be accomplished in one of the following ways A) Extended parley with an independent chairman at a venue agreed upon by all parties. B) If…"

"There is no such law!"

"Well now it's just your word against mine and I'm sure that's a situation neither of us want to get into. My ex-girlfriend swore, like a sailor as it happens, but also declared vehemently that she one hundred percent knew that I *hated* her mother. And let's be honest, you sound like someone who has been married maybe three or four times – don't you hate your mother-in-law? I wasn't even MARRIED but no, it was always – 'invite dear mother to dinner', 'cut her lawn', 'stop using locks of her hair to encourage demons to devour her soul'. What an idiot I was! Of COURSE the sour faced bitch didn't even HAVE a soul. And as for her mother…"

"RELEASE THE HOSTAGES NOW!"

"Which ones? We have a lot. There's the guys off this ship and then in the hold we've got a variety of others. What can I say? I love collecting them."

Now that Kennedy had the attention of the escort vessels, he made a cutting motion behind his back, knowing Paltos would see it and hurry to cut the grapples which tied the ships together. They had to keep their options open and letting the *Warrior* quietly drift away was relatively safe for the moment with the merchant crew on board his ship and the commander fully invested in shouting at him.

"ALL THE HOSTAGES!"

"Even Jim the personal trainer? Honestly, he's been so happy since we liberated him from what was pretty much slavery…"

A musket was fired from the cutter and the shot flew over Kennedy's head as he waited to deliver his punchline.

He doubted the Barsian would even understand the pun, but he knew his crew would enjoy it.

"I WON'T ASK AGAIN!"

"OK, you can have Jim too. Sorry Jim, buddy."

Paltos' guffaw was quickly smothered as another musket ball flew a little closer to Kennedy's head.

"Surrender now and mercy will be granted to your crew!"

"Oh, go on then." During the somewhat unusual negotiations, Kennedy had heard a definite exclamation of triumph from Arke in the merchantman's hold so he guessed that one of the suppressors was offline and he hoped she'd found the second one as he made his final play.

"What?" The Barsian commander appeared to be somewhat taken aback by his reply.

"You said mercy, right? In that case, I, Philip Kennedy, humbly surrender myself." He knew the Sky Guards' definition of the word was entirely different to his own, but his offer would buy a few more moments for some sort of Arke-related miracle.

"Throw down your weapons!"

"Of course!"

Kennedy obligingly undid his belts, throwing his swords and pistols over onto the *Warrior's* deck as it slowly started to move away from the merchant. Then he stripped off his long coat, hanging it neatly on the wheel and taking a moment to brush down the sleeves while he made surreptitious signs to Paltos to keep pushing the two ships apart. Turning back to the looming escort vessels, Kennedy spread his arms and then knelt on the deck.

As he'd expected, the escorts were tentative in their approach but finally one of them lashed themselves to the merchant vessel. Eighteen well-armed men leapt aggressively onto the deck and fanned out in front of the kneeling pirate captain who greeted them with a broad smile.

"And a frantically good day to you. Triumphant and majestic all."

Their officer strode straight up to Kennedy and levelled a pistol directly at his forehead. "Give me a reason not to pull the trigger."

"That's a tough one; I'll need a moment."

The weapon smacked Kennedy around the side of the head, knocking him to the deck and as he lay there, he saw three more escort vessels join their fellows as they hovered next to the merchantman. Six cutters, all armed with cataclysms and out for blood. Kennedy suppressed a deep sigh as he realised the *Warrior's* luck had just run out.

However, as he lay prone, sore, and dispirited, blood trickling down one cheek from the impact of the pistol to his face, Kennedy detected a faint whiff of smoke filtering up from below the merchantman's decks. That was his first step back to confidence – his second was spotting the briefest of shimmers moving towards him. With a flash of recollection which brought a smile back to his face, Kennedy remembered one of his mother's favourite sayings. Two words: one was luck and the other rhymed with it.

"Might I get back up so you can hit me again? It's no fun beating a man when he's down and believe me, I've tried. I kicked a rock instead of a head and broke my foot in three places."

The Barsian officer grabbed Kennedy by the shirt, ripping it as he hauled him back onto his knees. "Do you ever shut up? Talk, talk, talk and all of it utter nonsense. I don't know what's more criminal, your actions, or your words. In the name of the Barsian Conglomerative Customs Commission I hereby sentence you to the cessation of life, effective immediately."

Two of his men grabbed Kennedy's arms, twisting them behind him to present a bare neck to their commander who stepped to the side and drew his long and impressively shiny blade with a flourish.

Turning his head awkwardly to address the officer, Kennedy tutted with disappointment. "That was a terrible death proclamation; maybe you should try 'By Order of the Barsian Authorities and the power vested in me I pronounce you very well executed?'"

The officer just glared back.

"Fine," Kennedy continued, "what about some last words? I have plenty prepared."

"How about these? I am going to REALLY enjoy the silence of your death." The commander measured his blade against Kennedy's neck before raising it high, ready for the killing blow.

Four things happened almost instantaneously as the Barsian officer's sword swung down to decapitate Kennedy. First was the resounding clash of metal on metal as the strike was blocked, the heavy impact with an invisible barrier cleaving the shocked commander's weapon in two. Second was the sudden appearance of Stabbington's blade as it dropped to the deck in front of Kennedy. Third was the officer's expression changing from surprise to terror as an invisible person, cursing bitterly about the pain in her hands from blocking the strike shoved him away from the failed execution. The fourth was that expression turning to abject horror and disgust as Arke returned to the visual spectrum, straightened up from her shoulder charge and vomited all down his chest.

While the men restraining him had their attention wholly held by the chaos, Kennedy easily slipped out of their loosened grips, grabbed Stabbington and stood up. The moment that they saw their captain free again, the previously silent *Warrior* crew started cheering and stamping their feet so loudly that it sounded like a distant drumbeat.

The increasingly green-faced commander was busy trying to get away from Arke, who had a white-knuckled grip on his arm as she continued to retch uncontrollably.

"Anyone got a tissue?"

Kennedy kept his sword down and his smile radiant as he looked around at the confused soldiers who kept looking at their commander for direction. Unfortunately for them, he was entirely preoccupied, not only with his vomiting assailant but also his own rebellious stomach if the pale-faced gulping he was doing was to be believed. Kennedy's smile grew wider still as he pushed his advantage, addressing the small crowd in a warm and affable manner. "It's a bit embarrassing really, she has terrible nausea issues with adaptive camouflage, not being able to see her own nose makes her toss her cookies. Or sausages. Oh yes, those are definitely *sausages*."

At the final and far too gleeful mention of food, the commander abruptly lost the battle against his own dignity. His stomach started to heave and with a decisive burst of strength, he shoved Arke away before stumbling desperately to the port gunwales and venting his breakfast.

The soldiers stood awkwardly, watching Kennedy warily as he held up a placatory hand and slowly stepped towards Arke. "I know, this is all *super* awkward right now so I'm going to remove my vomit comet and we'll sashay back onto our ship while you deal with your boss's emetophobia. We can still handle this like adults."

It was a bold and decisive move but unfortunately, the Sky Guards were not entirely as dumb as they looked. One ran to their indisposed commander for instructions and a few others stepped in front of Kennedy, blocking his path towards the Soulbound.

"KILL THEM!" The unmistakable voice of their commanding officer gurgled a single hoarse instruction from the side of the ship and his men sprang into action, charging en masse.

Stabbington had been silent while Kennedy tried to talk his way clear but as soon as the enemy started to attack, he began to help. His normally casual manner was completely absent as he barked instructions in Kennedy's head, helping him duck, dive and dodge his way backwards across the deck as most of the guards decided he was the major threat.

※ ※ ※

ARKE WAS LEFT with only two Sky Guards, both with their swords raised and eyeing her with more than a little trepidation. She sighed with irritation as she looked at the crowd almost tripping over themselves to attack Kennedy as he leapt and parried his way around the rear decks with perfect poise.

"You know what I hate more than vomiting?"

The two men looked at each other in confusion. Their orders had been to kill but this woman was unarmed, had very recently been quite unwell, and was just standing there in front of them.

"Lots of things, but in this situation we'll go with unequal opportunities," Arke continued. "How many of your friends are trying not to stab each other in pursuit of the big bad MALE pirate? And I got TWO. AND you aren't even TRYING to hurt me! Do you even know how sexist that is?" Arke looked from one man to the other and shook her head disappointedly before her tone changed from angry to coldly informative. "You have three seconds to start running."

"Us?" one of the guards questioned, his eyes wide as he caught sight of Kennedy surfing down the banisters of the stairs by the rear cabin.

Arke also saw the showboating and couldn't prevent a wry smile twisting her lips, despite her irritation. In an athletics contest between Kennedy and the Sky Guards, there was never any doubt about the winner. Kennedy was both fast and fit while the average Barsian sailor was just that, average. She watched him standing briefly alone in the middle of the deck before he dropped to flex out a couple of one-handed press-ups while he waited for the herd to catch up. Then with an imperative tap of her boot on the deck, the Soulbound began the countdown.

"One."

The two guards' attention was dragged back to their much less muscular charge. They looked at each other, expressions darkening, and took a step towards her, swords at the ready.

"Two."

"SHE'S A MAGE, YOU IDIOTS! KILL HER!"

A dagger came flying through the air from the recovering commander and Arke timed her dodge perfectly, twisting out of the way so that the weapon hit the man closest to her in the shoulder. As he staggered and fell to the deck, his colleague's blade slashed towards the Soulbound, but she was waiting for his strike and dived forwards, rolling neatly to her feet inside his guard. In one brutal move, Arke grabbed the man's sword arm with both hands and slammed it down over her knee, breaking his wrist as well as his grip.

"STOP PLAYING WITH YOUR FOOD!"

She heard Kennedy's shout and flicked a glance to where he was sprinting across the deck before leaping up the mast and climbing hard as the guards chased him like breathless hounds. It wasn't hard for her to spot the results of Kennedy and Stabbington's handiwork as wounded Sky Guard now littered the merchantman, all of them somewhere between merely limping or limp and bleeding. Crippling the enemy to thin their numbers was the perfect tactic and Arke nodded with grim appreciation.

"Why? Doesn't look like you need any assistance," she called back.

"Of course not! Why would I need help with all these men?" Kennedy shouted as he grabbed a rope, cut it and swung all the way to the quarterdeck, somersaulting as he let go and landing perfectly before clapping loudly as if to encourage the chase party to keep going, like a

PE teacher during cross country.

"So many jokes." Arke turned to where the fully recovered but rather unpleasantly scented Barsian commander was stalking across the deck towards her. "And here's another."

"Take a look at the bow and then tell me if you're laughing," the man growled, ducking to pick up a pair of swords from one of his injured men and rapidly closing the distance between them.

"I think you'll find that I haven't laughed once." The Soulbound picked up the sword that the guard had dropped when she broke his arm. She'd already seen another cutter about to grapple to the merchantman so had no need to take her eyes off the commander's cocky approach. "But maybe you should take a look over at the main hatch and tell me why I have no issues welcoming ALL your men on board."

The commander's eyes flicked briefly to the smoke which was starting to thicken and rise in ominous clouds from the belly of the merchant ship, before suddenly leaping at Arke, attacking with murderous intent, his swords flashing with a barrage of blows. At a distinct disadvantage with a single blade, the Soulbound had to retreat rapidly across the deck, parrying and dodging the Barsian's well practiced attacks.

As Sky Guard reinforcements arrived, the commotion briefly distracting her opponent, Arke sprang sideways and used her boot to flick an abandoned sword into her offhand. Whirling quickly to counter an attack, her lips twisted in a smile at finally having evened the odds and from having spotted Kennedy battling his way towards her. She knew they'd need to fight together against the greater number of enemies, but not before she'd finished the job in hand.

"Now we're equal." She parried his strikes easily and adjusted her grip on the new blade for maximum control.

"You and I? Absolutely not!" The commander's sour expression showed exactly how disgusted he felt by her comment.

"Good point. I'm far better."

The Soulbound might not have had his military training, but she had survived in a man's world for forty-three years and no-one with any sense ever bet against her. She had exceptionally fast blades and nimble footwork, and when that wasn't enough, she was an excellent clutcher, always managing to squeeze her way past looming disaster by the narrowest margin of pure grit, good instincts and a heavy dollop of luck. Now armed with two swords, it was her turn to press attacks against the heavier man, dancing around him and pushing him back across the deck as he tried to defend himself.

Unfortunately for her, the number of Sky Guard arriving on board all keen to watch the duel began to hamper both her footwork and ability to dodge. The Barsian commander spotted his opportunity and ordered his men to form a tight circle, taunting Arke that she couldn't hope to withstand his attacks once she had nowhere to run.

He wasn't wrong, and with a grim smile, he began to crash overarm blows against her weaker side, forcing her to stand and defend since she could no longer avoid them. After wearing her down with a barrage of heavy strikes, he feinted low to split her defences before slamming down another high attack, using his greater height and strength to push her own blade towards her head. He didn't ease his pressure for a second, feeling her arm begin to weaken and knowing she'd have to bring up her other blade to protect herself, since the press of men behind her meant that she couldn't duck away. The moment she did, he swung his other arm, the steel of his second sword slicing clean through her thick leather jacket.

"You're MINE now!"

"I'm *not* your possession!" Arke snarled, using the moment he was off balance from the strike to partially disarm him, twisting her swords expertly to launch one of his away over the heads of the soldiers.

"Blade!" the commander called, holding his empty hand out expectantly as he took a few steps backwards. Right on cue, a sword came flying through the air towards the Barsian and without hesitating, he caught the black bladed rapier's hilt.

"The lady is correct; she is not your possession. She is mine."

A deeply appreciative smile lit Arke's face as she watched the commander's horror-struck expression as he suddenly focused on the blade in his hand. Wicked amusement welled up inside her as he threw the weapon to the deck, warding himself frantically against its otherworldly energy.

"DEMON!"

The terror in his voice and the smell of burning flesh coming from what remained of his glove completely defeated any of Arke's attempts to suppress her mirth. She knew from experience that Stabbington was perfectly capable of heating up his hilt. Usually he did it to keep her hands warm, but she also knew he could get it so hot it would burn through any natural fibres, including skin.

"Oh, now that looks *super* painful." Unsurprisingly, the Soulbound's tone was perfectly lacking in any sort of sympathy.

With a rush of hoarse expletives, the commander dropped the blade from his uninjured hand and grabbed a pistol from one of the men next to him, firing at Arke as she dived away from his shot. Her reaction was quick, but not quite quick enough, and the bullet hit her in the arm, scorching its way across her bicep. It wasn't exactly the distraction she'd hoped for, but she wasn't about to argue with its efficiency. All eyes were on her as she dropped her swords and threw herself dramatically onto the deck before making far more effort to get to her knees than she actually needed. As a result of her play-acting, no-one noticed that the black rapier had suddenly disappeared. Although she'd guessed none of the Sky Guard were aware that some demonic weapons could be as easily recalled as resummoned, it was always best to err on the side of caution. Especially with the little surprise she had planned.

"I should have just done this to start with." The Barsian officer moved closer, levelling the pistol at her head and pushing the muzzle hard into the bridge of her nose.

"Me too." If Arke's bright smile was disconcerting, the lightning quick movement which spat the demon blade into existence again was even more so.

The commander looked down in absolute disbelief at the rapier's hilt which now protruded from his stomach. Catching the pistol as it dropped from his nerveless fingers, Arke spun it in her hand and fired, hitting the man full in the face from almost point-blank range. As the Sky Guard around them looked on in horror, she stood, taking hold of Stabbington again and drew him clear just before the Barsian officer dropped backwards to the deck, extremely and utterly dead.

"That was exceptionally gratifying, but I feel we may now be in trouble," Stabbington remarked, his voice in her head more welcome than his well-practiced ability to state the obvious. "Maybe you can use some magic?"

"With all those bottles I broke and mixed down there? Are you crazy? This ship's just one magical sneeze from oblivion." Looking from left to right, Arke eyed the wall of angry faces that encircled her, before suddenly realising that Kennedy's ghostly alter had appeared next to her and in the blink of an eye, the rest of him merged with it.

"And neither of you thought to mention that earlier?" Unsurprisingly, Kennedy didn't seem overly enthused by that knowledge. "I thought it was just a fire."

"Tell him I was having too much fun," Stabbington suggested helpfully. "Explain that I was reminded of all the happy memories when I taught him swordsmanship when he was so very small."

"He was supposed to say," Arke explained, throwing her demon under the bus without hesitation.

"You did not tell me to!" Stabbington objected.

"Wasn't it obvious?"

"We had other things to do, in case you had not noticed, being so busy with your *three* opponents."

Although Kennedy could only hear one side of the conversation, he knew the pair of them well enough to know when they were about to get distracted by a petty argument, and quickly jabbed his elbow into Arke's ribs to get her attention again as the Barsians raised their pistols.

"Well, I feel distinctly under-armoured for the occasion," Arke muttered, while listening to Stabbington unhelpfully counting the number of bullets she was likely to become personally acquainted with if their enemies chose to fire.

Kennedy brought the entire power of his Sunday best smile to the situation as he addressed the exceptionally hostile crowd. "I think this has all gotten a little out of hand, gentlemen; hot heads, brisk tempers, but I truly believe that with some kind words and forgiveness, we can all walk away with our dignity."

He'd barely even finished his ridiculously hopeful speech when there was an extremely loud and distracting series of explosions from the direction of the escort vessels. Neither Arke nor Kennedy hesitated, diving through the gaps between the shocked Sky Guardsmen before sprinting away across the deck. As they ran, the Soulbound glanced to the left and saw two of the Barsian cutters breaking up, their engine stacks now twisted and bent metal, the decks around them splintered and burning. That was more than perfect... unlike the brightly coloured bird who was coming in fast and clearly aiming to land in the middle of the deck of the merchantman.

"Ruby! NO!" she yelled, trying to deter the Ornithol from her determined approach.

"What the actual...!" Kennedy peppered his exclamation with an unusual amount of curses as both he and Arke skidded to a halt and watched their crewmate on what was likely to be a very final approach.

Chapter Seven
The Right Tool

AFTER OBEYING THE first mate's explicit instructions and dropping the bundles of magic potions cleanly into the exhaust pipes of two of the escort ships, Ruby had decided that since Paltos hadn't explicitly told her to come straight back to the *Warrior*, she would try and help Kennedy and Arke. As she swept towards the merchantman, she noticed their horrified expressions and she definitely heard them shouting something negative at her, but she wasn't about to leave them fighting alone. She didn't even bother to land to begin with, just swept over the railings as low as she dared and ploughed full speed into the mass of soldiers, some of whom were looking at her and some at the stricken ships. As her headlong attack slammed a bundle of them together like herring in a net with some very meaty thuds and crunches, she felt a familiar warmth rush through her veins. Round one had begun.

The moment she touched down on the deck next to the pile of groaning men, the Sky Guard who had managed to avoid her dramatic entrance fired their pistols. Gunshots rippled and cracked around the deck as multiple bullets shot towards the seven-foot-tall, rainbow coloured easy target in front of them.

The Barsians, much like the *Warrior* crew, didn't know that Ruby had been the undefeated champion of the Barsian Junior Cage Fighting league for the past ten years. The Sisters of No Mercy hadn't just trained her well, they had taken her natural talents and honed them with utter devotion. One of their tenets of belief was that reaction speed was the key to victory, so they'd regularly made her run around their beautifully kept gardens whilst under fire. She would be doing laps and Sister Evangeline, a seagull Ornithol, would suddenly roll out from under a hedge to throw firecrackers under her feet. Where Evangeline went, Sister Marietta was never far behind, and she'd use her penguin prowess to keep herself hidden in one of the many fountains before erupting in a shower of water and throwing knives. In contrast, the Mother Superior, as befitted her advanced age, had preferred to sit on a bench with a box full of pre-loaded pistols.

As a result, Ruby's reflexes were more than just good, they were borderline godlike. First she flattened to the deck like a dropped cookie, then rolled and leapt into the air, whipping strikes from her wings negating the few shots that managed to get close to her. Landing and brushing the final bullet away with a perfectly measured feather, she tilted her head and beckoned the Barsians on with one teasing wing tip.

"Round two."

Despite the fact that they'd already seen their new adversary bust some seriously mind-blowing moves to evade their bullets, the Sky Guards still rushed towards Ruby's challenge, clearly believing that a surfeit of swords should make her oven ready in no time at all. In the event, they were dead wrong, with heavy emphasis on the *dead*, as Ruby destroyed thirteen of them in seconds. She whirled and punched at the same time as she kicked;

even her wings acted independently, battering and pushing the men right into the path of her brutal blows. Bodies flew into each other, across the deck, over the side, down the open hatch. Once the thirteen became obsolete, Ruby launched into the air, grabbed the last two men who were trying to run away and dropped them into the hold before landing again and slamming the cover shut with a thud.

The only sounds on deck were the groaning of the fallen and the crackling of the fires in the hold as Kennedy beamed at Arke. "What an amazing crew member. I wonder who hired her?"

Utterly ignoring him, the Soulbound looked at Ruby curiously. "Where did you learn to do all that?"

"I thought you said you grew up in a convent?" Kennedy queried.

"I did… the nuns were really keen on dodgeball?" The Ornithol tried and failed to pull her gaze back from Arke's interrogatory eye contact.

"*That* was a little more than dodgeball."

With a self-effacing shrug of her shoulders, Ruby came clean. "OK, so I was also the Junior Cage Fighting Champion of Barsia for ten years."

"I can see why that would slip your mind." Kennedy shook his head with a deep chuckle before stepping forwards and shaking Ruby's hand enthusiastically. "Joking, by the way, that's awesome. And thanks, big thanks." He took a deep breath and looked over to his ship as it drifted slowly away. "I need to get back to the *Warrior* and see if they've fixed the problem."

"Let's hope so. Ruby, now I know you've got hidden talents, you and I need to get busy; there's still cataclysms out there." Arke squared her shoulders with grim resolution and nodded towards the Sky Guard ships as they manoeuvred away from the ominously smoking merchantman.

Kennedy looked at them with a frown but nodded slowly. "Ok, but before you go – Ruby, you need to know something that might save your life. The greater Arke's sense of humour, the greater the danger you're in. Don't ask me, I've never understood either. And remember the *Warrior's* number one rule – don't bloody well die." He looked over to his ship for a moment, cast his alter over to its decks, then flickered and disappeared.

⚔ ⚔ ⚔

THE GENTLE, RHYTHMIC humming from the engine had changed to a lumpy clanking and its jarring rattle slowly bled through the blackness in Sparkz's head. His eyes flickered and blinked weakly but did not open until the first desperate note of Ellie's voice as she thumped on the engine room door added urgency to his efforts to wake.

"SPARKZ! WHAT'S WRONG? DO YOU NEED HELP? SPARKZ!"

It took a moment to focus, but when he did, he saw a stranger in the uniform of a merchantman's commander standing by the door, a long wrench in one hand and a crowbar in the other. Slowly putting an exploratory hand to the blood and swelling on his temple, Sparkz straightened with a grimace and climbed silently out from his awkward position among the pipes. The man had his back turned so Sparkz walked carefully towards the control panels and started work to bring the engine back online. Unfortunately, the sound of switches clicking and the whirring of circuits as they realigned wasn't something he could silence, so the engineer moved as quickly as possible given the pain in his head.

"You must have an incredibly thick skull, grease monkey." The merchantman's commander turned sharply and strode towards Sparkz. "I thought I hit you hard enough to keep you down for hours." He sneered, his cut glass accent causing more of a reaction on his enemy's face than his words.

"See, that's the problem with us grubby manual labourers. We're so used to getting beaten down by you wet-nursed do-nothings that we just keep getting up and carrying on." Sparkz moved from panel to panel, his fingers swiftly re-aligning every miscued switch, lever and dial. "Anyway, fun fact... today's my birthday."

"And your Deathday." The man interrupted, rapping the crowbar on a pipe with a heavy clunk.

"I expect that sounded better in your head." A distinctly unimpressed Sparkz carried on working. "As I was about to say... my birthdays have always sucked harder than your father."

He wasn't lying. The day he'd been born Sparkz had been given away to a childless couple who he only remembered by virtue of their punishments every time he showed any hint of his magical abilities. When they'd died during a terrible outbreak of sloughing sickness, he'd escaped the official purge of their district by using those very magic talents to make himself small enough to slip into the sewers. Washing out to sea in a torrent of excrement wasn't exactly the tenth birthday he'd hoped for, but, if he was honest with himself, out of the twenty since that one, he'd definitely had worse. Over the years, his birthdays had never brought anything other than pain or distress and he was fully ready to share the load with someone who deserved it.

"Step away from those controls or I will show you what twelve years of martial training can accomplish!"

Sparkz's eyes narrowed as he turned slowly around. "This seems to be broken." One of his hands rested just below a crippled lever, a forefinger imperiously tapping the casing around it. "Did you happen to use your *incredible* martial skills to do something so demeaning as to whack it with a hammer?"

"This spanner did a fine job. Not quite a precision tool but it has its uses."

Sparkz looked briefly pained. It was a wrench – one of his own custom-made tools and he did not appreciate it being spoken about with such ignorant disparagement. But then he smiled a little, his eyes glittering with malice as he dipped his other hand into his pocket.

"Unlike you."

Noticing Sparkz's hand emerge with a tiny screwdriver in it, the merchant commander broke into derisive laughter. "You're threatening me with that?"

Turning back to the console, Sparkz snapped the wrecked lever off and stabbed the end of the tool in its place before using it to click the circuit to the on position.

"STOP!"

The crowbar swung fast at the back of Sparkz's head, but he'd been carefully watching the man's reflection on the panel's metal casing in readiness for an attack. He ducked away from the blow and propelled himself backwards into the officer's body, knocking him into the wall of pipework behind.

Staggering after the unexpected counterattack, the

officer curled his wrench-holding arm around Sparkz's neck but was completely unprepared for the teeth that bit deeply into the side of his wrist. He dropped the tool with a shout of pain and the perfectly weighted metal fell neatly into its owner's waiting hand. With a lurch, Sparkz pulled away, but only far enough that he could angle the wrench horizontally before slamming himself backwards again, stabbing the tool heavily into the stomach of the bigger man.

The commander doubled over, gasping for breath amid groans of pain, while Sparkz turned, his expression ice cold as he smashed the wrench over the knuckles of the hand still holding the crowbar. Twice was enough to release the commander's grasp on that as well and as it clanged heavily to the floor, Sparkz gripped his improvised weapon in both hands and crashed it against the man's chin.

"This is a *wrench*. It's adjustable. Spanners are not."

The merchantman's commander raised a weak hand in what might have been surrender but Sparkz ignored it and savagely cracked the tool against his enemy's wrist before stepping aside as his opponent slumped to the floor, unsuccessfully trying to say something through a broken jaw.

"The problem with you *highly trained* fighters," Sparkz growled as he dragged the commander's bloody and moaning body over towards the console by his non-broken arm, "is that you're so intent on parading yourself around, admiring your skills, that you don't bother to actually see what's in front of you." He wasn't even out of breath after his exertions, but his voice was dark and his words dripped with menace.

In one brisk movement, he shoved the man's face up against another damaged lever, this one only a couple of feet off the floor. He held the officer there as he spoke, the broken metal digging into his nose.

"Lesson one: this is a lever. *Someone,* someone very stupid, moved it to the OFF position and then snapped it in half. *Someone* clearly thought that would be sufficient to keep it from being turned back on."

Stepping back and delivering a single, sharp kick to the back of the man's head resulted in the officer's face becoming part of the lever. Despite the ensuing scream of pain, Sparkz kept his boot on the back of the commander's head, forcing him ever closer to the console as he spoke, his voice becoming louder and angrier as he vented.

"I'm no-one to people like your *exquisite* self, just a grunt who spends all day covered in oil or grease. I'm invisible until you need me and if I can't do what you want because you haven't given me the training or the tools then *your* problems become *my* fault. But it's OK, even though you aren't a *precision* tool, I finally found a use for you. Happy birthday to me."

Sparkz dragged the man slowly upwards by the collar, the lever taking a while to move but finally moving into the ON position with a muffled click. He yanked the man's head clear of the console and let him slide to the floor.

"Lesson two: once a part is irreparable, get rid of it."

Leaving the merchant's commander in a barely conscious heap, Sparkz strode over to the door and unlocked it, only to find a very angry Ellie on the other side, sword raised, ready to attack.

"Not now, Ellie!" His expression lightened immediately as he saw her in full-on feral mode and quickly held up his hands in mock surrender.

"Are you alright?" She sheathed her weapon and looked at his bloodied face with concern.

"Of course. The other guy's over there, dripping all over my floor." Sparkz turned and hurried back to continue fixing the damage to the engine controls. "What's going on topside?"

Ellie's vitriolic reply was more than seventy-five percent curse words and the only thing that stemmed her furious tirade was seeing the state of Sparkz's opponent. Her scowl was suddenly replaced with a grin of cold satisfaction, and she started to drag him away, leaving a wide blood trail on the engine room floor. As she reached the door, she bellowed for Urzish to come and help her teach the saboteur – or what was left of him – how to fly.

⚔ ⚔ ⚔

IT WAS EXACTLY the moment that the Ornithol folded her wings and dived straight down towards the deck of the nearest escort vessel that she realised Arke wasn't a massive fan of bird-style headlong descents. She herself found absolutely nothing disconcerting about plummeting vertically downwards, but it wasn't hard to work out that the drawn-out, four-letter word that the Soulbound was yelling as she was carried towards the Barsian ship indicated her discomfort. However, there wasn't much that could be done to assuage Arke's misgivings except land as quickly as possible. Judging her approach perfectly despite the distraction of her passenger's noisy anxiety, Ruby waited until she could almost count the rivets in the deck planking of the Sky Guards' cutter before flaring her wings and landing next to the ship's wheel with a featherlight touch.

While the Soulbound recovered from the flight, Ruby took the initiative and grabbed the helmsman, stabbing her beak into his face before throwing him down to the main deck like a bowling ball. His body crashed into his own men, knocking some of them flying, while the others stared in shock, the Ornithol's pre-emptive strike having slowed their reactions to the bird-borne attack.

Ruby was already committed to a flying roundhouse on another Sky Guard when he suddenly stopped moving, white-blue frost covering his body and icicles hanging from his fingers. As the Ornithol's foot connected, the unfortunate man shattered into thousands of pieces that clinked down onto the deck in a tinkling melody of icy dismemberment. She looked around quickly, almost comically surprised to see the entire crew frozen in position, weapons still raised, angry expressions etched in shining crystals of ice.

"That was you?" Ruby fastened her eyes on Arke as she blew on her hands as if to warm them up.

"No, some other idiot with talon piercings in her shoulders."

"Oh, I'm sorry! I'm not used to carrying people around and I didn't want to drop you."

"My skin and I could tell."

It was hard to know whether Arke was angry or not, but there wasn't time for Ruby to muse any further on the matter as the Soulbound headed below decks. The Ornithol hurried after her crewmate as she slid down the ladder and stamped on the floor, sending waves of blue light rippling away into the dimly lit corridor.

"Time to clip this bastard's wings. Kick it down." Arke stopped in a doorway where the blue light had gathered and stood aside while her companion broke the lock with a single, powerful blow. "Magic keeps these hypocritical bastards' ships in the air. I'll deal with that, you wait here."

Ruby fully expected to hear Arke destroying some form of device or arcane engine. But as she heard voices rather than sounds of destruction coming from the room, she peeked inside.

Inside the dark and fetid cabin, she saw two people chained to the side of the ship – two unwashed, withered, beaten people, dressed in nothing but filthy underwear. With mounting horror, she realised that the magic that made Barsian ships fly didn't come from a series of runes, an artefact or a process, it came from actual living mages who were kept like animals in airless, windowless prisons.

She had to put a hand to her beak and hold it shut to stop her anger springing out as she listened to Arke's voice, her tone unusually soft as the prisoners cowered away from her.

"It's OK. Look." The Soulbound held up a hand, touching her fingers together and making them light up. "I'm one of you and I'm here to get you out."

The two mages stopped cowering and shaking their heads, spoke almost as one.

"The chains are warded, unbreakable."

Arke looked closer, and her shoulders stiffened in frustration.

"There is only one way we can leave." The second

115

prisoner bowed his head fatalistically. "Kill us."

"Please." The first nodded in agreement.

"Lie on the floor." Arke commanded, her jaw clenched tight.

Ruby's eyes widened as both mages got to their knees and then lay down as best they could. Each one was secured in a similar fashion, one hand held up by a chain so perfectly measured that their skin never left contact with a crystalline band that seemed to be built into the hull. She couldn't bear to watch as Arke's fingertips lit up with power and winced as she heard the first of the crackling energy blasts hit.

After a moment, Ruby realised that the Soulbound was still firing, over and over and opened her eyes again. She saw that Arke's target was not the living batteries, but the point where the first prisoner's chain was fastened to the side of the ship. Her expression was pure and intense with concentration as her magic pummelled the thick planks around the rivets into matchsticks. Ruby wasted no time in joining her, shouting to be heard above the sound of the heavy impacts.

"I can help!"

With a curt nod, the Soulbound started work on freeing the second mage, her repetitive strikes beginning almost before their ears had recovered from the first bout. Ruby stood to one side of the first prisoner, calling on Chromatia to aid her in channelling her rage and horror into solid blows that did not cease until she had destroyed what was left of the wood.

"We'll have to carry them," Arke ordered as the mages rolled free. "And fast. I don't know how long we have before this heap of shit falls out of the sky."

Neither burden weighed enough to trouble their rescuers as Ruby and Arke carried and boosted the pair up the ladder to the main deck where the mages stood on wobbly legs, blinking owlishly in the daylight.

"You fly, right?" As the men nodded, the Soulbound pointed to the south. "Nidea's that way, no laws against magic there."

With effusive thanks that Ruby noticed Arke could only awkwardly acknowledge, the mages took a few deep breaths before using their magic on themselves for what must have been the first time in years. As they took off, Ruby also hopped into the air and hovered above Arke, suggesting she hold onto her legs as a talon-free way of travelling. While the Soulbound experimented with several arm locks, Ruby watched the ex-prisoners flying upwards, gaining more and more confidence as they felt the pull of the wind.

"Ready!"

Arke's call to Ruby came just as the ice spell on the crew of the escort vessel ended and some of the Sky Guards aimed pistols in their direction. However, the Barsians' time would have been better spent running for the racks of lifebelts as, with a lurch, they and their entire ship suddenly learnt about terminal velocity in a very personal way.

On the short flight to their next target, Ruby's mind was awash with questions, but the musket balls being fired in their direction meant that it was definitely not the best time to ask them. It was far more difficult to weave around bullets whilst carrying someone, especially someone swinging from your legs, so the Ornithol simply dived away under the ship, gaining momentum so she could slingshot up the other side. Swinging almost horizontally over the railings, she kicked Arke clear near to the hatch with a shout of "GO!" while she continued onwards, throwing herself bodily into the middle of the Sky Guards.

⚔ ⚔ ⚔

THE SOULBOUND HAD never entered combat via being launched like a bomb, skidding across the deck on her back and promptly falling down a hatch. She resolved never to do so again as it was not only disconcerting and deeply undignified, but it also really, really hurt and she took a few moments to get her breath back while she checked in with all her limbs.

"You are fine, get up already, or are you feeling your age today?" Stabbington was his usual caring self, and his host chose to ignore his jibes as she peeled herself off the floor.

This ship was older than the first and with a quick assessment of her surroundings, Arke knew she didn't have to use her powers to find the mages. She could smell them, and she could hear them. Without Ruby to kick the door in, she simply fired a couple of energy blasts at the lock, shattering it. The sound alerted a Sky Guard who rushed down the corridor towards her, but Arke didn't even bother turning around to battle with him. It was far simpler to just hold a hand out in his direction and summon her sword the moment before the man came into weapon range. The soldier was doubtless surprised when he was impaled on a magical blade but undoubtedly even more surprised when he was swung around and launched into the stinking cabin. His screams and the bestial noises within told Arke all she needed to know without even needing to look. Minds gave way after years locked in the dark.

"You cannot save these." Stabbington's tone was suddenly entirely different, his words clipped and curt. "Do not try."

Forty-three years together, living as outcasts and pirates meant that Arke and her demon had experienced a lot of the worst things life had to offer. Whatever he did with his unpleasant memories she did not know, but she worked hard on locking all of hers in boxes and throwing them away. As she stood in the doorway and prepared herself, she knew that this particular room would create a memory box she would need to wash down with an awful lot of alcohol.

A few moments and a few devastating magical blasts later, Arke sprinted down the corridor and threw herself up the stairs, immediately looking around the deck for Ruby. The giant, rainbow coloured bird wasn't hard to find even amid the mass of Sky Guard trying to attack her. Arke sprinted towards her crewmate, slamming a series of crackling bursts of energy into the fray to clear herself a path. As the deck trembled under her feet, she shouted a warning and leapt towards the Ornithol who reacted instinctively, grabbing her crewmate and flaring her wings as that ship too started to plummet away beneath them.

"What happened to the mages?" Ruby asked breathlessly, hauling Arke up and holding her so they were almost face to face as she headed towards the cutter that was coming around behind the *Warrior*.

Her question hung heavily between them as they flew towards their next target.

Chapter Eight
Defying Gravity

WHILE URZISH THREW the saboteur clear of the *Warrior*, Kennedy ran down to the engine room where Sparkz and Zeke were running a huge, armoured cable from the end console to the generator.

"Gentlemen, miracle workers, beacons of light and hope."

"Stick your bullshit where the sun doesn't shine," Sparkz replied with a few extra swear words for emphasis. "Give us two minutes, she'll be ready to go." He hauled the heavy cable into position and started to strip the sheathing with a knife. "I've just got to connect this to a power source and we're away."

Kennedy tried to look casual as he delivered an instruction he doubted would be well received. "Cool. But I actually want you to turn it off."

"WHAT?" Sparkz's knife slipped, cutting his finger and he spat out a curse before sucking the wound quickly. "It's off now!"

"I mean ALL of it. We'll drop without exposing our exhaust to their cataclysms. Straight down." Kennedy used his hands to demonstrate the plan, his tone overflowing with positivity.

"And then crash, saving them a magic bullet." Sparkz's was quite the opposite.

"Of course not! You'll restart the engines."

"I'll restart the... are you KIDDING ME RIGHT NOW? As we are PLUMMETING to the ground after a complete engine shut down, you want me to restart everything? A procedure that normally takes ten minutes."

Having nothing useful to say in response, Kennedy decided a wide and confident smile was his best option. He couldn't help but notice that Sparkz was not smiling so he looked away and cranked his happy expression to the max before meeting his brother's eyes again. Despite Sparkz's continued accusatory glare, Kennedy chose to believe that his brother was thinking about how the miracle could be accomplished and not about castrating him with a pair of bricks and a hair band.

Finally, Sparkz broke eye contact and sighed heavily. "And you want me to do it now?"

"About three minutes ago actually. We have a Barsian ship coming around astern of us."

Sparkz tucked his knife and screwdriver in a pocket and hurried to the main control boards, grabbing his wrench on the way. "You could've said that earlier. If you want to be at the wheel when she drops then you'd better run."

"Count to twenty and restart." Kennedy was already on his way out of the engine room. "And then I'll need full power."

"And I'll rip myself a new ar..."

Kennedy didn't hear the rest of that word as he leapt up the stairs and sprinted across the deck to grab the wheel. The main stabilising wings were already loose, Paltos standing by one and Urzish the other, ready to push the locking pins back into place the moment the

Warrior stopped falling. The smaller outriggers would hopefully be enough to keep her steady, but they couldn't risk the large ones in a rapid descent. Everyone else, even the merchant crew, were sitting on the deck, holding tight and looking extremely nervous. No-one wanted to drop out of the sky and simply hope the engines could be restarted in time to save them being a smudge on the ground. However, they were also aware that the instant and guaranteed permanence of being blown into atoms was a far less desirable option.

As Kennedy reached the helm, the Barsian ship that was coming around behind them managed to fire both of its bow chasers with loud cracks and clouds of magical smoke. That was all he had time to see as the *Warrior's* deck shuddered and the entire ship began freefalling. Several of the merchant crew started to scream and Kennedy shut his eyes, concentrating on hanging onto the wheel. He gritted his teeth, trying to persuade his flame-grilled sausage breakfast to stay where he'd put it and desperately hoping that their descent would be terminated by his brother and not the ground.

"...Nineteen...Twenty...Twenty-one...Twenty-two..."

Realising that the ability to count accurately while surrounded by terrified screeching and the insatiable hunger of gravity was not one of his strong suits, Kennedy resolved never to try to do so again. By the time he reached twenty-three the only thing stopping the urge to vomit was the guilt that constricted his throat. He'd doomed them all, all the lives on his ship. As he kept counting, he realised the pressure on his body had been changing long before he'd even noticed. The ship was falling more slowly. Plummeting became hurtling, hurtling became dropping, and finally the *Warrior* oozed to a gentle stop. Then he heard a very smug cough from the engine speaking tube followed by his brother's voice.

"Miracle enough for you, Kennedy?"

Kennedy cleared his throat, forcing his voice to its normal pitch and not the hoarse squeak he suspected would otherwise emerge.

"Do we have propulsion yet?"

After a lot of muffled noises that he chose not to listen too closely to, the next voice he heard was Zeke's.

"Sparkz wishes me to inform you that you are an insufferable prick who regularly achieves biological impossibilities with yourself, and that if he hadn't burnt all the skin off his hand disrupting the power to the crystal before slowly resuming the connection, firstly, you would all be dead and secondly, he would be running up to the main deck and punching you squarely in your perfectly chiselled chin."

Kennedy grinned at the Bior's detailed interpretation of what his brother was clearly ranting about in the background. "Tell him he's my hero. And then ask him if we have propulsion."

There was silence from the other end of the tube and Kennedy turned to watch the nearest Barsian ship as it dived recklessly towards them.

"One closing in and another a decent distance behind." Paltos pressed his telescope to his eye as he too watched their pursuit.

"Ellie, please let Gurdi know that my brother needs medical attention," Kennedy ordered, hands gripping the control levers impatiently. While the stomach-churning vertical drop had given them a head start, they still needed to finish the getaway.

"The engine is online, Sparkz requests that you treat the control levers like you would a beautiful woman." Zeke's voice was its usual robotic self as he delivered a heavier burn than the one he'd reported on Sparkz's hand. "Run away and let someone more qualified deal with her."

Pretending that he couldn't hear the snorts of laughter from everyone within earshot, Kennedy eased the levers forwards to engage the crystal powered propulsion. The ship began to come alive again: the hum of the engine increasing, the wheel vibrating under his hands and finally the wind pushing against his face as the *Warrior* finally got underway.

"Cutter firing!"

⚔ ⚔ ⚔

"*WARRIOR!*" RUBY GASPED as she saw the Barsian cataclysms fire. "Praise Chromatia, they missed again!"

"Chromatia, my arse," Arke muttered to herself before raising her voice so the Ornithol could hear her. "Get us on that ship NOW!"

This time the Soulbound didn't react as Ruby folded her wings back and dropped like a stone towards the cutter as it put its nose hard down to pursue the *Warrior*. Arke was ready for her ejection this time and gritted her teeth as she was launched down the sloping deck towards the left cataclysm cannon, its long, rifled barrel still wreathed in cyan smoke. Time seemed to slow as she lost her footing and slid spread-eagled down the deck while Stabbington unhelpfully compared her current position with Ruby's effortless ability to remain balanced while fighting her way towards the right hand gun.

Crashing into the netting by the bow with an uncomfortable thud, Arke still was trying to extricate herself when one of the gun captains appeared next to her and thrust his handspike towards her chest. She managed to bring Stabbington's blade into play in time to deflect the heavy iron-shod pole so it glanced off her shoulder rather than delivering a full blow to her breastbone.

"He is saying some of my favourite bad words, and I do *not* like his pronunciation." Stabbington's tone was nothing short of acidic until he noticed Arke's extended and defiant middle finger, and then he started to laugh. "NOW the stupid man will shut up."

With a hiss of magic, the Soulbound threw one of her punchier spells at her attacker, blue flames instantly covering him from head to foot. Arke stood up just as her victim fell down, magical fire dancing devilishly around her as she turned a deliberately ominous gaze on the rest of the gun crew. That was enough to break their nerve, all of them desperately clawing their way up the steeply sloping decks to get away.

"Ruby, crack open the red barrel on your left."

If the Ornithol thought that was an odd instruction while in the middle of combat on the deck of a diving enemy vessel, she didn't show it. With one yank, she ripped the lid off the container and exposed its contents, pink tinted sand that seemed to sizzle as it reacted with the air.

Arke grabbed one of the crates of ammunition sitting next to the guns and dragged it awkwardly up the tilted decks towards Ruby.

"Magic suppression sand – pour it over this ammo."

Ruby quickly set to work, but as Arke slid across the deck towards a second box of cataclysm ammunition, the hairs on the back of her neck stood up.

"INCOMI…"

Stabbington didn't even have chance to finish his warning as a magically produced lightning bolt hit Arke squarely in the chest, launching her into the side of the cutter with an impact that smashed all the breath from her body.

"Ruby has also been hit with the lightning, and SHE is back fighting already," Stabbington goaded. "Get up before you embarrass yourself any further!"

Empathy simply did not exist in Stabbington's battle dictionary and a lightly toasted Arke had to regather her scattered senses to the dulcet sounds of her demon's disappointment. She sat up and spotted Ruby slamming fists, feet and wings into a crowd of emboldened Sky Guard. The well balanced Ornithol was perfectly at home on the angled decks and was busy making the most of the fact her attackers were not. Arke ignored Stabbington's unpleasantries as she hauled herself to her feet and tried to concentrate on activating her ice spell to help her crewmate.

"You're not the only mage on this vessel, but you are the only illegal one."

The Soulbound heard a woman's voice behind her an instant before she felt a painfully large fist try to displace her left kidney. As her knees buckled with the blow, pain firing through her entire body like a wave of burning acid, a pair of orc sized hands grabbed her by

126

the neck. Arke could barely breathe enough to struggle as she felt herself being hauled across the deck before her head was forced down into the magic suppression sand.

"This is *my* ship and I'm not losing it to a pair of pathetic pirates!"

From the other side of the cutter, Ruby grabbed the man in front of her and lifted him up before slamming a palm to his chest so hard that he flew across the cannons and crashed into the hulking Barsian who was torturing her friend.

The orc barely flinched at the impact, but she did let go of Arke before turning to hurl a lightning bolt towards the Ornithol. With her assailant distracted, the Soulbound finally managed to lift her head from the sand and gasp in a ragged breath.

The commander hauled Arke upright, spinning her around before grabbing her by the throat and effortlessly lifting her off her feet. Her face contorted with rage as she slammed a single heavy fist into the Soulbound's ribs. "I saw what you did to the other ships! This is for them!"

Another flailing soldier flew across the deck and crashed into the orc's back, but again she barely seemed to notice the hit. Concentrating fully on her captive, she closed her fingers more tightly around Arke's throat and punched her again.

As a result of her inability to take a hint, the next thing to hit the commander was Ruby's beak as she launched herself like a missile and stabbed the woman in the side of the neck. That attack was followed by both fists flying at eye-watering speed and pummelling the orc like a mountainous punchbag. Arke was dropped to the deck where she heaved in a few shallow breaths and tried to ignore the searing pain from the magical burns all over her face.

Ruby managed to land a blow that knocked her opponent to her knees, but instead of a moment of respite, the Ornithol was the recipient of a cluster of lightning bolts, one of which hit her directly in the head, staggering her backwards. Taking her opportunity, the orc commander quickly swept Ruby's legs from under her before scrambling back to her feet.

Behind her Arke leant heavily on the barrel and scooped up a handful of the suppression sand, grimacing as her skin began to react to its touch. "Is that ALL you can do? Lightning. And more lightning. Maybe some lightning?"

The orc commander reacted immediately to the taunting words, changing the target for the next handful of lightning at the very last moment. Ruby had just regained her equilibrium enough to see the magical bolts arc towards the Soulbound who reacted by launching her handful of sand into the air. With a flurry of sparks and sizzles, it intercepted the lightning with ease, negating every single attack before it hit.

"All I needed was a helping... sand." Arke dug both hands back into the barrel. "No? I wasn't sure about that line either but sometimes you need to try these things out."

The orc started to climb the short distance of deck up towards the Soulbound but was suddenly assaulted with handfuls of flying sand, peppering her with painful magic suppression. "I've never tried sand blasting before. How am I doing?"

Arke was waiting for a chance to move and her barrage meant that the opportunity didn't take long to arise. Beset by the painful, sandy onslaught the commander lifted her huge forearm to protect her face and the Soulbound dived away, sliding feet first down the deck towards the last box of ammunition.

With a cry of frustration, the orc chased after her. However, having been allowed some time to recover from the lightning attacks, Ruby was ready for some perfectly weighted revenge. As the commander charged down the deck, the Ornithol leapt across, clotheslining the woman with a sinewy forearm which put her down and followed up with a heavy kick to her forehead which made sure she stayed there.

Their officer beaten, the remaining Sky Guard started firing their weapons. Ruby flattened herself to the deck and slid to where Arke was struggling to lift the ammunition, both of her hands as well as her face now blistered from the sand. As bullets started to thump into the ship around them, the Ornithol grabbed the box.

"Throw it overboard. We're going home." Without another word, the Soulbound jumped off the cutter's bow, leaving Ruby to follow her.

Having spent most of their journey scolding an entirely unrepentant Arke about throwing herself off sky ships without any warning, Ruby finally landed them both safely on the *Warrior's* deck. She saw Kennedy's smile on seeing them arrive clouding to a frown as he saw the sheer amount of feathers missing from herself and the livid burns all over Arke.

"Don't tell me you're OK," Kennedy looked expectantly at the first mate who sighed and started to head towards the Soulbound.

"What gives it away?" Arke croaked. She sat down heavily, trying and failing to rub some of the sand off her face with an equally sandy sleeve.

Far above them, there was a massive explosion as the merchantman finally blew itself into pieces and the Soulbound sighed with weary resignation. "NOW you explode. Not earlier when it might have been a useful diversion."

Paltos took a long look at her predicament before eyeing Ruby, a grin quivering on his lips. "Birds bathe in sand to get rid of parasites, right? How come Arke's still here?"

Kennedy snorted with laughter while Arke took slow, deep breaths and shook her head wearily. Finally, the first mate reached down and carefully hauled the Soulbound to her feet.

"Let's get you washed off, then you can go and swear at Gurdi because she must be getting lonely. It's been what, ten days without you as a patient? She must think she's on holiday."

After Ruby watched Paltos ignore Arke's exhausted attempts to stop him helping her below decks, the Ornithol gave Kennedy a quick version of events on board the Barsian ships. When she'd finished her story, she turned her gaze to the merchant sailors who Urzish and Ellie were lining up on top of the captain's cabin and supplying with hefty tots of rum.

"What are you going to do with them?"

"Still two cutters out there but they'll have to stop to pick up some men overboard," Kennedy replied. "We can solve our passenger problem and our stalker issue at the same time." He gave a thumbs up to Urzish who tapped the first sailor on the shoulder.

"But...!" Ruby watched in horror as the man launched himself off the side of the ship and disappeared. With immense relief, she saw him reappear again as the life preserving belt he was wearing activated and floated him gently upwards in the *Warrior's* wake.

One by one, the captured sailors took their turns jumping over the side until they bobbed behind the pirate vessel in a long line.

Kennedy steered the *Warrior* towards a nearby cloudbank before turning to look at Ruby again. "Post battle rule one – everyone gets checked over by Gurdi. However, no harm waiting up here for a bit while she recovers from treating her least patient patient."

"Least patient? More like feral," Paltos remarked with a chuckle as he climbed back up to the main deck, carrying mugs of coffee in his huge hands. "Once I had to put her in a headlock and drag her into the infirmary."

"Was that the arrow in the eye or the time her hand was nearly hanging off?" Kennedy leant his forearms on the wheel and sipped his drink slowly.

"Couldn't tell you, it all blends into one."

"She doesn't like healers?" Ruby puzzled. She had always enjoyed her time in the Apothecarium back at the convent; a let up on training and an excess of ice cream was always good.

"Arke doesn't like anyone," Paltos chuckled. "Bad ass and pain in the ass." He opened his hip flask and took a long, satisfying swig before washing it back with a mug of coffee and smiling over at the Ornithol. "Still want to be a pirate, Ruby? There's time to get away before you're stuck with us forever."

Ruby looked around the deck, tilting her head this way and that as she considered his question. She'd always dreamt about flying on a sky ship, but the reality seemed very different to her imaginings. Adjusting to her new life had been more stressful than she'd expected, but it wasn't anything to do with her missing feathers, the violence or the battle she'd just been in. Instead, she'd been dealing with her own internal frustrations. She'd been aggravated by her inability to coil rope, tie different knots or remember which part of the ship was which, as well as being plagued by the guilt that not worshipping her god had unexpectedly produced.

She'd recently dealt with the last issue by telling Kennedy about her childhood as an acolyte of Chromatia and thus revealing the source of the divine magic she'd used in Gorki's office. His instant, warm acceptance had emboldened her enough to ask if she might look for a place for her daily devotions on the main deck. She'd explained that the rainbow god was deeply connected to the weather, of the cycle of good coming after bad, the sunshine following the storm and had voiced a hope that she'd find a connection to her outside somewhere. Having received his approval, she'd searched the ship until, with a moment of pure joy, she'd spotted endless tiny rainbows twinkling in the *Warrior's* exhaust gases. After that surprising affirmation of Chromatia's blessing, she'd known without a doubt where she belonged.

She took a sip of the incredibly strong coffee, feeling its briskly invigorating touch flood through her like a warm wave, and nodded decisively. "I'm exactly where I want to be."

Chapter Nine

Those Murderous Men on Their Flying Machines

THE *WARRIOR* FLEW into a thick bank of clouds which shielded the ship from sight while Kennedy slowly changed course to head for the Greyspine Mountains again. Their haul from the merchantman would bring a good payout from their long-time ally, Mr Crimbles, who made his living in several nefarious ways, one of which was supplying illegal magic potions to every corner of Barsia. Back when he was taking his first steps towards being a captain, Arke had insisted Kennedy learn about flying smaller ships. That had led to two years in charge of one of Crimbles' high-powered delivery clippers distributing his illicit products around the Empire. It had been an adrenaline filled job and the young captain had come away with skills as well as scars but more importantly, he'd gained a powerful friend. The magic dealer would always buy what Kennedy acquired and that made his life an awful lot easier.

After their close call with the Barsian escorts, the *Warrior's* crew were twitchy and distracted. Normally it only took a couple of days for morale to improve following a near miss, but as they flew closer to the

Greyspines, negativity reigned supreme. Sparkz's expression was a constant frustrated scowl, as with his burnt hand heavily bandaged, he could only supervise while Zeke repaired the damage in the engine room. Arke, burdened with a memory she needed to destroy, had disappeared into her cabin after returning from the infirmary and spent two days very much less than sober.

Kennedy spent a lot of time with Ruby, answering every single question the Ornithol had about the *Warrior* and its history as well as the realities of life that she'd been shielded from in the convent. In return, she told him more about herself, especially what it was like being raised by cage-fighting nuns. Before meeting her, Kennedy's only experience of Ornithols had been Porro, whose plumage was brighter than his personality, so Ruby's eager intelligence and positive outlook gave him an entirely new perspective on their race.

During a conversation with Ruby about cage fighting training, Kennedy suddenly thought of the ideal activity to rouse the crew from their doldrums. At breakfast the next day, he put his plan into action, asking everyone to report topside at two o'clock for some professional development. He chose to ignore the deafening silence that followed his order and walked out of the galley with a spring to his step. It was obvious to him that some fresh air and team building would soon zap the crew into a more positive frame of mind.

"This is more like it! I told you a little exercise would work wonders on morale," Kennedy enthused as his crew shouted hearty encouragement to Ellie who flew through the air in a jumble of limbs before slamming onto the crash mat for the second time in a minute.

"As long as none of them get launched overboard or snapped in half." Paltos was sitting on a coil of rope, sipping from a tankard of coffee with a placid expression on his face.

"They'll be fine," Kennedy replied with a grin. "Would you look at that? She's quite incredible."

He applauded vigorously as Urzish staggered backwards, blood pouring from her nose after a precision elbow from Ruby. She regained her balance quickly and charged her opponent, taking advantage of the fact that the Ornithol was still concentrating all her blows on Krugg's stubbornly static defence. Almost as if she had eyes in the back of her head, Ruby whirled around at the last moment, nearly folding herself in half to avoid Urzish's heavily weighted fist before using the orc's own momentum to launch her headfirst into Krugg's meaty forearms.

The first mate handed Kennedy a florin with a rueful sigh as Urzish slid slowly down the ogre's legs and landed in a heap on the deck. "You win. Is seems that neither Urzish nor I saw that coming." He swigged another mouthful of coffee and wiped his mouth. "I'm glad I don't have to fight her, I'm way too old for all that."

"Oh, didn't I say?" Kennedy chuckled. "We're up next."

There was a frigid moment of silence as Paltos turned slowly to face his captain, landing his gaze squarely on Kennedy's face. "I'm sorry, what?"

It was barely ten minutes later when Arke finally emerged from her cabin and blinked owlishly in the weak afternoon sunshine. As Kennedy watched her sweep the deck with a glance, he wondered if the

Soulbound thought she'd happened upon the early stages of the Ornithol Uprising. Ruby was fine, in fact she barely had a feather out of place, but around her in a defeated circle, sat or lay most of the crew nursing bruises in every conceivable place. Paltos was flat on his back with a cold compress covering his eyes and Kennedy himself was strapping up an ankle while sporting a wad of bloody tissue wedged in each nostril. Over to his left, Ellie was pretending she hadn't kissed the crash mat so many times she was tempted to take it out to dinner and nearby, Urzish was styling out her bruised coccyx by never getting to her feet again.

Kennedy raised a hand in greeting, only to witness one of the most damningly disappointed head shakes he'd ever seen Arke deliver.

"I would ask if you're OK, but I can see that you're all idiots."

"The captain wanted me to teach the crew some new moves." Ruby looked and sounded utterly dispirited despite Kennedy's attempts to persuade her that she'd done exactly as he'd asked.

"Doesn't look like you've been very successful. They already knew how to get the shit kicked out of them." Arke's tone might have been laced with deep disapproval, but she couldn't hide her wickedly amused grin as she passed Ruby on the way to the main hatch.

Noticing the Ornithol stand that little bit taller after the Soulbound's moment of offhanded solidarity, Kennedy smiled to himself, then winced as his battered lip split open again. Clearly their recent shared experiences had created something of a bond, and he loved nothing better than seeing his crew make friends.

After their bruising afternoon, Kennedy decided that rest was probably the best option for raising morale. The ship was steadily increasing altitude as she flew directly towards the edge of the Greyspine range which rose like a giant cliff directly from the sea. The closest peaks looked large enough but the ones behind were bigger, darker and far more oppressive. As the *Warrior* ascended towards the wall of rock, the icy air grew more and more painful to breathe, and everyone bar the watches stayed below deck. It was clear that no-one was relishing the forthcoming job although everyone was fully committed to the promised reward. The crew's expressions grew more grimly determined with every hour that saw their ship climb to a height that would clear the outlying mountains and expose them all to the winds so furious they scoured rock to the glassy cleanliness of weathered bone.

The Greyspines had a terrible reputation for good reason and although everyone was prepared for the weather, no-one was ready for the added unpleasantness of horrifying dreams which started to plague them the moment they crossed over the first frost-glazed peaks. Not a night went past without dread and terror haunting all attempts to sleep. Exhaustion hit quickly from the physical exertion of keeping the ship on course in the increasingly stormy weather, compounded with waking from whatever rest they could get with an overwhelming sense of doom. Kennedy felt his crew's collective anxiety keenly and made sure to maintain a reassuringly confident expression even while struggling to handle his own uncertainty. He'd agreed to the job, but the further they flew, the more worried he became.

Thankfully for Kennedy's own morale, he didn't have the time or energy for much introversion. Steering the ship and keeping track of their course in the turbulent and stormy conditions was incredibly difficult and when he wasn't taking turns on the wheel with Urzish, he was checking and rechecking his charts.

On their third day over the mountains, while forcing down cold coffee and going over his latest attempts at calculating their position, the bell in his cabin jingled, summoning him to the wheel yet again.

He glanced at the clock which indicated it was just after midday, though the lack of light coming through his windows made it seem more like dusk. Kennedy gritted his teeth as he grabbed his sou'wester, its folds still stiff and dripping from his last excursion. Everything he'd heard about the Greyspines' weather was right. Although he'd started to tune out the sound of the wind howling and the hail smashing down, going outside in it wasn't something he ever wanted to get used to.

Forcing his arms through the heavy sleeves, Kennedy steeled himself for the outside world. He'd lost count of the times that he'd been called to the helm that day. The *Warrior* wasn't only battling weather so foul its crew had to rig safety lines across the deck; there had also been frequent reports of ominous dark shapes moving in the clouds. Kennedy had always responded to the alerts, but each time he'd fought his way to the wheel, there was nothing to see other than the screaming tempest that whipped shards of icy rain into such a frenzy that they bruised any unprotected skin.

Pulling the drawstrings of his hood tight, Kennedy stepped out onto the windblown deck, trying not to wince as the hail lashed across his face. He grabbed the guide-rope, feeling the ice around its fibres crushing under his glove as he made his way towards the bow where Urzish had her arms braced hard against the kick of the huge wheel.

"I'm here," he shouted, having to raise his voice to be heard over the shrieking wind and thunderous hail.

"The storm's getting worse. Visibility is dropping, and I can't see the mountains anymore," Urzish announced hoarsely. She looked exhausted as she struggled to hold the ship steady, her movements stiff and her posture hunched.

"Can't we go up to find some clear air?" Kennedy asked, cupping his hands around his mouth as he shouted the question.

"Don't think so, the subcurrent is holding us down while the vortex is pulling us on. The engine is already struggling just keeping us in the air."

Kennedy looked at the control levers, able to see they were at one hundred percent even with the ice crystals coating the glass dials. He hadn't yet resorted to the ship's emergency power which would give them a small boost, but neither the crystal nor the engine around it could maintain the overclock for very long. Kennedy knew that if they were struggling now, it was likely that even with an extra ten percent of thrust, there wouldn't be enough energy to lever the *Warrior* out of the storm's clutches. With the way the entire structure was warping and creaking in the high winds, he wasn't even sure if the ship herself could hold together with the shearing forces that would be involved in such a manoeuvre.

"Any other ideas?" he asked, in case there was anything he was missing.

"Pray?" Urzish fought with the wheel as a massive blast of wind hit the stern.

"I'll get Ruby then." Kennedy smiled wanly as he attempted to make light of the situation but then a thought hit him with almost as much force as the hail. His eyes opened wide and his body suddenly filled with the rush of energy that came with hope. "Ruby can scout ahead! She might even find us a better course."

In what might have come as a surprise to absolutely no-one except the briskly enthusiastic Kennedy, the Ornithol seemed much less keen on the idea when he charged wetly into the crew quarters to suggest it to her.

"Out there?"

"Yes! You can fly, you'll be fine."

Ruby held up a box which had been resting in her lap and showed it to him. Inside was a bedraggled, exhausted-looking tern, its wing carefully splinted.

"Look at this! Arke found it on the deck earlier and gave it to me to look after. *This* is what happens to birds in this sort of weather." She stroked the creature with a gentle finger before setting its sanctuary back down in between the two pillows on her bunk. "It plummeted to the deck, completely encased in ice."

"That's just a small bird, you are way, way bigger and stronger," Kennedy reassured. "Just help us avoid the mountains until the weather calms down a little."

"I've never been stupid enough to fly INTO a storm."

Seeing Ruby's beak tapping itself together with anxiety made Kennedy's positivity waver. He was suddenly reminded just how young and inexperienced the Ornithol really was, and how much he hated having to put such pressure on her.

"I appreciate your honesty and I wouldn't ask unless we absolutely needed your help. It might make a lifesaving difference." He left it at that before struggling back to the wheel and helping Urzish hold the storm-battered *Warrior* steady as the winds intensified yet again.

It didn't take long for Ruby to appear, shoulders hunched, tension evident in every movement. She held onto one of the lines and looked hard at Kennedy before suddenly shaking her wings loose. The wind snatched at them almost immediately, the rainbow colours blurring into one another as they flared and flexed in the vicious weather.

"I used to think I wanted to be a bird," Urzish shouted. "I don't anymore."

⚔ ⚔ ⚔

"FOLLOW ME!" RUBY called and leapt into the air, exploding upwards clear of the *Warrior*, but struggling to hold her form as she was tossed around in the gale. After a few terrifying moments, she adjusted her tactics and began to find the rhythm of the storm, soaring with the power of the wind rather than fighting across it.

The ship began to track its rainbow-coloured beacon as Ruby's birdlike instincts found a slightly clearer path through the relentless weather. Her new course brought the *Warrior* from the bank of permanent punishing hail into a zone of rain and occasional snow. A warm sense of satisfaction grew within her as she realised what a difference she was making to her ship. With that inner glow and the adrenalin that flying through a storm provided, Ruby barely noticed the freezing temperatures around her. Her focus was so perfect that she could feel each and every feather as it moved and adapted to the wind currents. She knew instinctively where the next punishing blast of wind would come from and how to skim effortlessly across the gusts.

It was so mind-blowing to feel such deep connection with the weather that Ruby only just spotted an odd shape looming in the clouds ahead. Not a mountain, but something else. She blinked, twisting her neck to try and follow its path, but the roiling darkness around her confounded even an Ornithol's super sharp eyes.

Unable to dismiss that brief vision from her mind, she scanned the clouds more intently while she angled her wings to edge her to follow the calmer air. And then she saw it again, a blurry shape flitting past a brief gap in the cloud. This time it was definitely larger, definitely closer, definitely real, and definitely heading towards the *Warrior*.

"SOMETHING'S COMING!" Ruby, like all Ornithols, knew how to project her voice and the wind did the rest, carrying her warning cry back down to the ship.

ⵝ ⵝ ⵝ

"BATTLE STATIONS!" KENNEDY yelled, more from force of habit than from actually believing anyone would hear him over the howling winds.

Urzish reached for the lever that sounded the general alarm as Kennedy summoned his alter into existence so it could take its usual station guarding the engine room. He briefly wished he hadn't told Sparkz to stow their new defences away, but quickly realised that flamethrowers active in the middle of a storm would be an all-round terrible idea. He checked his pistols were still dry under his coat and his swords free in their scabbards, then scanned the sky for whatever threat Ruby had seen as everyone hurried topside, ready to fight.

They weren't waiting for long as three men riding odd-looking wyverns burst from the clouds and dived straight for the deck, battle fury amplifying the beasts' keening roars to a volume that cut through the wind as they landed, the deck shaking under their assault. Kennedy's gaze was instantly drawn to the nearest monster as it snaked its bony neck and hissed menacingly. This was unlike any wyvern he'd ever seen – he knew them as vibrantly coloured purveyors of death, not patchworked zombie creatures whose eye sockets were empty and whose paper-thin skin was mottled in every possible shade of putrid grey. Any merchant trying to sell such ancient and tatty monstrosities would instantly attract the attention of Trading Standards, even in High Haven where the bar was set indecently low already.

When the broad-chested rider slid off his mount's bony back and stepped into view, Kennedy was relieved to see that his enemy, at least, was most definitely alive. He absolutely loathed fighting the undead with their shambling gaits and dreadful body odour problems. Anything was better than that, even a Bonelord, although it was a close-run thing. Everyone had heard grim tales of the tribal warriors who roamed the Greyspines like the deadliest tour guides. They had no itineraries and took no bookings, but if you entered their mountains you could guarantee they'd be nearby to help you along the last excursion of your life.

The tribe were particularly secretive, and only a few lucky souls had ever survived to report back on their existence. Kennedy knew more than most people about them, courtesy of his father's insistence on the importance of understanding the geo-political landscape of the *Warrior's* territory. Boring as that was, and despite young Philip's dislike of lectures, he had retained the basic information that had been patiently and persistently explained to him. The Bonelords were one of the deeply isolationist groups referred to by Barsians as the 'sordid folk' who lived in the most inaccessible mountain ranges of the Empire. The Greyspines' inhabitants were made up of a conglomeration of races and their clan was characterised not only by its extreme violence but also by its armour.

As that last fact bounced into Kennedy's head, he noticed, in a moment of grisly discomfort, that their attackers all wore what looked like a flexible carapace made from scraps of rope that wove bones of humanoid origin together. There was flexing and then there was '*I'm literally wearing my enemy's skeleton as armour*'.

As their masters dismounted, the flying monsters snarled, snapping their disappointingly serviceable jaws, and clearly ignoring the fact that their own sell-by date was several centuries ago. Kennedy locked eyes with the nearest enemy, a stony-faced hulking creature, whose oversized, hooked blades looked like they'd been hewn from granite. This was no law-ridden Barsian or pride-fuelled noble; this was simple, life or death, no negotiation or quarter would be given.

With a sudden flurry of wings and an astonishing number of blows, Kennedy watched Ruby land on the deck behind one of the Bonelords, pummelling the man into unconsciousness before he even had chance to react. His wyvern screeched as it saw its master fall, and before it had even finished the final dissonant notes of its call, the battle began.

✕ ✕ ✕

WATCHING FROM HER position by the captain's cabin, Arke scanned the initial melee to see where her magic would be most useful. Over on the starboard side of the main deck, she saw Kennedy's flashing swords draw first blood from the hulking Bonelord he'd been staring down. He was in his element, so she had every confidence that he'd be fine. Her attention moved to Sparkz, who was positioned close to the central hatch, as he leapt to the left when the nearest wyvern lunged at him. In an impressively quick move, he spun sharply back around to stab his pair of blades deep into the base of the creature's skull before it could pull its head back out of reach. She knew that on a normal beast, that would likely have been a paralysing blow, but with both a disappointing lack of reaction or indeed anything resembling blood, the wyvern continued to fight.

She swung her gaze to port where the other two patchworked monsters were trying to make a giant sandwich with Paltos, attacking him with teeth and talons in a whirlwind of violence. Realising this was where she needed to intervene, she began creating her ice spell, concentrating on building the power of its magical chill in her fingertips. Suddenly a blast of savage energy hammered into her ribcage, forcing her to stagger backwards, and her spell sizzled into nothing as she lost focus. Still reeling after the crushing impact, she spotted her attacker, the third Bonelord, his eyes glowing and fingers sparking with magic as he prepared another attack. Quickly dropping to one knee behind some nearby barrels, she received a hefty dose of Stabbington's magical painkiller while she tried to work out if the creaking noise was her laboured breathing or the grating of any broken bones.

"When will you learn to better your stance and take the weight more evenly on the balls of your feet?" Stabbington's tone was nothing short of judgemental as his host wheezed and winced with every shallow breath.

"I'm not bloody ballroom dancing!" Arke hissed. "My ribs feel like they're trying to join my spine, so shut up unless you've got something helpful to say!"

Trying to keep her head down but still find an angle to send some help towards Paltos, Arke peered around the edge of her cover to see Krugg bellowing in rage as he slammed his weapon of choice, a thick length of anchor chain, into one of the beasts who was double teaming the first mate. Another magical impact near her head made the Soulbound pull back and fire some unsighted energy bolts in the rough direction of the mage who had her pinned down. Popping her head up again, she spotted Urzish sprinting down towards the wyverns' battle but being taken down by a ball of roiling grey energy which slammed into her legs, sending her skidding across the deck like an orc-shaped skittle.

"Arke! Look ahead!" Stabbington's enhanced senses were sometimes as good as Ruby's and as the Soulbound turned towards the bow she saw the clouds parting directly ahead of the ship to show a very tall, very dark, very solid cliff. Hitting that would rank quite high on the list of 'Ways to die quickly', right above 'playing with sour-faced wyverns and their magic wielding riders'.

Her eyes widened in horror, and she shot a glance to the wheel, but it was unmanned. It was clear that there was no-one near enough to the helm to steer them clear in time. The battle on the port side was intensifying and as she glanced that way, Arke bore witness to Paltos being shaken like a rag doll by one of the wyverns who'd sunk its yellowed fangs into his neck. She saw the arterial blood spurting from the wound and knew there were mere seconds to save him.

"A collision will kill us all." Stabbington's succinct statement demanded her decision.

With a burst of bright blue magic and a sonic boom that shook the ship, Arke made her choice. Her method of teleportation wasn't even slightly subtle but it was effective and in the blink of an eye she appeared at the wheel, spinning it as hard as she could – so hard, in fact, that the *Warrior* heeled viciously to starboard, causing even more chaos on the main deck as everything slid sharply in the same direction.

As the ship tilted, she braced herself, battling to hold the turn that was swinging the bow away from the deadly mountainside. She wasn't watching the deck, but Stabbington was, and he quickly alerted his host to the sudden appearance of the Bonelord mage as the sharp turn summarily ejected him from his hiding place. Arke's lips twisted in a silent smile of perfect payback as she focused on the man as he used the railings at the side of the ship to struggle to his feet. It only took a few seconds for her to calculate the optimum place to hit that would catapult the enemy clean over the edge. The fact that that place was right in his crotch afforded her an extra moment of job satisfaction as she fired off a handful of her icy blue, snake-shaped projectiles.

The magical strikes landed with perfect precision and the now Boneless-lord was spectacularly launched both backwards and up. His hands might have instinctively clutched his groin but the glowing eyes that glared in her direction showed that the mage only had vengeance in mind as he flew through the air. For a brief moment, Arke admired the self-control that allowed him to cast a spell under such trying conditions, but that quickly faded as she tried and failed to throw herself clear of the nebulous bank of grey smoke he'd conjured into existence for her personal displeasure. There was only enough time to see his body drop away before the fog threw itself into her mouth and nose, forcing itself down into her lungs with burning inevitability. As the dark cloud started to shrink-wrap her, Arke heaved in breath after pointless breath, feeling every drop of energy leeching away as the magic mist wreathed itself around her. Choking, disoriented and unable to control her limbs, she staggered away from the wheel and fell onto the main deck, landing heavily, her hands clawing at her face to try and clear the invisible barrier that was preventing her taking a breath.

"One day you will learn to dodge!" Stabbington snapped as the cloud started to dissipate, but not even his barbed remark earned him any sort of reply.

The spell might have ended but Arke was struggling to recover, hauling in ragged breaths but just as quickly coughing them out along with a lot of dark grey smoke. Her reddened eyes streamed with blinding acrid tears and she scrubbed them away with a sleeve, frantically trying to clear her vision.

Stabbington's voice shouted in her head as she struggled painfully to gulp down any clean air between smoky coughs. "Behind you is the door to the lance controls, get to your knees and crawl in there until you can be useful!"

Stubbornly, Arke turned towards the sound of the nearest combat and struggled to get to her feet.

"I know what you are thinking but you are WRONG! You cannot help them until you are recovered. I WILL TAKE OVER IF YOU DO NOT LISTEN!"

That was Stabbington's ultimate threat, one he absolutely knew would get her attention, and finally Arke listened, fingers having to clutch twice at the door handle before she managed to open it and disappear inside.

Chapter Ten
Primed for Oblivion

BACK AMIDSHIPS, SPARKZ was remembering why he worked with engines and not animals, especially ones who used the excuse of already being dead to avoid getting killed. The zombie wyvern he'd been trying to subdue was proving to be a stupidly tenacious opponent, attacking with its teeth, talons and tail with the same ferocity as it had when it first landed. Well, one of its talons anyway, as the roundhouse kick from a passing Ruby had managed to remove the other with the stomach-turning sound of rotten wood tearing apart. Sparkz might have cringed, but the beast hadn't even flinched. All in all, it was fair to say that the monster's refusal to go down was becoming a source of great irritation to him. That and its handiwork, for its bites and strikes had shredded his clothes in multiple places.

As he lurched away from another swipe from its talon, Sparkz decided he was in need of a new wardrobe, for which Gorki would definitely be providing funds. That was a pleasant thing to think about, unlike the pain from the myriad of slashes underneath the ripped fabric and the blood he could feel soaking into his shirt and see dribbling down onto his hands. In general, Sparkz had no real opinion about the sight of blood, unless it was his own, in which case he was strongly opposed.

With the fraying of his temper as well as his clothes, he suddenly decided that the idea he'd discounted three attacks ago for being far too risky was now the best one he'd had all day. The creature swung his head around, mouth open, just as the tattoo on Sparkz's inner wrist suddenly flashed red. Instantly, the swords still embedded in the beast's neck began to glow, and it roared in fury as the long-dead skin around the blades started to burn. With a swift reaction, it struck at him with its tail, but Sparkz had been ready for the move and jumped, landing neatly on the pointy end of the wyvern with both feet.

"Not today, you decrepit excuse for a monster. Have a bit of pride, look at yourself – not even enough leather for a handbag."

The beast thrashed around, trying to throw him off, but Sparkz leapt closer to its body and styled it out with ease; he'd developed both tenacity and excellent balance climbing around on the masts and spars of the sky ships he'd served on. Neither the beast's teeth nor talon could reach him, and as he saw how quickly it burnt, he smiled grimly to himself – this lizard was toast, really vile smelling, overcooked toast.

☒ ☒ ☒

THE SOUND OF swords clashing from the starboard side had been ongoing through the entire battle as Kennedy and the hulking Bonelord fought one on one. Kennedy was strong, but his enemy had muscles so large that they battled each other for space on his body. This wasn't a fight that would be won by delicate thrusts and parries, it was one of grit, strength and smashing blades together until someone got tired.

It felt like hours, though it had barely been a few

151

minutes at maximum effort, before Kennedy was panting and dripping with sweat that crystallised almost immediately on his unshaven face. But he was winning, his strength enough to force his enemy to expend energy blocking his swords while his speed and agility kept him out of the way of the Bonelord's mighty strikes. He could see that his opponent was struggling, the veins standing out on his temples, several bones of his breastplate completely cleaved in half and dark blood dripping down his forearm. Kennedy attacked again, blades whirling, but was suddenly hurled backwards by a solid blow to the chest as the enemy fighter gave up trying to best him with weapons and started casting spells instead.

Ignoring the burning pain that rippled across his body, Kennedy dropped his swords and sprang back to his feet like an acrobat. As he landed facing the Bonelord, he drew his magically enhanced pistols, firing both without hesitation. If magic was round two, he wasn't going to be left behind.

The bullets' arcane energy launched his target backward like a rag doll, but instead of a look of satisfaction, Kennedy's eyes widened with concern as his opponent began to shimmer with magic potential. Another spell was on its way. However, after the impact of a sudden blast of bright blue energy, the airborne Bonelord's concentration was shattered and the glow around him dulled to nothing. Revenge ruined, the muscle heavy mage continued on his unwilling flightpath and disappeared over the side. A smile flitted across Kennedy's face as he sheathed his pistols and bent to pick up his swords – he was sure it was Arke's magic that had saved him from a second magical hosing. That or the Bonelord had a bad case of projectile dysfunction. Either way, he needed to get busy helping his crewmates clear the decks.

He swept a glance over the battleground, spotting that amidships Sparkz's wyvern was well alight with his brother tail-riding it like a true rodeo king. Over on the port side it looked a lot messier. Krugg was being yanked off his feet by the chain he'd managed to wrap around one of the monster's necks while Urzish slammed her axe over and over against its flank. At the same time, a blood covered Ellie was crouched behind a cluster of barrels as Ruby tried to force the other wyvern backwards, her fists, feet and wings buffeting the creature relentlessly as they fought nostril to nostril. Kennedy knew for certain that staring into the cavernous eye sockets of an undead monstrosity wasn't on anyone's bucket list, but these were mountains that just kept on giving.

As Kennedy flicked his gaze towards the bow, he also knew, with a surge of adrenalin, just how generous the Greyspines could be.

"HOLD ON!"

He doubted his bellow was even audible above the joint cacophony of the weather and the battle, but as he created and instantly merged with his alter by the unmanned wheel, he knew there was no time to do anything else. If it looked like a mountain, loomed like a mountain, and darkened their decks like a mountain, it was definitely a mountain. And it was far, far too close. He spun the wheel hard over and the *Warrior* lurched, decks tilting to an almost untenable angle as the ship clawed its way around.

The moment that everything twisted a full forty-five degrees, Kennedy saw many of the combatants struggling, and quickly failing, to avoid premature disembarkation. He was still clutching onto the wheel to keep his ship in its lifesaving turn, so could only watch in stunned silence. With his one action, everything had changed so radically that even chaos must have been surprised by its own success.

The wyvern Ruby had been pummelling, still reeling from her heavy blows, was the first to tumble, quickly followed by the Bonelord she'd stunned before the battle had even begun. While those two departures were more than welcome, the sight of Urzish being launched over the side by a tail strike from the third beast, was not. Kennedy looked for Ruby, shouting to get her attention when he spotted her running back up the steepened deck towards Krugg.

The ogre was still holding onto his chain that ran around the last wyvern's neck in a twisted noose. As the ship's deck had tilted, Krugg had been on the highest side so had grabbed the nearest railing with his free hand to hold himself in position, clearly not noticing that his choking opponent was sliding quickly away. It was only when the chain started to pull tight that the ogre finally seemed to realise that its free end was still firmly wound around his own forearm. Kennedy watched the unfolding drama with mounting certainty about how the tug of war was going to end. Krugg bellowed his defiance to the laws of physics just as Ruby's piercing call boomed across the deck towards her friend.

"LET IT GO!"

Knowing just how much Krugg loved a hearty

physical challenge, Kennedy was not surprised when the ogre did nothing of the sort. He watched with helpless acceptance as the monster on the end of the chain slid completely off the ship, instantly making Krugg exactly one dangling wyvern heavier. Gravity was giving a masterclass and although the ogre was incredibly strong, he could only deny its existence for as long as the wooden railing held; so, in the fewest of moments, he and the ancient monstrosity were plummeting together.

As Ruby dived away after her friend, Kennedy was able to bring the *Warrior* back out of her steep turn. When its decks tilted back to a more sustainable angle, he was relieved to see Sparkz was still on board. Granted, he was lying flat on the wyvern's twitching tail, arms and legs wrapped around it, cheek pressed against skin that crunched and flaked under his weight, but he was safe. Or as safe as anyone could be while clinging to an undead monster as it smoked and guttered like the vilest of candles. The stench of death on fire would have been impossible to bear if it hadn't been for the icy wind that carried it away.

Kennedy was scanning the deck for Arke when a fourth enemy drove his wyvern down towards the *Warrior*. The creature came in fast, touching down at speed before bracing its wings to try and slow itself before it crashed into the bulkhead below the helm. Its dwarven rider slid off before his beast had even stopped, landing dramatically and drawing a pair of curved swords, each blade easily four inches wide. His was clearly a commanding arrival, but as Kennedy saw Ellie leap from behind her barrel sanctuary to land on the back of his wyvern before driving her sword repeatedly between its weathered shoulder blades, he felt it was fairly clear that she'd been less than impressed.

✗ ✗ ✗

A DISTINCTLY CONCUSSED Arke lurched out onto the deck from the lance controls just below the helm. She'd recovered from the Bonelord's spell just in time to save Kennedy from a similar fate but when the *Warrior* had thrown itself almost on its side, her head had fought with the nearest wall and come off decidedly worse. Although she'd groggily refused to let Stabbington take control of her body, she had agreed to rely on him to navigate the multiple spinning worlds she appeared to be in.

"The first thing to do is delegate! We have people overboard and you cannot do everything, unlike me; I must be your eyes and your ears and your sword and your power and..." Stabbington could be irritating at the best of times, and this was certainly not the best of times.

Arke tuned her demon out after his first few words and quickly summoned her favourite almost canine assistant. "Dozer – man overboard!"

The Rottweiler's tail nearly wagged itself completely off in delirious joy at finally getting to chase something more exciting than a ball and he plunged over the side. Arke heard a slap of infernal leather as his wings materialised, followed by his joyous barking.

"He knows to bring back one of the crew and not one of the enemy, right?" A distinctly troublesome mental image of Dozer dragging a reluctant wyvern back to the ship had popped into her sideways brain.

"That would appear to be a 'you' problem,"

Stabbington remarked coolly. "Unlike the new Bonelord who has just landed, so take three paces forwards, listen to me, aim as I direct and we shall prevail."

Unfortunately, the demon's targeting solution proved to be more confusing than his host's battered brain could handle.

"Eight o'clock... down five degrees... twist your wrist a little."

Arke quickly stopped listening and put a hand over her right eye as a much simpler solution to her double vision.

Surprising absolutely no-one, the Soulbound's hack was nowhere near safe working practice when firing blasts of arcane energy. Her first attempt went so completely awry it managed to hit Ellie in the side of the head, sending her flying off the wyvern to lie in a crumpled heap on the deck. At Stabbington's furious urging, she stepped back, bracing her unsteady hand against the doorframe and re-aimed, the rest of her magical strikes managing to connect with the actual target. To begin with, the Bonelord had been too busy swinging his giant blades as he strode towards Sparkz to notice her appearance. However, after Arke's first shot hit him, he tried desperately to turn and face her but the heavy impacts that threw him down the deck were just too rapid to fight. By the time the fourth slammed into him, he was already ten feet off the ship, head lolling on his chest, perfectly primed for oblivion.

As the Bonelord's wyvern shrieked and flew in pursuit of its handler, Stabbington kept Arke moving. "Now collect the first aid satchel that is hanging by the door. If we are lucky, Ellie will not remember how she ended up on the deck."

"And if she does, is that a 'me' problem?" Arke replied, struggling to grab the emergency medical kit as it taunted her by hanging perfectly still on its hook.

"After so long you should know that is correct. Either *we* win or *you* lose."

She was just crossing towards the halfling when she saw multiple versions of Ruby hauling Krugg up over the side and dumping him onto the deck. Arke turned to look at them and instantly regretted shifting her focus as the movement made her head thrum with pain.

"Keep walking. As we agreed, I will be your eyes. There appears to be no more enemy, Ruby and the ogre look fine, Kennedy is safely at the wheel and Sparkz's slow roasted wyvern is finally dead." The demon paused and Arke saw a fast moving black and tan blur, carrying what she assumed was a body, shoot across the deck to land at her feet. "Ah. Crouch down and get the wound sealant from the kit. You will need that very quickly as I do not remember orcs growing limbs back like salamanders."

Dozer sat in a decidedly noble pose beside Urzish, his tail beating out a happy rhythm as he knew he'd been a *verygoodboy* despite the orc's missing arm and the copious amount of blood that was pouring onto the deck. Stabbington remarked wryly that since the hellhound didn't seem in the least concerned about only bringing back 95.03% of his target, he wondered if the Rottweiler had needed a quick snack on the way back to the ship.

Arke continued her double vision hack by keeping one eye shut and finding the bottle of *Sealit Bang*. Its label was unmistakable, as murky brown as its contents, and she shook it hard before pouring copious amounts over the orc's ragged stump. The instant sealant was not only incredibly effective but had also become an overnight success after a marketing intern had sold his soul to the god of business in exchange for the slogan of his career. There was barely a single Barsian who hadn't seen the classic advert: "Use *Bang* 'til your wound is gone!"

Carefully selecting a smaller sized canister of *Just Say Go* from the kit, Arke took a quick swig and poured the rest into Urzish's mouth. The fluorescent green liquid was a fortified magical shot which hit with the equivalent of twenty espressos. If you didn't wake up with that, you weren't even trying. The orc's eyes fluttered open and she groaned as Dozer loomed over her, licking her face with his usual rough intensity.

"He didn't… eat your arm, did he?" Arke asked quickly, the go juice already starting to flood her system with healing energy.

"Wyvern did," Urzish croaked and reached her remaining hand up to pat her rescuer on the shoulder. "Dog saved my life. Wouldn't let go of me."

"Good boy." Arke was almost flatpacked as Dozer leapt over Urzish to bury his head in her aching ribs, waiting for the cuddle he always expected after his two favourite words. She was happy to oblige him while the *Just Say Go* finished working as both she and Stabbington were well aware of what must come next.

⚔ ⚔ ⚔

"Are we even a pirate ship without a missing limb or two?" Kennedy had needed a moment to think of that line after watching Urzish's wretched return, but eventually he managed to force a smile and a breezy remark to his lips. The orc gave him a weary thumbs up in reply as Krugg carried her below decks.

"We did OK, all things considered." He patted Dozer on the head as he bent down to grab a couple of bottles of *Just Say Go* from the kit next to Arke. "You look rough, so stay there, I've got the others."

Kennedy uncorked the first bottle as he strode over to Ellie before crouching down to open her mouth and drip it in. He started counting down from five but had only got to three when the halfling's eyes snapped open and she shuddered and swore her way back to full consciousness.

"Welcome back to reality, the doors are here, here, here and here. Looking good, looking fine. Next patient." Kennedy always enjoyed watching the magic potion get to work and was still smiling as he walked over to Paltos, tapping his foot against the giant's boot as he reached him. "Hey, big guy, let's get you back on your feet."

He hadn't expected an answer, but nor had he expected his old friend to be so pale, so still, or surrounded by so much blood. As Kennedy's smile vanished and he stepped level with his first mate's head, it started to rain heavily. Huge cold droplets suddenly pelted the deck just to emphasise his stomach-churning realisation that Paltos was dead. Not even an emergency dose of *Jumpstart A Heart* would bring him back. It was obvious that he'd bled out so quickly that he'd died where he fell.

Kennedy's chest constricted so painfully that he could barely breathe. Even when he'd seen him lying on the deck, he hadn't been able to think the worst. Paltos was the inexorable mountain who had stood at his parents' side, at *his* side. He'd always been the first to fight and the last to stop. He couldn't be dead, it just wasn't possible. Kennedy had always seen his first mate through the eyes of the boy who marvelled at the giant who'd once carried an entire golden throne two miles home to the *Warrior*. Today that same man was pale and dead in front of him and Kennedy's head felt like it was going to explode with the sudden pressure of grief. He couldn't stop the tears and he didn't want to.

"It was quick." Ellie put her hand on his shoulder and squeezed it gently. "He didn't suffer. We tried to get to him, but it was... we couldn't. I'm sorry."

Almost bent double with the sobs that wracked his body, Kennedy heard Arke's voice from behind him, her tone utterly businesslike despite the body lying next to them.

"Are you injured, captain? If so, you need to go to see Gurdi. Ellie too, Sparkz has already gone, Ruby has the wheel. Zeke is coming up from the engine room to take the watch and..."

"DON'T YOU DARE!" he shouted, turning to glare at her through tear-sore eyes. "Don't you DARE pretend he meant nothing to you! LOOK at him!"

Arke simply raised her gaze to meet his, her expression stiffly neutral. "Go and get checked over."

"Paltos is dead."

The Soulbound's composure didn't waver. "Yes, captain. I'm fully aware of that."

Kennedy grabbed her by the arm and dragged her across in front of him, his other hand on the back of her head to make sure she saw the gaping wound around the giant's neck and the blood that soaked his clothes as well as the deck around him.

"Well?" His voice trembled with emotion as he stood holding her so she faced Paltos' body. "You have to FEEL something."

"Cold, sore and increasingly wet." Arke's voice was as expressionless as her face and she yanked herself out of Kennedy's grasp. "If there's nothing else, I'm going to my cabin."

He said nothing else, fury having won out over his gnawing grief and watched the Soulbound walk stiffly away with Ellie hurrying after her. The halfling caught up before she'd even got ten feet away, her voice a hoarse whisper, as if Kennedy wasn't close enough to hear every single word.

"You couldn't have just PRETENDED? He needed that from you! You're so far up yourself that you can't SEE he's in pain?"

The Soulbound stopped before replying, her voice firm and laden with meaning. "What he needed was exactly what I did. He's the captain and he needs to act like one."

"And you're going to want to chuck Paltos over the side too, I bet. Before you say anything – that's NOT happening." Ellie stepped in front of Arke, her posture bristling with animosity.

"Nothing good ever comes of keeping corpses for sentimental reasons."

"He deserves a proper funeral!"

"So do you, but we've lost enough crew today."

Arke went to step around the halfling, but Ellie

moved with her.

"Alright, let's do it. You and me, right now. Since you can't even focus your eyes I reckon I've got a good chance."

"You're not worth the energy." The Soulbound's tone was icily dismissive.

Kennedy was just about to make a move to stop the impending fight when his brother called over from the main hatch.

"Ellie, Gurdi's ready to check you over."

Arke took the moment of distraction to sidestep around the halfling as Sparkz limped across the deck towards them, his voice smoothly persuasive.

"C'mon Ellie, you're soaked, let's get you out of these wet clothes; Gurdi's got a tall glass of post-battle smoothie ready for you." He put an arm around her shoulders and eased the halfling towards the hatch. "She's trying a new flavour, *apparently* it's bacon."

After moving Paltos' body to the galley freezer, Kennedy took over the helm, steering the ship through the rainy tail of the storm and out into a clear, cold sky. Everything was shades of grey; the sun was bright but bore no warmth, and below them the sharp-edged mountains pointed up hungrily. Unlike his mind, his body was thoroughly numb after downing Gurdi's bright blue potion. He didn't read the label; he knew what she called the disgusting gloop and he didn't need to cry any more.

The empty bottle of *Never Gonna Let You Down* rocked gently on top of the barrel next to the wheel as Kennedy checked the chart he had tacked inside his coat to keep dry. By his reckoning the *Warrior* was only a few days from the treasure chest the sailor had drawn on his maps, and though he wanted nothing more than to lie down and sob, he knew Arke had been right – the crew needed their captain.

Chapter Eleven
To Cast a Shadow

THE BONELORDS MIGHT have been gone but the nightmares remained. As the ship plunged into a foggy no man's land that appeared to wreath the inner peaks, the indescribable terrors spread their shapeless dread until every single person on board was assailed by their touch every time they closed their eyes. As they flew on, a single ship suspended in a grey, ethereal world, even the boundaries of night and day seemed to blur. Time lost all meaning amid smothering cloud and slithering nightmares and the crew fell prey to a grating bitterness that seeped into every corner of their vessel.

The only person whose temperament was unaffected by the night terrors was Arke. After all, what was one more terrifying dream after a lifetime of them? It had been over forty years since she'd been scared enough to ask for her demon's help to deal with the lurking doom that haunted every sleep. She'd hoped for some sort of intervention, perhaps even a warm presence to help her stand her ground against the shadows, but what she'd actually received had been a Stabbington special. His words had been cold, logical, and far more horrifying than any dream.

"Nightmares, my Arke, are just your own fears given a brush to paint with. Their pictures cannot hurt you, unlike every awful thing that is *really* out there." His fallback career was not as a motivational speaker.

After a few days ploughing through heavy cloud and heavier dread, dawn finally broke over the *Warrior* in a clearly visible manner. As the Soulbound exited her cabin she was greeted by the surprise of an open sky; the fog banks lay behind them and an icy blue expanse stretched over the raking peaks ahead. Looking around the main deck, she spotted Kennedy dozing at the wheel and walked quietly to the starboard side, bringing out her telescope to survey the nearest mountains. Yawning widely, she started looking for something that would explain Stabbington's early morning wake-up call. The icy wind was brittle as it whipped her cheeks to full wakefulness and made her shiver despite her extra layers. The Greyspines sucked especially hard early in the morning when you'd been annoyed out of a perfectly warm bed. She wished she could have ignored her demon alarm, but his instincts rattling like a tail had correlated with Kennedy's estimate of their position the night before. They were close to one of the marks on the unfortunate sailor's map. Whatever had possessed him was close and she wasn't about to let Kennedy's usual headlong tactics give it any more opportunities to scramble minds.

Seeing nothing obvious on the starboard side, she crossed to port, put the glass to her eye and with one wide sweep, found their destination. There was no way that the monstrous pathway which looked to have been hewn geometrically into the side of a mountain was a natural feature. Between that obvious clue and the dark murmurings from Stabbington as she focused in on the sharp-edged cliffs, Arke knew that this was the place.

Checking that Kennedy was still unaware of her presence, she moved quietly around the back of the cabins, knowing that dawn was Ruby's prime prayer time. As expected, the rainbow coloured Ornithol was perched on the stern rail, wings spread, eyes closed. Arke waited for a moment, politely hoping that Ruby would either notice her presence or finish soon, but after a few minutes the Soulbound got bored and cleared her throat. The Ornithol jumped in surprise, nearly falling over the edge of the ship.

"Arke!" Ruby used her wings to steady herself and tilted her head quizzically to one side.

"I need you to fly me down there," Arke jabbed a thumb in the direction of the mountain she'd seen through her telescope. "There's a potential site I want to check out."

"Good idea." Ruby looked at her for a long moment. "You don't grow up in a convent without learning to recognise the signs of a breakout. The captain doesn't know, does he?"

Arke just raised an eyebrow and made a little shrug with one shoulder. "Ready?"

Taking only the briefest moment to ponder her response, Ruby flexed her wings and waited for her crewmate to climb aboard. "Visibility's great, so it makes perfect sense to scout the area; annnnnd I really need to get off the ship, everyone's so bad tempered right now, even Porro. I didn't even know Ornithols could spit until Ellie shouted at him for putting three sugars in her coffee and not four."

⚹ ⚹ ⚹

THE ODD-LOOKING LANDMARK on the mountainside

Destiny's Boot

stood out like a sore thumb, and although Ruby took a more cautious approach than perhaps her passenger would have liked, the pair of adventurers eventually touched down on the smooth, cold rock of whatever it was that this place had once been. Ruby looked around with furious curiosity as they stood in the middle of an unnatural canyon which had such a uniform appearance that it looked like a giant scoop had gouged away a section of the mountain with one pass. In contrast, Arke was distinctly less excited by the experience, especially as Stabbington was busy giving her dire warnings about 'something' that was already aware of their presence. Nevertheless, she swung a measured glance around their landing site, both seeking clues as to its purpose and any threats that might lurk unseen.

The cliffs on each side were tall and sharply vertical with perfectly spaced alcoves halfway up, each containing a weathered statue so old it was virtually featureless. To the far left was the impenetrably dark mouth of a cave, and opposite that, right at the other end of the cut, was a stone platform positioned so it was hanging over the edge of a terminally high drop.

Having assessed the area, Arke strode decisively towards the cave with the Ornithol quick to follow her lead. The closer they got to the disturbingly flat and featureless darkness, the more Ruby started to feel the oppressive atmosphere.

"This doesn't feel right."

"It's not supposed to. Just keep your eyes open."

"Ok."

The Ornithol took the instruction to heart, scanning all around her, listening hard and looking suspiciously at every faceless statue or shadow in the rock as they walked.

As they reached the threshold to the cave, where icy light turned to silent gloom, Arke stopped, her expression serious and her tone laced with dire warning.

"Stay here and keep watch. If things go bad, get straight back to the ship."

"You're going in on your own?" Ruby's eyes widened as she glanced into the yawning maw of darkness.

"Yes. Whatever possessed that sailor is nearby, can't you feel it? And when I say nearby, I mean in its dire warning of a cosy lair." Arke pointed quickly at the cave before looking up at the Ornithol. "It's probably the same thing that's been messing with all the crew for the last few days – even you."

"Oh." Ruby thought for a moment, remembering with more than a little shame how, just a few days ago, she'd shoved Zeke into a bulkhead when he'd got in her way and the more recent savage argument she'd had with Porro about his kitchen hygiene.

"Exactly," Arke nodded. "It doesn't affect me and so I'll be the one going in."

"Do you know why?" The Ornithol felt keen to learn what set Arke apart from the rest of them. "Sorry if you think I'm prying, only the nuns always said that every weakness could be countered if you understood it."

"I honestly don't think knowing will help you." The Soulbound looked up at Ruby before offering a wry smile with an even wryer comment. "You need light to cast a shadow. Surprising as it is, I'm not known for my sunny disposition."

That clearly amused Arke, but judging by the

Ornithol's increasingly anxious posture, it had done absolutely nothing for her state of mind.

"Ah, but you forget that Kennedy told her that when you start to be funny, things are going downhill faster than a polar bear on skis," Stabbington remarked. "She is inexperienced, and it is unfair to leave her alone out here."

"Nicely volunteered." Arke replied under her breath before returning to her normal volume. "Stabbington will stay with you; do exactly what he says. If he can keep me alive for all these years then you'll be no problem. If he says get out then you go, OK? No questions."

She drew her sword and offered the hilt to Ruby, who hesitated, clearly expecting to be assaulted by terrifying demonic energy the moment she touched it.

"That was not what I meant!" the demon retorted. "We should wait for back up!"

Eyeing the blade warily, Ruby looked back at its owner. "Will it possess me?"

"Of course not, *he's* mine." Arke's reply was instantly repressive, but then her tone softened, and she smiled a little. "Don't worry, Stabbington can be very good company when he wants to be; but don't ever assume that every demon is as nice... is like him."

"Arke, this is a BAD idea."

The demon's warning in Arke's head went completely unheeded.

As Ruby held out a hand, the Soulbound's eyes twinkled, and a wider smile danced around her lips. "Also, don't call him *it*. He has an alarming repertoire of songs to irritate you with if the mood takes him. Behave yourself, Stabbington, I'll be back soon."

The Ornithol tensed as her fingers closed around the perfectly tooled hilt and it settled comfortably in her palm.

"A fine phrase to come from her lips, I am not the one who ever needs reminding to behave." Stabbington grumbled, knowing Arke could no longer hear him. Then switching to a far friendlier manner, he addressed his new companion. "Hello Ruby, I will be your danger sense today; please do not worry, I am far better company than my host. Maybe we can sing a little duet?"

The voice in her head was not what Ruby had expected, there were no sepulchrous growls, otherworldly dissonances, or threatening overtones. Instead, his tone was light, his accent not unpleasant, and he was clearly the owner of what seemed to be an agreeable sense of humour.

"I don't really… sing," Ruby replied uncertainly.

"Everyone sings. Arke has a beautiful voice, although she would hate me telling you. Perhaps you should forget that I mentioned it."

While the Ornithol came to terms with the voice in her head, Arke slipped away into the darkness of the cave. Goodbyes of any sort had never been her style.

⚔ ⚔ ⚔

THE CAVE WAS far quieter than a cave should be. It was also darker and longer, with a clagging taint of arcane power that seemed to cling to every breath. However, as Arke headed deeper into the mountain, she was far less concerned about the spooky silence, interminable length, and bitter-tasting magic residue than she was about the sheer number of spiders which seemed to be increasing in size the further down the passageway she walked. She swallowed dryly as her magical light illuminated a huge web to her right, which completely flouted her first rule of cavern living: spiders should stay up high and out of the way. Out of her eyeline. Or just Out. She'd heard every argument about the benefits of the creatures and appreciated their use to the ecosystem, but for the love of all the gods could they please not be where she was. If that wasn't possible, then could her eyes please not pick up every movement of the hand-sized hairy-legged heinous crimes against her nerves that littered the tunnel. The Soulbound, who lived with an actual demon in her head, who specialised in dark places, bore death and disaster stoically and could withstand pain and threat without flinching, was scared of spiders.

Trying to ignore both her fears and the cave's residents, she kept walking, focusing on the winding passage ahead of her as it led deeper into the heart of the mountain, and definitely not on the thick layers of dust-laden webs above her head. Unsurprisingly she'd never had reason to consider what spiders of advanced size ate for lunch when living at altitude in a barren mountainous region. However, as she looked at the somewhat familiar bones littering the floor of the tunnel, she strongly suspected the answer was 'anything they can get' and hurried her step. Possession-hungry entities didn't make her skin crawl nearly so much as people-hungry arachnids with bodies the size of occasional tables.

As Arke rounded a corner, ducking under the draping lace of the largest web she'd seen and then frantically brushing hands through her hair to remove the teasing touch of imagined silk, her own spider sense pinged like a particularly ironic handbell. The sound was somewhere around F sharp, that peculiar not quite right but not quite wrong note, and it was enough to make her stop cleaning a whole lot of nothing from her hair to see that the walls ahead of her were free of both webs and their inhabitants. Arke's interest was suddenly piqued as she noted that not only had she reached the end of the spiders' territory she'd found the start of a set of carvings that covered wide swathes of the stone walls ahead.

Walking without hesitation through a ring of runes that marked the change in the passageway's purpose, Arke was suddenly hit by the idle thought that one day she'd take one step over the wrong threshold and simply explode. That briefest of dark contemplations was distinctly unhelpful given her circumstances, so she quickly shoved it aside and slowed her pace, using the magic light she'd conjured around her hand to investigate the pictures carved into the rock.

Not even dust seemed to cling to any of the scenes that were painstakingly immortalised on the walls and Arke took her time attempting to understand the story that the artists had been trying to tell. The pictures were stylised in a manner she hadn't seen before and had clearly once been painted, though time had dulled the vigour of their pigments. With absolutely no sense of shock, the Soulbound saw a lot of suggestions that the platform at the far end of the cutting had been a place of sacrifice. Over a few separate frames there were multiple incidences of what appeared to be worshippers being flung into the void, but none of them had any depiction of the creature they were appeasing or appealing to, just a deep set of scratches that appeared in a similar position each time.

The final tableau was the only one which still had some colour to it, suggesting that it was more recent than the others. Arke stopped in front of it for quite some time, noting with interest an obviously victorious female figure, standing with a baby in one arm and what looked like a goblet in the other. Behind her were many figures celebrating, weapons in hand. Peering closer, the Soulbound was fairly sure that what she'd first thought of as the woman's clothing actually looked more like bone-based armour. Suddenly things started to fall into place, and she nodded slowly as she pieced the puzzle together. The people in the carvings, possibly ancestors of the Bonelords, having beaten whatever they'd worshipped as a god, had immortalised that moment and then decided to visit every other image to scour their fallen idol from record. History belongs to the victors, after all.

Rounding a corner, Arke peered at some oddly shaped bundles of something that flanked a dead end. Four in total, one still upright, held there by stones that had been piled up around it, the other three collapsed to the ground. She took a closer look, finding that whatever was inside the thick animal skins had been wrapped in coils of blackened rope. She'd seen mummified remains before, on not entirely religious trips to ancient burial mounds, and recognised these as similar. It wasn't outside the realms of possibility that this place, with all its grisly history, had been repurposed to act as a tomb and the magic she could feel was simply here to guard whatever bodies lay further on. Maybe the mind-mangled sailor back in High Haven had been right – for where there were well-protected burials, there was usually treasure. She swept her light around the end of the passage until a faint line of wards carved into the stone floor caught her eye.

Putting her hand on the wall next to them, she opened her senses to the arcane and suddenly all she could smell was the sweetness of perceptive magic. A good illusion was a thing of beauty, and whatever was really here was doing a great job of pretending to be a solid rock face. She smiled with instant confidence, knowing that while she could always use her powers to end a spell by force, breaking and entering wasn't necessary if you could find the key. Shutting her eyes, she tracked the sugary tang to its strongest point before opening them again to see her gaze directed at a well-worn rune on the floor. At this point, smarter people would be trying to work out what the carving meant, bolder people would just have dispelled the magic, and wiser people wouldn't even be at the end of a spider infested tunnel in the middle of the Greyspines. But Arke was specifically, uniquely and chaotically herself. So she put her foot on the middle of the stone and pressed down.

With a soft hiss, the illusion of a wall disappeared and instead, Arke saw a huge pair of wooden doors held shut with a heavy cross-bar. They looked like they had been made many centuries ago, the thickly hewn wood old and dry, the bronze hinges tarnished with age. Without hesitation she lifted the bar, pushed the doors open and found herself entering a room whose edges were shrouded in darkness so thick that it looked solid.

The senses she'd deliberately heightened in order to identify and track the source of the illusion at the door were instantly assaulted by swirls of powerful magic so disorientating that her vision began to blur. She stopped, concentrating on turning her internal dial in the opposite direction in order to tune out the overwhelming arcane energy around her before continuing. Ahead of her sprawled a magnificent heap of treasure – coins, ingots, silver, jewels; a hoard any dragon of legend would be proud to own.

Behind her the doors slammed shut with a loud thud as the bar crashed down into its slot and what had been merely the illusion of treasure shimmered into nothingness.

Arke turned full circle, the vivid darkness preventing her from seeing any more than ten feet in each direction. As she looked around, a whispering, murmuring hiss began from deep within the impenetrable blackness. She couldn't make out any sense of language, but knew it was moving rapidly closer, its volume increasing as it swept towards her, raising the murmurs to screams and the whispers to shrieks. Her mind was filled with images of violence, each a bloody moment of excruciating torment on a helpless victim, every mouth contorted in a silent scream. The scenes cascaded in increasing horror as the shadows swirled around her, smothering even the magical light on her hand.

Dread was on her lips, in her ears, in her mind as she stood in the middle of the whirlwind of darkness, feeling air rush past her face, chilling her skin and clawing at her hair. Sudden pressure roared in her temples, throbbing through her skull as something scratched at her, pushed at her, threw itself at the centre of who she was and demanded this useless mortal vessel give herself to its dominion.

Eyes shut, jaw clenched, hands in fists, she could only endure the onslaught which grew in intensity and fury every second she denied it. Then it stopped, the images faded, the shrieks became silence, the darkness receded and Arke, head heavy with ebbing horror, sat down quickly before her legs gave way.

As she struggled to recover, instinct jangled its F sharp again. She knew she must try and open communications with whatever this presence was before it slammed into her head once more.

"My name is Arke." She needed more time to bounce back from the first attempt that had made her brain feel as if it had just been scraped along concrete. "Who are you?"

"You are nothing. Give yourself to me." A deep, masculine voice, savage in its denial of everything she was, flooded the cavern around her, echoing its brutal message off all the walls she could not see.

Arke chose not to respond, aiming to keep her mouth from spitting a reply that would certainly not help matters. She wasn't well known for her ability to stay silent in the face of judgemental arrogance, especially when she was in difficult situations. She might be able to block this being from possessing her, but could she stop herself making things worse?

"You've already allowed a paltry, pathetic demon inside your body," the voice continued. "Why do you resist something so much more powerful?"

She didn't even have time to wish it hadn't picked on

Stabbington before she bit back. She'd been insulted so many times before that she barely heard the words anymore, but no-one had ever been so dismissive about her partner. Without thinking, she reacted angrily, spitting a vicious retort into the void.

"So how long has it been since your supplicants defeated you?"

The darkness lurched forwards, swallowing her in a cacophony of pain and pressure. This time the being was shouting at her as it launched against her will, telling her of the agony she could expect every time she refused its possession. She felt the breath being crushed from her body as she was picked up, held in the air and screamed at by a creature who had not been spoken to like that in its entire existence.

Arke resisted. The fire that had sparked in her with the comment about Stabbington helped her fight the demanding waves that crashed in perfect rhythm, trying to hypnotise her into leaning into the darkest of songs. Everything about this attempt was primal, as the being tried to isolate her from the world, wrap her in nothingness and resonate within her until obedience followed fear.

While she recovered from the bone-jarring impact that occurred as her body was smashed angrily back down to the ground, Arke's confidence in her ability to hold onto herself began to grow. The injuries would heal but the creature would not own her. She eased herself back to a sitting position and waited for its next gambit.

"It takes no great intellect to see that I am imprisoned here." The deep voice finally came again, washing through her senses, still trying to disorientate her but with a much milder sentiment, the tone more even.

"Who are you?" she demanded.

"If you must ascribe a name to everything that I am, then know that others have called me Irash."

The expectant silence after the name drop suggested that the being expected Arke to know who it was, but she genuinely had no idea. However, not wishing to lose the progress she'd made, she decided silence was a better plan than admitting that its name meant nothing to her.

"I am an *Ancient One*."

There was a long pause as Arke tried to work out what response was appropriate given she still had absolutely no clue who or what he was. Finally, she decided to just try and move past what might be an awkward dent to Irash's ego with a change of subject.

"Look, I'm just here because you scrambled a sailor's brain."

"He was weak."

"All he could say was 'treasure' as he drew a map of this place."

"Ha! You mortals are greedy for power, duplicitous and self-serving. I knew the promise of treasure would bring someone here."

"I'm not denying it; but you baited the hook with imaginary gold. Doesn't sound exactly non-duplicitous on your part." Arke was careful to keep her tone well away from any hint of accusation as she pushed a little further into the discussion. She needed to try and find out what he wanted and whether there was anything she could do to get herself out of the cave with her mind and body intact.

"I must do what I can to escape. He was the first

179

mortal I have found in so many years that they did not manage to kill! They, my own servants who imprisoned me here!" His explosive explanation was full of frustration and fury, his words echoing around her.

Arke smiled a little as she began to feel her way more confidently through the negotiation. "And I thought people hated me. You must be extra."

"You have no concept of what I am!"

"Something locked in a cave who wants my help?" It was a bold statement and part of her expected an angry response, her fingers curling into fists in expectation of another attempt to take over.

However, there was no immediate reply and Arke relaxed a little, using the silence to contemplate her predicament. She was certain, after the first few salvoes, that Irash hadn't expected his attempts at forcing himself into her mind to fail. Conversations with lesser beings were clearly not his forte, but he was having to try, even if he had to take a frustration break every so often. She also had no doubt that if killing her and using her body had been an option, Irash would have done so without a thought. It was obvious that he was the only thing that mattered to him. Desperation might bring him to negotiate, but it didn't make him any less dangerous; she knew she mustn't let her guard down.

"I can help you too. You are a prisoner of your demon, and I can free you from him." There was his first offer, his voice calm but clear.

"I'm really not." Arke was heartened by the opening of a new phase of the discourse, so deliberately kept her tone neutral as she replied. "And anyway, your 'help' would probably leave my mind in a useless mess, just like that messenger you sent."

"He did not even come close to this place, just climbed the cliffs nearby, crying for his pitiful life. I used words of power, sent him visions and thoughts of treasure; it was a mere moment's work to bend him to my will and hope that someone stronger would make it to my prison instead. And you are here, and I do not know how you have resisted me so far, but I do know that I grow TIRED of having to talk to something so beneath my notice!"

In an eruption of power around her, Arke felt the unyielding pressure on her temples begin again as the entity tried to take control once more. It was becoming clear to her that each time he tried, he was growing weaker and more desperate, though the process of denying him was no less painful. She gritted her teeth and concentrated on counting backwards in threes from one thousand, a trick that usually silenced Stabbington too; order subduing chaos.

"You are exasperating!" Irash retreated in a frustrated rush.

"I'm here to help you, not for you to help yourself." Arke rubbed at her temples with a small smile. She'd have to remember to use that on Stabbington too when he was being pushy.

"Then help me! I want to leave this place!"

"So stop trying to possess me!" Arke snapped as she felt his presence loom over her again. The blackness pulled back in response to her demand, and she nodded, pinching the bridge of her nose to try and distract herself from the pulsing of an Irash-induced headache. "Let's talk about why I should let you out into the world when you keep filling my head with nothing but terror and doom. And while we're here, what about the nightmares everyone on my ship has been having? Is that you too?"

"Nightmares?" Irash sounded perplexed at the term.

"Frightening dreams. They started as soon as we crossed over the first peaks."

"I would not be so indirect. However, my servants do not want anyone to find me; certain among them could do such things to warn people away." He paused for a moment, giving the impression that he was marshalling his thoughts. "Mortal minds open to me when they are under stress; so fear and anxiety are the words of power – the keys I have always used. It is not what I wish to bring to this world on my release. My sole desires are to leave this prison and return to my own plane."

"Riiiight." Arke's tone was heavy with distrust and there was a long pause before Irash made his most reluctant offer.

"I only need to be within you to leave here; I do not need to be in possession of your mind. If I am only a passenger, then I cannot do anything directly."

Arke was more than familiar with possession and recognised the basics of what he said to be true. However, she also knew there was nothing stopping more attempts to take over once he was hitching a ride. It was a more than dangerous proposition whichever way she looked at it, but instinct told her that was probably the best she was going to get.

"And if I don't agree?"

"We both leave or neither of us do."

Arke sighed and hauled herself to her feet. "Ok,

passenger only. How do we do this?"

The darkness sucked back immediately, showing the brightly shining, absolutely unmistakeable shape of a chalice on the far wall of the cavern. Arke immediately wished she'd stabbed the tarot-wielding goblin woman right in the face; and as she expressed herself freely, Irash learnt some words of power that he'd never heard before.

Chapter Twelve
All in the Mind

EVEN SLEEP DEPRIVED, it hadn't taken Kennedy long to miss two of his most obvious crew members and even less time to locate the obviously unnatural chasm in the mountainside. After a few personal moments in his cabin where he'd heaped heavy curses on Arke's name, he'd instructed Ellie to put the *Warrior* into a holding pattern while he sent his alter down to the surface in the ship's gig. With a little concentration, Kennedy was able to fully control the other version of himself, to see what it saw, hear what it heard and direct its every movement. He hadn't been wanting to leave his ship unless it was absolutely necessary, so sending his substitute was the perfect solution to finding his missing crew.

The ship's boat took a few minutes to release from the network of ropes that held her firmly to the mooring station on top of the *Warrior's* main cabins. Despite rather too many patches and dents in the little craft, her wood still shone, courtesy of the oil that was painstakingly applied to her hull whenever she ceased to glisten. She was a mini-*Warrior* in every way, even powered by a tiny scrap of aetheric crystal that sat in a pint-sized version of the larger vessel's engine. The box that covered it was clearly marked *'Do NOT sit, you bloody idiots'* in Sparkz's best scrawl, but the warmth of the machinery beneath meant that the very seat-like structure had seen the lodging of plenty of disobedient buttocks in its time. The alter settled himself by the tiller, reaching to toggle a lever which flicked the stabilising wings out in a thud of stiff canvas before engaging the power and lifting smoothly off the top of the cabins.

An impatient Kennedy sat through what felt like an interminable flight down to the mountainside with his eyes shut and hands clasped into fists. It took a lot of effort to keep control of his alternate self over long distances and he was already sweating as the gig came in to land. He'd judged the approach carefully, sensibly choosing to set down in front of the stone platform, well away from the abrupt and windblown cliff face. After cutting the engine, he focused his alter's attention on the unmissable figure of Ruby who was standing with her back to one of the walls further down the perfectly symmetrical cutting. He was relieved that she seemed perfectly fine; less relieved but not at all surprised that Arke was nowhere in view. He widened his search area, even though the moment he'd seen the dark fissure that led into the mountain he'd had a pretty good idea where the Soulbound would be. However, he wasn't about to jump to the most obvious conclusion without making a full survey, but as he looked up at the cliffs, the hairs on the back of his neck suddenly spiked with cold anxiety.

It wasn't the sinister cave mouth, nor the faceless sentinel statues that had alarmed him, but the line of distinctive figures who were walking with stiff and silent intent to the cliff edges above.

Although it was both physically and mentally taxing to merge with his alter over long distances, Kennedy didn't hesitate. Joining and rejoining in close proximity cost only a simple millisecond of blurred vision, but when the other him was too far away, the experience was thoroughly draining. Taking a deep breath and concentrating his mind on rejoining the two versions of himself, he felt a cascade of shattering images shake his body as he burst through the ethereal plane at mind numbing speed.

With a shudder that radiated from head to toe, the two versions of Kennedy became one. Pulsing lights thrummed in front of his eyes and his heart thundered in his chest as he focused on recovering from his ethereal shortcut. As the distress ebbed away, he leant on the gig, hunching his shoulders against the icy winds blasting up and over the edge of the cliff behind him. Once the visual disturbances eased, he focused on what had brought him to the mountainside, the unmistakeable forms of Bonelord soldiers who were taking position on the cliff tops overlooking the cave and the cutting that led to it. It was hard not to be impressed by their steps which fell with absolute unity but as his gaze passed over the left-hand horde, he realised with mounting perturbation that all of them were perfectly matched. Same height, same build, same weapons, same armour. Turning to look at the figures on the right, he suppressed a strange desire to shudder at the sight of yet more identical forms. He narrowed his eyes, squinting through the blustery wind to identify their race. Orcs. All of them. Muscular, lean and disturbingly silent as they stood with their arms raised in some sort of ritual. Though briefly caught up in trying to spot even one misfit among their ranks, he knew that their appearance, no matter how jarringly uniform, was going to herald behaviour that was the opposite of friendly.

He also knew that fighting what looked like about two hundred furiously powerful soldiers in the middle of the Greyspine Mountains wasn't even close to how he wanted to die. He wasn't keen to lose the use of his very serviceable, sturdy and entirely necessary bones any time soon. He needed to get Ruby and they needed to leave before the Bonelord army lit the match to their funeral pyres. Once back on the *Warrior*, they could bring the aetheric lance to the party before going back down to find Arke.

⚔ ⚔ ⚔

FROM HER POSITION midway along the cutting, Ruby had watched Kennedy arrive twice, once as the gig landed and once into his alter, his form flickering briefly as the two versions merged. Stabbington had been warning her for the last few minutes that they were not alone, his tone changing from its previous warmth to distinct concern. He had Ruby constantly checking the entire area as if her head was on a swivel and his obvious anxiety was not calming her whatsoever.

The instant that the incredibly long line of Bonelords appeared on the top of the cliff opposite, Stabbington made up his mind.

"It is time to go."

"But… Arke?" As overwhelming at the odds seemed to be, Ruby was deeply reluctant to leave her friend behind.

"Do as I SAY!" the demon commanded, his exotic accent slipping into something far more akin to Arke's for just a second before he regathered his composure. "Without hearing from her we must do as she instructed:

leave when bad things appear." Sighing heavily, he continued. "I cannot warn her, and I do not know what she is doing as I have not been able to sense her since she went into that place."

"Is she…?" Ruby could not bring herself to finish the question, but she did tuck the blade into her belt before unfolding her wings. The wind caught them instantly and she paused, testing the flow of the air currents before taking off and starting to fly down the long cutting.

"Dead?" Stabbington finished her question with a snort. "No. Stupid? Yes. Impulsive? Also yes. Annoying, argumentative, stubborn, feckless, reckless, lost, broken… I could go on. And maybe I will kill her myself when we get out of this! Yes, maybe I will finally snap. Do you know how hard it has been to keep her alive all these years?" Listing the ways in which his host irritated him seemed to get Stabbington back on a more confident track and he continued his detailed litany of complaints as they flew towards the gig.

While Ruby would normally have been interested in the demon's rant, after the first few sentences she had barely heard any of it. Her headspace was being increasingly overtaken by the strangest thrumming chant. It had started so softly that even her sensitive ears had to strain to catch the details but as she focused on it, the sound rapidly increased in volume, starting to reverberate around her body until it felt like every feather was vibrating to its rhythm. She did not know the words or what they meant but they filled her head with images she could barely comprehend. The moment she reached her captain, violence bubbled up inside her in an uncontrollable rush of fury.

⚔ ⚔ ⚔

"Ruby?" Kennedy peered into his crew member's face with increasing concern as she landed in front of him, her entire posture nerve-janglingly wrong. One glimpse of her eyes, now unnatural inky pools shining dully in her face, told him everything he needed to know. "RUBY! Snap out of it!"

Without a flicker of emotion, she slammed a fist into her captain's chin, the power of the blow snapping his head back. He staggered with the unexpected impact, his legs giving way and depositing him unceremoniously onto the ground. In one long stride, Ruby was standing over his fallen form and as Kennedy struggled to disperse the painful starbursts taking centre stage in his consciousness, her strong fingers closed around his wrist.

"Desecrator. You will die." Her voice was guttural, the words barely recognisable in their delivery.

Ruby started walking towards the precipitous drop, dragging Kennedy alongside her as he desperately tried to prise her fingers from his wrist. When he realised there was no chance of unpeeling her brutal grip, he sprang his alter and merged with it in front of his possessed crew member. This time he was prepared for her attack, athletically ducking her first and second blows, distinctly thankful that whoever was controlling her lacked the ability to activate her cage fighting skills.

"RUBY!" Finally realising that shouting did nothing to help remove the hostile takeover, Kennedy dived into a full body roll to avoid another selection of the Ornithol's multi-attacks. As he rose to his feet once more, he noticed the demon blade tucked into her belt.

"Stabbington! Do something!"

Ruby swiped low just as a huge, dark shape swept over the pair of them and the unnatural voice burst from her throat again. "All of this is ours. This place and the One. You are nothing but bones."

Suddenly her eyes flashed the brightest of blues and she shuddered violently as the hold on her body was broken. Dropping out of her fighting pose she stared at Kennedy in horror.

"Captain, I'm sorry... I couldn't stop myself."

"Wasn't your fault. No need to apologise." He reached out and rested his hand on the hilt of the demon blade in Ruby's belt. "Thank you, Stabbington."

"That took longer than it should have; these Bonelords have disgustingly oily magic, I will never be clean again." As Stabbington spoke in Kennedy's head, his weak attempt at humour was undermined by the edge of weariness to his voice.

"*You* freed me?" Ruby tapped her beak together in evident confusion.

Kennedy made a mental note to have a long chat about Arke's demon with the Ornithol over a cup of tea when this was all over.

"Yes, yes, me," Stabbington replied quickly. "There are rules where I come from; it is extremely rude to possess people without asking, especially with words of power that do not belong in a mortal's mouth."

Kennedy let go of the sword and turned, levelling his glance at the cliffs as his priorities shifted. Ruby was now back to herself, so next was getting away before the Bonelords made their move. He shoved the worry about Arke to the back of his mind with the finesse of a finely honed snow plough. One problem at a time.

"We need to go now."

As Kennedy looked up towards the Bonelord overwatch once more, he had cause to wish that his inner monologue hadn't just tried to spin a little positivity about their situation. A reassuring thought that had said *At least there's no wyverns this time* was clearly a big enough middle finger to Fate that she had to immediately stomp his hopes into puddles of acid. The sudden sight of a cluster of patchworked creatures flying over the clifftops and heading in the *Warrior's* direction elicited an expletive-ridden phrase which was delivered with such vehemence that it made his bloodied lip split apart again.

The Ornithol saw them too and flared her wings in readiness. "I'm faster, I'll go ahead and warn the others."

Kennedy was still watching the Bonelord mirror army as they finished whatever ritual or prayer they'd been busy with, and as every one of the identical heads turned slowly to look at them, he began running towards the gig. "Go!"

"On it." Ruby leapt into the air and hovered there for a moment, pointing a hand towards the cave. "Arke went in there."

"She'll find her way out." Kennedy wasn't at all sure, but he had his ship and crew to look after first. Plus, only a fool bet against the Soulbound.

Ruby accelerated upwards, her wings powering her towards the heavyweight clouds that had begun to push in across the mountains, obscuring the *Warrior* from view and Kennedy leapt into the gig. As the little craft thrust itself into the air, the icy winds began to buffet its hull and he held tightly to the tiller while he concentrated on muttering to himself. Screw Gorki, screw untold wealth, screw everything. His own frustrations were far better company than the unearthly battle cries that suddenly echoed around the mountainside behind him.

Tirade briefly spent, Kennedy couldn't help but be curious about the noise. Glancing behind him, his hopes were briefly raised as he watched the strange sight of Bonelord soldiers simply leaping off the clifftops. Sudden ground-based deceleration was exactly what he'd wish for those particular enemies. However, as their descents slowed, Kennedy sighed with the dissatisfying but unsurprising realisation that magic was lowering them carefully to the ground. As more and more landed safely, their perfectly matched ululating shouts ricocheting off the granite walls, he turned his back on their concert of sinister vocal athletics to concentrate on piloting the gig.

As he pushed the pint-sized aetheric engine to its limits, Kennedy made another valiant effort to snow plough the Arke-related worry from his mind. Although he kept telling himself that she'd been in bad spots before and always made it out; his inner voice, beaten down from the positivity it had tried before, was not being helpful. Asking himself if previous unpleasant situations had involved an entire army of magically homicidal mountain dwellers was not conducive to the level of guilt he was feeling as every second left her further behind.

Still battling his uncharacteristically downbeat thoughts, Kennedy broke into the dank and dreary first level of cloud, angling the gig's nose to push through it as quickly as he could. As the smothering moisture wrapped its freezing tendrils around his face, drilling spikes of ice into every pore, he gritted his teeth in stoic endurance against the conditions both outside and inside his head.

Finally flying into a patch of clear air, he blinked the frost from his eyelashes before sighing with deep dissatisfaction. Discontent fully vented, he forced a smile onto his face and waved a merry greeting at the pair of wyverns who were turning away from the *Warrior* and aiming towards him. Fretful anxiety paled in the face of the threat of imminent death and Kennedy's brain finally stopped spinning its wheels, quickly getting down to the business of making a plan to stay alive.

⚹ ⚹ ⚹

ALTHOUGH SHE WAS standing in a dark cavern, deep in the heart of a mountain, it wasn't entirely true to say that Arke had no idea what was happening outside. Granted, she had no knowledge of the Bonelord army who were slowly massing at the tunnel entrance, but courtesy of Irash, she knew a lot more than she wanted to about the dangers looming around the *Warrior*. The magical darkness had changed to a grey curtain against one of the granite walls as the weirdest shadow puppet show in the world began to play upon it. A stony-faced Arke couldn't fail to recognise the unmistakable forms of the *Warrior*, the gig and all the attackers as they all began to converge.

"You must make your decision quickly. I can help you defend your ship." Irash's voice hovered around her, whispering his words first in one ear and then the other.

"How do I know this is even real?"

"I would have made it appear far more perilous if I was creating this to manipulate you."

With a reluctant nod, Arke realised that his logic made sense, but she still needed more information about what Irash wanted her to do. There had to be more to it than just letting him hitch a lift in her body. Where did he want to go? What did he need to do to return to his home plane? As the shadow puppet show continued, she saw that time was clearly of the essence, but that didn't affect the fact that she didn't trust him or his motives in the slightest. The only positive was that he had stopped trying to forcibly possess her – for the moment at least.

"So you just want to leave this world. That's it?"

"Yes, it is all I desire."

"OK. So how?" Arke's hands gripped into fists as an ominously large shape loomed into view on the wall. It was much larger than a wyvern, and even more worryingly, she could see a tiny figure that looked like Ruby heading towards it. It appeared that Stabbington's idea of keeping the Ornithol safe left a little something to be desired.

"Find an item that opens doorways between the planes – we used to call such a thing an Orbiculum – and then I can leave this miserable place."

"You make it all sound so simple. But if it is, why haven't you done it before?" Arke dragged her eyes away from the shadows and refocused them on the hovering chalice with a sense of irritation. She did not want to slip into destiny's pocket, but it seemed that she no longer had a choice in the matter.

"It *is* simple once I am outside. Make your choice so that I can help you destroy everything that is attacking your ship. I know that you do not wish your friends to die."

Irash's voice emerged as a hiss, bending the air around her head with the insidiously alluring promise that the only thing she had to do was agree and everything would be easy.

With a long exhalation of breath, Arke looked from the chalice to the shadow show and made up her mind. She absolutely knew that Irash, this violent and autocratic force which operated via possession and terror, was imprisoned in a cave for a lot of dark reasons, and having met him she could understand at least some of them. But having seen the wyverns, she knew that the powerful Bonelords were back and hellbent on destroying the *Warrior*. She needed to get out there and help. Having spent her life diving from hunch to clutch and back again, Arke always went with her instincts, and those were adamant that it was time to bend a knee to fate.

"Let's do it. Passenger only."

"I can free you from your lesser demon too. I do not like to share."

"No deal. I told you to leave him alone."

"Very well." The chalice flashed across the chasm. "You must carry this."

As the golden, rune-carved goblet hovered in front of Arke, her hands were already reaching for it. The moment she touched the freezing metal, Irash shot into her body. Icy waves of pain crashed over her, shocking every cell and launching her into tumultuous inner darkness. This was clearly the instant he'd been waiting for and as he poured himself into her, she was consumed by his lust for control. Her eyes flickered, dull blackness struggling to overwhelm them, breath stilling in her throat as his words of power threw themselves from one side of her shaking body to the other. The whirlwind writhed within every part of her, pushing at every boundary, pummelling her muscles and scarifying her nerves as Irash fought for the possession of her entire being.

Arke had no idea what her middle name was, or even if she had one at all. But if she did, it surely would have described her seemingly endless reserves of grim determination.

"I – don't – have – time – for – this!"

She ground the words out in a voice laced with hoarse frustration, as Irash started to fall back in the face of her implacable resistance. Finally, with a rush of blissful peace, everything went silent within her as her passenger acquiesced to his role and the resulting calm allowed the Soulbound to take a deep breath. After a few moments regaining her equilibrium, she flexed her aching shoulders and lifted her chin with triumphant purpose, rekindling the magic light around her hand.

"Let's go."

The door swung silently open in front of her as she walked out past the mummies that lay ignominiously outside the chamber.

"They believed a quick death would bring them closer to me." Irash's voice sounded in her head as she glanced at the cloth-bound bundles. "So the usurpers made sure these priests took weeks to end their existences."

"Right." She strode on past the wall carvings without a single glance. "And were they right? Die in a hurry, be one with your god?"

"Of course not."

"And you didn't tell them?"

"It was their assumption." Irash's ego was untouchable, his answers boredly dismissive.

"You weren't even a god."

"To an ant, a horse is a god."

Arke rolled her eyes expressively. She had her own opinions on deities and this interaction wasn't changing any of them. Reaching the end of the frescoed area, she ducked carefully under the giant web that hung across the width of the tunnel and tried to resist the urge to scrub the imaginary dust-coated spider silk from her head as she marched on.

She was still running tentative fingers through her hair when her bobbing light made her the perfect target for whoever was coming down the passageway.

Chapter Thirteen
All in the Flesh

ALREADY WELL AHEAD of her captain, Ruby pushed her body to its limits as she battled the winds by taking the straightest route to the *Warrior*. Suddenly, her sharp eyes noticed a colossal, dark shape materialise among the clouds to her right, its silhouette bigger than a wyvern by far. The closer she flew to the monstrosity, the more of it she could see. The massive leathery wings, wedge-shaped head, spiny body and snake-like tail, all of its parts identical to the drawings in books that told of the long dead behemoths which had helped build the world. She had no doubt in her mind that it was a dragon, and noted that whoever had decided they were extinct had failed to inform this particular one.

Altering course to intercept the monster, Ruby realised that this was yet another day of deeply unpleasant firsts for her. She'd never been possessed before, and she'd never seen a dragon before. Bad things always came in threes, and after the awful nature of the two she'd already experienced, she certainly didn't want to think what the third might be. Completely ignoring Stabbington's dire warnings, she shot upwards in a near vertical climb, deciding that preventing the monstrosity from reaching the *Warrior* had to be her priority. Since she couldn't even hope to turn the gargantuan creature by force, she powered higher, her eyes raking down through the scudding clouds. The wyverns had had Bonelord riders and she doubted this creature would be any different.

Positioning herself directly above the dragon, Ruby's sharp eyes finally found the brains atop the brawn. Without hesitation, she pinned her wings back and dived hard, aiming for the tiny figure perching on a shining bone seat that was strapped to the dragon's back. Armed only with the confidence of youth, she ignored the ominous grey aura and the bevy of skulls that clustered menacingly around her enemy as she prepared to make an incisive strike.

Dropping like an arrow, Ruby planned to land fists first on top of the Bonelord who sat on a bone throne aboard the monstrous dragon. It would have been the most brutal of strikes had her opponent been one of the Bonelords she'd fought before. Unfortunately for the Ornithol, the dragon rider, who was clad in red painted bone armour and wreathed both in grey magic and hanging skulls, was far more powerful than the others.

As the rainbow-coloured attacker fell out of the sky, an unearthly shrieking pierced the air. The rider stood, looked upwards, and waved an arm in a gesture that was less greeting and more 'releasing agents of chaotic death'.

Vacant-eyed skulls flooded upwards, the screeching noise growing louder as they spread out, littering the sky like shrieking, grey, necromantic flak. Like shrieking, grey, *heat-seeking*, necromantic flak. In sudden agreement with Stabbington, Ruby banked hard – they were not buying whatever the bony defenders were selling. As she changed her trajectory, the skulls mirrored her movements, some of them accelerating harder and starting to throw their ear-rending selves directly at her. Their screams were only extinguished amid explosions of dark energy when Ruby swiped her wingtips through the empty eyed bones.

However, she couldn't afford to waste time using heads as batting practice, for every moment she was dealing with the moving magical minefield, the dragon and its rider were getting closer to the *Warrior*. With a moment of inspiration, Ruby raided her memory of Stealorama where she had participated in her first ever conga line. While she had thoroughly enjoyed that experience, it hadn't included many screaming skulls or potentially life-threatening partners. Nevertheless, that flash of genius inspired her to make a sweeping turn back up to gain altitude, making the minefield spread out to cover her movements. Then she dived again, wings wrapped around her, rotating as fast as she dared while buzzing right along the underside of the dragon.

Shrieking and explosions followed her as the magic skulls learnt about aerodynamic forces the hard way while conga-ing with the spinning Ornithol next to a super-sized solid object. Correcting her rotations before she got to the bitey end of the giant beast, Ruby soared away to the right, wings at the ready for her remaining dance partners, silencing them with some satisfaction before making her second attack run.

The renewed confidence of youth took a good battering as the blatantly smiling Bonelord mage slung spell after spell at her would-be attacker. After the third near miss, Ruby finally agreed with Stabbington that simply throwing herself out of the sky at the dragon rider was only going to get her feathers melted, burnt, or ripped out by their roots. None of those options were tremendously appealing to her, as while she didn't care about her physical appearance, she definitely did care about being able to keep herself in the air.

Ruby remembered Kennedy saying that it was vital to have a Plan B. From the conversations they'd had about tactics, she was pretty sure that her captain believed in having C through M ready as well. However, she was not Kennedy and would happily settle for a single alternative. She flew on under the relative safety of the dragon's belly, trying to work out how she was going to get to the rider since there was no way anything she could do would be enough to knock the giant beast out of the sky.

"Are you willing to listen to me now? You do not need tackle the mage directly. You simply need to wear them out. As you know, magic uses energy, the bigger the spell, the more effort it takes. Bait and run, well, fly." Stabbington's advice was delivered with the world-weary tone of someone who had been dealing with a headstrong host for many years. "Just do not die. I will never hear the end of it."

Flying upwards around the dragon's cracked and leathery flesh, Ruby launched a handful of harmless rainbows at its rider and quickly dived back down to safety as a roiling ball of energy spewed from the mage's hand. Speeding around the beast, she avoided its heavy wingbeats and reappeared from the opposite quarter, posturing as threateningly as she could while conjuring a raincloud in front of her enemy and shooting away to avoid the next retaliatory attack. She wasn't sure if she could do this all day, but she could definitely keep the

Bonelord mage too busy to concentrate on the *Warrior* as the dragon powered through the skies towards it.

※ ※ ※

IN A CLEAR patch of air between the thickening streams of cloud, Kennedy held the gig steady against the wicked buffeting of the icy wind. Eyes narrowed, he aimed the bows straight at the nearest wyvern as it flew towards him, concentrating on the enemy for any small movement that would tell him which way they were going to turn. The man's spear was already raised, magic crackling around its tip as he urged his mount on its collision course with reckless abandon. Kennedy waited with icy composure. He'd never lost a game of chicken and didn't intend to start now. Then his eyes caught the almost imperceptible movement as the wyvern's rider shifted his weight to the left. Message received.

The distance between them was rapidly decreasing and Kennedy fancied that he could even smell the monster's rancid breath before its rider suddenly kicked hard left, throwing his spear as he did so. He was more than adequately prepared for both actions, instantly swinging the gig's tiller hard over to follow the turn as he dropped to his knees in the bottom of the boat to let the wickedly whining spear whisk harmlessly over his head.

As the gig came sharply about, he slammed the engine controls to full throttle and glanced at the more distant Bonelord as his mount swooped into an attack run. The little boat leapt eagerly towards the first wyvern who was now just ahead of them. Suddenly seeing the oncoming danger, its rider urged his beast into another sharp turn. Kennedy adjusted course to follow before quickly conjuring his alter directly behind the other attacker, bringing it into undetected existence sitting casually astride the back of the second patchworked flying lizard.

It seemed that undead wyverns had far slower reactions than breathing ones and that fact, combined with Kennedy's excellent piloting skills, worked perfectly in his favour. Gushing magical smoke, the gig's engine smashed its bows into the first creature's ribcage, the little craft splintering its way in with cracking inevitability. The rider turned, eyes wide in horror, as his mount shuddered with the impact, its wings faltering. Kennedy waved a jaunty goodbye before merging with his alter.

The instant he shifted to his new position, he drew his swords and drove them precisely into the unwitting Bonelord now sitting a few feet in front of him. During his years of training, Kennedy had learnt many things about manipulating anatomy and although near-death strikes weren't a skill he was particularly proud of, there were occasions where it was necessary. Understanding how to wound an opponent badly enough that they were unable to fight back but not quite dead wasn't something he'd ever boast about, but it had been useful on more than one occasion. In this case he was keen that the Bonelord didn't die, as he wasn't taking the chance that the wyvern they both rode would cease to function at the same time as its master. Swords still skewering the man in front of him, Kennedy kicked the beast hard in the side, turning it back towards his vessel, as behind him, the *Warrior's* boat and the other wyvern plummeted away, locked in an embrace which would last until they hit the ground.

"You owe me a gig."

XXX

THE PROMISE OF imminent death had been enough to yank Arke out of any arachnid-based anxieties and back into the moment. After a heavy-hitting spell slammed into her shoulder and knocked her into a patch of sticky silk, she no longer cared about the web's owner, an extremely hairy spider that thought it had just won the dinner lottery. Flexing her arm with a wince, she took a moment to catch her breath. She could just make out three shapes in the passageway ahead and though she couldn't see exactly who they were, she was painfully aware that their magic packed a hefty punch.

"KILL THEM!" Irash's fury rushed through her like molten lava as the impact of a second spell slammed her to the right, her body instantly crushing the hapless spider as it basked in the glory of its greatest ever catch.

Rolling away from the arachnid pancake she'd just created, Arke narrowly avoided a third attack and launched a wall of blue tinged ripostes down the tunnel towards the dimly lit mages.

"Not like that! You are so IGNORANT!" Irash was more of a delight than Stabbington.

Bristling with irritation, Arke snapped back. "Who's more stupid? The one who doesn't know how or the one who does and doesn't explain?"

Diving away from a dangerous looking ripple of magical fog that whickered down the tunnel towards her, Arke slipped on some bones, almost face planting in yet another web. She just managed to push off the nearest wall in time and re-oriented herself, brewing up a fistful of ice which she unleashed on the enemy before simultaneously throwing some magical light across to the other side of the tunnel and extinguishing the glow on her hand.

"Use your tiny mind. Picture an action and it will become real."

"Anything?"

A series of sulphuric explosions from the enemy mages hit Arke's decoy light, destroying it in seconds. Irash waited until his host had stopped coughing from the noxious fumes before replying, his voice eminently casual as he announced his true title.

"Anything which will annihilate them. You use the powers of Irash the Destroyer."

"The – DESTROYER?"

Arke took a moment to fully understand the ramifications of that particular bombshell before hurling a curse-laden rant down the tunnel. Fury at both her passenger and her attackers led her to multitask, venting her rage through the medium of expletives while simultaneously dealing with the mages. It was unexpectedly satisfying to concentrate the power she felt within her on making the enemy's heads detach themselves from their bodies the moment they heard swear words so perfectly enunciated they were almost poetry.

A cold silence descended and Arke relit her hand, ready to repulse any attacks that targeted her as a result. She couldn't see or hear the enemy but that didn't mean her first attempt at wielding Irash's magic had worked.

"They are dead. Did you not feel their agonies stretching into consummate nothingness?"

The delight in Irash's voice was as unmistakeable as the pleasure he radiated within her and Arke frowned as she strode down the tunnel. She was so unnerved by the continued gloating of the connoisseur of death inside her head that she barely noticed the swarms of giant spiders which had already clustered over the three bodies, sucking at the warm flesh and clawing their way deeper into the corpses.

Turning a sharp corner, she saw a faint glow ahead of her and realised with relief that she'd nearly reached the cave mouth again. Then she stopped, suddenly aware that what she'd assumed was the howling of the wind was actually something quite different.

"Yodelling? I know it's useful in the mountains, but seriously?"

"A battle cry." Irash's reply was far more casual than the subject matter demanded.

"Oh, that's OK then." Arke drew in a deep breath and exhaled slowly before started to prepare herself for combat, flexing her shoulders and cricking her neck, firstly to the left and then to the right. Now she understood why she'd seen Ruby in the shadow puppet show. Stabbington wouldn't have let her stay outside the cave with what sounded like an entire army as company. She walked closer to the exit, the noise growing louder and louder as she approached. "Apart from aural torture, what am I facing here?"

Irash launched into a scathing explanation and Arke began to wish she had phrased her question more precisely. She could think of better times to indulge in a little monologuing and as he spoke, she could feel more and more of his rage building inside her.

"Those who imprisoned me chiselled away at my power, stealing more from their prisoner than I had allowed them to use as their god. They are nothing more than vile leeches who seek to keep me away from the world, to keep me enslaved for their own benefit. Yet they have no ambition; they do not use the magic they take to become great. Their lives have remained the same for hundreds of years, for even now they still wear the bones of the fallen as armour. They must be riven into fragments, torn apart, crushed, annihilated, exposed, and utterly destroyed!"

"Now the fighting makes sense," Arke replied dryly, finally understanding exactly why the Bonelords protected the Greyspines so fiercely. She tried to regulate her breathing and keep her voice calm, fighting to remain controlled despite the flames of Irash's anger which roared through her once more, frantically attempting to ignite her to full fury.

"KILL THEM ALL!"

Images from the Soulbound's recent memories came crashing into her mind, thrown there by her passenger as he opened boxes she'd only just locked shut. Paltos' body, cold and empty eyed as the rain poured down on him. The bloody stump of Urzish's arm. Kennedy's wretched grief.

Arke could hold him back from possessing her, but in discovering her memories, Irash had found her weakness. She kept them locked away for a reason. Rage erupted within her as she remembered what the Bonelords had done to her friends and she strode towards the cave exit, her mind white-hot with the need for revenge. Her eyes did not flash black as she marched out onto the plateau; she remained entirely herself. She wanted nor needed the alibi of possession.

Ahead of her stood the horde of identical Bonelords, weapons raised. The moment they saw her, their yodelling intensified and they lurched into a charge towards her. In any other frame of mind, Arke would have taken a moment to comment on the unnerving experience of being attacked by what looked like a couple of hundred clones, all in perfect step. However, pure unrelenting wrath did not allow for more than the most basic of observations, and with bloodlust building with every second of hate, she concentrated Irash's power on the body armour of every single enemy sprinting towards her. The bone protection over the chests of these particular troops extended upwards into eerie cages that encircled their heads and spread along each limb in exquisitely aligned articulation. Arke felt the reverberations from each matched stride rippling through the ground under her feet, she felt the powerful echo of their increasingly high-pitched yodelling as it bounced between the chasm walls, and she watched dispassionately as their charge suddenly faltered.

The Bonelord soldiers stopped in their tracks, in the midst of their battle cries, in the moment of their deaths, as their very armour crushed the life from them. That which had protected them for so long, had been stripped from corpses, painstakingly cleaned and prepared, woven with care and skill into each terrifying carapace, tightened instantly around their wearers. Some bones splintered under the pressure of sudden constriction, driving themselves through skin and into flesh, digging hungrily into the bodies below. Some amputated limbs, some heads, others crushed ribcages, sternums, skulls. Filled with a desolate, raging fury, Arke destroyed the entire force with a single powerful thought. Then she waved a hand, sweeping the fallen to the sides of the cutting and willing the grey, faceless statues to tumble from their alcoves, mashing what was left of the army into unrecognisable pulp.

The ground ran with blood, her boots splashing in the gore as she strode onward. The massacre had thrilled her passenger, but the intensity of Arke's anger drained as quickly as it had arrived. She felt empty of everything except the need to return to the ship and help her crew.

"Use my powers. Fly," Irash's voice whispered in her head.

She rose in the air and accelerated at an incredible rate, heading straight for the *Warrior*.

Chapter Fourteen
Undead Flightmare

CROUCHING OVER THE aiming scope for the aetheric lance, Sparkz tried to keep his voice calm as he directed Ellie's hand on the helm above him. In the absence of Kennedy's solid presence, the mood on board had been twitchy enough without the appearance of a bloody dragon. In retrospect, his rallying cry of "They don't exist!" had not been the most useful thing to shout when there was actually one of the monsters cruising towards them. Like the wyverns, the beast's subscription to life had been cancelled many years ago but the gargantuan, grey dragon clearly wasn't about to let minutiae like that hold it back.

However ill-conceived his line, Sparkz did not regret it, or he wouldn't once they'd survived the encounter and his black eye had stopped throbbing. As it turned out, Ellie had one hell of a left hook when she was roused from blank-eyed terror to indignant rage and he was convinced he could milk her guilt over his bruise for at least a couple of days.

Surviving was, of course, a priority in their situation, and after the halfling's decidedly cheap shot, Sparkz had shoved her back towards the helm with a comment of "Do that to the dragon instead!" before heading to the lance control room. After the last encounter with Bonelords, he'd spent a lot of time musing on the best plan to deal with a wyvern but since bloody dragons didn't bloody well exist, he hadn't thought to include them in his hypothesis. Still, he did have a super powerful aetheric weapon at his disposal, so he'd decided that the beast would have to join its fellows in the annals of history via brute force rather than smart thinking.

"Port five, Ellie."

The dragon had been brazen in its direct approach to the *Warrior*, despite the clear figure of the Ornithol weaving her way around the beast in an attempt to distract its rider.

"She's coming round again. Sparkz, we can't fire with Ruby there!" Ellie's voice was taut with tension.

"With her super hearing she'll know the lance is charging. She's a lot of things but stupid isn't one of them."

"But…"

"'Midships."

Sparkz cut the halfling off before she planted any more seeds of doubt in his mind. He couldn't worry about Ruby when the *Warrior* was at risk. Checking the scope again, he satisfied himself that the monster's massive bulk was fully covered by the crosshairs and took a few deep breaths as what felt like every muscle in his body tensed anxiously. The distance between the ship and the creature he really wished was extinct was closing rapidly. The lance had never taken so long to charge.

As the thrumming around him reached a crescendo, all Sparkz could see in the lens was the monster's patchworked chest. He flicked the offset switches either side of the console that were the failsafe activation mechanism.

"FIRING!"

He didn't really need to tell Ellie that, since the silence which suddenly echoed around the *Warrior* informed everyone aboard that the lance was about to spit forth a gout of aetheric energy. However, saying it always felt good, especially now when all they'd been able to do so far was watch the terrifying creature soar towards them. He leant back from the scope, knowing from painful experience that the blinding beam of magical energy would render his eyesight defunct for precious minutes if he was stupid enough to watch it through the crosshairs.

The expletive filled roar of triumph from Ellie that echoed down the speaking tube and through the boards above his head was enough to tell Sparkz that their weapon had hit home. He clicked the switches to the OFF position and ducked to the scope, seeing the dragon reeling from the aetheric body blow but still stubbornly aloft and heading towards them. Sparkz set his jaw in furious defiance and started the weapon's recharging cycle.

"We're on a collision course!" Ellie's hoarse voice didn't tell Sparkz anything that he didn't already know. "Do I turn us away?"

"We hit it!" Grimlet popped his head in the door and Sparkz kicked it quickly shut again. The last thing he needed was the over-enthusiastic young orc blundering around in the control booth.

He ducked his head to the speaking tube again. "And open our flank to it? Not a bloody chance."

"We can't ram it, it's too big! Grimlet, it's not safe up here! Get below with everyone else!"

"The lance will charge in time." Sparkz could only hope that his voice held as much conviction as his brother's would have done in the same circumstances. "Hold her steady."

Unfortunately for the *Warrior*, the dragon, clearly enraged after its free, no commitment, laser surgery, was now within range of its own main weapon. Sucking its patchworked neck up and back, it blasted a roaring stream of magical grey fire against the front of the ship in a crackling wave of instant death. Ellie just managed to dive for cover behind the fire suppression barrels as the monster's devastating power washed over the bows. She was perfectly placed to hear the tortured scream that rent the air and more devastatingly, able to see Grimlet enveloped in a ghastly cloud of flame and smoke.

Sparkz also heard the scream and then a heavy thud outside the control room. He yanked the door open, seeing the last of the ominous grey magic whisk away from the deck. Grabbing the first aid satchel hanging on the wall, he stepped out of the booth and stopped, eyes widening in silent horror. He'd seen an awful lot of awful things in his lifetime, but never the aftermath of an undead dragon's breath. It was obvious that there was no need for the kit in his hand, and with numb fingers he replaced it on its hook.

Grimlet was dead, fully and utterly defunct. Whatever magical energy had spewed from the monster had suddenly, brutally, and catastrophically reduced his body to a skeleton, his clothes and flesh stripped away like so many dead leaves. The pile of bones lying on the deck glistened white as if they'd been bleached, moisture from them sizzling into steam which was chased away by the wind. Not a single piece of anything recognisable remained; Grimlet had been purged of his identity just as instantly as he'd been purged of his life.

Stepping back into the booth and closing the door, Sparkz forced himself to unclench his jaw and take some deep breaths before speaking into the tube.

"Ellie, lash the wheel on this course and get under cover. We can't miss now, it's too close."

"Is he…?"

"There's nothing we can do for him except make sure we take that thing out of the sky forever."

"It's going down even if I have to rip it apart with my bare hands," Ellie hissed.

Ducking to look through the scope, Sparkz watched the dragon loom larger. He guessed that it, like their lance, was recharging, and knew it was now a race against time. Whoever was ready to fire quickest would be the winner.

ⅩⅩⅩ

Powered by Irash's magic, Arke made it to the battle in seconds, arriving in time to see the *Warrior's* bow covered in the monstrous dragon's grey fire.

"You'll need to get close. I have yet to recharge from our last encounter," Irash warned as she began to plot the giant creature's demise.

"How close? Polite greeting or intimate massage?"

"I can always do this if you aren't sure."

Two-word denial appropriately delivered to her conniving passenger, Arke made her plan – there weren't many beasts she knew that could survive having their head removed. Without further deliberation, she headed straight for the creature's mouth as it opened, preparing to deliver another roaring cloud of magic across her ship. Diving right through the open jaws until she reached the back of its throat, she used Irash's power to create a wave of explosive force, pushing it away from her in all directions to try and burst the beast's head open from within. The percussive blast busted shards of bone and long dead flesh away from the dragon's skull, scattering them liberally in its slipstream, but although the creature was wavering and wobbling in the air, its head barely functional, her efforts hadn't been enough to finish it completely.

"It was your fault that did not work; let me take over."

Irash was uncomfortably persistent, his hunger for control so strong that Arke could almost taste it. She didn't even bother to answer, concentrating instead on channelling enough of his energy to finish the job.

Destiny was, however, winding up for a gigantic sucker punch. At such close proximity, Arke could hear that the *Warrior's* aetheric weapon had almost recharged. The noise was unmistakable, the pitch increasing as it finished priming. Then the sound ceased abruptly, throwing the next second into a trough of eerie silence as the charging conduits cut out. The weapon was ready to fire. Arke knew what would happen next.

Time seemed to slow down as she felt the boom of the power unleashed and saw the sharp light slicing towards the beast's neck. It couldn't miss at this short range.

Clarity came quicker than the explosion – she was a vessel, just like the *Warrior*. Except her passenger was a scorching, searing, rending, caustic power. She felt his rage and his nihilistic delight in destruction. She knew he'd goaded her to massacre the Bonelord army when she could have just flown away. She knew how powerful his possession attempts were and doubted anyone on her ship could avoid his control. Could she chance him being loose in her world? Or even on her ship with all the people she cared about? Could she trust herself as his host when he was able to manipulate her to murderous rage so easily?

She knew the dragon was going to be obliterated when the beam hit.

"MOVE!" Irash screamed in her head.

As she looked at her ship one last time, Arke caught sight of Kennedy riding what had to be a hijacked wyvern towards it, his hat gone, blond hair flying in the wind. He was OK and the *Warrior* would be safe.

This moment was hers; this was how she could protect the rest of them. The Greyspines would swallow Irash once again.

Arke obeyed her instincts and shut her eyes as the bright light seared its way into the dragon.

⚹⚹⚹

RUBY HAD SOARED clear of the blast at the last moment. She watched with satisfaction as what had been a monster was instantly reduced to a headless body, its wings hanging limp. What had been its neck and head were now no more than chunks of grizzled jerky and bone dropping out of the sky, brushed aside by the giant carcass as it plummeted. The Ornithol's sharp eyes focused quickly on the ex-dragon's rider as they followed their mount towards the long distant ground. While she was relieved to see her enemy falling, she was too far away to stop them launching a spell towards the *Warrior*, grey energy spewing from their finger like a javelin.

Ruby headed quickly back to her ship, ready to help with any damage control. She'd expected the mage's final 'screw you' to be something nastily simple like some sort of fiery ball or hail of acid. However, what she saw as she approached the main deck was far, far worse, and definitely her third horrific experience of the day. Over by the aetheric control booth was a glistening white skeleton, its bones wreathed with the mage's grey magic as it lurched to its feet. She was watching in mute horror as Ellie came under attack from the conglomeration of body parts when Stabbington started vibrating urgently in her belt.

"ARKE! She is falling!" The demon's voice was both accent-less and uncharacteristically strident as he shouted his warning, his sudden fear shaking Ruby to immediate activity. "Somewhere close by!"

The Ornithol hadn't realised that the demon's connection to his host was so strong, but at that moment, nothing else mattered but saving Arke. She looked down, eyes rapidly scanning the sky and spotted the Soulbound's limp and bloody body plummeting towards the wide expanse of the Grey Valley River. Ruby threw herself straight into a headlong dive, wrapping her wings tightly around her body to find every sliver of extra speed.

Closing the distance rapidly, her sharp vision noticed something that struck her as decidedly out of place, a strange looking goblet falling a little distance from the Soulbound. Bizarre as random airborne drinking vessels were, Ruby ignored it, needing to concentrate on the rescue in hand. As she grew even closer, she noticed with a moment of beak-clenching concern, that Arke was tumbling through the air with a huge, distinctly fin-like triangular piece of dragon bone sticking out of her back. Ruby knew that was going to make the catch extra tricky, so as soon as her dive brought her close enough, she made a grab for the Soulbound.

With a bump, her fingers met Arke's disconcertingly limp arm but as she tried to secure her grip, the piece of bone slammed painfully into her chest and she lost purchase. Stabbington's instant verbal reaction was both distracting and deeply shocking for an Ornithol who had been raised in a convent, but Ruby was too breathless as well as too polite to tell him to be silent. She flared her wings to change course for her second effort before diving once more.

The lower mountain peaks were already stabbing icily through the clouds and the froth-capped river was coming up fast by the time Ruby was in position for another rescue attempt. As she waited for the perfect moment to make another grab, the dragon rider in her red bone armour suddenly dived purposefully into view, only to clasp her hands around the odd-looking goblet and fly immediately upwards.

"CONCENTRATE! You must get her this time!" Stabbington shouted, as if that wasn't obvious. His incessant imperatives combined with her own anxiety were making her head ache horribly.

With one final effort, Ruby shot forward, twisting in the air so that her entire body was underneath Arke's. She couldn't afford to miss and this was the best way to ensure a catch, even if by far the riskiest. As the

Soulbound slammed into her chest, she wrapped both her arms and legs around her friend as tightly as she could. Then, as the demon's urgings changed abruptly to ones directed at his unconscious host, she flared her wings, fighting to control her orientation before finally flying as fast as she could back towards the *Warrior*, desperate effort burning every muscle.

✘✘✘

As HE URGED the hijacked wyvern towards the *Warrior*, Kennedy was still celebrating the way the dragon had been carved into unrecognisable chunks by his ship's aetheric lance. However, his joy grew a little less carefree as he spotted a pair of Bonelords and their standard sized mounts about to land on the *Warrior's* deck.

Fierce, cold anger overtook him and Kennedy dropped an unusually personal slur in the slumped Bonelord's ear before angling their mount for a stealthy final approach. Kicking the beast into a turn, he put it on a course that would swoop toward the stern and out of the marauders' sight.

At the precise instant his temporary mount came level with the back of his ship, Kennedy brought his alter into existence on top of the cabins and quickly merged with it as the ancient beast flew on. No longer held upright by his rigid blades, its helpless rider began a lazy tumble away from his mount. Kennedy watched for a second, nodding in cold satisfaction, before turning to assess the situation on board.

He briefly noticed Ellie fighting something behind the helm before switching his attention to the Bonelords who'd just dismounted their wyverns amidships. He saw one of the enemy sealing the main hutch shut with swirling grey magic just as someone from below was trying to push it open. Kennedy's lips tightened and he slid his bloody swords into their scabbards before drawing his pistols, flicking the switch that loaded two magically charged gemstones into each. It was an expensive move, but he needed to make his shots count. He knew the crew would be racing to the smaller hatchways, but he intended that there would be nothing left for them to do once they arrived. These Bonelord dicks could get the hell off his ship.

Just as Kennedy was taking aim, he saw Sparkz step out of the aetheric booth at the far end of the main deck. With a single defiant crack of his whip, the engineer captured the Bonelords' full attention. Taking advantage of the distraction, Kennedy engaged Plan B and backed up along the roof of the cabins, making room for a good run up. Then he sprinted forwards, leaping high into the air and, aiming his pistols at the wyvern on the left, fired.

His magically enhanced shots seemed to be inspired by the airborne assault and both bullets went true, smashing into the creature's skull, crumpling it instantly to the deck. Sadly, Kennedy wasn't able to appreciate the satisfaction of that beast-crushing moment as he'd already tucked himself into a backwards somersault. His mother had been the queen of acrobatic attacks and though Kennedy had always preferred face to face duelling, she had spent hours making sure her son could both fight and flight. The moment he passed the apex of his rotation he dropped the pistols and drew his swords in a reverse grip.

The Bonelords were only just turning to find the

origin of the pistol shots when Kennedy landed between them, knees bent to absorb the impact and control his perfect landing. Straightening explosively, he pushed up and backwards with his swords, powering the blades through his enemy's bodies. He angled the weapons with deadly precision and as he looked from one stricken Bonelord to the other, his expression radiated grim contentment at a plan perfectly performed.

Looking up, he saw Sparkz had launched himself at the last wyvern, dodging its lunging jaws by the narrowest margin and spinning away from its secondary claw strikes while he positioned himself to attack. After their last encounter with the beasts, Kennedy had spent a few coffee fuelled hours with his brother, discussing the optimal way to subdue giant, irritable, flying lizards and while neither of them had expected to test their theories this soon, Sparkz was clearly ready. Aiming his whip at the beast's head, he let it fly, pulling the lash tight around its bony jaws; then dived on the thrashing tail, probably gaining a whole new set of bruises while he struggled to tie that to its nose. As the last knot tightened, the struggling wyvern fell with a heavy thud, writhing helplessly on the deck. The engineer stood up and brushed his clothes off with a satisfied grin as he looked over at his brother.

"Told you that would work."

"*This* is how the *Warrior* rocks."

Kennedy nodded in brisk appreciation as he yanked his swords clear of the Bonelords. The wyvern riders fell senselessly forwards, dead before they hit the deck and he looked at his brother expectantly as their ancient beasts dissolved into dust.

"Fine, but I'm only saying this once." Sparkz took a deep breath. "This is how the *Warrior* rolls."

Kennedy was about to continue the chant when what looked like a humanoid skeleton came hurtling over the rails from the helm and landed with a scuttling splat of bones nearby. He froze, his face wreathed in confusion, as it rose again, everything finding its anatomically accurate place in the creepiest shuffle he'd ever seen.

"Watch out for... that." A panting Ellie leant on the railing by the helm, blood dripping from her face and neck.

The skeleton charged at Kennedy, throwing itself through the air, leg bones wrapped around his waist as it clawed and pummelled at his face. Sparkz grabbed its head, expecting the skull to detach from the rest of it, but as he struggled to yank it away, found that the creature was held together with invisible bonds that seemed impossible to break.

The three of them fought harder than anyone would think was necessary in order to control animated bones. They finally managed to peel the forceful skeleton away from Kennedy's body and launch it unceremoniously over the side, watching it fall away into the deep river valley far below them.

"What the hell was that?" Kennedy leant breathlessly on the railing, blood dripping down cuts on his face and neck.

Sweeping her gaze across the enemy-free decks, Ellie heaved a deep sigh. They'd survived. Grief was next.

"Grimlet. He got caught by the dragon's breath and then his bones... somehow came back to... life? No, not life. Something else."

Silence reigned. Kennedy's eyes widened in horror and he peered helplessly over the railings. Then his shoulders drooped with defeat as the news sank in and his hands gripped the hilts of his swords until his knuckles showed white.

"Don't go into fostering any time soon."

With a tone as brusquely discomforting as his words, Sparkz headed across the deck to deal with the bodies of the dead Bonelords.

Chapter Fifteen

Possession is Nine Tenths of the Law

SPARKZ WAS JUST grabbing his whip from the pile of
wyvern dust when he looked up to see yet another
Bonelord lowering themselves to the deck nearby,
a strange looking chalice in their hand. The engineer
had already had an utter gutful of these nasty mountain
dwellers and this one, who looked like they were just
about to ask for a goblet of sugar, had landed right on his
last nerve. He didn't care how wreathed in magical grey
smoke and dressed in blood red armour they were, they
weren't welcome aboard the *Warrior*.

Before the Bonelord even had a chance to bring any
magical powers to the party, a small yin-yang tattoo on
Sparkz's neck glowed purple. The red armoured mage
was hit by a cascade of flashes, their form growing
smaller with each dazzling pulse, until they'd shrunk
from standard sized to football sized in a matter of
seconds. The chalice, however, did not change, and fell
to the deck with a heavy clunk as it grew too heavy for
its bearer to hold. Sparkz ignored it and did the very first
thing that came to mind. Taking a quick run up, he
punted the now tiny and confused Bonelord far out over
the edge of the ship. The scream they uttered as they fell
was ear-shatteringly high-pitched and as he watched
their flailing body describe a perfect arc, Sparkz took a

moment to admire the distance he'd achieved with his kick. Finally, a wicked grin splitting his face, he pulled a grubby handkerchief from his pocket and held it up.

"Hey, you forgot your parachute!" He looked around for an audience, but the deck was empty, and he sighed with disappointment. "Never anyone around to appreciate the delivery of such fine lines."

He was just fastening his whip back on his belt when a flurry of tired wings heralded Ruby's appearance amidships. His expression darkened as she deposited a badly injured Arke onto the deck and shoved Stabbington under her friend's limp hand, muttering that she hoped that he could help. It was obvious that this was beyond serious – the Soulbound's skin was deathly white and her breath was ragged and rattling in her chest.

"Get this in her now." Sparkz rifled through the nearest first aid satchel and handed the bottle of *Jumpstart A Heart* to the Ornithol. There was no point in trying anything weaker, Arke needed the emergency strength go juice and she needed it now.

"Me?" Ruby frowned. "I've never…"

"Consider this on the job training. Open an eye and pour it in."

Ruby yanked the cork from the bottle of rainbow-coloured liquid and tipped a hefty amount into the Soulbound's right eye, praying to Chromatia as she poured. The pearlescent liquid hovered around the eyeball for a second and then with a hiss, disappeared completely.

With a sudden jolt, Arke lurched to a sitting position, crackles of multi-coloured lightning visible all over her, the power of the magical potion even setting her hair on end. She was breathing rapidly and obviously disorientated but not so much that she couldn't snarl at her demon.

"Do you *ever* shut up, Stabbington?"

She was clearly going to be OK. Even Sparkz cracked a smile as Ruby rocked back on her heels and heaved in a hugely relieved breath. However, as his eyes fell on the fin-shaped dragon bone sticking out of Arke's back, his good humour quickly faded. He took no time at all working out that he did not want to be the one to remove it. Thankfully, before any awkward extraction related conversations could be had, with a magical shimmer and a huge amount of relief, the bone dissolved into nothing but a sprinkling of dust.

As Sparkz watched Ruby look between what remained of the bottle of *Jumpstart* and the grisly wound in the Soulbound's back, he was aware that what was about to come next would undoubtedly be his fault. However, the devilish temptation to enjoy what was about to happen prevented the intervention he knew he should make. He shoved his hands in his pockets, decided to deny he'd seen anything, and waited for the magic to happen.

Since this was the Ornithol's first experience of *Jumpstart*, she had no idea of the effect an application would have on a conscious person, and innocently tipped the rest of the bottle into the wound that the dragon bone had created. In an instant, Arke erupted off the deck with a startled yelp, followed by an absolute cascade of jerky curses and the brittle crackling of rainbow static that sparkled its way up and down her entire body.

"Is she alright?" Kennedy looked down at the scene from his position at the helm with confusion and relief.

Sparkz felt mostly sure that his brother hadn't intended to drop such a ridiculously naïve question, but the result of Arke hearing it was a thing of absolute beauty.

Pointing a shuddering arm in Kennedy's direction, the Soulbound unloaded words that were undoubtedly spicy but hilariously incoherent due to the magic potion wracking her body.

"Sorry, you're going to what my what now?" Kennedy interrupted her tirade, his lips quivering with amusement.

"Aren't you old enough to be his mother?" Sparkz asked, trying desperately to keep a straight face.

Unluckily for the bucket that Arke threw at his head, her aim was distinctly compromised by her inability to withstand the magical shocks that were still rampaging up and down her body. And as it disappeared over the side of the ship, both Kennedy and Sparkz gave up trying to contain themselves. Their roars of laughter seemed to release something in Ruby, and she started to giggle, then chortle before she finally gave up the battle against full blown mirth. The more the three of them laughed, the more swear words Arke massacred as she paced up and down the deck, all the while struggling to put Stabbington into his scabbard with a hand that was twitching uncontrollably.

In the background of the Soulbound circus, Ellie appeared out of the main hatch, the magic that had held it shut having died with its master. Sparkz spotted her approach and turned to greet her, guessing she'd want to know what was going on. However, her glassy-eyed look and automaton tread silenced both his laughter and explanation immediately. As Sparkz watched her walk towards the strange chalice lying on the deck, his hand flew to the whip hanging at his belt.

※ ※ ※

"No! don't touch it!"

Arke's control had returned just as her vocabulary had run out and she yelled a warning as she spotted Ellie reaching for Irash's vessel. Her words went unheeded and as the halfling's hand closed around the goblet, her eyes suddenly glowed with black energy.

With a sharp crack, the lash of Sparkz's whip wrapped around the chalice and spun it clear of Ellie's hand. The Soulbound watched as the halfling's eyes returned to normal just before she passed out, landing with a heavy thud on the deck. Without hesitation, Arke scrambled over and grabbed the golden chalice. The moment she touched the cold metal, Irash's voice boomed in her head, his dark images flooding her mind as they rejoined their battle for control. She endured as she had before, right up until Stabbington decided to intervene with a fierce possessiveness that took her by surprise.

"This woman is MINE! You get out! Get out now!"

Her fingers were still twitching after the double *Jumpstart* and the shock of her demon's fury made them drop the chalice which rolled across the deck and down through the open hatch.

"Stabbington!" Arke sprinted after it as it disappeared. "You IDIOT! What have you done?"

"This is NOT a time share," he responded with full venom. "You cannot invite other things over to party! Not on my watch, not when I am here, and I give you your power. When we have been together so long why would you want another?"

"This isn't about YOU!" She reached the hatch and froze in horror as she looked down to see Krugg walking up the stairs towards her, eyes fully black, the chalice tucked inside his shirt.

"Now this body is STRONG!" Irash was clearly very happy with his new residence and slammed the ogre's fist into Arke, the blow launching her across the deck and out of his way.

As Ruby helped her up, the Soulbound tried to ignore her rapidly swelling left eye and looked over to where Kennedy was talking to Irash-Krugg, waving the others back as he tried to negotiate. All this was what she'd feared would happen and why she'd accepted her fate when the lance's beam hit the dragon. She clenched her jaw and began to inwardly shout at Stabbington who was more than ready to fight back. After so many years of living the same life, the pair had a long list of grievances which they traded furiously, opening old wounds, starting new ones. It was Ruby who inadvertently broke up the private row, touching Arke's shoulder and whispering that the captain was making a deal with 'the thing' in Krugg.

That was enough to get the Soulbound and her demon to save the rest of the brutal argument for later. She headed quickly over to Sparkz and engaged in a terse conversation after which the engineer hurried below. The rest of the crew, who had now appeared on deck, listened intently, if also warily, to the business-like discussions taking place by the helm. As Kennedy started to plot a new course, it was obvious that he'd been convinced that finding an orbiculum to open the door to Irash's home plane was the best way forward.

"If anyone knows where to find one of those things, it's Crimbles. We'll go straight to him, it's probably only a few days travel once we get out of these mountains."

"What is Kennedy DOING? We can't set that thing loose in the world! He can do whatever he likes while he's in Krugg's body!" Arke hissed from between gritted teeth.

"But is he OK? Is Krugg still in there?" In her fear for her friend, Ruby didn't notice the forbidding expression on the Soulbound's face.

"Is that the ONLY thing you're thinking about right now? Giant ogre possessed by a being so powerful he can do pretty much exactly as he pleases? Yeah, let's worry about poor Krugg and not about the guy in his body getting fed up and tearing everything to tiny pieces."

"You didn't say that's what was controlling him." Ruby lowered her voice and looked away from Arke, arms folded.

"I haven't had chance! What, should I just blow a whistle for half time and break out the oranges? Team talk, folks, don't touch the shiny chalice and don't play with beings you can't control."

"We had no idea, so no need to be a bitch." Clearly having taken Arke's deeply patronising rant personally, a pale faced Ellie staggered to her feet and glared at the Soulbound.

"That is absolutely never true."

At that precise moment, the *Warrior* began to slow, the engine noise changing from a harmonious hum to a halting growl.

"What is this treachery?" Irash-Krugg snarled, glaring at Kennedy through narrowed eyes. "You are trying to trick me. Do not think I am a FOOL!"

"I'm really not!" Kennedy looked around for a clue before noticing his brother was no longer on deck. "Honestly, this is nothing to do with me. Let's go and see what's happening in the engine room."

After her brief discussion with Sparkz, Arke knew exactly what was happening. The engineer was busy sabotaging the engines just enough to slow them down until they had an Irash solution. It was more than obvious that they couldn't trust him, but equally evident that they were in an incredibly perilous position if they stayed where they were. Sparkz had been confident that he could make an easily reversible amount of damage look impressive and get out before he was caught. However, he hadn't had nearly enough time to do the job as well as get away, and knowing what Irash thought of lesser beings, Arke realised she had to stop Kennedy showing him to the engine room, no matter the personal consequences.

"Philip, I need to tell you something!" She tried to put herself in between Kennedy and the stairs. Whatever she said needed to be enough to stop him in his tracks and there was only one thing she could think to say that would have any chance of distracting him. "I killed your parents! They haven't retired, they're dead. And I did it. Having a near-death experience made me want to tell you, to clear my conscience."

As confessions went, it was absolute fire. As successful distractions went, it sucked.

"She has had many near-death experiences, I believe

this is a merely a diversion," Irash-Krugg noted dispassionately, using the ogre's giant hand to shove the Soulbound out of his way as he went down the steps to the middle deck, ducking his head under the low ceiling.

"I saw you coming out of the house that night, I've always known," Kennedy added, his voice dripping acid. "Nice timing, by the way. Thanks for that."

As counter-confessions went, it was incandescent.

Arke blinked in shock as her entire world shook around her. It took a moment to recover from that bombshell, but her long practiced self-discipline just managed to hold back the reaction she felt bubbling up inside her. She'd deal with that new information maybe, sometime, never. Open a box, chuck it in, stay in the present. Trying to stop them without violence hadn't worked – desperate measures were needed. Even if he didn't punish Sparkz for his sabotage, they couldn't risk taking Irash into the world while he was in full control of any other being. She'd seen what he could do with her as a conduit and she absolutely didn't want to know what he could do when he could choose his own actions.

Easing Stabbington from his scabbard, Arke looked at Ruby and pointed ominously after the captain with the tip of the demon blade.

"We have to stop them."

They slid down the main stairs as silently as they could and slunk along the corridor, Krugg's booming voice covering the sound of their approach.

"You will have the engine fixed," Irash commanded as he and Kennedy made their way along the corridor towards the engine room. "I will give you instructions and you will make your crew do what I say. I feel your leadership is weak so you will need help to subdue the crew." He looked around, like a dog sniffing the air before smiling darkly. "Ahh yes, this will help them perform their duties with alacrity."

From the galley to the right came a parrot-based scream of pure unadulterated terror and the crashing sound of a zombie giant forcing his way out of the ice room as Paltos returned to what wasn't exactly life but was definitely existence.

"Of course, I will absolutely order them to...."

Kennedy thudded senseless to the floor as Ruby's lightning strikes knocked him unconscious. Arke moved quickly around him, realising with horror that Irash was nearly at the engine room, the ogre's hand reaching for the door.

"Get that thing out of him," she commanded and with sheer desperation, threw Stabbington's blade with every bit of energy she had, directly at Krugg's back.

The sword pierced deeply into the ogre's body and Arke held her breath. However, this time the possessor was fully in control and replied to whatever the demon blade had said with casual disdain.

"Enough. You are the work of a moment." Then Irash-Krugg turned slowly to look at Arke, eyes still pools of black, her sword stuck deep within him.

Knowing exactly what Irash was capable of, the Soulbound felt a brief wave of desperation wash over her. Her gamble had failed and there was absolutely no doubt in her mind that he was about to make her pay for trying to thwart him. If she was dead, then the *Warrior* had no chance against him. She had to make it right, whatever it took, and her best defence had always been to look confident but clutch like a drowning man.

"Have I got your attention now?" She squared her shoulders, glaring her challenge directly into the dark orbs shining coldly in Krugg's face.

"Yes. Though you will regret it."

"The ogre's body is muscular but he is not accustomed to magic, so your immense power will burn him to ashes the moment you use it." Arke knew absolutely nothing of the sort, but she did know that anything vaguely flattering delivered with enough conviction to a being whose ego was the size of a small country was always worth a try. "I've proved that I am strong enough to be your host and I promise that I will help you to leave this plane."

The tension in the corridor was almost palpable as Irash considered her words before replying, Krugg's meaty finger poking her blade as it stuck out of him. "Your pathetic lesser demon must go first."

If that was the price to get Irash contained inside her, in the only body that could resist his will, then Arke had no choice but to pay it. She walked down the corridor towards the ogre, stopping in front of him as the same finger that had touched her blade landed heavily on the top of her head. A blast of pure heat seared into her skull, spreading rapidly down through every bone in her body and she staggered backwards, slamming into a wall with a force that paled beside the pain inside her. Caustic power cut Stabbington free from her, dug him from the centre of who she was and dragged him away in a torment of agonising emptiness. She heard him begging her to help him fight against the separation, but she knew she must not. Finally, his voice dwindled to nothingness and she crumpled to the floor, sweat beading on her forehead, weakness flooding her limbs.

As her entire body tremored with shock, she felt something being pushed indelicately against her chest. Even with her eyes shut, she knew it was the chalice wielded by Krugg's huge hand. Numbly, she forced her arm to wrap around it. She knew what came next, the images, the words of power, the deep dark dread that would try to sap her will. She resisted because she knew no other way. She dug her fingertips into the palms of her hands as Irash tried once more to wrest control from her. Weak as she was, Arke would still not give in and as a sudden silence settled inside her head, she realised he'd given up. This attempt at possession was over.

Once she regained her senses, the Destroyer's energy forced itself on her with an icy blast that instantly re-invigorated her, striking through her body with glacial force. All her injuries were immediately healed and she felt like she'd just downed an entire week's worth of coffee rations.

"I cannot have a weak host. Get up."

She obeyed, turning as she heard the Paltos zombie crashing around in the galley and realising that finally she could do what she'd wanted to in the first place. Dead bodies should never be kept on board. There was sudden silence as she used the little energy her passenger had left to drop the giant off the ship.

"You will get the engines fixed," Irash ordered tersely. "And take me to find an orbiculum."

She didn't even glance at the ogre as she stepped past him and knocked on the engine room door. "I have the chalice, Sparkz. Can you get the engines running again?"

"I can give you snail speed," Sparkz shouted. "Anything faster will take about a week."

"A week?"

Irash's tone was already harsh enough to convey his intense irritation without slamming the dial up to maximum volume inside Arke's head, but he did so anyway.

His host blinked painfully before replying. "Do the best you can." Then without a single glance at anyone else, she turned on her heel, walked up to the captain's cabin and locked the doors behind her.

᙭ ᙭ ᙭

DOWN IN THE galley, Kennedy was being given hot sweet tea and a run-down of the events he'd missed when he was face down on the floor. He sat quietly listening until the end and then looked at Sparkz and Ruby accusingly. "You could have told me the plan!"

"Wasn't time," his brother remarked offhandedly as he poured himself a coffee.

"You were distracting him really well so we just let you carry on," Ruby added, with a far more apologetic tone.

Suddenly a heavily accented voice erupted with rage from the doorway. "You are all fools! Are you not doing ANYTHING about the abomination inside her?"

It wasn't for the first time that day everyone turned to look at Krugg – or more accurately, Stabbington-Krugg.

"Stabbington's in Krugg now?" Kennedy asked incredulously, marvelling at the intensity of the piercing blue eyes that now shone from the ogre's face. "I didn't know he could do that!"

"Is Krugg still there too?" Ruby asked anxiously.

"Yes, yes, he is here, sleeping I think. I am just borrowing his meat suit. He is fine. But me? I am mortified that I must break my own rules and be in this lump of an ogre because Arke wanted me GONE from her. I do not know how I can EVER forgive her! She let him *peel* me away like a used plaster! *Chew* me off like a hangnail! *Slice* me clean away like the rind of a cheese! She replaced ME, ME who has always been there for her! It is outrageous and horrible and terrible, and I cannot bear it. Any of it! But if she thinks I will just LEAVE? No, I will not!"

It was very apparent that no-one knew quite what to say when faced with a super-sized crewmate who was suddenly speaking with a strong otherworldly accent, flinging his hands as he talked and expressing emotions that none of them expected from either an ogre or a demon.

"None of you will help me? I do not, I cannot even START to understand you people. This will end badly! Very badly."

Stabbington-Krugg stormed out of the galley, bashing into the doorway several times before he managed to negotiate the obstacle and left, crashing into the stairs as well before he managed to get his new body to climb them. Ruby hurried after him after letting the others know that she was going to try and make sure the demon didn't do anything rash.

"Good for you," Sparkz grunted, grabbing a loaf of bread and a lump of cheese before turning to Kennedy. "I'm going to the engine room and locking the doors. The only possessions I'm interested in are things you own, not things that own you. Making and fixing, yes please; playing host to some invisible demon, not now, not ever."

As his brother strode out, Kennedy looked around the galley, feeling more than a little lost. He didn't want to think too much about what had just happened, making the excuse to himself that his head was hurting after Ruby's lightning fists. He could hear Porro in the storeroom making a very bad attempt at fixing the ice room door – so soon both Kennedy and Porro were in the storeroom making a very bad attempt at fixing the ice room door. It would take time and effort to adequately bodge a job like that and that was just perfect.

Chapter Sixteen
With Imp-Like Tread

For the next few days, despite relatively clement weather and the absence of any Bonelords, the half speed *Warrior* was a distinctly uncomfortable place. Kennedy was sleeping with the rest of the crew below decks, Sparkz had slung his hammock in the engine room, Arke was barricaded in the captain's cabin and Stabbington-Krugg was drinking his way through every drop of alcohol on board with complete devotion to his task. The other crew members kept out of their way, all bar Ruby who tried to post food under the door to Arke three times a day and attempted to learn the names of the tools Sparkz was using so she could act as his assistant.

She'd found out that when Sparkz had run into the engine room to start his Irash related sabotage, he'd had to deal with Zeke, whose natural instincts were to fight back against any damage to the machinery, no matter the source. Since he didn't want to hurt the Bior but had no time to debate his actions, Sparkz had simply used his magic to weld Zeke's head to one of the pipes. Naturally, the atmosphere between them could now be described as unseasonably frigid since one refused to apologise and the other refused to forgive.

Ruby spent at least an hour in the engine room every day trying to improve her negligible technical skills while utterly failing to make conversation with Zeke.

The Bior had engaged creepy stalker mode and spent his time silently shadowing the engineer. Although Sparkz didn't seem even a little bothered by the distinctly judgemental scrutiny, Ruby couldn't help but feel that Zeke's soulless eyes and unrelenting silence were almost as disturbing as anything she'd been witness to recently.

Much of the rest of her free time was spent sitting with the possessed ogre, trying to persuade him to eat and soak up even a little of the alcohol he was sometimes quite literally throwing into his face. At first she was trying to protect Krugg's body from what she thought was anger, but soon realised was actually Stabbington's plunge into deep melancholy. Of course, the drinking only numbed his feelings briefly, so the entire middle deck had to listen to the sounds of the exceptionally morose ogre sobbing and moaning about his misery way into the night. Ruby offered the occasional supportive word when she had a chance, but mostly just sat in silence while he talked about his feelings and she continued to re-arrange her world view on the nature of demons and possession.

When she'd first met Arke, Ruby had assumed that her dour disposition was entirely due to having a demon inside her, keeping her trapped and miserable. The Ornithol's convent schooling had taught her that demons were the worst, they destroyed everything, they would tempt the unwise in order to devour their souls – there had been no small print which said that some of them were good company, reliable friends or prone to emotional outbursts.

Back on the mountain, Ruby had remembered Arke referring to Stabbington as nice. She'd also called him charming and while he wasn't that currently, he absolutely did have a good singing voice and a wide repertoire of songs, just as she'd said. Now Ruby had time to dwell on the subject further, she started to challenge what she'd been taught – for if all demons were wicked, terrible entities, then why was this particular one lying in a corridor pouring mixed spirits down his throat and hiccupping his way through sad songs? None of the things he was doing really fitted in with the blanket view that all demons were evil. He just seemed really sad.

One afternoon, while Kennedy was peeling potatoes for the evening meal, Ruby expressed her concern about Stabbington's state of mind. After hearing her out, Kennedy nodded slowly.

"Honestly, I was surprised that he didn't drag Arke's soul away for breaking their deal. I'm pretty sure I would have."

"He could do that?" she asked, eyes wide.

"She's a Soulbound – literally, her soul is bound. She receives magical powers in the now and when she dies, Stabbington owns her soul. Like any big sale, there's a contract and I've heard that those things are savage. I mean they have to be, there's a lot at stake. There's bound to be a clause, or fifty, about ways the demon can collect if you try and break the deal." Kennedy paused in his meal preparation and looked earnestly at Ruby. "Don't worry though; this is Stabbington we're talking about. They've been together since she was about your age – that's a lot of years. It'll work out. If I had to guess, I'd say he's hanging around to get her back once Irash leaves." He scratched his nose awkwardly with the end of the peeler. "You know, Stabbington's not just Arke's demon, he's more like… well, family, I suppose. He used to babysit me when I was a kid, even taught me to sword fight when I was only just big enough to hold him without falling over." His face crinkled into a warm smile at the memory.

"I didn't think demons could be…" Ruby tilted her head to one side and struggled to find the right word to describe Stabbington-Krugg's current state of distress. "…emotional?"

Kennedy looked up at her thoughtfully. "Maybe try not to think of him as a demon, just as a guy dealing with a messy break up. Some might say he's actually the less demonic of the pair; I couldn't possibly comment."

That only confused Ruby more. Although the number of messy break ups in the convent had not been nil, it still wasn't an aspect of life that she had any real experience of. "Maybe you could speak to him?"

"Ah." Kennedy dropped the potato in the pot and grabbed another, weighing it in his hand as he spoke. "Normally, I'd have been the first to try to talk to Stabbington, but the way I'm feeling, I doubt I'd be any good as a counsellor. Everything that's happened since we left High Haven has left me thinking that lying in a corridor blind drunk and crying sounds more than quite enticing."

※ ※ ※

UP IN THE captain's cabin, Arke opened the door and kicked out the stale food that Ruby kept squeezing underneath it. Pizza with the topping scuffed off, some sandwiches that looked like they'd been rolled flat to get through the gap, broken crackers, dried out slices of fruit – Arke hadn't wanted any of it. She knew where

Kennedy kept his private stash of junk food and on arrival in his cabin had quickly decided that when she was self-isolating with a monster in her head, sugar and carbohydrates were her new best friends.

For days she'd done nothing but tell endless stories and eat copious quantities of noisy snacks to keep Irash too tired to think about exploiting any weakness. She'd had a warning of his intentions after one unfortunate incident when she'd only been in the captain's cabin for a few hours. It was the simple act of unbuckling Stabbington's empty scabbard that had undone her instead. Just looking at it on the side table had triggered something primal within her. Without even thinking she'd grabbed it with such force that the metal cut her palm, and then with a furious effort, thrown it at the wall. She had trusted him, but it was obvious he hadn't trusted her. The emotions she had been holding back with such determination flooded her body, the rush of blinding anger almost more painful than the dark surge of grief which had twisted in her stomach.

"I can help," Irash had hissed, picking his moment perfectly.

Arke's eyes had flashed instantly black. She'd let him drag her backwards, promising that he would take her pain away if she just rested for a while. She'd felt broken and empty and angry but more than that, she'd been so very tired of everything.

Blood had dripped from Arke's injured hand to the wooden floor, and she'd felt its impact as it landed. The thud of liquid on solid had resonated through her entire body, instantly driving the blackness from her eyes. Inexplicably, she'd suddenly heard beautiful music pouring from the crystal powering the engine and tasted the corded sweetness of the timbers around her. She'd felt another drop of blood spread itself on the deck and more reverberations had cascaded upwards through her body like a fountain.

Letting go does not mean giving up.

The handwritten words had drifted in front of her eyes, then dipped, drawing her attention down to where the next red drop had rolled to the edge of her palm, ready to fall. It had glistened in the light, shining, glimmering, magical. Arke had instinctively closed her hand, cradling it to her chest to stem the bleeding.

In an instant everything had returned to normal, which had been a huge relief as she'd never wanted to know what Kennedy's dirty socks tasted like or how tears smelt. She'd wiped them away and moved to pick up the empty scabbard, but as she'd reached for it she'd noticed that her cut had already healed, leaving a strange-looking scar on her palm.

After that episode, Arke had quickly decided that silent misery was not an option, she needed to throw herself into something which would keep her so busy that both Irash and her feelings would stay locked down. Her lips had twisted in a half smile, and she'd dragged Kennedy's ominous black chest labelled 'Socks' from under his bed. She'd been well aware that it did not contain anything but a colourful smorgasbord of tasty snacks and availed herself of plenty before she'd settled in a chair and begun introducing Irash to Barsian children's stories.

"When I was four, I walked into the woods one day and found an empty cabin…"

A few days later, as Arke scraped the stale food out of the captain's cabin, she noticed Ellie busily sweeping the decks and quickly avoided her gaze, not wanting to give her passenger any ideas about jumping host.

"Go and check on the engines," Irash said for the fourth or fifth time that hour.

Arke stepped back inside and shut the door before opening another bumper box of dry roasted peanuts and putting her boots up on the chart table. "But I haven't told you about what happened when I was eight."

"Your ridiculous lying kept me amused when I was resting. Now I am feeling stronger I wish you to *check* on the engines and *cease* with your fantasies. You were *not* raised on a mountain top herding goats. Your adventures did *not* lead you through a mirror *nor* to steal porridge from forest creatures."

"Ok you got me. The truth this time?" Arke settled back in the chair and threw a peanut into her mouth.

"You promised that before you told me an interminably long story which ended with you dying of the plague. Although even that was more believable than you wearing a ballgown and dancing with a prince."

"K." She started munching her way through a handful of peanuts.

"AND STOP WITH THE CRUNCHING!"

Arke did not, in fact, stop with the crunching. She'd had so much caffeine and sugar she didn't know if she would ever sleep again and gently tormenting her passenger was becoming more and more amusing.

"Once upon a time…"

"No! Stop this NONSENSE!"

"When I was eight…"

"Engines!"

She poured more peanuts into her mouth and crunched as Irash groaned expressively, but their battle of wills was suddenly interrupted by a knock on the door.

"Cap..." Urzish cleared her throat and began again. "Arke, we've spotted a shipwreck ahead. It's in a similar position on the charts as the one we were sent to find."

"The prototype engine." Arke was suddenly interested.

"*This* ship is the priority, I must get off this miserable plane," Irash growled.

Arke stood up, brushing her hands, coat and trousers clean of all the crumbs. It took time, there were an awful lot of crumbs. "The prototype engine is supposed to be incredibly fast."

Irash took in the implications of her words for a moment. "Then why are we still here?"

The shipwreck sat grounded on a huge lump of rock that nestled in the shadow of two peaks. As she approached, Arke saw that the vessel was still partially powered as it seemed to drift backwards and forwards over the rock without having enough energy to push itself skyward again. It was a small, sleek craft, built solely to fly fast and seemingly carrying no armament or cargo. There was some minor damage, but she didn't think it was enough to bring it down. She flew closer, looking for any evidence of what had gone wrong.

It didn't take long to find out. Hovering ten feet off the deck the smeared bloodstains were pretty obvious. She even thought she spotted a bare piece of spine sticking out from between two damaged planks. Things had got brutal, possibly the Bonelords or even something as mundane as a mutiny if this crew had been more affected by the nightmares than hers had. She looked curiously at an unusual structure located at the stern before moving in for a closer inspection. It appeared to be a cage of some sort, and though the inside was dark, she could make out what looked like pipework and ropes hanging from the top. There was the hint of a sulphurous smell around it, and knowing what she knew about those sorts of scents, Arke doubted very much that whatever had been kept there had left completely. Getting closer still, she saw that there was something else in the far corner – a body of some sort, hanging harnessed from the ceiling. In fact, all the rest of what she had thought were ropes were actually harnesses. However, all bar the one which was still in use were ripped or torn as if the creatures usually held prisoner by them had gnawed their way to freedom.

"Irash, what is that hanging there at the back?"

"I'm surprised you couldn't recognise an insignificant infernal creature."

Arke ignored her inner bitch and shouted in her most imperious manner. "Nice try at an ambush. Now get out where I can see you. I know you're there and you do NOT want to displease me."

Nothing happened for a moment but then slowly, almost as if they were materialising out of the gaps between the ship's deck planking, slunk a group of scruffy and mismatched imps. Some were short, some wide, most hideously ugly and every single one utterly obsequious as they peered up at their visitor.

"Can we control them all?" Arke asked quietly,

counting sixteen by the time they had finished assembling on the deck.

"Look at them fawning already, they know power when they see it. They will obey."

She landed on the deck and eyed the group. "What went on here? That cage – those harnesses?"

One of the taller imps was reluctantly pushed forwards by his fellows. "We were the power. We were used." He showed his teeth in a feral grin. "We escaped."

"Excellent. Now get back in the harnesses." As they went to complain Arke held up a finger repressively, making sure to glare at every one of them as she spoke slowly and with meaning.

"But they're broken!" the tall imp protested, wringing his hands in an attempt to look pitiful.

"Then – fix – them." Arke ground the words out and she took a deliberate step towards the group with each syllable.

They looked from her to each other and then bolted for the cage, scrambling into their harnesses, tying bits together and frantically plugging the pipes back into their bodies. As each one came back online the ship's hum became louder and it rose a little more from its position on the rock.

Arke moved to the wheel where she found herself a coil of unbloodied rope to sit on and wrote a quick note before summoning her friendly flying hellhound as delivery boy. The note read: *Have new ship. Get underway to Crimbles at the flotilla. Pop a flare if you need an expert.* She patted the dog on the head and sent him off to the *Warrior*.

"Ok, you lot," she said as she tried to get comfortable.

"Imp-ulse speed!"

The imps were simple creatures and just gazed at her in confusion until she yelled. "GO!"

The ship shot forwards at speed, gaining height effortlessly.

"When I was nine…"

"Anything else. ANYTHING!" Irash demanded.

Arke checked her compass and took a new heading before settling back against the rope. "This orbiculum. What's the deal? How does it work?"

The explanation while brief, wasn't exactly what she wanted to hear. The planar door needed at least one specially trained mage who could attune Irash to it in order to locate the right destination. He was also sketchy on just how many people could be alerted to the magical activities as the ritual started, how long it would take, or how vulnerable he would be while it all spun up. Arke identified so many problems even off one short description that her teeth hurt from clenching her jaw so tightly. There had to be another solution.

She sighed heavily. "So, tell me about where you want to go."

"You cannot comprehend my home."

"When I was nine, I met this puppet maker…"

"It is pure energy." Irash hurried his words before she got into the flow.

"And? What does it look like? Are there others like you?"

"It is energy, there is nothing to see with your limited human eyes. There are others but we are not like you mortals, incessantly polluting your surroundings with sound and clutter."

"Giant hole of nothingness then?" It sounded like Arke's personal nightmare world, empty of form and feature, no trees, no rivers, no earth or stone.

"Do not mock! I was pulled through to your plane against my will. It is disgustingly mundane. Everything is so... solid and restrictive."

"It's way better than permanent nothingness. The feel of the sun on your face, the smell of freshly cut grass, all the good food, sweet, savoury... and better than that – beer, wine, rum, whisky, sherry, vodka."

"And other people. You have some very interesting interpersonal memories..."

"STOP RIGHT THERE!" Arke stiffened suddenly, her face freezing into a scowl.

"But..."

For the next few minutes both the imps and Irash were forced to listen to an overloud tale of a strange woman with a penchant for eating animals of increasing size, peppered with Arke's explosive exclamations of "STOP!" and "Get OUT of my head!". Just before the all-important denouement of the story, Arke gave up and folded her arms crossly.

"OK, I'm done with you rummaging around. Let's talk about something else. Are there any more of your kind here, in this world?"

Irash took a moment and then growled out the words. "There used to be."

"Can you call to them? If they're still around then maybe they can help you leave."

"We were hardly close, I doubt they'd help."

"Don't know if you don't try."

Irash just grunted stubbornly.

"Look, now I know more about it, I'm telling you that using an orbiculum is going to be risky. More than risky. Search my mind but NOT for the things you sought before. Check I'm not lying when I say there are people who would kill to get hold of you, and I doubt it would be for your winning personality. You're a creature of immense power and we're no longer the backward savages you knew. There are a great many who would stop at nothing to secure you as an asset."

Both were silent for a long moment, Arke's eyes flickering with black veins as Irash accessed her mind before sending out a message.

"I have tried to make contact. Now be quiet, for I must rest."

Getting slowly to her feet, Arke leant her forearms on the wheel as she watched the sun drop below the horizon and the sky darken until the mountains below her disappeared into blackness. Although it was incredibly cold, the night was perfectly clear and as she felt Irash withdraw his attention from her actions, she started steering in a series of lazy circles which would keep her faster ship in the same area as the *Warrior* while they headed to the flotilla.

Satisfied with her course, she looked up again, breathing in the stars and feeling their delicate touch on her face. Without thinking, she reached to her belt, but her fingers found only emptiness where Stabbington's hilt should have been. Struggling to control the instant pang of loss before it took hold of her entirely, Arke squared her shoulders, balanced her weight more evenly on the balls of her feet and began to tell a new tale with her voice no more than a whisper as she steered the night-kissed vessel through the darkness.

"This is my favourite book in all the world... and it really is..."

Chapter Seventeen
Be Careful What You Fish for

KENNEDY HAD ONLY been back in his cabin for a few minutes when the door opened and Sparkz stuck his head in.

"Engine all fixed."

Broom in hands, sleeves rolled up, Kennedy halted mid-sweep and looked up with a frown. "I thought you said two days?"

"I KNEW you weren't listening to us when we told you about the plan." His brother rolled his eyes with the blatant disrespect that seemed to come naturally to him. "I'm not going through it again." He walked in and put Arke's note on the chart table. "This came via that creepy thing she says is a dog. Look, I'm no more of a fan of this shitshow than you are, but she's calling the ball and there's no-one more experienced in being some invisible creature's glove puppet than her. If Arke says go, we go. I know we've found some storm free air and that's great but personally, I can't WAIT to be out of these bloody mountains before they try and kill us again."

Kennedy glanced at the note before balling it up and throwing it on the floor with the rest of the rubbish Arke had left behind. "Look at this place! It's going to take me hours to clean it up."

"Sure that's the *only* reason you look like a squirrel

who lost his nuts?"

Shooting his brother an unusually dour stare before turning towards the open door, Kennedy called over to the helm. "Keep heading west and bring us up to full speed. Avoid any suggestion of heavy weather. Once we're clear of the mountains we'll run south down the coast and start looking out for the flotilla beacons."

If anyone knew where an orbiculum was to be found, it was Mr Crimbles, and the flotilla was his home.

After Sparkz left, a scowling Kennedy went back to cleaning up. That angry expression was the exact opposite of the one he'd had a few minutes earlier as he ran up the stairs towards his cabin, knowing it was now free of Arke and her passenger. Quite understandably, he'd been having a hard time dealing with everything that had happened over the Greyspines, so the prospect of having some personal space to restore a little normalcy in his life had given him a sudden and very welcome burst of happiness.

However, the moment he'd opened the door and taken in the sorry state of his room, his happy expression had completely disappeared. His eyes had travelled slowly over the absolute destruction of his not-so-secret-as-he-thought snack supply, the mountain of crumbs on the chart table and the splintered wood around a deep hole in one of his cabin walls. With a sudden rush of fury, he'd lost his shit completely as the final straw that had been resting on his last nerve burst into a geyser of flame. Slamming the cabin door behind him, he'd launched into an incendiary tirade against Arke and every rude, unpleasant, or downright appalling action she'd ever taken.

His rant could have gone on for days without even struggling for subject matter, and he'd barely started when he'd been interrupted by Sparkz's arrival. However, his brother's visit had only stalled the cathartic process and the moment he left, Kennedy immediately returned to sweeping the floor with brisk, furious strokes while blasting out a litany of long-bottled complaints and damning character indictments.

He was still going full bore when he spotted his workbench with its toolbox open and Arke's empty scabbard sitting on it, the leather belt hanging untidily over the edge. All the words queuing to spew from his mouth were swallowed back as he picked up the sheath for a thorough examination. The end was utterly crippled, the metal bent and flattened. There were some amateur tool marks around the damaged areas, but Kennedy knew it would need more than a hammer and some pliers to make it useful again.

With sudden realisation, he turned to look at the hole in his wall, his wrath evaporating with every connection he made. Crossing the room in three strides, he took his time investigating the damage, comparing the point of impact to the scabbard in his hands. It was a match. However, there was no way a casual throw could have made such a mess of both wood and metal. She had to have hurled the thing like a javelin and then some. The only conclusion he could draw was that Arke must have been angry, but not the icy, calculating fury he'd seen from her before; the splintered planks and bent scabbard had to have been the result of uncontrollable, incandescent rage. Kennedy frowned in confusion, he'd seen her defiant, he'd seen her on her knees, he'd seen her struggle, he'd seen her win. But he'd never seen her lose control. She'd always been a cold-hearted bitch.

Or had she? Something niggled at him, chipping away at his certainty, and as he looked down at the well-worn scabbard, a memory flashed unbidden to his mind. He remembered Arke's laughing face looking down at what must have been a young version of himself as he tried, extremely unsuccessfully, to pull the demon blade from the same sheath he now held in his hands.

He hadn't recalled that moment for years and as he unwittingly opened the floodgates to the past, pictures started to pour back into his mind, some scenes painful, others warm. Drowning in vivid memories, Kennedy sat down heavily on his bed, the scabbard resting on his knees as he struggled with the torrent of thoughts and emotions that were throwing themselves at him.

It had been so long since he'd been truly honest with himself, years since he'd papered over the chasm that losing his parents had created. Everything had changed when they died; he'd had to battle his grief and anger alone before finally forcing himself to re-invent Philip Kennedy as a captain, and not a son. The man he'd had to become had taken the emotionless Soulbound at face value and deliberately forgotten what his old self knew about the woman she'd been before that day. He'd had to believe that she was completely unable to feel, utterly immune to the consequences of her actions; for otherwise how could she live with herself after what she'd done? He'd always known she'd killed them; the delivery he'd been allocated on that night hadn't taken as long as it should have, and he'd dropped by his parents' house on the way back to the ship in the hopes of a second dinner.

He'd arrived just in time to see the unmistakeable figure of Arke striding away down the street as smoke started to curl from the windows.

Even though they'd never discussed it with their teenaged son, it had been obvious for weeks that his parents were running from something. Young Philip had felt their anxiety grow into fear as they became more desperate in their attempts to evade whatever it was that would not let them go. The family hug that he'd squirmed through earlier that terrible evening was given awful new meaning as he'd searched the house, struggling through smoke and flames before finally reaching their bedroom. As his eyes had become accustomed to the dim light, the first thing he'd seen was the glint of empty bottles on the table. He'd looked closer to see magical sleeping potions and bottles of wine piled on top of trays holding the remains of a sumptuous meal for two.

Kennedy clutched Arke's scabbard tightly as he recalled the sickening dread that had gripped him that night and the way his hand had trembled uncontrollably just before he'd pulled aside the curtains around his parents' bed. He'd stared down at his mother and then his father, the sight of their bodies searing into him with indelible horror. He'd hardly been able to comprehend it at the time, but as the shock seeped away, he realised the course of events had been obvious, the careful planning unmistakable. His mother and father had eaten their last meal, finished their wine with potion chasers before falling asleep, hands entwined, faces aligned. The last thing they'd seen had been each other. Their deaths had been at the hands of a master, the matching incisions across their necks precise in every way. Everything they'd been had ended in painless seconds.

Even if he hadn't seen Arke leaving the house, Kennedy knew that the only person his parents would ever have trusted to do the job would be her. Joy and Philip Senior had planned their deaths how they'd lived their lives, with panache and determination. The only thing they'd surrendered to in the end was alcohol, some serious magic potions and the precision strikes of their best friend.

Months after that day, young Kennedy had finally believed that he was strong and experienced enough to avenge them. For obvious reasons he couldn't talk to Arke about what had happened, so waited until he had the chance to ask Mr Crimbles. There wasn't much that the magical entrepreneur didn't know, but after some determined provocation to get to the truth, Kennedy had wished he'd never asked. He'd learnt that his parents had had to die to stop a tremendous debt being collected from everyone around them, especially their son. Not even Crimbles with all his contacts had been able to protect them, and he was adamant that he'd say no more since the only thing that would come of any ideas of revenge was exactly what Kennedy's parents had sacrificed themselves to avoid.

In the weeks, months and years that followed, Kennedy had believed Arke when she acted as if nothing she ever saw or did bothered her; when she brushed off tragedy and sadness as if it meant nothing, for he knew she could kill her best friends, lie about it to their son and get straight back to work. But as he sat quietly with memories he hadn't roused for years rushing through his head, Kennedy clenched his jaw, swallowing back the emotions that flooded him. He recalled the Arke he knew from his childhood, with warmth in her expression and teasing words on her lips. He saw her and his parents out on the deck of the *Warrior*, heard the sound of their laughter rippling through the air, and remembered the nights she and Stabbington had sat out on the deck with him, making shapes from the stars.

Sitting on his bed, in the cabin that had been his parents' and was now his, Philip Kennedy Junior started to see things very differently. He knew how he'd had to change in order to overcome his tragedy, to find a version of himself that could carry on, and as he let his memories linger, he realised she'd done the same. He'd been too young, too grief stricken and too angry to even want to empathise with Arke; but now he did and although it was late, maybe too late, he was going to start.

Holding her scabbard gently in his hands, Kennedy moved to his workbench and sat down, picking up his tools with quiet determination. There weren't many things he could do to help the current situation, but he could mend what was broken and he could start to see Arke in a very different light. She could lie to herself and the rest of the world, but Philip Kennedy would no longer be fooled.

✕ ✕ ✕

DAWN BROKE ACROSS the prototype ship and Arke woke with a start, her head uncomfortably wedged between two spokes of the wheel. An imp was standing in front of her with what looked like a cup of steaming coffee and an unrecognisable food-like substance in a battered dish.

"Breakfast, sir."

She blinked and tried to stifle a yawn, surprised as well as relieved that Irash hadn't taken advantage of sleep to possess her. Taking the mug while idly wondering if the drink was poisoned, Arke decided the best way to tell was with a quick sip and instantly shuddered at the taste. Whatever it was, wasn't so much coffee as disgusting crunchy sludge with scum on top but at least it was hot and wet. If it was poison, it wouldn't taste nearly so bad. She sipped some more with a grimace before eyeing the imp who was hovering nearby in a totally-not-suspicious-at-all manner.

"What?"

"Sir. Just… I mean me and the gang were wondering if you'd… tell us what happened next?"

It took a long moment for her tired brain to work out what he meant. During those seconds of confusion something behind the imp caught her eye and she suddenly downed her drink in one vile, scalding mouthful. One was a good start, but she was uncomfortably aware that a single coffee may not provide enough energy as she might soon be expending, for while she'd slept the little ship had wandered off course so much that the *Warrior* was clearly visible to port. It was going to be horribly tricky to explain its appearance to Irash for two reasons; firstly, since she'd told him that she was taking him directly to the flotilla and secondly, because suddenly and some might suggest, miraculously, her old ship was very obviously back under full power.

"Arke."

And there he was, right on cue.

"Ah, so I fell asleep…"

She started on an excuse but was quickly interrupted.

"When imps say things you don't understand, you know you're being particularly dense. He means the story! The story from the book with the green cover that you keep under your mattress. We need to know what happens next."

Not quite sure whether she was dreaming, Arke nodded slowly. She wasn't about to complain about being let off the hook or incriminate herself with an explanation, so she deliberately didn't look at the *Warrior* while she casually steered to starboard so that the bigger ship would be out of sight as quickly as possible.

"More coffee," she demanded.

"Yes sir." The breakfast monitor started to slink away dejectedly.

"Then I'll continue."

The imps quickly muffled what had definitely been a cheer, since everyone knew infernal beings were not supposed to enjoy story time. Irash was less reticent and as Arke continued the tale she had to put up with his distinctly distracting background commentary until she snapped that he was making exactly the same points that *someone else* had made when she first read it with him.

"Can't use his name yet? Ahhh you are still so angry at that pathetic creature. I love it." Irash hissed.

"Do you want the story to end here or not?" Arke downed yet another cup of coffee and tried to dowse her emotional response with what was possibly the second or third most disgusting drink she'd ever had in her life.

✗ ✗ ✗

WANDERING BACK UP from the hold with a pouch of something special for his friend Mr Crimbles, Kennedy cast an eye over the flotilla as the *Warrior* made its final approach. Ahead of them and spreading in every direction, was a huge number of ships, all arranged like spokes on a wheel around a central floating walkway which was held aloft by brightly coloured balloons. As well as the usual traders and pirates moored out on the fringes, there were specialised flying boats for every eventuality, taverns, hotels, shops, brothels, and emergency services all tethered close to the central hub. After so many years doing business here, Kennedy's reaction to its sheer size and perfect organisation was distinctly jaded. However, as he stood at the helm and watched Ruby's awestruck reaction, he was reminded of the first few times he'd visited the flotilla and smiled with genuine warmth at her excitement.

"Don't forget to breathe." Kennedy patted Ellie on the shoulder, knowing her too well not to notice that the enormity of being left in charge of the ship for the first time was causing her serious stress.

She tried to force a smile but it looked more like a grimace and her hands clutched the wheel tightly.

"You trust me, right? Then trust my decision – you are the perfect person for the job. Don't try to be his replacement." Kennedy held up a finger. "Before you say anything, obviously do the things first mates need to, but do it all your way."

He made sure to give her his most supportive thumbs up just before he was carried off the *Warrior* by Ruby who proceeded to spend the entire flight to the flotilla putting words to her overstimulation as she continued to marvel at everything there was to see. Getting a word in edgeways was difficult but Kennedy persevered, managing to direct her towards a particularly brightly coloured ship which was held aloft by two massive balloons. Slowing her down before they got too close, Kennedy bellowed out a passphrase, knowing that Crimbles did not react well to unannounced visitors. With a fizz, the magical forcefield around the vessel dissipated and he instructed the Ornithol to set him down on the deck before going back for Sparkz.

"Captain Kennedy, it's been months!"

The hail came from a comfortable-looking cushion over by the main cabin, and more specifically, from its owner, an exceptionally large cat with an eye for expensive jewellery and the sleekest coat magic could provide.

"Good to see you, Mr Crimbles."

Proffering the pouch of catnip he'd brought over from the *Warrior*, Kennedy watched the giant tabby cat sniffing delicately at it before purring in warm appreciation.

"Oh, the good stuff, of course. You know what I like."

"Of course." Kennedy turned away respectfully as the cat availed himself of a large sample. He knew better than to intrude on such a deeply personal act, so spent a few moments watching Ruby flying back with Sparkz towards them and landing on the deck nearby.

"You have new friends. Welcome, welcome," Mr Crimbles called before offering his broad head for Kennedy to stroke as the others approached.

Noticing Sparkz's and Ruby's shocked reactions, Kennedy realised that he probably should have mentioned that his ally was a well-furnished pussycat.

Crimbles wasn't a catlike humanoid, nor was he an illusion, a puppet, or a front. He was just a very well-to-do stripey cat, such as you'd see toasting its toes in front of grandma's roaring fire. Except this one wasn't so much into torturing unfortunate rodents and leaping in the air at the sight of a randomly placed cucumber, as building a massive magic-smuggling empire. Kennedy decided to make rapid introductions and hope neither of his friends would mention the whole feline issue before getting straight to business while Crimbles was still in the throes of catnip heaven.

"Mr Crimbles, Sparkz, Ruby. Yes, yes, they're delighted, you're delighted, we're all thrilled to be here. Anyway, I'm looking for an orbiculum. Do you have one?"

The tabby, with his eyes half closed, made no suggestion that he was surprised by the request. He merely tilted his head so that he could be rubbed under his chin. "Not your usual fare, dear boy, hardly any call for those these days. Are you sure that's what you require?"

Kennedy took a deep breath and the entire story came flooding out. While telling it, he made sure to look directly at Crimbles and not his brother. He was well aware that Sparkz had seen him spill the beans before, but that had only been one type. This time it was everything – baked, kidney, cannellini, broad, green, butter, black – all tumbling out in front of the plumply arrogant tabby cat.

"Bro," Sparkz said as the confession finally ended. "Really?"

"It's fine, he's an old friend! We've worked together

for years."

Mr Crimbles nodded his head sagely. "All true and of course not forgetting that I owe Captain Kennedy my life, or one of them anyway. However, back to business. As is the strange and interconnected way of such things, the vagaries of destiny or the dabbling's of fate if you will; I recently had a yard sale of sorts, during which I cleared out a very dusty section of my ship's hold. There was an orbiculum in that pile of junk and I sold it to Madame Chalet, owner of the *Gravy Boat*. She's moored over on the other side of the flotilla, you can't miss her, just follow the smell of overcooked hash browns. Oh and, do not, under any circumstances, try the fish."

"I know the place, but what would she need with an orbiculum?" Kennedy queried. "Is it also a cure for heartburn?"

The cat turned and angled his head as if he knew that a curious Ruby wanted to smooth his luxurious fur, padding with his front paws on the cushion as she did so. "Rather incongruously, this particular orbiculum is in the form of a frying pan; apparently she simply cannot get enough solid cookware that will last."

Suddenly, lights began to blink all around the ship and Mr Crimbles turned slowly to look at the exact spot where another vessel was approaching. It was an extremely expensive-looking conveyance, small, fast, and obviously luxurious.

"A different class of customer?" Kennedy questioned, assessing the visiting craft with a single glance.

The cat said nothing, but from the deck of the new ship came an unpleasantly familiar voice, one they'd last heard in Gorki's office back in High Haven. And to their extra spicy displeasure, she was calling out the passphrase. Kennedy frowned, looking at Sparkz and Ruby who were both wearing similarly dark expressions, and as one, their heads turned to level accusatory glares at Mr Crimbles.

"I have no idea who that is." The tabby casually sniffed the air before standing and attempting to walk off.

Kennedy was quick to react, picking the cat up and cradling him firmly in his arms. "Oh no you don't, buddy. Who the hell are you in bed with? She seems to know the correct greeting and I didn't think you needed to advertise."

"Especially in *Bitch* magazine." Ruby's sharp eyes were fixed on the red-headed elf as she waited for her ship to dock, and every one of the Ornithol's feathers were bristling with discontent.

This time, it was her turn to be stared at, her crewmates' mouths falling open briefly before they started to laugh.

"We broke her already," Sparkz chuckled, applauding slowly.

"Nice, Rubes, nice," Kennedy grinned. "I like that, lots of levels to it. Excellent burn."

If Ornithols could blush, Ruby would have, but as the sleekest of ships nudged up against Crimbles', Kayla's imminent arrival was enough to dampen her brief moment of triumph.

"Hello there! Good to see you again Mr Crimbles and, of course, Captain Kennedy and friends. Is this a private party?" Gorki's assistant, a smug smile plastered all over her face, vaulted onto the deck and headed towards the small group.

"Please can I kill her?" Ruby whispered. "Arke would let me."

"Arke would absolutely not. Happy faces people, happy faces." Kennedy fixed his smile and stepped forwards, ducking his head to whisper to Mr Crimbles. "Have NO idea who she is, eh?"

Kayla and Kennedy traded fake smiles while Ruby folded her arms and Sparkz examined his nails in great detail.

"SO pleased to see you alive, Captain. Have you anything to report?"

He took a long moment to pretend to think about his answer before shrugging. "I don't think so."

"You've done nothing *at all* yet?"

"Short staffed, had to pull in here to get some more crew."

Kayla looked hard at him, as if trying to will him to explain further, but Kennedy just smiled, for even *he* had limits to the people he'd overshare with.

"I hope nothing TERRIBLE has happened to your friend. What was her name? Barka? Tarka? It's so nice that you're making sure the older members of society have gainful employment."

"*Arke* is busy elsewhere." Kennedy remained unmoved, his smile never fading.

Kayla nodded understandingly. "There are some excellent nursing homes if she's started, you know, *wandering around*. Don't be afraid to get her the care she needs."

"She's currently working on another ship, hence our staff shortage."

"I see." Kayla stared unblinkingly into Kennedy's eyes as if trying to hypnotise him to tell her more, but he just stared back, expression unwavering. "I know I'm a serious upgrade, but I could temporarily take her place on the *Warrior*? Two birds – one stone; I can help you out while keeping an eye on a certain investment."

"That would be amazing." Kennedy beamed with an appreciation he most certainly did not feel. "Our guest cabin is perfectly situated next to the forward head, so you'll never be alone there, especially with Porro's cooking. Conversation at all hours." The advantage, thought Kennedy, as he kept his smile in place, of being assumed to be an unintelligent lump of muscle, was that he could get away with statements like that.

"She's in luck – it's even cleaning day tomorrow so the smell won't be as awful, unless we get bad weather and have to close all the hatches," Sparkz remarked, with the warmest expression he could muster.

"We look forward to having you on board." Kennedy added, stroking Mr Crimbles' head with so much pressure that even the cat's whiskers were pulled inexorably backwards.

"Shall I go there now then?" Kayla looked from one to the other, seemingly a little taken aback by their enthusiasm.

"Help yourself, though we're just going to get a bite of to eat if you'd like to join us?"

"I've already eaten, thanks. See you another time, Mr Crimbles." Kayla turned abruptly and walked back to her own vessel which reversed away before heading towards the *Warrior*.

They all watched her go, Ruby muttering a prayer to

Chromatia for a bolt of lightning to obliterate Kayla's limo ship while Kennedy and Sparkz stayed quiet until the vessel was well out of earshot.

"And if you SHOULD choose to tell anything of what I told you to that soul-sucking bitch then I'll take that life of yours I saved and a few more besides." Kennedy's expression was as murderous as his words as he dumped the cat unceremoniously back on his cushion.

"I'm offended that you think so little of me after all we've seen together; I would never betray you." Mr Crimbles started to wash himself diligently, almost as if he was trying to remove Kennedy's touch from his fur.

"We'll see." Sparkz looked at Ruby. "Time to go."

"Wait, please. I am always in your debt, Captain." The tabby leapt off his cushion and padded to a set of drawers just inside his cabin door. "Given what you told me it's probably best if we're able to keep in touch. Do you know mouse code? Sorry, morse code; cat joke." He opened a drawer and gestured to its contents with a paw. "Emergency line straight to me, I'll get the message wherever you are."

After pocketing the completely unironically designed bell that was small enough to go on a cat's collar, Kennedy led the others to an air taxi rank. Their destination was a good distance away across the busiest part of the flying port and though Ruby had offered to take them, he wasn't sure how well she'd manage in heavy traffic. Wisely choosing not to mention his doubts, Kennedy made sure he explained his decision to take a cab as an opportunity for her to see the sights of the flotilla in comfort.

Chapter Eighteen
Panacea

AS THE BRIGHT yellow gig, piloted by a distinctly sullen gnome, flew across the flotilla, Ruby filled the silence with such animated chatter that all Kennedy needed to do was nod at appropriate moments. Sparkz, however, spent the trip musing on his misgivings about his brother's relationship with a talking cat and what he felt sure was some sort of set up with Kayla. He'd lived most of his life keeping people at arm's length because on the whole he'd found that they were duplicitous, greedy, amoral jerk-offs with all the redeeming qualities of week old road kill. The possibility that he was the same as everyone else was something he'd always neatly sidestepped, usually by distracting himself with more rewarding ideas.

"Greasy Spoons always do incredible bacon rolls."

"That was... random," Kennedy replied, looking at his brother curiously.

"What?" Sparkz pointed to the huge ship ahead of the taxi. "You can't get greasier than that place, there's even an oily tide mark up the hull."

The flying taxi pulled up to the floating dock next to the vessel that couldn't be mistaken for anything other than the *Gravy Boat*, mainly because of the giant letters spelling it out on the side. Kennedy cleared his throat, then did it again as Ruby was still talking. Eventually she noticed his increasingly unsubtle signals.

"Sorry! I'm just... this place is so... it's... I can't..."

"I think her adjective bank is finally in the red," Sparkz remarked with a wry smile.

Kennedy frowned. "Her what now? Anyway, about what happened back there with Kayla – don't tell Arke."

"There's only one of us here who's that stupid."

Their agreement was unanimous and when Kennedy held out a fist for a reassuring bump, Ruby met it immediately, and even though his brother's physical affirmation was merely a shrug, it was enough. They had enough on their plates without the guaranteed explosion that would occur if the Soulbound knew her nemesis was around.

As he walked up the *Gravy Boat's* gangplank behind the others, Sparkz was assailed by a barrage of pungent aromas that completely erased any yearning he might have had for a bacon sandwich. He wasn't a fussy man, but there was no way that he was eating in a place that smelt as if its entire clientele were unwashed and unable to control their bodily functions. The top deck was half covered with tables, while at the other end was an open area with a huge bar; people were sitting, standing, or lying everywhere, in every state of insobriety between merry and unconscious. The entire place was basically a deeply insalubrious open-air tavern; the floor was sticky, the tables were dirty, and clouds of smoke hung randomly over hatches and people.

"Good thing we didn't bring Stabbington," Kennedy remarked, ignoring the squalor and looking around at the huge kegs of beer that were queued up ready to be tapped. "I don't think I could afford the bar bill."

"Man's a mess; last night he was trying to lick the empty barrels and got his head stuck." Sparkz shook his head disappointedly. "I think I preferred him drunk and miserable rather than sober and pathetic." Suddenly realising that his brother had gravitated over to chat with a group of men who had a decidedly piratical air to them, he shook his head at Ruby. "Keep him out of trouble while I find this magic pan." He grinned. "And stay out of trouble yourself – fowl mouth."

Sparkz was still chuckling at his own joke when he found his way down the staff stairs to the massive, bustling kitchen. It only took a few questions to the ladies butchering a giant centipede to locate Madame Chalet. He followed their directions over to what appeared to be the dessert section of the preparation area to find an enraged orc wearing a dressing gown and flip flops throwing dishes at a few cowering juniors.

"Is my Spotted Dick Surprise a joke to you? Tell me now! You know I can't make it myself, not with my frozen shoulder." A chafing dish was summarily launched at the little crowd of young chefs. All dodged clear bar one unlucky specimen who took it straight in the forehead and toppled backwards, his fellows quickly throwing themselves underneath him to break his fall in what looked to be a well-practiced team building exercise.

"We're sorry Madame Chalet, only it's that Gustavus here said you wanted us to add Ladyfingers to the Spotted Dick, and…" The smallest chef's squeaky voice tailed off as around him the other youngsters began to snigger and snort with laughter.

"And this is a problem BECAUSE?" Madame Chalet picked up a bundt cake mould and threw it at the group on the floor.

"There should be no problem, for your Spotted Dick Surprise sounds nothing but delicious." Sparkz stepped smoothly between Madame Chalet and the juniors, making sure he kept his expression totally serious.

The apprentice chefs took full advantage of the distraction and ran for it, leaving the unlucky Gustavus laid out on the floor, a lump building on his forehead. Madame Chalet grabbed a pair of pans and turned, ready to launch them at her retreating staff when Sparkz eased both from her hands with an air of earnest concern.

"You look like you need a cup of tea; I don't know what's going on with the younger generation, they can't seem to apply themselves to anything."

The orc looked at him with sudden appreciation and nodded. "You are SO right; camomile tea it is! Come with me, whoever you are."

Letting her get a couple of steps away, Sparkz quickly looked down at the dirty pans. A tattoo on one of his fingertips pulsed and suddenly they lost their grimy coat of grease, instantly appearing brand new. He swiftly tucked the pair of them under his jacket and caught up to the owner of the Greasy Spoon as she led the way to her office.

With a broad smile, Madame Chalet went to an urn at the side of the room and poured what looked like dishwater into strangely delicate bone china cups. Trying not to wrinkle his nose, Sparkz took a sip and nodded in a warm appreciation his tastebuds certainly did not feel.

"Who are you anyway? I don't think you work for me – you don't smell of grease." The orc burst into almost exactly four seconds of mirth and slammed her cup down on its saucer, shattering it instantly. "Ha! I get through so many of those. What did you say your name was?"

This was his moment and Sparkz took a deep breath before launching into his spiel. "It's your lucky day! I'm from the local branch of Gnome Depot, and you, Madame Chalet, are the lucky winner of one of our 'New for Old' prizes. It's as simple as simple could be. You give me *one* old frying pan, and you, Madame Chalet, will receive *two*, yes *two* entirely new ones!"

"Gnome Depot? But you're not even a gnome!"

With a wink and a conspiratorial smile, Sparkz leant forwards. "Let's just keep that our little secret?" Then, carefully putting his cup down, he whipped the two shiny, new looking pans from under his jacket with a flourish. "These are state of the art, they'll cook anything you have the temerity to put in them."

Madame Chalet watched carefully as Sparkz turned them this way and that, making the most of their impeccable shine. "I'll be honest with you, I've never even heard of Gnome Depot."

"And that's the way we like it. First rule of Gnome Depot…" He tapped a finger on the side of his nose conspiratorially.

The chef seemed to relax, a slow smile spreading across her face. "Ok… and you want a frying pan?"

"Yes, feel free to offer your oldest or most useless frying pan in exchange for this marvellous pair of new ones." Sparkz's face was beginning to ache with the effort of keeping his happy expression firmly in place.

"Very well, just wait here a minute." Madame Chalet walked out of her office and returned a little while later with an armful of disgracefully filthy pans. "Choose whichever you want." She dumped all twenty-seven of them on the floor with a crash.

"Wonderful." Sparkz smiled, concentrating his senses on the task of finding the magical one in the giant heap of slimy, half-washed pans, hoping it was near the top. He might have known that wasn't going to be the case, but he did expect it to at least be there. However, after a few minutes up to his elbows in foetid cookware, the man from Gnome Depot realised that none of it was even slightly magical.

"I'm afraid that none of those qualify for our 'New for Old' drive. Do you have any others?"

Madame Chalet smiled toothily and pulled a single pan from behind her back with a flourish. "So, I was curious why you shined up a couple of my old griddles; yeah I saw you, this place has a LOT of reflective surfaces. I spoke to a few folks who'd seen you arrive from Crimbles' direction and things started to make sense. This here is the pan I bought off him; you want it? Two hundred florins and it's yours."

Sparkz took a deep breath, wishing he'd just clubbed the bloody woman senseless the moment he met her. "It's not worth that."

"Must be to you. Two hundred florins."

"Ok, you got me." He sighed defeatedly and offered her a handshake.

"We have a deal?" she asked, eyes sparkling greedily.

Sparkz shrugged, waiting for her to take his hand. The moment she did, he yanked on her arm, twisting it until she dropped to her knees with a strangled yelp.

"My frozen shoulder!"

"Of course. You think I didn't notice which arm you weren't throwing things with?" He twisted it viciously, making her whimper in pain. "Your place is such a shithole even the rats eat elsewhere! You don't need to kill the things you cook – they'd drown in all the oil. I've been in prison, and we ate better slop than the 'food' you serve here. You want me to let go, just drop the pan, and you'll never see me again."

"You're hurting me!"

"No shit, unlike your health hazard of a ship. Drop it now or I'll twist some more."

Madame Chalet threw the magical pan down and as Sparkz let her go, she sank to the floor, trying to stifle her agonised sobs. Grabbing the pan, he tucked it inside his jacket and shut the door behind him. Walking briskly back through the kitchen deck, he smiled and nodded to the staff as he passed them, all the while praying to any god that would listen that his brother and Ruby would be ready to go when he got back topside.

Unfortunately for Sparkz, either his direct line to the divine was out of service or none of the gods gave even a single shit what he wanted. As he looked around, he spotted Kennedy talking animatedly to a group of strangers and immediately recognised the sound of his brother's cheesy recruitment spiel. Kennedy was hiring again.

Hurrying towards the group, Sparkz couldn't help but notice the very odd one out. Parked next to his brother was the unmistakeable form of a Vonti, giant swirled shell, shimmering slime and all. If he'd had more time, he'd have yanked Kennedy aside and asked him whether he had rocks in his head for recruiting a literal snail. Vonti were slow, deliberate creatures, reputedly incredibly attuned to the world around them, but what good would that be on a pirate ship where reaction time and combat ability was key? He dragged his disparaging gaze away to the next candidate, a grizzled halfling dressed in a military style, a blunderbuss over his shoulder. He looked a lot more useful, even if he clearly designed his own uniforms with far too much gold thread. Sparkz instantly dismissed what appeared to be a malnourished scrap of a boy standing behind the halfling and turned his attention to the last of the group. He was a Tiax, a sharp-featured race with tremendously thick body hair and triangular ears that stuck out sideways from their heads. Without exception, Tiax were known to be tenacious fighters and this one looked particularly battle ready, his clothes covered in protective metal rivets, a huge broadsword on his back.

"Sparkz!" Kennedy called as he spotted his brother, his face wreathed in a bright beaming smile. "We've got some new crewmembers. Giro the navigator, Volk, Gabbi and Klaus. They've just signed on and are ready for action!"

"Brilliant. Shall we go? *Now?*"

With an almighty squeal which made several drunk pirates simply fall over in shock, the ship's tannoy burst into life.

"Hello my friends, customers, clients, lovers. I have a very special offer on today: Free breakfasts for a YEAR to anyone who kills the smooth-talking scumbag who attacked me." It was very obviously Madame Chalet's voice booming over the loudspeaker and Sparkz flicked a warning glance towards his brother before gesturing towards the gangplank. "Bring me his HEAD, so I can boil it till his eyes pop! He's heading off the ship right now, dark hair, skinny runt of a body, doesn't stink of grease. No-one disrespects me on board the *Gravy Boat!*" She took a wheezing breath, her tone softening back to that of a persuasive saleswoman. "And don't forget the Spotted Dick Special is twenty percent off until the end of the week. Kisses!"

The tavern deck was coming to life around the group, multiple eyes following them and the unmistakeable sound of weapons sliding free of their sheaths. Some of the pirates on board were already moving to surround them, while others ran for the exits, diving into some of the little boats moored there and heading away.

"So this is awkward." Kennedy sighed, realising there was no obvious escape route, especially with a Vonti in tow.

"Fight, fight, fight, fight!" The Tiax shouted excitedly, his accented voice high-pitched with excitement.

"They're going to fight *us*, you fool!" Volk scowled, unshipping his blunderbuss and checking it was loaded before snapping at his completely dry-eyed servant. "Stop crying and get down, Gabbi!"

"Yes sir, sorry sir." The scrawny servant obediently hunkered down behind his master.

Ruby unfurled her wings and jumped into the air, hovering just above their heads. "So, captain, maybe we should send up that flare now? Arke said she'd be around if we needed her."

As the growing crowd of distinctly menacing

customers closed in, Kennedy nodded quickly to Sparkz who sent a flurry of pyrotechnics straight up from the deck of the *Gravy Boat*. Some of the more inebriated enemy stopped to watch the shiny twinkles, giving the old and new crew of the *Warrior* the opportunity to act first, leaping towards the enemy as one.

⚔ ⚔ ⚔

"You win." Irash sighed as the series of coloured lights flooded the sky. "You said there'd be trouble so we'd need to be close by."

Over the course of their five-day journey to the flotilla, Arke had become aware of a massive shift in her relationship with her passenger. His frustration had all but gone, replaced with genuine curiosity about the world outside his mountains. He'd started to ask questions about everything: Barsia, people, animals, politics, life experiences, life itself. A lot of them were mundane and easy to deal with; others far, far too personal to respond to with anything but a stone wall and a line of curses; then finally there were the mind-boggling or flat-out existential ones which were almost impossible to answer. No matter how hard she tried, she still couldn't explain to Irash what love was or why pineapple on pizza caused some people such outrage; and she refused to even start to think about the reason for her own brief existence when framed against the endless loops of time.

It was on the day they finally spotted the beacons that alerted sky travellers to the nearby flotilla that Irash had come clean about why he'd been asking such questions. They'd already talked at length about the fact that the world had moved on since he'd been imprisoned.

People knew more and wanted more, and Arke had been totally honest when she told him that his powers made him a valuable item. She'd almost said 'relic' but decided against it at the last moment, and the way he'd reacted to being called an item had made her glad of that snap decision. If they couldn't get an orbiculum or find a safe haven, she could see no future other than the one where eventually his powers weren't enough to protect him. As Arke steered the little ship to intercept the flotilla, Irash reluctantly admitted that there was another option. It was possible to download himself into a vacant body – permanently. Doing so would mean giving up a lot of his powers, but at least that would make him much less of a glittering prize. Obviously, he didn't want to do that before they'd investigated all other options, but it did explain why he'd been asking her what it was like to be alive.

After that little bombshell which revealed both another solution and the far more rational personality that her passenger was developing, Arke felt a lot more confident about explaining that they were keeping pace with the *Warrior*. Irash had snorted with dark amusement and barely even tried to refrain from smugly pointing out that he could not fail to see what she saw so yes, of *course* he was aware of that. However, the new and improved Destroyer had also agreed that the logic behind her decision had been perfectly sound; Kennedy had a good relationship with the magic broker, and it was eminently sensible to let him take any risks.

Their rapprochement and the fact that there had been no more attempts at a hostile takeover meant that Arke had been asking questions of her own. Mainly practical ones, such as 'Are you feeling stronger yet?' and 'How am I supposed to know how much of your power we're going to need?'. His evasive replies were met with increasing irritation on her behalf: 'I don't care how much weaker you are since the Bonelords used you as a battery or that you'll be back to normal in a month, a year or a hundred years! In case you haven't noticed, we're on the clock!'. She was adamant that he needed to replenish at least some of his energy as, in her experience, even a casual visit to the flotilla often included a brawl or seven. It had to go smoothly, and if that wasn't an option, then it had to go bang. Finally admitting that he wasn't yet even partially recovered was the first step to fixing the problem. The second was... gross.

"So how do we juice you up?"

"There is a way, but you aren't going to like it."

Arke pursed her lips over a very wry smile. "Not the first time I've ever heard that."

"See those imps? Walking bundles of energy conveniently packaged in crispy skin."

He was right, she didn't like it. Not at all. However, there were no other options. Even knowing the infernals would reconstitute back in their own plane hardly made the decision any better. Whichever way she looked at it, it was grim.

She was standing at the bow, only a couple of minutes into her deliberations about what to do, when the coffee-making imp cleared his throat behind her. As she turned around, she saw four of his colleagues already bound and gagged, lying by the ship's wheel.

"Volunteers."

"And they're tied up because?" Arke had no illusions

about what had happened the moment her back was turned.

The infernal grinned as he sauntered back to the cage, giving a desultory kick to one of the unlucky fellows as he passed. "Wouldn't want them to be changing their minds, sir."

Having reluctantly decided that the safety of her friends was the most important thing, Arke began to steel herself for the forthcoming experience. However, at the point she was ready to begin, her equilibrium was wrecked by Irash's bellows of laughter when she asked him if she had to eat the imps raw. And when her head stopped resonating to his incredibly hearty amusement, she was hugely relieved to learn that she wouldn't actually need to chew and swallow them.

However, a few minutes later, as she sat on the deck with her head between her knees, she realised that her relief had been deeply misplaced, and that she probably should have asked her passenger for a little more detail on how they were going to ingest the infernals. He'd simply told her to put a hand on the first one's head, and she'd done so, assuming the energy would just flow up her arm in what would effectively be the reverse of a standard spell. She'd been very wrong. Hilariously wrong, according to Irash, whose burgeoning sense of humour was becoming exceedingly tiresome.

At the touch of her hand, the infernals' bodies had dissolved into what could only be described as 'imp-based smog', swirling for a moment in a mini tornado before launching up her nose with pure brute force. Having sinus cavities full of sulphurous smoke not once but four times was arguably less preferable than a three course dinner of imp liver pate, followed by imp à la mode with imp suzette to finish. She wasn't sure she'd ever be able to smell anything except sulphur again.

"After all that you'd better have enough power when things go south at the flotilla," Arke snapped.

"When? Surely that should be 'if'. All they're doing is trying to find an orbiculum, not start a war. You're worrying over nothing."

Chapter Nineteen
Pan-demonium

A S BATTLE RAGED on the *Gravy Boat*, the pile of bodies around the *Warrior* crewmates kept growing and growing as a seemingly endless supply of enemies appeared from all directions. The first of them had been fairly drunk and decidedly disorderly, so dealing with them had been simple. However, the supply of rowdy idiots seemed to be running out and their more able replacements were proving trickier to handle.

While the brawl was ebbing and flowing in the tavern area of the main deck, a group of chefs dressed in what used to be white aprons arrived and started to cook up some distinctly unusual spells. The Saucerors didn't join the melee directly, choosing to keep their distance while hurling magically created food at Kennedy and his crew. The only person who appeared to be enjoying their talents was Gabbi, the scrawny teenager, who was sheltering in the middle of the *Warrior's* defensive circle. He seemed to be a particular fan of the spam fritters that had thwacked everyone with crispy wetness before dropping to the deck to add to the already hazardous work environment.

"We need to get off this bloody ship!" Sparkz, dual wielding his short swords, was suddenly drenched in a gazpacho downpour that washed a glob of Thousand Island dressing down the back of his neck. "And where's the *Warrior?* You can't tell me they didn't notice all this?"

"Ellie looked tired this morning – she's probably asleep at the wheel. I wonder why." Kennedy fired a pistol at one of the Saucerors as he began to conjure a barrage of liver and bacon, then shot his dishevelled brother a very old-fashioned look. "Walls are thin, you know."

"We were celebrating her promotion. You honestly want to talk about this *NOW?*" Sparkz was being attacked by a woman with incredibly muscular forearms who was wielding a wicked-looking bread knife in one hand and a muffin pan in the other. He ducked her attempt to bludgeon him with the metal tray while parrying the serrated blade as it swung towards his throat before stepping in to skewer his opponent and shove the flour-covered baker away.

"I don't want to talk about it at all; but yeah, why not here?" Kennedy headbutted an elf then grabbed him to use as a shield against an incoming gnome who was whirling his toasting forks as if he was cheerleading for his college casketball team.

"It's not serious, OK?" Sparkz sidestepped a one-eyed waiter with a carving knife in each hand, kicking out as the man went past so that he nose-dived to the deck.

"Does she know that?"

A roar rumbled around the deck and a heavyset ogre lumbered into a pounding run towards them. Kennedy quickly drew and fired his other pistol, already primed with a sleep enchantment. As the magic projectile hit the massive man square in the chest, he sank to the deck like a deflating balloon, grabbing a rotary whisk wielding goblin as he fell and snuggling him firmly to his chest as if he was a particularly bony teddy bear.

"What kind of arsehole do you think I am?" Sparkz stopped fighting for a moment and looked at his brother, eyebrows raised.

"Ahh…" Kennedy began, with all the awkwardness the situation would allow.

"Trick question, I'm all of them." A flying wooden spoon hit Sparkz square in the side of the head and he spun round to see Gustavus at the gangplank, his face radiating shock that his throw had been so accurate. "But not this time. Right at the beginning she told me it was her rules or nothing. Strictly casual." He turned back with a wide grin and stuck a sword out, effortlessly impaling a bartender as the man leapt towards them. "She is an awesome woman… in every way."

"That's fine. Good. Wonderful. Enough. Shut up!" Kennedy shouted, busily defending himself against a pair of full height candlesticks wielded by the most athletic orc he'd ever seen. Where the decorative light fittings had come from on this filthy ship wasn't immediately obvious, but they were being spun at a rate that demanded his full attention.

Behind Kennedy and Sparkz, Giro the Vonti had done the most sensible thing he could in a fast-moving fight and retreated into his shell, but in doing so, his new crewmates had found a new weapon.

On Volk's call, his servant sprang forwards, shoving the Vonti across the slippery decks like a bowling ball, bulldozing everything in his way. Then the boy hunkered back down, reeling in the line they'd attached to the shell until he was ready to launch again.

On the fringe of the main fight, where the seating area met the open deck, Ruby and Klaus were fighting a much more mobile battle. The Ornithol was flying crazy patterns around the melee, kicking people backwards or slamming wings across faces so hard her victims' cheeks had feather prints on them. Behind her, the Tiax leapt athletically from table to table, scything through the unwary with his broadsword. Together they were creating an ever-higher barrier of bodies between the restaurant section and the bar.

However, no matter how many they took out, there were always more to take their place. Staff were still pouring up from the lower decks and a long line of folk clearly eager to earn free breakfasts for life stretched down the gangway, all heading straight for the *Gravy Boat*. All the *Warrior* crew could do was keep fighting and hope that help arrived before they were overrun.

The first suggestion they had that their 'expert' had arrived was a juddering impact that tilted the greasy deck for a moment. Seconds later, an authoritative shout rang out across the melee.

"KENNEDY! Did you forget to leave a tip?" There was no doubt about the owner of that voice – Arke was back.

"With this service, are you kidding?" Kennedy grabbed a candlestick in each hand and rolled backwards, using his feet to launch the orc over the top of him to where Ruby was waiting with a double-fisted knockout.

"Arke! Arke!" Having dropped the orc into a puddle of what was probably soup, the Ornithol waved a distinctly bloody hand as the Soulbound came into view, climbing on the imp's cage so she was able to see onto the top deck of the *Gravy Boat*.

A Sauceror had also noticed the new arrival, his hands magically whipping together a batch of pepperoni pizzas and launching them one after another straight towards her. Arke had already seen them coming and sidestepped neatly, grabbing the last one as it was about to fly past and sent it back frisbee style with Irash's magic as an extra topping.

"I didn't order pepperoni!"

Her lips curled in a brief smile as the pizza delivery boy was hurled backwards by his own handiwork. Then, her expression changing to one of wry disapproval, she took stock of the entire chaotic battle and the impressive queue of idiots lining up along the pier. Finally, she settled her eyes back on Kennedy who'd just had a rotten cabbage pass so closely to his nose that he instantly remembered his first and only day at school. He turned and spotted two dwarves armed with kitchen dustbins, ready to hurl more rancid vegetables in his direction. Everyone knew that in a food fight, fresh or freshly magicked was fine but jellied lettuces or furry burgers were simply not acceptable. Barging aside an elf wielding a pair of broken bottles, he dropped to the deck and slid along until he could grab the dwarves by their cankles, then leapt back to his feet, effortlessly turning the garbage-flingers upside down.

"PUT THE RUBBISH DOWN AND GET OVER HERE!" Arke bellowed as Kennedy gave his assailants a good shake.

With a slurping slurry of impacts, another Sauceror had served dessert and everywhere was suddenly pelted with cream and custard delights. One hit Kennedy right in the face, its thick gelatinous ooze slipping slowly down around his nose.

"I'm a *trifle* busy!"

"Is that your nanny?" One of the dangling dwarves, having tried and failed to pummel Kennedy, attempted some emotional damage instead.

"Maybe it's bedtime for baby boys?" the other added with an unpleasant chortle.

"At least she taught me to take out the trash." Kennedy dropped the pair straight into the rubbish, slamming the lids down on their uncalled-for remarks about his punchline. "Whatever, lads; at least I'm not a has-bin."

As he turned sharply away, undoubtedly wishing he'd had more time to prepare a killer line, Ruby flew past, holding a waitress by the throat as she pummelled her mercilessly with her feet and then launched the limp body away as she landed by Sparkz, quickly extending a wing to deflect an airborne can opener from his face.

"Kennedy, we've got this! Go!"

He turned and sprinted across the deck towards where he'd last seen Arke, ducking, diving and dodging the attacks that came his way. However, she'd already given up waiting and jumped down to the wheel of the imp ship, muttering to herself as she eyed the various unmarked levers next to it.

"I'm not a helmsman, how am I supposed to know what does what? Stop and go, sure, I'm all over that. The rest is all bullshit. Why does no one ever label things?"

In the absence of any helpful instructions, she tried each control in turn, but nothing happened until she finally found the one for reverse and shot the prototype backwards just as Kennedy leapt over the side of the bigger vessel. Spotting the distinct lack of deck to land on, he made a desperate grab for the bowsprit and swung there one handed for a moment before hauling himself on board, cursing heavily.

Arke seemed utterly oblivious to his exertions. "At last. Get over here and drive this stupid thing."

"Seriously? I've shown you so many times how these things work!" He wiped a distinctly tangy mixture of food from his face as he strode towards the helm.

"Why have a dog and bark yourself?" Arke stepped aside, rolling her eyes impatiently as he took a long moment to admire the craftsmanship of the ship's wheel, his hands appreciatively stroking the beautifully polished wood. "Stop or you'll go blind. Capsize that disgusting hovel already."

"Really? Can this ship manage it?"

She gestured towards the cage. "It's running on infernal power, so yes, of course it can."

Kennedy turned to see the unblinking beady eyes of all the imps in their harnesses silently judging him and shuddered a little. "Well, there's the reason Gorki wanted this back. Can't say I'm a fan. How do they... work?"

"Say go. Or stop. They're simple, you'll get on well."

Ignoring the sideways remark, Kennedy quickly manoeuvred the smaller ship so it was angled to create maximum pressure on the side of the *Gravy Boat*. He looked at the imps and said "Full power. Please."

The infernals looked boredly at him for a moment, but after a second of insolence their eyes widened with another emotion entirely. Kennedy braced himself as the two ships came together with a meaty thud and Arke stood behind him, one hand holding herself steady, the other still poised menacingly, pointing at each imp in turn as if selecting her next noseful.

With surprising ease, the much smaller vessel's impressive power began to rotate the bigger ship, the sticky decks sloping away quickly from the combatants. Pirates started to leap to safety as one side of the *Gravy Boat* rose rapidly to a vertical position and then just kept going. Everyone still aboard tried to find something to grab hold of as the ship reached the point of no return, but as ever, gravity liked to make a point, and the deck was suddenly all but empty. Falling away, the Saucerors were desperately trying to make giant tortillas into parachutes and the goblin teddy bear frantically wound his whisks against the ogre's head to wake him, but they too dropped away, still cuddled together.

⚔ ⚔ ⚔

THE MOMENT THE decks began to tilt in earnest, Sparkz sprinted over to the Vonti, knowing that there was no chance that the snail would ever make it off the vessel in time. Telling him, with pun fully intended, to hang tight, he tied the rope that Gabbi had threaded through the grey shell to the nearest solid object before continuing over towards Klaus. The Tiax was caught up in a vicious sword fight against what looked like a trio of goblins with cheese graters on their heads and pokers in each hand. The engineer kicked one of the attackers aside and leapt towards Klaus, managing to grab him the instant before the *Gravy Boat* was poured.

"Ah, hello! Sparkz isn't it? We didn't get time to be properly friends, so it is good to make a greeting. I am so sorry though, I have no ability to fly." Klaus's natural accent was unusual and the way he lisped as he talked made his words even more musical.

"You do now." The tattoo of a pair of wings under the engineer's ear lit up in a suitably sky-blue colour, and suddenly neither of them were falling. "You've only got a few minutes of airtime so don't hang around. Drop me off on the top of this stinking ship and go back for that other guy." Sparkz pointed above them to where Giro's shell was swinging back and forth under the capsized vessel.

"And I take him to Kennedy in the little ship, yes? What about you?"

Sparkz grinned. "Tell big bird to come get me, I'm just going to add a little more oil to the gravy."

✠ ✠ ✠

ABOVE THEM, ARKE had a telescope to her eye as she checked on the rest of the flotilla's ships, some of which were rather ominously getting underway in their direction, clearly also keen to claim Madame Chalet's bounty. She looked between Kennedy and the imps with a frown. "We need to get out of here before things get really messy. You lot better do what he says, or I'll eat you the old-fashioned way."

Just at that moment there was a whistling, rushing noise from two harpoons that had been fired from the nearest pursuer. One hit the wheel, grazing Kennedy on the way past and retracted with a hiss of rope. The other struck Arke in the thigh, the razor-sharp tip piercing deeply before its line also pulled back, dragging her helplessly away until she was yanked off the deck, swinging through the air upside down.

The imps winced theatrically as they watched her

unwilling exit and Irash's newly discovered sense of humour kicked in as he chuckled in Arke's head. "Catch of the day?"

Hanging grimly onto the harpoon as she swung in a wide arc towards the whaling ship which had fired at them, his host cursed heavily as she sawed at it with her dagger. "This *isn't* funny."

"Maybe not for you." Her passenger was still amused. "You know there *is* an easier way."

With a mouthful of heartfelt expletives, she hauled herself up the harpoon until she could reach to cut the rope, then used his magic to fly upwards. She was in pain and distinctly irritated by the voice in her head, but more to the point, she was Arke, so it was time for a little overkill. As she came level with the whaler, she focused her gaze on its main deck and spotted that it had a recent kill on board. With a wicked smile playing on her lips, she began to channel Irash's renewed power towards the unfortunate creature, remarking under her breath that there had to be some benefit to snorting all those imps.

The dead whale's revenge began with a full body shudder, then it started to expand at an exponential rate before exploding with a massively powerful blast that blew the sailors, their ship and their excruciating weapons into oily chum and matchstick rain. Grimly satisfied, Arke looked down at the harpoon that was stuck deep into her leg, experimentally trying to break it in half and then stopping quickly with a grimace of pain.

"You just blew up a WHALE! And you can't work out how to get rid of a stick in your leg?" Irash's amusement had worn off and been replaced with exasperation. "How are you mortals so numerous when you're so stupid sometimes? Most of the time. All of the time."

"I snorted imps, that's got to do something to your brain. Now shut up." Arke took a deep breath and quickly re-imagined the harpoon as a big bandage which wrapped around the wound in her thigh before flying back to the ship in much less discomfort. She landed heavily in front of the imp cage, instantly silencing the infernals who had been getting rowdier in her absence. "The next one I see putting less than their full effort in gets made into sushi."

With a sudden rush of her rainbow wings, Ruby landed by the imp's cage, dropping Volk and Gabbi in a heap as she hurried over to greet Arke whose attention had been gathered by the odd figures she'd spotted flying towards the ship.

"Kennedy, would you know why there's a foxy guy carrying a snail on a rope flying towards us?"

"You think he's cute?" The glare that an amused Kennedy received in response to his question was more than enough to make him chuckle even harder before dropping a casual reply. "New crewmates, Klaus and Giro."

"You went to get an orbiculum, not start a zoo."

Kennedy's mouth dropped open. "I'm going to pretend you didn't say that!"

It was at that precise moment that a pair of warm, feathery arms as well as two rainbow-coloured wings swallowed Arke up in the softest and most claustrophobic hug she had ever endured. When she was finally released, the Soulbound didn't make a sound as she patiently removed a few downy feathers from her mouth, but to the Ornithol's surprised delight, as Arke walked away she actually reached out a hand and quickly patted her on the back.

The Tiax came in to land with gloriously dramatic effect, dropping Giro in the middle of the deck before touching down with a forwards roll and a bow as he leapt to his feet.

"Klaus reporting: I have a message from Sparkz; he says that he is making oily gravy for a ship flambé and requires a Ruby-taxi."

"He's what?" Kennedy asked, in obvious confusion. "Ruby?"

"There he is!" Her sharp eyes had already spotted Sparkz on the hull of the upturned boat and she watched for a moment as he walked across the ship, pointing a finger behind him as he went. "I'll go get him!"

Arke followed her friend up into the air and hovered to get a better view of what was happening on the other side of the capsized ship as well as further back in the flotilla. She could see a rescue tender heading towards the *Gravy Boat* and a serious bucketful of others from both sides of the circular floating town heading in their direction. Further back still, she could just make out the *Warrior* under heavy acceleration, carving a path directly towards them.

Focusing on Ruby again, the Soulbound watched with curiosity as she airlifted Sparkz from the hull and accelerated away to a reasonable distance before stopping and turning. Suddenly a gout of magical flame shot from the Ornithol's hand, the wind trying and failing to extinguish it before it landed square on the stern end of the ship. Whatever Sparkz had been doing up there had created the perfect conditions for ignition and with an echoing *whoosh*, the hull of the Gravy Boat became an inferno.

"The bird is a very useful mobile flamethrower," Irash chuckled, deeply appreciative of the entertainment.

"She's been wanting to use that ring ever since Sparkz gave it to her."

"What had she done for him to get a gift like that?"

"Nothing, ever." Arke hadn't intended for her reply to come out quite so protectively but as Irash's chuckles turned to laughter, she told him exactly where to stick his amusement.

Her deep irritation at his mirth completely spoilt her appreciation of the excellent job Sparkz and Ruby had done on the *Gravy Boat*. Irash was still chortling in a deeply aggravating fashion when she saw the rescue ship start to tackle the conflagration and noticed the way they were pouring water from their giant deck-borne tank on what was clearly an oil-based fire.

The voice in Arke's head suddenly dipped to a deeply wicked whisper. "The plan you're considering has my full and complete approval. I will freely admit that sometimes your intellect manages to reach one notch above pure ignorance. Do it."

With a glance to check that the imp ship was at a survivable distance, Arke concentrated her passenger's power on turning all the water in the rescue ship's reservoir into alcohol. Pure, finest grade alcohol which flooded down the hoses, hit the flames and instantly carried them back up into the tank, turning that and the vessel itself into a massive fireball, with a final detonation that disintegrated it entirely. And in an unexpected turn of events, either the shockwave, its inversion, or the raging fire on the *Gravy Boat's* hull must have ignited its fuel source. With an even more apocalyptic explosion, the greasiest of greasy spoons was permanently closed for business.

⚔ ⚔ ⚔

Everything close to the *Gravy Boat* was either destroyed or damaged so badly they could no longer continue their pursuit. It couldn't have gone any better if Arke had tried, and as the smoke cleared, most of the vessels coming from the western side of the flotilla began to turn back, clearly deciding that they had better things to do with the rest of their lives.

"That was a rescue ship!" Kennedy yelled.

"We don't need rescuing!" She clearly wasn't in the mood to argue semantics and anyway, her gambit had been incredibly successful, for there were only a couple of ships still coming from that direction. Unlike the crowd gaining headway from the other side of the floating town. "Not yet anyway. Can you handle the last ones from this side while I dissuade the rest?"

With a confident smile, Kennedy looked up at Arke as she hovered above him. "Of course! Just be careful!"

He looked back down before any misgivings he felt about her current situation showed in his face. He was still deeply uneasy about Arke keeping control of Irash, but he couldn't deny that they needed his power right now. There were a lot of enemy vessels heading their way and though the imp prototype was fast, it was also small and without a single cannon to its name.

"Maybe try not to kill everyone?" He glanced up again with a hopeful expression, but she'd already gone.

Concentrating on keeping the prototype flying at optimum velocity, Kennedy ordered Klaus and Volk to take station either side of the stern to watch for any pursuit still heading their way. He gripped the wheel tightly before forcing himself to relax his grasp and loosen his shoulders as he waited for whatever was coming to break through the oily smoke cloud left from the explosion of the *Gravy Boat*. It was just another day in the office. A different, much more fragile and defenceless office.

"One ship, almost directly astern, Captain!" Klaus reported. "I see bow chasers and... things dropping from their hull."

"Things?" Kennedy queried, glancing over his shoulder to see what could only be described as a stylish pirate ship scything its way through the cloud of smoke, her sails billowing, puffs of smoke already evident from her forward guns and the oddest dark shapes dropping below her.

Almost as if the enemy had heard his question, a chorus of voices from the pursuing vessel reached their ears. "Shark! Shark! Shark! Shark!"

"Someone please tell me they're just shouting the name of their ship?" Kennedy pleaded, concentrating on squeezing every ounce of speed from the prototype.

"They're just shouting the name of their ship," Volk agreed, telescope to his eye. "Named it after all the sharks they keep on board."

"The *flying* sharks. They're VERY cool," Klaus enthused as he watched the creatures fan out into a perfectly spaced formation and start gathering pace.

"There's at least twenty-five out there and it looks

like each one has wings and an engine," Volk observed. "Someone over there has far too much time on their hands."

Kennedy watched as the beasts surged through the air, smoke trails behind each providing clear evidence that they were possibly not so much magically but mechanically powered. "Let's hope we can keep ahead of them until their fuel runs out."

Chapter Twenty
It Had to Be Sharks

THE SHOCKWAVE FROM the *Gravy Boat's* explosion hit Ruby and Sparkz when they were barely a third of the way to the imp ship, the sheer force of it yanking the pair apart and sending them tumbling blindly through the air in different directions. Sparkz didn't even slightly enjoy the sensation of freefall during the seconds it took the Ornithol to collect him, but her reassuringly bright plumage zooming closer kept him from panicking and using his own energy to cast a second flight spell. He found locomotive magic far more draining than his other abilities, so if a ride was available, he would always take that option.

"You do know that you're our designated life saver now? I'd ask for a raise." Sparkz grinned as Ruby's arms plucked him from the air.

"I can't do that, I've only just joined." She paused for thought as her wings powered them both upwards. "But maybe I could get a badge?"

As much as Sparkz disliked most people before he'd even met them, there was a lot about Ruby that didn't irritate him. He'd given her the magical ring he'd won in High Haven not only because it was practical to have a flying flamethrower but also because he genuinely liked her. In fact, he liked a lot of the other crew too, and it was all Kennedy's fault for maintaining an environment that encouraged friendship, loyalty and teamwork rather than backstabbing, lies and greed.

"Sparkz…" Ruby hovered for a moment and turned in the air to point out a dark line of weird, winged creatures flying towards them.

"More like sharkz!" he responded. "Sometimes I know we're being trolled. First Arke with a fin in her back and now actual flying bastard sharks."

"Basking sharks? They don't look quite the same."

"BASTARD sharks!"

"More like great whites."

With only a beak, Ruby's facial expressions were limited, but Sparkz was almost sure she was deliberately mishearing him as they watched the formation approach.

"They're pretty fast. We should get moving."

"Yeah." He pointed towards the sharks. "That way."

"Sparkz, are you OK? Why would you want to go *towards* them?"

"They're coming on faster than you can fly with me slowing you down; I say we hit them in the face rather than get bitten from the rear."

His reasoning was impeccable, and Ruby wasted no time getting closer to the formation while Sparkz studied the new enemy. The creatures looked as if they'd been relocated by someone who'd taken 'finding new habitats' far too literally. Their bodies, once sleek and aerodynamic, were now a tangled repository of badly stitched surgeries topped with metallic wings and a jetpack. A very interesting looking jetpack. Sparkz's eyes lit up; he had no opinions about the sharks themselves, but he did like the look of their engines.

"Ruby!" he called, pointing to the nearest hefty-looking creature. "I want you to drop me on top of that big one, then get back to help Kennedy."

"You want to do what now?"

"Jump the shark. Well, onto the shark."

He was not only adamant but also strangely excited, so with deep reluctance, Ruby carefully manoeuvred into position above the chosen beast and lowered Sparkz down. To his relief, the shark barely noticed its passenger, and continued to fly towards the imp ship with the rest of its squadron while the Ornithol raced along above them, her natural wings soon outstripping their mechanical speed.

The moment he landed astride the creature, Sparkz forgot everything but the shiny engine purring away behind him. Being able to fly was exceptionally useful when one lived on a sky vessel, and he'd always wanted to build a single person flying machine. However, time, opportunity, and materials meant he'd never got past the testing phase, so having a working one right next to him was beyond exciting. There was only one tiny snag; he needed to get it back to the ship.

Sparkz always had ideas for many things in his head but 'how to ride a flying shark' was definitely not one of them. However, he'd try anything for a really good bit of machinery. First, he tried wrapping the cord of his whip around the beast's neck and trying to steer with it, but the shark completely ignored him, intent on staying with its fellows. Turning rather perilously around so he could concentrate on the part without irritating opinions, Sparkz looked along the creature's back, examining the metal unit that housed both the wings and the engine. To his immense pleasure, the rig looked very simple, having clearly been designed to be fitted quickly. What went on fast also came off fast. He grinned as he eased an adjustable wrench from his jacket pocket.

"This is going to be great!"

⚔ ⚔ ⚔

"THIS IS NOT great!" Kennedy yelled as the imp ship slewed sideways, rapidly losing speed. He couldn't see what damage a double hit from the bow chasers of the pirate ship had done to the propellers behind the imp cage, but the effects were undeniably worrying. He unleashed a few choice curses at the situation. The nasty-looking sharks were approaching fast, Sparkz was not on board and their speed had just been halved. There was no point in having the best power sources if they had nothing to power. "Anyone fancy trying to fix the damage?"

Volk was quick to volunteer, and Kennedy watched him vault over the railings to traverse the narrow ledge towards the stern with a surety that only came from a life fully spent on board a ship. The little man moved nimbly, even managing to avoid snagging his expensive-looking dress coat on some splintered timbers just before he disappeared from sight. It didn't take long to diagnose the issue, Volk sending Gabbi to report that, in his master's expert opinion, the problem likely originated from the cannon ball that had wedged itself in the propeller. A few of the fins had buckled but the rest looked viable, or they would be once Volk was able to 'assert his dominance over the offending iron shot'. As the young man hurried back to help his master, Kennedy wrinkled his brow at the phrasing Gabbi had used. He thought he'd met a lot of unique people, but then the world just kept on giving.

On the other side of the stern, Klaus still had his telescope trained on the pirate ship, calling to Kennedy when he could see that they were about to fire so his new captain had more chance of steering hard away from the unpleasantly accurate gunnery. It was probably the glint from his glass that made the Tiax the sharpshooter's first target, the bullet going straight through his shoulder and dropping with a wet clunk to the deck.

"Take cover! They are very good shots." Klaus clutched a hand to his wound as he slid to the floor. "I will be fine in a moment or two."

"Hurry with the engine!" Kennedy shouted in Volk's general direction and then winced as something hit his leg. Almost immediately after, he heard cannon balls whistling towards them and had no time to do anything but work the trim and spin the wheel to try and avoid any more shot smashing into the nimble, little ship. Injuries could be dealt with later; keeping an intact vessel in between his crew and the ground was the only thing that mattered right now.

⚔ ⚔ ⚔

THE NOW-WINGLESS SHARK was doubtless quite surprised as it fell away below Sparkz who was sitting precariously on top of his jury-rigged flight pack. He'd isolated the fuel line as the most basic way to control his speed and held that in one hand. The other was fully entwined with the cord of his whip which ran through several now empty bolt holes on the metal frame. Almost holding his breath as the seconds ticked past and the machine kept running smoothly even without its connection to its previous owner, Sparkz finally relaxed a little, knowing he wasn't about to fall out of the sky. He untwisted the hose to increase the power below him and slowly leant to the right, using his bodyweight as a very blunt steering apparatus to head towards the pirate ship.

It didn't take him long to get close enough to hear the thunder of the cannons and the crack of rifle fire even over the sound of the engine that vibrated noisily beneath him. Clumsily manoeuvring his new toy, he finally got close enough to activate the yin-yang tattoo on his neck while concentrating on an area right in the middle of the ship's keel. The enemy vessel suddenly shuddered and creaked as an integral part of its structure shrank to a fraction of its original size, and the frame of the entire vessel began to warp and twist as it flew.

"That should screw with your aim!"

Carefully leaning back to the left, Sparkz steered away from the pirate ship and spotted the very welcome sight of the *Warrior* at full speed as it smashed its way through the pier that had once led to the *Gravy Boat*. It was a lot nearer to him than the imp ship was and his route to it was not lined with flying sharks. There was no decision to make, especially as Sparkz had no idea how much fuel was left in his flying metal tray. Angling himself to intercept their course, he opened the fuel line almost all the way and shot towards his ship.

⚔ ⚔ ⚔

"THE PROPELLER IS fixed!" Volk called triumphantly as he leapt back on deck, right before shouting "Gabbi, you IDIOT!" as his servant pushed him clear of an incoming cannon ball.

Jumping straight back to his feet, the halfling yanked the blunderbuss from over his shoulder and unscrewed the end, turning the wide bore into a rifle, before flipping a set of sights up with a practiced hand. He concentrated, finding his target at one of the bow chasers and fired.

"Take THAT you rogue! You see Gabbi? *That* is how you deal with cannon fire."

As the wheel started to vibrate more strongly under his hands, Kennedy knew the ship was speeding up again. Looking over his shoulder with a frown, he could see that the shiver of sharks had made up a lot of distance while they were at half power. Another cannon ball came whizzing in and crashed hard into the hull, making the ship shudder heavily but she kept going and he patted her wheel appreciatively.

"Volk, can you do anything about the sharks?" Kennedy called. "Don't fancy our chances if they want to hitch a ride."

"Aye captain, with much pleasure!"

"Just don't shoot the big rainbow-coloured bird!" Kennedy grinned as he spotted Ruby diving to the deck. "Welcome back! Where's Sparkz?"

"Hijacking a shark?" When he just stared at her, confusion on his face, the Ornithol gestured behind her to the pack rapidly approaching. "They have engines on them."

Kennedy managed to both nod and shake his head at the same time. "Volk, if you see one being ridden by my brother, make sure to shoot him first."

There was no time for anyone to reply before Klaus wobbled his way across the deck towards the helm. "Enemy incoming." The fact that he looked up was not a good sign, and as the others followed his lead, the intimidating sight of a ship that appeared to have sprung brown fur-covered wings diving down towards them only reinforced their sense of foreboding.

"Beware the hare in the air? Hang on!" Kennedy slammed the wheel hard over while fettling the trim levers to sideslip the entire vessel out of the way of the new attacker.

As the deck tilted, Ruby grabbed Klaus, quickly ripping his shirt to use as a bandage to staunch the blood from the bullet's exit hole before settling him down by the imp's cage, sword in his good hand.

"Watch our backs, will you?" Volk asked him, before sighting and firing at one of the sharks, hitting it square in the forehead and causing it to crash into the one next to it before dropping out of the sky. "Oh that's the ticket, you beast! Reload faster, damn you Gabbi!"

As Kennedy sent full power back to both propellers, the new enemy levelled out, wings folding back against its sides as it aimed its bow directly at the side of the imp powered vessel. It was clearly a trapper's ship, beast cages and barrels all over the decks, and at its wheel was a gnome dressed in what looked like a zebra skin coat who was busy bellowing in Nidean while pointing angrily to a small container which was stationed right at the bow.

From a distance, the barrel had appeared unexceptional, but now that the enemy ship was close enough, Kennedy could see that it was definitely not. Glowing magical runes obscured most of the wood, and mighty chains covered those, lashing it firmly to the deck. Finally obeying his captain, an obviously reluctant member of crew crept towards the cask, flicking the hasps on each side of the chain open with a long pole before turning and running. He became the aperitif. A monstrous purple tentacle with green suckers shot out from the tiny prison, grabbing the unlucky man before retracting so quickly that his body was pared down to a central core as it was dragged into the barrel with a wet gurgle.

Whatever the creature was obviously appreciated the snack and was keen for more as suddenly its container shuddered and a myriad of similar tentacles poured out like water, lurching across the narrowing distance towards the imp-powered vessel, each sucker slapping wetly as it locked onto the hull. Once the last arm was firmly in place, whatever was contained in the barrel started to retract its limbs with tremendous power, hauling its prey towards it with unstoppable energy.

"Take a moment to rest, but when I say go, I need everything you've got, unless you want to be that thing's dinner!" Kennedy shouted at the imps as he battled with the controls, trying to angle the bows downwards.

The sound of a broadside shattered the air as the pirate ship fired. Everyone aboard the prototype cringed, expecting multiple impacts, but as Kennedy watched, all the hits landed on the trapper's vessel. Everyone knew there was no honour among thieves, and it seemed as if the saying also applied to the would-be bounty hunters. As iron shot crashed at random onto the main deck, cages and boxes were knocked over. Some lucky creatures found their prisons were no longer able to hold them and their jailers close enough to extract a little revenge for their imprisonment. Kennedy heard Ruby's voice suddenly shouting encouragement at the oddest of beasts as they wreaked havoc on the other crew.

"The pirate ship's in trouble," Volk called. "Firing that broadside nearly ripped their hull apart; they're listing heavily to starboard."

"Thoughts and prayers," Kennedy replied through gritted teeth, still struggling with the trim of the ship as the tentacles writhed around the hull, crushing and dragging it closer. After a few more seconds of wrangling, he finally managed to get the nose angled downwards.

"GO IMPS!"

The ship leapt forwards and ripped at the monstrous purple tentacles to no avail. Kennedy glanced behind him, shouting at the infernals to give him everything they had. While exhorting them to greater efforts, he noticed Ruby had dragged her eyes away from the critter war on the trapper's deck and was trying to use a broom handle as a lever against one of the suckers that was attached to their hull. Just as she was trying to work the wooden pole into position, a far more ragged broadside hit the trapper's vessel. Crates and boxes that had been damaged by the first fall of shot were now completely shattered and even more creatures emerged, indiscriminately attacking both each other and the crew.

The largest animal, a shimmering jaguar-shaped ball of confusion laced with claws and teeth, roared as an orc swung at it with a pike tipped with a glistening magical aura. As the weapon connected, the monster shuddered, the zap of lightning echoing across both decks. Ruby didn't hesitate, pulling back her arm and launching the broom handle at the animal abuser. Accuracy honed by righteous anger made the ersatz javelin a weapon of orc destruction, and the second after her target took a broom to the face, he also took a crystal jaguar to the chest, and the stomach, and the intestines, and the kidneys. Once the beast had finished its grisly revenge, it sniffed briefly at the broom handle before swivelling a pair of luminous pink eyes around until they landed on Ruby who waved a tentative hand in greeting.

"You're welcome?"

"It's not time to make friends, Ruby! IMPS COME ON! If Arke doesn't eat you, I will!"

The infernals dug deeper, straining into their harnesses, giving absolutely every ounce of effort just as the crystalline jaguar that had no business existing in this particular plane, slid down one of the straining tentacles and leapt onto the deck, its eyes never leaving Ruby's face.

"IT'S WORKING! MORE!" Kennedy bellowed and with a sudden, tearing squelch, the suckers from the trapper's ship finally released and the smaller vessel shot forwards, nose down, gaining speed rapidly. "YES! COME ON BABY! COME ON!"

His elation faded somewhat as he noticed their extra passenger. "Ahhhh. Someone?"

"I'll take care of him." Without hesitation, Ruby stepped towards the creature, its beautiful shimmering coat reflecting the light like a multi-faceted diamond.

"Does she mean take care as in kill or…" Kennedy muttered to himself as he watched the Ornithol crouch down and make 'here kitty kitty' noises. "Right, so not that sort of 'take care' then." He raised his voice a little, trying not to spook the creature but also trying to warn his crewmate. "Ruby, that thing is definitely growling at you. And it has really big teeth and absolutely giant claws… Oh. Ouch."

He winced as the beast leapt on Ruby, using those giant claws and teeth to try and take care of her the very non-gentle way.

"If she wanted a pet, she just had to ask." He sighed, watching the strangest wrestling match he'd ever seen unfold in front of him as the Ornithol struggled to detach the giant cat from her body while making soothing noises and telling it that she understood that this situation was very scary.

"Captain, I'm shooting as many of these bloody things as I can but there are still some coming!" Volk called as the sharks dived towards them, gaining just as much speed as their target.

"I – could – help." Giro had been amassing his power as he watched the squadron approach. "I – can – create – wind."

There were so many jokes but no time for any, especially given the speed that the Vonti spoke.

"Keep those tentacles off us first," Kennedy ordered, watching as the trapper's ship put its nose down and the waving purple arms reached out towards them once more.

As Giro's spell began to frustrate the hungry barrel beast, Kennedy found himself watching round two amidships as Ruby made another attempt to calm what was absolutely not a scared pussy cat. That attempt went the same way as her first.

Finally, he heard a familiar voice ring out across the deck as Arke returned from dealing with the rest of the pursuing ships.

"For the *second* time today, this is not a bloody zoo! Put it down or I will."

With almost comical reluctance given the amount of blood pouring down her feathers, Ruby leapt into the air, and with one of her lightning strikes, slammed a double fist, double wing blow on top of the beast's head so hard that everyone on board could see the stars dancing in its blank eyes. The shimmering jaguar toppled helplessly to the deck, and she quickly started hog-tying it with a coil of rope handed to her by a nervous-looking Gabbi.

Kennedy raised a hand in greeting to Arke and then pointed to the trapper ship. "I know I said we could deal with the two but is there any chance you could do something about…"

She was about to reply when a beam of aetheric light shot out from their port quarter, skewering the enemy amidships with a resounding crack, followed by a muffled boom as something inside the trapping vessel exploded.

"Ah, don't worry. We got it." The wide smile that flooded Kennedy's face was so infectious that even covered in blood and scratched to ribbons, Ruby started to cheer.

"GO *WARRIOR!*"

"About bloody time *Warrior*," Arke corrected with a shake of her head as she watched the enemy vessel drop behind, flames starting to cover its decks from whatever the aetheric lance had ignited. She turned to look at where Giro was working to hold the last few sharks off their decks while Volk blasted them with his blunderbuss. "No zoo also means no aquarium."

"I'll deal with them." Kennedy grinned confidently. "This is the captain's part. Ruby, take the wheel!"

"Fine, showboat all you like, I need a coffee." Arke limped heavily down the steps to the galley, the bandage on her leg now more red than white.

"There's two left, captain." Volk fired a final shot and grinned, patting his gun with true affection before handing it to Gabbi to clean.

"Giro, time to let them come on in." Kennedy rolled his shoulders, still smiling, and marched out onto the open deck. As he walked, he felt something pop in his leg. Then the tiredness hit. He could hardly put one foot in front of the other. And his right boot was sloshing. He looked down and saw that his leg was soaked in blood. That wasn't good. He remembered feeling something hit him earlier in the chase just as everything went dark.

"CAPTAIN!" Ruby yelled, her horrified voice cutting through the sudden silence as one of the sharks sank its huge teeth into Kennedy's arm. The other bit into his already bloodied leg and dragged him around like a ragdoll, smearing blood as he went. Klaus lurched to his feet, swinging his sword and bisected the first as Ruby punched the other so hard on its nose that it let go and was immediately set upon by two imps, who dragged its writhing body back into their cage and slammed the door behind them.

⅍ ⅍ ⅍

ARKE WAS ALREADY half-way across the deck before anyone else had moved. Horrified eyes fixed on Kennedy, she slid to her knees beside him and slammed her fingers into the arterial wound in his leg.

"Did I get them?" Kennedy's eyes fluttered open as she began to dam the flow.

"No! No, you didn't! I turn my back for one minute and look what happens! You bloody useless waste of human organs! I've worn trousers with more ability to defend themselves!" Arke ranted. "This is a bullet wound; I know because I can feel the bullet!"

"Forgot about that, it wasn't bleeding before, I promise." His smile was boyishly embarrassed as he tried to pretend he hadn't utterly forgotten how to pirate.

"YOU DON'T FORGET YOU'VE BEEN SHOT!"

While Arke shouted furiously at the fallen captain, Ruby was desperately wrapping his arm with Gabbi's shirt to try and stem the bleeding there while Klaus used the rest of his on Kennedy's lower leg.

"No need to be mean."

Kennedy shut his eyes tiredly and Arke slapped him hard across the face, then backhanded him for good measure.

"There's EVERY need! Stay awake! Irash, can I fix this?" She knew her passenger was weary, as it had taken a lot of energy to set fire to enough pursuing ships to persuade the rest that their efforts would be better spent absolutely anywhere else.

The voice in her head snorted with brief derision. "The Destroyer, not The Healer." Then he sighed and continued. "But yes, if you can visualise it, then it will happen – but you must be precise or you could do more damage. The easier way, of course, would be for me to possess him; it is a lot easier to heal from the inside out."

"Possess him?" Arke hadn't even considered that option.

"NO." Kennedy opened his eyes again, glaring into her face. "I'd rather die."

"You'll die when *I* say you can, and not before," she replied with the stern assurance of an almost-parent. "Now let me concentrate."

A few minutes later, speeding through the air with the bloodied captain in her arms, Arke dived down into the *Warrior's* main hatch without even sparing a glance for a startled looking Ellie at the helm. As she landed at the bottom of the stairs, she struggled towards the sick bay, having to use Irash's power to give her enough strength to carry Kennedy's dead weight, shouting for Gurdi as she went.

The door ahead of her sprang open, revealing the surprisingly sprightly dwarf who was probably older than the timbers of the ship she sailed in. Her face was leathered, but her eyes were sharp despite the torrent of time that had wrinkled and warped every inch of her skin.

"Looks like you've been in the wars." Gurdi smiled down at Kennedy with warm affection. "Not to worry, I'll get you all fixed up."

"I've taken the bullet out of his leg and sealed the blood vessel there. The rest was flying sharks."

"What else could it be?"

The healer threw a new sheet over the treatment table and helped ease a barely conscious Kennedy onto it, starting work immediately, her eyes glowing as she channelled powerful healing magic into his wounds. Arke watched anxiously until she was waved away, then turned and left the room, trying so hard to disguise the limp from her harpoon injury that she didn't notice a bleary-eyed Krugg coming out of the crew quarters.

"Arke, you are covered in blood."

"It's Kennedy's. He…" She suddenly looked up at the ogre in abject horror as the familiar voice cut through her worried thoughts. She had had no idea what had happened to her demon, and no-one had dared to tell her. "Stabbington?"

"I am here, yes. Is he going to be alright?"

"He'd better be," Arke replied with a frown, her attention captured by a pair of insanely bright blue eyes with snake-like vertical pupils while confusion washed over her as she desperately tried to fathom what fresh hell she'd discovered.

"So *he* is worth saving while *I* was not?"

In her head, Arke heard Irash say "Mi-aow!", and without even thinking she punched Stabbington-Krugg straight in the balls.

If you've ever heard a demon-possessed ogre take a blow to the testicles then you'll know the unearthly sound that came from Stabbington-Krugg's lips as he crumpled to his knees, holding his groin. Arke looked him over more closely and wrinkled her nose in disgust.

"You stink like a tavern's toilets! How much booze *have* you had?"

"All of it. And now there is no more so I am sober. Sober with aching balls," he explained through hissing breaths, still cradling the point of impact.

"All of it?" She couldn't comprehend how even an ogre could have got through all the barrels and bottles of alcohol the *Warrior* carried.

Indignance suddenly seemed to outrank the pain in his groin. "Yes, I have been here in this body since you *threw* me away. Plenty of time to drink everything!"

Fury overtaking her, Arke punched Stabbington-Krugg right under the jaw, snapping his head back sharply. "I did NOT throw you away you *pig-headed, snake-eyed,* waste of time!"

The bright blue eyes glinted with rage as he recovered from the blow and returned his gaze to hers. Krugg's body was still on his knees, so Stabbington was able to glare straight into Arke's face as he ground out his reply. "I – own – your – soul! I could have claimed it for breaking the contract."

"Do it now then if you want to." Grabbing him by the shirt, she leant in so she could shout right in his face. "DO IT! I dare you."

Her challenge hung like a blade in the air between them, neither sparing a muscle to take even a single breath. Stabbington's eyes glowed even brighter for the briefest of seconds but then he reached up, cupped Arke's face with Krugg's meaty hands and kissed her.

It was not the embrace of legend. It wasn't average or even tolerable. In truth, it felt like she was having her face sucked by a huge, wet hoover.

Arke desperately tried to get away, but the ogre was three times her size so, for the second time in a minute, she delivered a crushing blow to his groin, this time with a foot. As he released her, doubling over in pain, she disgustedly scraped the moisture from her face with one hand.

"THAT IS NEVER OK! If you're going to drag me to hell, kill me properly, not by trying to suffocate me with slobber!"

A movement to the left caught her eye and she turned, spotting that the sick bay door had swung open. Her eyes met Kennedy's for a long, awkward moment. He waved a weak right hand at her before Gurdi, utterly failing at being subtle, slammed the door shut with her foot.

Meanwhile, Stabbington-Krugg had taken the opportunity to quit while he was behind and was crawling back into the crew quarters. Arke ignored him as she turned to leave and noticed Sparkz leaning on the rail at the bottom of the stairs with an extremely amused smirk. He didn't flinch as she limped towards him with a forbidding expression on her face.

"Maybe you shouldn't be so picky, you aren't as young as you used to be."

Without a word she flicked the ogre slobber from her hand at him and headed up the stairs. Sparkz's smirk turned into laughter behind her, his amusement echoing down the corridor as the *Warrior* escorted the imp ship to clearer skies, leaving only chaos in its wake.

Chapter Twenty-One
It's Not Easy Being Seen

THE *WARRIOR'S* UNINJURED crew had barely slept as they made good their getaway from the flotilla alongside the imp-powered ship with Giro's solid form at its helm. With Kennedy in sickbay, Arke had been in charge, and she'd spent the evening limping up and down the deck with a deep frown on her face until someone had snitched to Gurdi about the bandage around her leg. Having quickly obeyed the dwarf's terse summons, worried there was something wrong with the captain, she'd been completely blind-sided by the healer handing her a post-battle smoothie while reassuring her about Kennedy's condition. Sitting by his bedside, feeling nothing but relief, an exhausted Arke downed the potion without thinking and never even noticed sleep slamming her eyelids down like shutters. With a satisfied smile, Gurdi sent word to Ellie that she was now in command and started treating the Soulbound's wound in a blissful zone of peace that was only interrupted by occasional snoring.

The night had not been an easy one for the crew, not because of any lurking danger, but more because of the first mate's stress levels. She was so anxious to keep everyone safe, keep the imp ship in sight, keep the flight smooth and keep watching the skies, that even Urzish had cause to complain.

"I know what I am doing. I do not need you to peck, peck, peck at me every ten minutes," the orc growled.

"When I am looking forward to seeing Arke so much I could hug her, this is when I know you are driving me crazy."

Dawn broke before any of Ellie's bones and to everyone's relief all they could see for miles around was beautifully empty sky. The watch was more than ready for breakfast by the time Arke limped back up the stairs, a freshly applied bandage around her leg and an oddly cheery air about her. As she checked their position, even managing to keep her usual scowl of mathematical frustration away while she did so, Ellie hovered nearby, waiting until she'd finished before asking for an update on Kennedy.

With what was definitely a chuckle, Arke turned to face the first mate, her eyes twinkling and a bright smile on her face. "Well, he's just been caught trying to escape. OK, so when I say escape, it was more of a hop and a splat."

"He's going to be alright? No amputations? Not even a finger?" Ellie asked quickly.

"Not unless he winds Gurdi up anymore. Might be close." Arke chuckled again, clearly basking in the knowledge that she was no longer sickbay enemy number one.

The fact that the *Warrior* still didn't have a captain with any body parts missing was briefly disappointing to his loyal crew, who were always the butt of jokes about Kennedy's inability to get properly maimed. Drunken conversations in dockside taverns invariably ended in fights if anyone queried whether they were even proper pirates without a captain with a peg leg or a hook for a hand. However, since they'd all been worried about their usually lucky leader, hearing that he was already well enough to try a breakout raised their spirits enough to start betting on when he'd actually manage it.

Leaving Arke in command and Sparkz on the wheel, the night watch hurried down to the galley, their overall vibe much improved even in the face of the breakfast ... soup, and whatever was bobbing inexplicably among the baked beans and sausages. While they ate, they quickly tweaked history with the skill of politicians. In other words, they completely ignored the actual truth in favour of a story that showed their side in a much better light. In the improved version of events, Kennedy, their heroic captain, had held back a tide of hungry predators single-handed as his incredibly talented crew pillaged their way through a massive treasure ship. The last monster, easily the size of a house, with its only vulnerable point located down its throat, had died after Kennedy thrust his arm into its mouth and stabbed it in the epiglottis.

Their captain's injuries now satisfactorily re-imagined, Ellie, Urzish and Porro huddled in a corner as they moved to an even more interesting topic of conversation: the incredibly juicy Arke and Stabbington saga. Their argument, followed by the kiss which Sparkz had described to the first mate in glorious technicolour, was also quickly embellished. Ellie's favourite version involved a tropical downpour, a barefoot dash across the puddled deck and finally a reunion so passionate that even the raindrops stopped to watch; followed by Arke knifing the ogre in the ribs because, well – Arke. They were all so inspired by the intense interpersonal drama happening right on their own ship that Porro's suggestion of writing a book was immediately seized on with great excitement. A new pot of coffee was made, and the epic novel began with a single line: 'Having killed men just for looking at her, the only person who could break her heart was the demon that owned her soul.'

In truth, Arke wasn't emotionally scarred after a torrid romp in the rain, she was just physically and mentally exhausted. Although she'd had a good few hours of Gurdi-induced sleep, as she lay on her own bed only the throbbing of her leg was keeping her even slightly awake. Irash, on the other hand, appeared to be full of energy, wanting to talk about the flotilla fight in far greater detail than his host. To Arke, a battle was only interesting while you were in it. She was not a fan of de-briefs or lengthy glorious re-tellings. Finally giving up on getting any sort of conversation out of her, her passenger asked to read some more stories like the one she'd told on the imp ship. That proved to be a great idea until his host nodded off with the first chapter barely even begun. Irash sighed heavily, loudly and pointlessly, as Arke was already fast asleep.

※ ※ ※

STABBINGTON, THE OTHER half of the new book's power couple, was absolutely-not-hiding in the hold, where he sat in the darkest corner he could find and occasionally held one-sided conversations with the crystal jaguar who was locked up behind an exceptionally sturdy door nearby.

It was a couple of days after the flotilla battle when he finally revealed his location to Ruby on her twice daily trip to feed her most reluctant pet.

"That is not a good choice of companion."

Stabbington-Krugg's voice was very loud in the confines of the hold and the deeply surprised Ruby flew upwards with a start, hitting her head on the ceiling with a painful thud.

"Ow. What are you doing down here in the dark, Stabbington?"

There was just a long heavy sigh in reply.

"I know about the Arke thing. Do you want to talk about it?"

"No."

This was new, and Ruby cocked her head to one side. Previously the demon had been all too ready to spend hours bemoaning his lot. However, since it was his choice not to talk, she carried on with what she was doing, opening the door to the crystal-coated beast and slipping slowly inside. Right at the back of the room she could see the cat hiding behind some barrels and hear it growling menacingly at her.

"It's OK, Kevan." She'd been trying out various names for her new pet to see what stuck, as she thought it might be harder for the others to kill the creature if she humanised him a little. She carefully slid the bowl she'd brought with her across the floor and stepped back. "I'll bring more later."

The jaguar stopped growling for a moment as it sniffed its meal suspiciously, then began again, nervously shifting its position as she slipped back out and locked the door.

"At least come up on deck, it's a lovely sunny afternoon." Ruby's kind heart would not let her walk away from the demon without one more try.

"I will stay here, where it is dark, and I will not see

her and that is good."

"Stabbington's here?" Ellie suddenly appeared in the doorway to the hold. "I had money on him being in the bilges. Didn't figure he'd let the new guy win that easily, he's out there with Arke right now, laughing, talking away together. Creeps me out but hey, whatever works for her. I thought I was wild, but I never had the new guy throw the old one out. That was straight up savage."

During what she thought was the most bizarrely inappropriate monologue, Ruby hurried over to her crewmate, frantically trying to get her to be quiet. When she'd finished speaking, Ellie grabbed the Ornithol by the arm and tugged her away, keeping silent until they reached the main deck.

"I give him five minutes, ten if he has a wash."

"What?" Ruby was baffled. "And Arke's not out here?"

"Of course she isn't… yet!" The first mate's eyes were sparkling with mischief.

The evil genius of Ellie's plan dawned on Ruby as she watched the halfling talking to Arke at her cabin door. It took mere seconds of conversation to transform the Soulbound's bleary-eyed weariness to adrenalin-fuelled rage. Slamming her door with extra verve, she stormed out onto deck and to Ruby's dismay, limped straight towards her and let loose.

"KAYLA was at the flotilla? Gorki's lapdog Kayla, pointy ears, pointy spear, pouty lips? And Kennedy told her to come on a ride along? What were you all THINKING? Ellie's just said that the only reason the red-headed bitch didn't stay on the *Warrior* was the stench coming from the forward head… I will never complain about Urzish's lactose intolerance again! But Kayla should never have been on board in the first place! Have any of you checked for ginger transmitted diseases? At the very least disinfected the decks? And oh yeah, totally NOT important but has anyone made sure she hasn't stolen anything, left a bomb or some shitty magic trap? Why don't we just go back to the flotilla and let them blow us up, save Kayla a job?"

"Ah." Ruby knew she'd made a sound in reply but she honestly wasn't sure what to say in the face of the Soulbound's unusually verbose fury.

Staring her friend right in the face, Arke bellowed her orders so loudly that the Ornithol's sensitive ears started to hurt. "ELLIE, turn out the crew to sweep every single compartment. By sweep, I mean search, scratch, sniff, seek, scrutinise, shakedown, survey, study, scan and scour."

The expression on the first mate's face was almost gleeful as she tolled the muster bell and while the crew began to gather by the wheel, Arke limped down the narrow walkway that led around the outside of the cabins to the stern, frowning as she concentrated on trying to locate any trace of unexpected magic.

If Ruby had owned a watch, she would have noted that Stabbington-Krugg emerged on the deck precisely nine minutes and thirty-seven seconds after they had left him in the hold. He'd washed and was wearing cleanish clothes as he looked around the deck, shading his eyes from the sun. From where he stood it was impossible for him to see Arke, but Ruby knew with mounting discomfort that it wouldn't be many moments before the inevitable happened. Ellie had primed them both for an explosive reunion and all that was needed was for Arke to walk back around the corner and bump straight into him.

The mustered crew were all watching expectantly, the first mate bouncing on the balls of her feet with triumphant mischief. Ruby quickly made up her mind and set off across the deck to intercept her friend before something awful happened. However, she hadn't taken more than a few steps when two new players entered the scene, completely ruining Ellie's scheme and causing Ruby to raise her eyes to the skies and murmur a heartfelt prayer to Chromatia. One crisis was in the process of being averted. Only one more to go.

⚔ ⚔ ⚔

"WHY IS THIS so difficult!" Kennedy's voice rolled onto the deck just before the top of his head appeared from the hatch.

Sparkz was second to appear, positioned under his brother's good arm, his expression both strained with exertion and distinctly exasperated. "Gurdi said to go up backwards, but no, you know best."

"Captain!" Ellie beamed with genuine pleasure as everyone watched his slow, painful progress out into the sunshine.

"I thought it would be easier, I used to bounce everywhere when I was a kid. Why is it so hard now?" Kennedy asked breathlessly.

"Because you're twenty years too late to play hopscotch?" Sparkz muttered.

The unusually pale looking Kennedy almost botched his next jump, banging his bandaged leg on the top step as his brother hauled him up. "Owww, bastard thing."

"You've just got out of sickbay after being mauled by mangy sharks and the FIRST thing you want to do is climb stairs. Who could have foreseen the difficulty?" Sparkz was breathing heavily after doing his best to keep his charge upright as Klaus, one arm in a sling, trotted up the stairs behind them.

Handing Kennedy the crutch he'd been carrying, the Tiax hurried to Ellie and pressed some florins into her hand. "Gurdi says ten feet."

"Ten feet?" Kennedy settled the crutch awkwardly on his good side and looked over at his crew with a curious expression.

The first mate shrugged nonchalantly. "Yeah, once she got that thing out of the stores, we started the book on how far you'd get the first time you used it. I've got you down for twenty."

"Your faith is nothing but inspiring. Ten florins say that I'm going to make it to…"

As a distracted looking Arke walked around the corner of the captain's cabin, her eyes first fell on the transfixed crew and then onto Kennedy. He might have been pale, sweaty and distinctly blotchy, but as he saw her, a bright smile split his face.

"To Arke. Hold tight folks, I'm about to rock it."

Letting go of Sparkz, he started to dot and carry himself forwards, trying to put all his weight on his good leg and crutch, with only the tiniest of toe touches from his injured one. It was clearly painful, awkward and probably very unwise, but he was accustomed to every one of those three words and determined to win the bet.

Kennedy saw Arke frown as he wobbled towards her, trying to work out the best placement for the crutch as well as what length of stride was most efficient. Every time he put too much weight on his bandaged leg he cringed and had to stop for a moment, pursing his lips with pain. To begin with, he halted every tiny step, but as he found more of a style and rhythm, Kennedy grew in speed and confidence. There were only a few feet left to cover when overconfidence hit and he nearly toppled after taking too large a stride.

"Flip!" Arke leapt forwards, ready to catch him.

Kennedy just managed to steady himself in time. "No! I'm OK. Back to where you were, I've got money on this."

She stepped away, watching anxiously as he made his way across the last few feet without error. As he stood in front of her, sweating, pale, and vaguely dizzy, she quickly ducked under his arm while he raised a wobbly crutch triumphantly in the air.

The crew erupted riotously, shouting, cheering and whistling, all dramas forgotten in the excitement of seeing their captain's victory over his shark related adversity, the surprise of seeing Arke's face brighten with a wide smile, and the reveal of what had to be Kennedy's childhood nickname.

He ducked to speak directly into Arke's ear. "You haven't called me Flip since I was tiny."

She shrugged and helped him into the armchair that Sparkz had carried over from the captain's cabin before gesturing to Ellie to get the crew moving on the search, seek and smell tour. Kennedy narrowed his eyes at her unusual behaviour; even when she was in command, the Soulbound simply did not run drills or find things for the crew to do other than their normal duties. And the way they were scouring the deck was absolutely nothing like a normal duty.

"So, what *is* everyone doing?" he queried.

"Oh, you noticed? Well done you."

Kennedy didn't need to see Arke's face to hear the sarcasm that dripped from her words. With a brow that furrowed deeper with each passing second, he watched as she pointed an imperious finger at Ruby who appeared to be making herself as small as possible in the background.

"Is there something wrong?"

Arke put her hands on her hips and turned around to face him, her smile distinctly chilling. "You – tell – me."

Behind her, Ruby walked slowly across the deck while trying to spell something out with her fingers. However, no matter how hard Kennedy and Sparkz tried to decipher her desperate efforts to pass them a silent message, they remained utterly clueless.

Turning to skewer the Ornithol and her hand movements with a dour stare, Arke raised a terrifying eyebrow. "Do you need medical assistance? Or has that cat thing given you fleas?"

Shaking her head quickly, Ruby's short and embarrassing career in sign language came to an end. She scurried over to stand by Kennedy who offered her a reassuring smile.

"I'm sure it's fine."

He soon learnt that it was not, in fact, fine. Not even close. Arke allowed a long and disappointed stare to wash over each of them in turn before speaking again.

"I think that the three of you need to work out *where*

you put your communal brain cell because it's pretty obviously missing." She sighed heavily, pinching the bridge of her nose with frustration. "So, was there any particular reason that you tried to recruit *Kayla?* Or sent her to the *Warrior* when you weren't even here? And why didn't any of you bother checking what she'd been up to when you got back?"

Letting her words sink in for a moment, Kennedy scratched at his stubble and wondered if it was too late to pass out or call dramatically for Gurdi who would probably defend him better than he could himself. Then he realised he had an ace in his deck and threw it on the table with what he hoped was a flourish.

"I was nearly dead." He gestured to his bandages with a boyish blink of his big blue eyes.

The Soulbound leant forwards, settling her hands on the arms of his chair as she went eyeball to eyeball with him. Her voice was quiet, icy, and utterly terrifying as she stared into what felt like his soul. "I can always help you go one better if you don't tell me how, and more importantly, WHY this all happened."

After a moment, she stood back, crossing her arms as the three conspirators looked at each other guiltily. Finally, Sparkz started talking, explaining about Kayla's visit to Mr Crimbles' vessel. Possibly wisely, given the expression on Arke's face, he only recounted the rough gist of the conversation, leaving out the inflammatory remarks that she'd made about the Soulbound.

"And did *none* of you think it was a bit of an odd coincidence that she arrived at the flotilla *exactly* when you did?"

"Of course! But with everything that's happened

since, I completely forgot." Sparkz looked Arke directly in the eye as he spoke, and the others were quick to agree with his statement.

She shook her head exasperatedly and turned away, muttering distinctly uncomplimentary things about all of them.

"Can I go and help the others search now? Please?" Ruby sounded understandably keen to slip away from the frosty atmosphere.

"I'll check in engineering and let you know if there's anything there."

Sparkz wasn't the type to ask permission and as he headed below, the Ornithol quickly followed him.

"I think she was looking for you," Kennedy said quietly, his eyes fixed on the Soulbound. "It was more than just personal. Have you searched our cabins yet?"

"Mine's clean; yours is next on my list. Enjoy the sunshine."

Chapter Twenty-Two

Break Out the Crayons

I T TOOK A good ten minutes of looking around the captain's cabin, putting a hand on every surface and wall, checking under the bed, in every drawer, behind the cupboards, before Arke found it: the item that explained much but changed everything. As she looked under the chart table she froze, pursing her lips as she forced a sudden burst of nausea away. A flat, brown gemstone was wedged underneath the tabletop, its surface entirely covered with deeply carved runes. It was too dusty and cobwebbed to have been put there during Kayla's most recent visit, so it wasn't what she'd been looking for, but it was what she'd needed to find. Although she hadn't seen many, she knew what she was looking at: a monitoring device. Every word that had been spoken in the cabin since it had been put there had been transmitted to someone else.

She left the room abruptly, shutting the doors behind her, her face an impenetrable mask. It took five minutes of standing rigidly at the railing before she spotted an unsuspecting seagull soaring nearby and obliterated it in a very unsporting contest of feathers versus roiling ball of death.

"You were wrong, Irash; that didn't make me feel better even when I pictured it as Kayla." Arke scowled and turned from watching the last tiny feather blow away on the breeze to see that Kennedy was asleep in his armchair. Limping over to him, she sat leaning against the chair's cushioned side, taking a few moments to rearrange her thoughts when Irash started to speak, his tone heavy.

"I didn't want to believe you when you said that people would want to use me, but I am able to admit that you were correct. That device was not newly placed, but I would guess it has been there since you took the job that led to me. After our days in that room, whoever was listening could not fail to know you are my vessel, but when you moved to the imp ship, they lost track of you. Then suddenly this Kayla appears with no explanation or obvious purpose other than asking about you. She was apparently desperate enough to force herself onto your ship to look for you, even while knowing you have my power at your fingertips. What is it that your people say? The noose is tightening."

"They also say if it looks like a trap and smells like a trap then it's not just a stray puppy in a box, it's probably also a landmine."

"You've been around some deviants," Irash remarked. "I'm almost impressed."

"Don't be. That puppy lived a long and happy life, unlike the scum that put him there." Arke felt the warmth of deep satisfaction at one of the memories she'd chosen not to lock away.

Her passenger sighed heavily, his mood clearly too heavy to be uplifted by the egregiously violent recollection that his host allowed him to see. "My traitorous worshippers imprisoned me to make use of my powers; I've only been free a few days and now more people want to do the same." He paused before grinding his words out with angry frustration. "How would you like being

Destiny's Boot

treated as a commodity? A thing that is only valued for what it can be forced to do?"

Matching him fury for fury, Arke's raw reply was the entire, painful truth. "Are you kidding me? I'm a *woman* in possession of demon *magic* who's lived in *Barsia* most of her life; I know *exactly* what it's like!" She rubbed her face with a hand and deliberately moderated her tone before continuing. "But you either get caught or learn to stay uncaught, so after all these years I'm a bloody expert in freedom." Quickly checking that her outburst hadn't awoken Kennedy, she made herself comfortable and started to problem solve. "They've heard our plans so let's use that to our advantage; they think we're going to take the orbiculum to Barry the Stump because he's the nearest mage who'll do anything for cash. Turns out starting your own cult gets expensive when the only people who join are smarter than you. Actually, thinking about it, maybe I'll retire to their island one day. Barry is an excellent chef even if he's the least-charismatic spiritual leader since that hairy old guy in Soleya tried to god-it-up wearing a mankini. Aaaanyway…"

She scrubbed her fingers through her hair, making it stand up in utter disarray before flattening it again with a dismissive palm.

"We've discussed going to Barry often enough in the captain's cabin, they'll definitely know that's our plan. We can make sure they still think we're going to get him to work the orbiculum for us, so they concentrate their resources in that direction. That'll buy some time and I can get more by sending an *imp*udent little present to whoever is waiting for us at his island, but long term I'm struggling with how to get you back to your plane before they catch up to us. We can't go to Nidea; you'd be shut in a little lamp and spirited away before anyone could even ask for a wish. So, it's Barsia or bust – but there aren't many high-level mages around. The number of those who'd let us find them is even smaller, and those who'd risk their lives by opening a rift between worlds is probably somewhere south of five. If I were Gorki, I'd be laughing right now, as it wouldn't take much to have a team watching every renegade arcanist in the empire."

"How does such deviousness come from such ignorant beings?" Irash sighed expressively. "And you would not be laughing, for you do not wish to enslave anyone. You would do what you have done this time; for all that your roots are in the dark, your head is in the light. I have enjoyed our time together."

"It's not over yet. I stand by what I said before, sometimes you can win just by not losing. Give me the word and we'll go to Plan B; I know it's a massive step, but you were the one who suggested it. And honestly, it's the best 'screw you' to that two-faced little prick I have ever heard. Letting go doesn't mean giving up – it just means that you take another path..." Arke's words tailed off as a memory hit her. She turned her hand over, scrutinising the odd scar on her palm, the result of the strange self-healing cut she'd obtained from hurling Stabbington's scabbard.

There was a brief snort of derision from her passenger. "You are FINALLY wondering about that? It has protected you from me more than your pathetic demon ever did."

"A scar?"

Irash was incredulous. "Unbelievable stupidity. Tell

me again why I'd want to live among you idiots?"

✕ ✕ ✕

WHEN KENNEDY WOKE from his sun-drenched sleep, Arke handed him a bottle of Gurdi's medicine, the taste of which made him grimace, and a cup of strong coffee to distract his palate. She waited until he'd finished before sitting on the arm of his chair, telling him about the listening device in his cabin and the radical new plan she had agreed with her passenger.

"And he's sure?" Kennedy asked, rubbing his forehead slowly. He was used to Arke's chaotic ideas and wild clutches, but this was so far out of left field, not even the giant cyclops fly with its multi-faceted eye ten foot across could have seen it coming.

"Yes. If we find the right body Irash will transfer permanently into it. According to him, the energy he will need to expend in the transition will drain him of most of his powers; after that happens he's both well-hidden and much less of a commodity. Given what we're up against, not losing is pretty much still winning."

"He'll be mortal?" Kennedy frowned, searching Arke's face for any hint that she was being manipulated by the entity inside her. "Do you believe him?"

She nodded. "I do, he's changed a lot since we met him; we talked a lot about it after I moved to the imp ship – being alive, having a body, pros and cons." A flicker of amusement suddenly lit her expression. "I guess if you've never had one, it's quite enticing in a lot of ways."

"What did you tell him? Actually, forget I asked as I'm pretty sure that I don't want to know." Kennedy shook his head slowly. A wry smile played on his lips, but that disappeared quickly as a sudden thought came to him. "So, the flotilla fight was a waste of time?"

"Blowing shit up is never a waste of time, and without going there we wouldn't have found out that they were listening." Arke tapped the top of his head with a finger. "For the record, I'm glad you're OK, even if Ruby's new pet has more brain cells."

"You'd better be glad, who else would put up with you?" Kennedy shut his eyes, rubbing a hand over his heavy stubble as he considered. "It's been a wild ride ever since High Haven, I won't deny I'm looking forward to getting back to simple looting and pillaging." He looked up at her with a decisive nod. "Let's get this party started. Bring me a chart, I don't want to waste any time getting your passenger a new home."

⚔ ⚔ ⚔

ARKE'S LIPS WERE pursed in a thin line as she released her 'fire and forget' secret weapon. She'd christened the imp ship *Surprise,* and in the absence of fizzy wine for the naming ceremony, she'd simply sloshed some of the imps' putrid coffee onto its bows instead. Standing alone at the rail, she watched the small vessel with its roughly patched battle scars fly into the afternoon haze at full speed, its *Warrior* flag flying proudly.

Her final meeting with the infernals had gone very well. They'd been unexpectedly excited and extremely motivated as soon as she'd outlined their part in her plan. Kennedy had supplied the heading which would take them to 'meet' Gorki's men who were doubtless waiting for them at the atoll. Eyes glittering and teeth almost chattering in anticipation, they'd assured her that as long as this 'meet' was full of potential meat, they'd love to go. The proposed delights of a large platter of murder and mayhem had created some rather unsettling salivary responses from the excited imps, but Arke just managed to avoid bringing back her lunch by pointing out the main downside of the mission. However, none of them seemed to care that it was probably a one-way trip, and the coffee monitor had cheerfully reminded her that in the event of any life-negating experience, they would be reconstituted back on their home plane. They would miss her stories, however.

Despite Irash pouring scorn on her actions, Arke had afforded the little infernals full respect for their services past and future. She had spent a good while with each of them, making sure they could get out of their harnesses to fight and explaining repeatedly that the *Surprise* had to be kept on its heading for three days before they'd get to their destination. Their rowdy cheers had rung out as the ropes were cast off and the powerful engine burst into life, while Arke's creepy coffee monitor stood proudly at the wheel, waving as they left.

"You wasted your breath, they're not going to do what you want, they're *imps*," Irash hissed and then paused, taking a moment to assess his host's mood. "What? You're sad? So you won't kiss an ogre but you'll shake hands with filthy infernals?"

Arke's eyes flashed with sudden, uncontrollable rage and she slammed her hand hard on the rail, opening her mouth to drop a multilingual barrage of vicious curses. The words never even got to her lips as the instant she hit the wood, a bright orange bolt of something magical shot from her palm, hitting the deck with a crackle. Anger dissipating as rapidly as it had arrived, she looked down in wide-eyed shock as a three foot square section around her erupted in orange fire, the flames high enough to engulf her boots.

"Irash! What did you do?" she hissed, quickly using his power to quench the mini inferno before checking around to see if anyone had noticed, but to her relief the only two people on deck, Urzish and Giro, had their backs to her. Both were over by the wheel, busy checking the course Kennedy had set and beginning to turn the *Warrior* slowly to the northwest.

"Prompted a little emotion." Irash laughed softly, deeply amused with her inability to see what was incredibly obvious to him.

"This isn't funny!" Arke looked at her hand once more, scrutinising the scar on her palm with rising horror. "There's another line on it now! Stop laughing and tell me what's going on!"

"I've given you hints; I've told you where to look. Do you need me to draw a picture?"

"Fine, if you won't tell me, I'm going to cut it out." Arke pulled her dagger from its scabbard.

"Let me find my crayons."

✕ ✕ ✕

IT WAS A voyage of discovery for all the crew as they flew towards the city of Theogenes in search of a willing recipient for Irash's consciousness. Ruby learnt that crystal jaguars were tricky to tame and needed three litter boxes completely cleaned out daily, but when they were happy, their opaque armour relaxed into super soft, deep fur and they purred like rusty metal. Kennedy learnt about patience, about trusting his body to heal itself and about not skipping any magical healing potions

Gurdi made him, no matter how foul they tasted. Sparkz learnt about personal flight machines and how much faster they were than using mere magic to fly with. He also became painfully aware how difficult it was to land them without smashing yourself into the deck.

The new crew members learnt all about the *Warrior* way of life and slotted into the pecking order with only a few attempted stabbings. The old crew absolutely did not learn to stop trying to create drama, but they did learn the consequences of it the day Ellie pushed Stabbington-Krugg too far with her pointed comments and he simply threw her overboard. Sparkz had been giving his new winged backpack a test run when he saw the first mate soaring into the air and heard Stabbington roar, "Flap your arms like you flap your mouth and you will fly just fine!" After that experience, the halfling agreed that it was wiser not to tease the demon-possessed ogre anymore, concluding that boredom was way better than death.

And Arke? Arke learnt too much.

Irash's simple lesson with crayons turned into an appointment with the headmaster. The information he imparted was brief and should have been instantly life changing. But he was talking to Arke, and she did not take the news well, or to begin with, *at all.*

His revelation that her entire self was infused with a unique form of magic – untameable, unquenchable, and unpredictable, was flatly and completely rebutted. Irash's description (also utterly denied) of this most unusual power, included the observation that she'd never seen it before because it had been locked away within her and only released when she lost control of her emotions back in the captain's cabin. The fleeting alteration of her senses she'd experienced had been a result of the magic surging into every part of her, briefly disrupting her entire body as it spread. She refused that explanation too. Her astonishingly stubborn disbelief roused him to frustrated fury.

"Yes, tell Irash that he was not witness to your feral magic's rage as it escaped its prison inside you. Tell the being who felt its burn when it leapt to protect you that it does not exist! Tell him it is not at the heart of you when he is watching its tides ebb and flow with feelings you can no longer control or conceal. You hide behind your own face, but I am here too, and I *see* you and all these festering memories you refuse to confront. Start thinking, and if that's too difficult for your mortal brain, join the dots instead! Someone put this orange flood within you, hid it away with such power even I could not find it until it found me. Something is coming, Arke, something not even you can run from. I do not know what and I do not know why. But I do know that you can choose. Do nothing and let it feed on your past, your guilt, and your pain, let it trample you to dust. Or look with eyes that want to see, make peace with what cannot be changed, and step out from behind your mask. Keep on cursing me if you like, I am watching your magic react to every single word, this very *real* magic that you refuse to acknowledge. It's volatile, stubborn, and elemental, so were you made for it, or it for you? You claim your demon has shaped *you* in *his* image? Look again and look properly. You have *always* been who you are."

341

Chapter Twenty-Three
Get to the Point

THE WEATHER HAD turned distinctly cloudy as the *Warrior* flew on, drizzle coating the deck in a slick film and mist clinging dankly to everything. Even gaining altitude in the hope of finding some clear air proved useless, as all they found was colder perma-rain. The only benefit from any of the miserable weather was that they were well hidden from any prying eyes as they headed towards the city of Theogenes.

Eyes, yes. Other things – say for example, undetected magical tracking devices – not so much. Devices that gave well-armed ships with violence on their agendas the *Warrior's* exact position no matter what the weather.

Dawn was only just pushing its way across the misty horizon when a cannon boomed and its shot flashed across the *Warrior's* deck, narrowly missing the starboard wing. Reacting quickly despite the shock of a surprise attack, Ellie slammed her hand on the general alarm and threw the ship into a dive, trying to gain enough speed to outrun whatever was attacking them. The *Warrior* was fast and manoeuvrable, but built to attack, not defend. A second cannonball crashed solidly into the hull, smashing its way into the hold, a shower of splinters exploding around the impact and falling away into the clouds below. At the helm, the first mate didn't even flinch, her concentration fully on the controls as she slowly eased the engine speed levers into the red zone.

The crystal didn't like to be rushed but she could feel the timbers beneath her feet starting to throb with a deeper rhythm as the power flowing to the engine increased.

The rest of the crew were still throwing themselves out of bed, grabbing their weapons and heading to battle stations when Arke strode across the deck. Water droplets were already tangling their way through her silver hair and running down her cheeks as she took stock of the situation with a sweeping glance.

"Where and what?"

"Port quarter. Flying bloody squirrels firing bastard nuts for all I know, can't see shit in this weather." Ellie scowled, her hands gripping the wheel tightly.

Arke opened her telescope, training it in the direction the first mate had indicated. It took a worryingly short time for their pursuers to fly close enough to become visible through the clouds. Two well-armed frigates were bearing down on them from the port side, one astern of the other. Neither bore any insignia and the misty rain obscured any crew uniform, but it could not obscure the fact that they were effortlessly keeping up with the *Warrior* as it dived away.

More cannonballs were fired from the bow chasers of the pursuing ships, one narrowly missing the captain's cabin before dropping away into the murky air. Ruby and Sparkz appeared on deck with the rest of the crew as Arke snapped the scope shut. She pointed at them as she walked backwards to the helm.

"MAKE SMOKE!"

"Can't you just click your fingers or something?" Kennedy appeared at the hatch, having finally made it up the stairs with his crutch, empty coat sleeve flapping.

The Soulbound looked at him with exasperation. "You're supposed to be in sick bay."

"We're being attacked!"

"I hadn't noticed," Arke replied dryly as a cannon ball flew past her before ricocheting off the sloping deck, splinters flying in a shower around the impact. "Ellie, they've got their range – evasive manoeuvres!" She strode across to Kennedy, keeping her voice low as she explained. "Irash is still recovering from the flotilla battle, I need to save him for emergencies, and *you* need to get below."

"But…"

The *Warrior* swooped sharply to starboard, and Kennedy nearly lost his footing. Arke grabbed his shirt to hold him in place. "GO! I can't worry about you as well as the ship."

With a reluctant nod, he acquiesced. "If you need me…" He started back down the stairs to the lower decks, Gabbi quickly ducking under his arm to assist him.

As she strode to the wheel, Arke was grimly satisfied to see that Urzish had taken over from Ellie who had scurried below to get her armour and weapons. The orc had many more years of experience at evading pursuers and was effortlessly using the very basic metal arm Zeke had made her to turn the wheel while expertly adjusting their trim with her remaining hand.

"One hundred and ten percent speed. Do I level us out?"

Cannon balls erupted through the magical smokescreen which was being created by Sparkz and Ruby. The Ornithol was wielding her magic fire producing ring which was creating copious amounts of acrid smoke as the rain hit the flames, while Sparkz was firing blasts of pyrotechnics from his wrist tattoo, aiming them to burst in the *Warrior's* wake and add to Ruby's homemade clouds.

More shots whistled narrowly past the *Warrior* and Arke's frown deepened. The smokescreen was already impressive and she knew it should be nearly impossible for the enemy to lay accurate fire on them as they twisted and turned through the sky. Should be, but clearly wasn't. Their attackers were still eerily accurate. Something was very wrong, and she made her decision quickly. If defence was impossible, there was only one option left.

"Bring her nose up," she ordered. "And charge the lance."

"But they're behind us?" Urzish looked over with a quizzical glance before her eyes widened in horrified realisation. "No, Arke. No, no, no, no, no! It was a stupid idea last time, and it's even stupider to try without something to tether to. I don't want to break another ship."

"I've got Irash this time. Be ready."

The orc almost swore that the Soulbound winked at her before ducking into the lance control room to start the arming procedure. However, there was no time to contemplate anything as another cannonball scorched across the deck, a glancing impact throwing Volk into the air and smashing him in an unconscious heap against the captain's cabin. Urzish threw the ship hard to starboard and then straightened her up again in a desperate effort to throw the enemy's gunnery off target.

"Sparkz, I need you on the lance." Arke hurried to

join him and Ruby, a coil of rope now slung over her shoulder.

"The – lance?"

"Yes, it's the thing at the front of the ship that blasts shiny light. Ring any bells?"

"But the enemy's behind us?" Ruby looked at Arke in confusion.

"Not for long."

"What?" Neither woman had seen Sparkz look nervous before but the anxious crackle in his voice was more than telling as he tried to balance what he knew with what Arke might be capable of. "You should know better than anyone that ships do not fly upside down no matter how much you want them to."

With what she thought passed for a comforting smile, Arke explained her plan. "Of course they don't. We're just going to drift this baby around; I want you to open fire as you bear, hit whatever you can."

Cannonballs flew overhead, still straddling the ship despite the heavy smokescreen.

"Just? We're JUST going to drift the ship? While we're at what, one hundred and fifteen percent power? How? And how aren't we going to die?" Sparkz was clearly wishing he'd never studied physics, knowing that then he'd be oblivious to his imminent demise at the hands of a certifiable lunatic.

"Magic for the win." Arke slapped him on the shoulder with a grin before turning to Ruby. "Keep the smoke going until we start the turn."

As the unmistakeable noise of the lance charging grew louder, Sparkz scurried into the control booth while Arke strode towards the stern, passing the word

346

for everyone to hold on tight as she went. The best form of defence was always offense, and no matter how they were managing to target the *Warrior*, wrecked ships couldn't fire cannons.

"Here should be about right." She tied one end of her rope to the rear mooring cleat before throwing the rest of it over the side. "Irash, it'd be a lot easier if I could think about it happening rather than having to use the hands-on approach. Are you sure you aren't just trying to kill me?"

"If I was there would be more mess and considerably fewer steps. Get down the rope; a direct application of magic has a much higher likelihood of success given my current lack of energy." Irash was nothing if not practical and amused himself by letting his host into some of his more murderous musings.

"Should I be flattered you've spent so much time thinking about my death?" Arke had to listen to her passenger's dastardly chuckling as she climbed over the railings and grabbed the rope, easing herself down until she was positioned midway between deck and keel.

Trying to ignore both Irash and the raking wind that buffeted her against the hull, she placed her hand against the ship and began to draw on his power. At first it was just a ripple, the wood pitting under her fingers as she infused the entire vessel with a protective coating of magic; and then as she called forth a flood, her touch boomed against the rear section of the hull and started to push the stern around. The stabilising wings threatened to buckle under the intense pressures as the ship slewed and drifted but were held together by the crackling grey layer of power that buffered the vessel against the incredible forces exerted on it. Then, as if the lights were suddenly turned on, the *Warrior* outmanoeuvred its own smokescreen, her bows coming around to a perfect firing position.

The sudden silencing of the ominous rumble of power beneath the decks was always the precursor to the blinding beam of energy blasting from the aetheric weapon at the *Warrior's* bowsprit. Sparkz's aim was brutally accurate, ripping into the first enemy and slicing it open from bow to stern as his ship kept turning until she finished her one-hundred-and-eighty-degree arc.

As its partner started to fall out of the sky, the second attacker responded by firing a rippling broadside as the *Warrior* came into sight. Arke heard the cannon fire as she climbed back on board and ran up towards the main deck, preparing to use what little energy Irash had left to deflect any incoming missiles. This salvo was the only chance the attackers were going to have as their ship would take time to turn, and hopefully by then the *Warrior* would be a long way ahead. She just had to keep her ship in the air with the damage to a minimum and they'd be home free.

Sprinting up the deck, Arke suddenly slowed and stopped as she saw the crew. Saw every single member of the crew frozen to the spot. Saw the cannonballs which were just about to impact the ship hanging uselessly in mid-air. Realised just how utterly silent everything was.

"Irash?" She moved to check Gabbi who was crouching beside Volk with a *Just Say Go* in his hand. He was warm and alive but she couldn't feel a heartbeat, nor did he blink or react in any way to any stimuli.

"Some sort of chronomancy. Time has simply

stopped for most of them," Irash explained. "Impotent against me, of course."

Ignoring his arrogance in favour of making her negative feelings on time-based magic exceptionally clear, Arke looked into the clouds around the ship to where she could just see a very slight distortion in the horizon that seemed to extend all around them in a sphere.

"By that I meant that my power also protected you from it. You're welcome, by the way," Irash added in case she hadn't appreciated his contribution.

"Where is it coming from?" Arke had no time for his ego.

"Below decks, somewhere in the centre of the ship."

He had barely finished his sentence before she was running down the stairs, leaping the last four steps and hurrying down the corridor. "Tell me where."

Her passenger's directions were precise and as she lunged towards the half-open door of the sickbay, her hands tingling with magic, ready to deal with whatever was in there, she heard a voice from inside the room which stopped her in her tracks.

"Arke, before you come in blasting I'm going to tell you about this little drop of something that I just fed to your precious Captain Kennedy. He is pretty cute, by the way, so it would be a real shame if I didn't get to use the spell that stops the potion from killing him the *instant* the time freeze ends. That's a long-winded way of saying – 'he's going to die unless you give me the chalice'. The choice is yours."

As Kayla's voice rang out from the infirmary, Arke's expression stayed immobile. The only movement she made was an automatic but futile attempt to grip her absent sword hilt.

"Nothing to say? Am I making you sad? Poor little Kennedy with his injuries, must have hit you hard. Not as hard as him obviously, he looks quite worn out."

In Arke's head, Irash began talking quickly. "She holds a commanding position, her plan is well thought out. The chronomantic spell is strong while I am currently – not. However, if you fight her, I believe that with my help, however limited, you would prevail."

"And if I do, what about Kennedy?"

The voice in her head was ominously silent.

"Still listening, Arke?" Kayla continued, her voice more authoritative. "Here's how this is going to work. I have a box in front of me. You will place the chalice in it before shutting and locking the lid – then you will step away. Once that is done, I will neutralise the poison. If you do anything but exactly what I say, then he will die."

"Letting go does not mean giving up." The Soulbound's voice was hushed. "I will get you back, I promise."

With a long exhalation of breath, Arke pushed the door open. As she walked slowly into the infirmary, she felt Irash's understanding wash over her. They both knew there was absolutely nothing that she wouldn't do to save Kennedy's life.

The *Warrior's* captain was sitting in a chair, perfectly frozen, a worried expression on his face as his hand gripped the arm of the chair so hard his knuckles were white. Kayla, her red hair neatly plaited and a confident smile on her lips, was standing behind him and she watched Arke enter the room before raising her right hand to reveal a tiny, empty bottle.

The Soulbound's eyes burnt hotly but Kayla's were cool and calm as they traded glares for a long moment. Finally breaking the stare-off, the elf looked meaningfully to the treatment table where an open wooden box was sitting. It appeared to be heavily warded inside and out, clearly ready to nullify the power of Irash's vessel and Arke felt her own frustrations building as she looked at the container, then back up to her adversary.

"You don't know what you're doing. Irash isn't who you think he is."

"Box."

"He's not a thing to be harnessed or used."

"You have no idea what *it* is. Make your decision, the clock is ticking, metaphorically speaking."

"*He*. And *he* isn't a commodity for your disgusting boss to enslave." Arke unbuttoned her jacket so she could open her shirt and ease the chalice from where it nestled uncomfortably against her side. "And so we're perfectly clear, I WILL be getting *him* back."

"Maybe you *are* getting soft in your old age. *Box*."

Arke reluctantly slid the chalice inside the waiting container. As she took her hands away, moving them to shut the lid, her world swirled nauseatingly with the sudden removal of her passenger. The room spun around her and though she could hear Kayla commanding her to finish the task, it took her an inordinate amount of time to comply. Finally, she regained enough equilibrium to do what she was told, watching the magical locks spin through combinations, clicking as the box became more and more secure. Obeying Kayla's instruction to step well away, she watched the elf put the container inside a bag which expanded to hold it and then deflated as if nothing was in it at all. As Kayla tucked her prize into a pocket under her armour she pointed to Kennedy with her other hand and hissed a few unintelligible words. A brief flicker of yellow light danced on his skin and then disappeared.

"Well, that was a painless transaction." With a dark smile, Kayla dipped her chin and raised a sardonic eyebrow, her words deliberately echoing Arke's own back in the harbourmaster's office in High Haven. "How does it feel being *totally* free of *any* possession?" She let that sink in for a moment before stepping out from behind Kennedy and smiling. "Business over. Time for pleasure." She lifted a locket from under her shirt and ran a finger over its shimmering surface before tucking it away again. "Plenty of time actually – I'm stuck here until the spell finishes, just *you* and *me*. I'll be honest, I've actually had dreams about this moment; I've had time to think about exactly what I want to do to you."

Arke wasn't in the least surprised at Kayla's dire intentions and continued buttoning her shirt back up slowly, while her eyes darted around the infirmary, noting the locations of anything that might be useful. She already knew that there was only one door to this room and Kayla was closer to it. Without Irash, without Stabbington, without weapons, with the entire crew frozen in time – she knew she had nothing but her instincts and whatever lay around her. So, in true Arke style she was coming out fighting, however one-sided that fight was going to be.

Levelling her gaze on Kayla, the Soulbound finally responded. "Have you thought about professional help?

I've heard there are some good dog trainers specialising in nasty bitches."

In instant reaction, the elf held out a hand to summon her nasty-looking spear before crossing the room in a whirl of speed and slamming the shaft across her opponent's body. As she pinned Arke to the wall, Kayla pushed in close, her dangerously narrowed eyes glinting with hatred and her voice hissing with malice.

"When I'm finished, you'll be begging me to kill you."

"Sounds like you've used that line before. Maybe on a lover? I mean your brother."

Using the brief moment of furious disconnect after her words hit home, Arke leant forwards and licked Kayla's lips, the unexpected and definitely unwanted intimacy instinctively causing the elf to recoil. As soon as the pressure on her chest was released, the Soulbound launched sideways over Gurdi's desk, grabbing a paperweight as she went. Neon yellow darts of energy from Kayla's hands flew after her, but all were the tiniest moment too late and slammed harmlessly into the wall. Without breaking her momentum, Arke threw the ornament towards Kayla's head at the same time as she rolled out from under the desk and dived for the exit.

The brightly coloured glass sphere soaring towards Kayla's face changed course mid-air, the elf magically re-directing it around her own body in a spinning swirl of colour. The extra revolution added additional velocity and with a single finger pointed at her enemy, Kayla posted the missile back to its sender. The paperweight slammed home, hitting Arke's left ankle with a solid crack, bringing her crashing heavily to the floor while the red-headed elf strode to the door and kicked it shut.

"For an infirmary, this place is pretty dangerous." Kayla looked down with a triumphant expression. She flexed her hand, yellow light sparkling from the magic she was readying in her fingertips.

Getting up slowly, Arke eased a crick from her neck and smiled. "If this isn't safe enough for you, how about I show you the morgue?"

"You – are – hilarious." Kayla's words dripped with sarcasm as she coldly slammed several neon darts into Arke's torso from close range. Her expression was darkly satisfied as she watched the impacts launch her opponent backwards over the treatment table only to slide off it on the far side and hit the floor heavily. "This is far too much fun. So, in the interests of keeping my word, I'll just pop this pretty captain of yours next door – I don't think either of us want collateral damage."

As Kennedy and his chair were teleported away, Arke was struggling to force air back into her lungs. Once she managed to heave a few breaths in, she tried to use the table to lever herself back to her feet, but a waiting Kayla smashed the paperweight down onto her hands one after the other. The crushing blows direct to her fingers made it hard not to cry out but Arke refused to make a sound. Clenching her jaw tightly as she dropped back to the floor, she tried to concentrate on anything other than the overwhelming pain. When that waned a little, she forced herself to look up and saw Kayla, elbows propped on the bed above, smiling beatifically as she watched her opponent's silent agonies.

"Must be tough without your demon to give you power." The elf examined her own fingertips one at a time, once again encouraging neon yellow sparks to jump and fizzle from the end of each one. "Do let me know when you've had enough." Spotting Arke's eyes going to the shimmering hourglass-shaped pendant around her neck, she chuckled. "So many people just look at my chest. Obviously, *you* wouldn't know what that's like, but I can assure you it's irritating when I'm so much more than my incredibly good-looking body parts. Anyway, don't even think about trying to grab this very expensive piece of arcane engineering; for a start it's not your style, whatever that is." She gestured dismissively at her enemy's usual black aesthetic. "Honestly aren't you a bit old to be emo? Some floral patterns and a blue rinse would be far more age appropriate." Carefully tucking the necklace back inside her shirt, the elf continued with gusto. "Where was I? Oh yes, this beautiful and functional piece of jewellery was created by a super paranoid mage, and she made sure that there were plenty of safeguards against sticky-fingered people like you. Can you say 'Boom'?"

While Kayla was clearly enjoying her patronising monologue, Arke had recovered enough to stretch out on the floor, aching hands positioned carefully behind her head, and legs crossed at the ankles. "I love story time; do we get cookies and milk?"

"Am I supposed to react to that?"

"Up to you, after all this is your fantasy."

Kayla flicked a glance to the cupboard on the wall above her opponent and the doors swung open as the contents flung themselves out. A pestle and mortar came first, smashing heavily on Arke's chest, quickly followed by a myriad of bowls, jugs, empty bottles and finally a large metal bedpan. Each item fell with extra speed as Kayla magically added to their momentum.

Just before the bedpan crashed on top of her, Arke's hand snapped up from underneath the pile of Gurdi's infirmary essentials and caught it. Without a word, she stood up, everything that had landed on her clattering to the floor as she turned away from Kayla and reached to put the chamber pot back on the shelf, all the while watching the room's reflection in the shiny metal.

Another barrage of neon yellow darts shot out from the elf's long fingers and Arke whirled with perfect timing, smashing them away with the back of the bedpan before holding it over her head as Kayla launched the paperweight towards her, magically shattering it mid-air, shards of glinting glass showering down and clinking as they bounced off the makeshift umbrella.

"That's Gurdi's favourite!" Arke exclaimed with almost genuine sounding anger, deftly flipping a measuring jug up with a foot and smashing it towards Kayla with the bedpan. She followed it with her more of the bowls, jugs and bottles from the floor, swiftly kicking each up into the air before thwacking them across the room. "Her mother's *eyeball* was in that!"

The elf had been easily parrying the missiles away with her spear, but the perfectly emphasised mention of the eyeball made her falter. That brief loss of concentration was just enough for her to mis-time her defence, and with a loud cracking sound, the speeding stone pestle hit Kayla square in the mouth.

There was a moment of complete stillness, almost as if the two combatants were caught in the time freeze. Then the elf spat two bloody front teeth into her hand

and threw them at Arke, lisping a furious spell as she did so. The teeth glowed neon yellow and swelled rapidly as they sped across the room. As they hit the waiting bedpan they exploded, drenching it with a hissing gel which instantly dissolved the metal into streams of silver liquid.

Kayla wasted no time following up her success by hurling her spear, but Arke was already diving away and the point hit the cabinet door, the shaft quivering with the force of the blow. The elf instantly recalled it to her hand, launching it again just as her nemesis was vaulting over Gurdi's desk. The razor-sharp tip caught the Soulbound in the top of the shoulder and carried her into the back wall, holding her there like a badly pinned specimen. Without hesitation Kayla fired dart after dart into her opponent's unprotected back, slamming her left and right with the impacts until the spear cut itself out of her shoulder and its victim slid to the floor, gasping for breath.

Chapter Twenty-Four
A Disproportionate Response

WITH SWINGINGLY TRIUMPHANT steps, Kayla sauntered around the desk, grabbing the Soulbound by the scruff and hauling her to her knees. "I just rescinded my offer – you don't get to tell me when you've had enough."

"Sorry, what?" Arke forced her words out between painful breaths. "Can't understand you without your front teeth."

Kayla brought her knee up towards her enemy's face, intending to exact a mouth-smashing revenge but as she did so, the Soulbound twisted out of her grip and grabbed her other leg, jamming her fingers hard into the back of the elf's knee. When it came to dirty combat, she was more than well-practiced; she only had to be conscious, and years of gritty experience did the rest. As Kayla's supporting leg gave way, the elf dropped to the floor, and with lightning speed Arke smacked the heel of her hand into the underside of her opponent's nose, breaking it instantly. That blow was followed equally rapidly by the top drawer of the desk as the Soulbound yanked it free and smashed it into Kayla's face. As its contents landed around them, she grabbed a fountain pen, uncapped it with her teeth and thrust it straight through the elf's cheek. With a shriek of uncontrollable pain, Kayla collapsed, eyes screwed shut as she held her face in helpless agony.

Arke's local knowledge was proving invaluable as her next move was to yank open the bottom drawer of the desk. Quickly grabbing some *Sealit Bang*, she shook it briefly before grabbing Kayla's hair to hold her still and pouring it over her eyes. The brown sealant hissed on contact and got to work immediately, sticking the elf's eyelids together and hardening like two murky monocles. Kayla's screams intensified and she rolled onto her side, fingers clawing at her face.

Utterly unmoved by her opponent's suffering, Arke grabbed a bottle of *Just Say Go*, ripping the cork out with her teeth before knocking it back with the usual shudder as the fluorescent green liquid surged through her body, healing and energising at it went. Tossing the empty bottle aside, she grabbed two doses of *Jumpstart*, yanked the caps off and poured their entire contents into her enemy's exposed ear. Disappointingly, although the new medication did result in the abrupt cessation of Kayla's high-pitched screeching, the rhythmic smacking of her head on the floor as she convulsed rather ruined the sudden peace.

Arke knew that she couldn't risk just yanking the pendant from Kayla's neck in the hope that that would put an end to the spell. 'Boom' was only a good thing when it was far away from her ship. However, the elf did have something she wanted back, and as far as the Soulbound was aware, the magical bag that held it was merely tucked into a pocket. Taking a deep breath as she watched the waves of sparks leap around the elf's body, Arke braced herself for the shocks which she knew would sting her hand the moment she made contact with a double Jumpstarted Kayla. This was her chance and for the very first time she hoped that what Irash said about this stream of power within her was right. She knew that magic would always find magic.

And magic did find magic. With a rush of warmth she couldn't explain, her cringing fingertips were drawn to her enemy's inner pocket and when she withdrew her aching hand, the small, empty-looking bag was firmly in her grasp. She had Irash back – now she needed to hide him. She knew there was no way she could open the magic locks on his box in a hurry and she wasn't going to give Kayla the chance to grab him back from her. While her opponent was still convulsing, Arke ran for the door, her mind busy with possibilities. She knew the elf's magic would doubtless be able to track the bag if she found out it was missing, so she needed to stash it somewhere incredibly safe. As the perfect solution hit her, she grinned with deep, personal satisfaction and, turning left instead of right out of the sickbay door, sprinted down the corridor to the hold.

She skidded to a halt outside the only storeroom which smelt distinctly of cat. Ruby's hand-drawn picture of her 'pet' was stuck at a jaunty angle on the door alongside a warning not to go in. Inside the room, the crystal jaguar growled menacingly as it heard her footsteps and Arke's smile grew wider. Her hunch had been right. The miserable creature didn't belong to this plane so, like Irash, it hadn't been affected by the time spell. Just outside the room was a box containing emergency meaty chunks – contingencies to distract the thing in case it got loose. Grabbing a slab of something slimy and unmentionable, Arke shoved the bag into the middle of the heap of meat and then opened the door. It was kitty dinner time.

One sniff was enough for the beast to swallow the offering whole and as Arke shut the door, sliding the latch across, her smile faded and a look of grim determination replaced it. She knew that even though the cat's magical origin would hopefully throw Kayla off the scent if she started looking, the best plan was to keep her distracted so she didn't even think to check for the bag until the time spell ended.

Getting the bad guys' attention was something Arke had never struggled with, and she headed quickly for the main stairs, making no attempt at stealth once she got past the sickbay door. Taking two steps at a time, she bounded towards the top deck, pain controlled, and energy supplied by the *Just Say Go* she'd taken back in the infirmary.

Four steps away from the hatch, Arke's progress suddenly halted as a series of impacts smashed into her lower back. Their raw power instantly flat-packed her, her legs giving way as she sprawled face first on the stairs.

"Gotcha." Kayla's voice oozed with triumph.

Arke forced herself to her knees. The *Just Say Go* was keeping her pain free, but she was well aware that she was a sitting duck. Stranded halfway up the stairs to the main deck, there was nowhere to run and nowhere to hide.

"So you did." She turned slowly to face her nemesis, grim acceptance in her movements. She wanted to see it coming.

What she saw, however, destroyed her in a completely

different way. Kayla stood outside the sickbay door, every part of her face its own little nightmare. Around her eyes were raw, red circles where she'd ripped the *Sealit Bang* from her skin. Her eyelids and eyebrows were bare and swollen, also victims of the abrupt sealant removal. Her nose was jammed with cotton wool and one cheek was puckered around the bloody wound the fountain pen had inflicted. In a final blow to the woman's mirror loving self, the smugly satisfied smile she wore was ruined by the jagged edges of her two broken front teeth.

"Loving the new look." Arke didn't even try to hold back her amusement. "Zombie chic is *so* underrated."

Roaring an expletive laden reply, Kayla launched her magical spear with the full effect of her fury. With overachieving accuracy and extra venom, the tip hit home, instantly slamming Arke back against the stairs, a good three inches of metal sticking out from the back of her knee.

The potion still coursing through her system was just strong enough to stop Arke passing out immediately from the pain but that was about all it could do. She was trying and failing to claw her way back up the stairs when Kayla strode over, grabbed the haft of her spear and dragged her crippled opponent up to the puddled deck where crewmates and drizzle alike were still frozen in time.

"This is a far more painful piercing than the one you gave me." Kayla put a foot on Arke's leg, a murderous smile on her face as she wiggled her spear. "You know I could just recall this in an instant, right? But since it's you, I think I'll do it the old-fashioned way." She slowly started to push the shaft all the way through the wound. "This is going to take a while, seems to be a lot of resistance. Maybe you should try and relax?" She altered her grip, adding extra weight to her task. "Or should we talk about what *super-talented detectives* you all are – you found the tracker I left in your crew's disgusting toilets. Oh wait, no you *didn't*, because it's still there, pinging away merrily – how else do you think my ships could keep firing so accurately? I have no idea how you even got this far with so few brain cells on board."

The elf kept talking as she prolonged every moment of unnecessary pain for Arke, who was curled in a ball around her leg, trying to brace herself against the unbearably agonising movement of the spear shaft.

"It is a shame you managed to take down one of the frigates, but I needed to make sure you and Irash were aboard," Kayla continued. "For all your bullshit posturing, you're ridiculously pathetic. I knew if I put enough pressure on you, you'd use his powers to protect your stupid little ship and your stupid little friends. And now look at you – helpless and hopeless."

She finally finished pulling the gore-covered spear out and dismissed it from her hand with a wicked smile before leaning to draw a bloody K on Arke's forehead.

"Got to sign my work, let your friends know exactly who killed their big bad bitch." She checked her pendant again with a nod. "But I'm not in a hurry, so you can just lie there a bit longer. Feel that burn." She straightened and walked from crew member to crew member, drawing a K on their faces too.

Arke's dull eyes watched her go, her vision swimming and ears thundering with the pressure of enduring so much pain. She could barely even lift her head let alone try to get up, even though she knew she had to. Where was this magic of hers when she needed it? Her eyes roamed the deck, slipping in and out of focus until they came to rest on a figure standing by the railing on the starboard side about fifteen feet away. His ogre body blurred and then came into sharp focus. Stabbington. Arke felt the searing pain from her injuries dull as the sharper ache of her twisted emotions gripped her. And then it started, a burning heat in her left palm, sudden pressure wrapping around her wound. She looked down to see that her right leg was being rapidly encased by what looked like vines that were erupting from the deck, cradling the injury, bandaging it from foot to thigh. Her natural magic, the power she'd been ignoring and denying, had finally come to the party. She couldn't control it or understand it, but she was suddenly more than grateful for its presence.

Concentrating on Stabbington, she forced herself to move, eyes fixed on him as she struggled to her feet. Standing next to Urzish at the helm, Kayla watched in disbelief as her downed and beaten enemy rose once more. The elf's fingers twitched and she fired off a furious barrage of neon darts, her astonishment only growing as each one was smacked away by what looked like a leafy sapling attached to Arke's ruined leg.

She fired more as the Soulbound started to limp across the deck, but the same thing happened. Fury growing, Kayla summoned her spear, launching it with venom, but that too was knocked aside by the sapling. The elf recalled it to her hand and strode from her position at the bow towards Arke, every step slamming down with thunderous malice.

"I'm going to end this properly – right – now!"

Arke stumbled and limped her way to the ogre, desperately grabbing hold of his hand as she reached him. "Stabbington. Krugg's body may be frozen but you're not from this plane, so you *must* be awake. Can you hear me?" She turned towards Kayla who had already stormed her way across half the deck and then looked back again. "I *need* you. Please."

There was no reply, so with grim determination she reached her other hand to take a sword from Krugg's belt, ready to make her last stand. Suddenly, she felt a ripple of anti-magic free the ogre's body and wonderfully familiar healing energy flood into her from her demon who was squeezing her hand as gently as his huge fingers could.

"This body is hard to motivate. But you said you needed me, and here I am." He crouched down to look at her, his bright blue eyes quickly taking in the intensity of her injuries. "What has happened? And where is that vile creature you replaced me with?"

"Kayla happened. She was going to kill Kennedy, unless I gave her Irash's chalice," Arke whispered, leaning to speak into his ear, her voice hoarse and exhausted. His magic had dulled her pain but with every passing moment she was getting weaker. "She thinks she still has him… she doesn't. I stole him back after I gave her a little makeover." A wicked grin flitted across her pale face and Stabbington turned his head so she could see him smile in response.

"Of course, she has no idea how disgustingly tenacious you are. But tell me everything in tiny detail later. Right now, I would like to hear you say you need me, just once more."

"Who are you and why are you moving?" Kayla stopped a few feet behind them, magic crackling up and down her spear.

Stabbington-Krugg turned towards the elf, eyeing her with dark distaste. "One minute please, this is a momentous occasion." He looked back at Arke, his face softening as he raised his eyebrows expectantly. "Say that you need me again."

A yellow dart hit his hand but he ignored it. Then the spear came flying at him and Arke's whip-like sapling defence pushed it aside. Stabbington-Krugg snapped his head round angrily just as Kayla's hands channelled lightning towards them. His eyes flashed, sending lightning of their own which hit hers head on, dissipating the spell instantly. As he straightened up, his voice boomed across the silent ship.

"Arke and I have had some serious issues recently and this is our breakthrough moment – the one where she says she needs me. And YOU are interrupting. Did you not have enough attention when you were a child? Is there love missing from your life? I can see you need professional help. Maybe you can find a dog trainer who likes bad bitches, yes?"

Arke started to laugh weakly, remembering she'd said almost exactly the same thing back in the infirmary. A furious Kayla charged at Stabbington, spear in hand. He sidestepped with surprising speed, grabbing the shaft and swinging around before letting go, launching Kayla in the air to land thirty feet away, her body crashing heavily to the deck.

Carefully sitting Arke down on top of a barrel, Stabbington locked eyes with her once more. "Now please, say it so I can deal with this exceedingly unpleasant woman."

"Do NOT kill her, or take off her stupid pendant – if you do, we may all go boom."

His eyebrows twitched in dark response. "I will not end her; although I do feel that an entirely disproportionate response is about to occur. But *not* before you tell me one more time."

She looked up into his startlingly blue eyes, her expression earnest and her words hushed. "Of course I need you. But I can't have you back until I've put Irash into a new body."

Stabbington was about to reply when Kayla sat up again and slammed more of her neon darts into his back. He sighed with extreme irritation before shouting at the elf.

"We are having a CONVERSATION!" With a deep, cleansing breath, he lowered his voice to talk to Arke again. "I can feel the time spell ticking away; once it has done, she will leave."

"Yes, we need to let her think she's still got him until it ends. But stop letting her hit you!"

"One advantage of this ogre's body is its resilience. Although yes, her magic does smart a little, so if you are OK here, I will start hurting her now."

Arke nodded tiredly. Stabbington-Krugg gently ruffled her damp hair and then turned around, swatting the curtain of darts away with a dismissive hand as he strode towards Kayla.

"*Now* I will deal with you. Firstly, did you know you

367

are missing a couple of things?" He pointed a meaty finger at Kayla's mouth. "Manners. Also teeth. Or if there are two teeth missing is that three things? I am not sure."

The elf's reply was to throw her spear hard at his stomach. This time Stabbington took only a half step to the side, barely even wincing as the razor edge sliced through the skin at his waist. As it hit, his blue eyes started to glow an even more intense hue. Winding up a middle finger in laconic response, he engulfed her body in a wall of electric blue flame. However, he didn't stop there, using his forefinger to shoot off a cluster of similarly coloured snakes that writhed their way through the air, each hit smashing her burning form backwards.

Kayla crashed against the starboard railing, immolated in blue fire and struggling to breathe as Stabbington-Krugg's huge hand grabbed her by the throat, lifting her effortlessly into the air before slamming her to the deck and holding her down, fingers digging into her windpipe as he spoke, his voice soft and entirely terrifying.

"If you think my Arke is vicious, I would like to introduce myself. My name is Stabbington Bear."

As the demon's blue eyes glared into hers, Kayla's skin turned blue where his hand gripped her throat. Ice began to form on her neck, spreading in milliseconds to encrust her entire body so fully it even stuck her tightly to the deck. Stabbington released his grip before stamping down on one of her ankles with a resounding crack and then rolling his weight around for maximum damage.

"I shall count, for extra dramatic effect. That was

one. Perhaps you know what comes after one?"

The elf was perfectly immobilised by the ice, her eyes wide in horror under the mask of frost but utterly unable to scream. The demon moved to the other side and did the same again with an even more intense sound of bones snapping.

"You were correct, well done. That was two. Two teeth, two legs. You deserve so much more." His blue eyes sparkled coldly as he looked down at Kayla whose terror finally burst through his spell, the ice shattering as she teleported herself away to the top of the captain's cabin. As she struggled to sit up, she shouted agonised obscenities at him, her shaking hands grabbing for the time pendant.

Stabbington glanced at Arke as she sat on the barrel, her face deathly pale but her lips twisted in vengeful mirth.

"Are you enjoying the show?"

"Of course, but I don't think she is. You weren't singing your shark song to her, were you?"

"No, that is only for you, of course, my lady." The demon put a meaty hand over Krugg's heart and bowed his head mockingly. "But thank you for reminding me, as I am so joyful that we are once again talking I feel that glorious tune in my heart. I will be back momentarily to begin the most magnificent rendition ever heard aboard this vessel."

Stabbington reached the ladder to the roof, climbing it in two giant steps and waving a terrifyingly cheery greeting to the elf. She was already dragging herself away from him, firing her yellow darts in frantic defence. With utter indifference to her attacks, he slowly herded her ahead of him until she got to the railing where she had to stop. Stabbington also stopped, a humourless smirk on his lips as he watched her desperately checking the hourglass pendant.

"Only a few more seconds!" Kayla shouted, a sudden smile washing over her battered face. "You hear that Arke? There's no time for him to get it back from me now! I win!" One of her hands slipped under her armour, feeling for her prize.

Her expression changed in a single, desolate instant. "No! How? No!"

"All of the winning. Well – done – you." Stabbington mocked and then stepped aside, revealing a hovering cannonball which was frozen in mid-air, its trajectory perfectly arced to hit Kayla's helpless figure. Her eyes widened in terror, but it was too late.

Time suddenly started again. The heavy iron shot flared into life, flying across the last few feet to meet its new target. Kayla was effortlessly punched through the railings, the iron shot carrying her away like roadkill.

Around the ship other projectiles were finally released to strike the *Warrior* with fresh force. The crew, oblivious to what had just happened, continued what they had been doing the moment everything had stopped and Stabbington-Krugg coolly descended the ladder to pick Arke up.

"You need the infirmary."

"I'm in command and I need to stay on deck."

Stabbington raised an eyebrow as she struggled to get the words out. "I have had more commanding sandwiches. I believe you are beginning to go into shock. So I will help that along by starting to sing."

"You're a monster, not a demon. Fine, OK, you win. Call Ellie over."

After being assured by the first mate that the remaining frigate wasn't pursuing them, Arke's increasingly foggy brain forced her lips to give the order to destroy the tracker located in the toilets. Then she turned her attention to a worried looking Ruby, pointing emphatically at her with a distinctly shaky hand.

"Bring all the kitty litter to me."

Chapter Twenty-Five
Flying High

CAPTAIN KENNEDY WAS confused. In fact, he was utterly baffled. He'd been sitting frustratedly in sickbay one moment and then sitting equally as frustratedly in the galley the next. He'd leapt to his feet the instant his scenery changed and headed for the door, feeling his ship shudder as cannon balls slammed into its hull and hearing the crew responding to the attacks on the deck above his head.

"Hello?" Porro peeped over the top of the counter. "Oh, captain, it's you! Where did you come from? And what's Gurdi's favourite chair doing here?"

"I have absolutely no idea but I'm going to find out."

As he limped out of the galley, Kennedy saw the sickbay door swinging open and almost bumped into Gurdi herself who had just walked out of the crew quarters.

"Where are you going? You're supposed to be staying below. Oh f..." The dwarf dropped a massively unexpected curse as she took one step inside the wrecked infirmary.

"I was in there just a second ago and it was fine!" Kennedy was quick to assert his innocence as the medic's accusatory gaze scoured his face. "I didn't do it!"

"Well someone did. It doesn't take a genius to work out there was a fight in here!"

As Kennedy looked into the normally neat room, he

knew Gurdi was right. There were impact marks everywhere and behind her wrecked desk was an absolute war zone. It started with a blood trail smeared down the wall, leading to more blood on the floor as well random splattered trails of it on the furniture. There were emptied potion bottles, smashed drawers and a very gory looking pen with a twisted nib resting forlornly in the middle of the desk. None of it made sense to him. One second he was in one room, the next another and he knew the sickbay had been pristine when he'd been there.

Pondering the mystery, Kennedy took a moment to check in with his ship's situation. He could feel that the *Warrior* was now level and flying fast – all he could hear of the crew were their feet moving about. There was no more shouting, and more to the point, nothing seemed to be firing at them. Whatever had been attacking had gone and that meant he was safe to go topside to find out if anyone knew what had happened.

He limped out of the room and was just heading to the stairs when he saw Stabbington-Krugg carrying a clearly wounded Arke down from the main deck.

"What happened? Are you OK?"

"*Warrior's* safe, just… long story." Arke's voice was quiet and slow, her clothes soaking wet, and a strange wooden cast was encasing one of her legs, making it stick out awkwardly.

"She intends to resume her career as a ballerina in just a few hours," Stabbington added, smiling down at his burden as he carried her past Kennedy. Then it was his turn to drop a booming curse at the devastation in Gurdi's room.

The medic stopped cleaning up to grab a sheet from one of the untouched cupboards, shaking it out with her usual alacrity as her patient was carried in.

"Lay her carefully on the bed."

"So I am not to drop her from a height? Throw her across the room?" Stabbington's response to being told something so obvious leant heavily on his well-honed sarcasm skills, even though the ogre's voice box was clearly not built for nuance.

"Stop being a dick." Arke muttered as she was exaggeratedly eased down onto the table. "Sorry about the mess, Gurdi."

"Of your body or the room?" The dwarf's tone was matter of fact, her expression unsurprised. She had ceased being shocked at her worst patient's ability to get injured a good many years ago and quickly laid a hand on Arke's forehead, flooding her body with healing magic as Kennedy and Stabbington-Krugg stood shoulder to shoulder next to the bed.

"Are you turning into a tree?" Kennedy peered curiously at the branches wound around the Soulbound's right leg.

"You can stop being a dick too." Even badly injured, she couldn't let an irritating commentator go un-insulted.

Gurdi waved an imperious hand around the infirmary. "If you're going to stand around then at least do something useful and clear the place up." The medic kicked the brakes off the table and started to wheel it into the corner. "Now, my old friend," she sighed, levelling a gaze at Arke. "Let's do this by the numbers. *One* is where you lie to me about how badly you're hurt.

Two is where I threaten to believe you. *Three* is where you swear at me. *Four* is where I wish I'd chosen another profession. *Five* is where you pass out and I can treat you."

"We don't need to do any of that, I just need Irash to fix me." Arke tried to sit up and nearly fell off the moving bed in her attempt to escape.

"Where is he?" Kennedy caught her with his good arm, pushing her back with an exasperated shake of his head.

The dwarf rolled her eyes with an 'I told you so' expression on her face.

"He'll be out soon. Hopefully." Arke lay back against the pillow exhaustedly.

"Out? Gurdi – surely if she's well enough to try and throw herself on the floor she can tell us what happened?"

"That isn't how any of this works. Let me examine her while you two clean this place up." Gurdi locked the brakes back on and pulled a curtain firmly around the bed as her patient sighed heavily and awkwardly started to unbutton her jacket.

The two men busied themselves first with picking things up and then with scrubbing and mopping, while Gurdi instructed Arke to let her help; then remarking that yes, of course it would hurt worse if she didn't have the sense to allow the completely uninjured person in the cubicle to assist, and quite honestly if she didn't stop trying to take her own shirt off she'd make the wound bleed again. Just like that.

Half an hour, a bundle of removed saplings, a plethora of potions and an entire bottle of some literally smoking purple elixir later; Arke, dressed in warm and comfortable looking pyjamas, was sitting up in bed. A blanket hung on a cradle over her legs and her arm was in a sling to support the healing of her thoroughly bandaged shoulder wound, but overall she looked much less nearly dead and was clearly ready to tell her story.

Kennedy and Stabbington had used their time productively; the infirmary was once more super clean and neat, even the drawers had been mended, though the fountain pen would never be the same again.

"All done. We couldn't do much with the paperweight I'm afraid. It was completely shattered," Kennedy apologised as the medic pulled back the curtains.

"It's a horrible thing anyway, I'm not sad," Gurdi remarked with a shrug. "Who wants a paperweight with an eye in it anyway?"

The dismissive words sent Arke into paroxysms of pure mirth, her whole body shaking with a laughter she could not control. Kennedy and Stabbington-Krugg looked between her and the medic with astounded incomprehension.

"Gurdi, I told her it was your mother's eyeball. It was a beautiful moment!" The longer Arke looked at their dumfounded expressions, the funnier she seemed to find them. Finally, she managed to draw enough breath to explain the source of her uncharacteristic behaviour. "I've had SO many drugs."

"She is possibly even higher than the *Warrior* right now," Gurdi corroborated, her face nothing but serious as she explained. "She needs to be. There is no way I can fix her leg here, unless I cut it off; even in a hospital I don't know if it could be saved." The healer shook her head slowly. "But apparently Irash can fix it, she's adamant. However, I'm going on the record – waiting even a few hours is a very bad idea. The ongoing risk of infection in the leg wound is huge and although I can mitigate it, I'm not in the least comfortable with taking the chance. I have made this all clear, but at the end of the day it is her decision, so I've given the absolute maximum dose of my strongest blends to keep her comfortable and in one place. There are side effects but apparently she'd rather have those *and* risk her life than lose her leg."

"Nothing wrong with a metal leg. We'd be taken more seriously as pirates if you had one." Kennedy, as always, was nothing but supportive.

"I'm *not* losing a leg to that red-headed uber-bitch. Her spear went right through my knee; Gurdi said I don't even HAVE a kneecap any longer. Totally gone! It's probably on the deck somewhere!" The drugs had clearly worked as Arke could barely stop chuckling throughout her whole grisly explanation. "Probably fell out when Kayla dragged her spear all the way through. Flip, you'd better send a search party to find it! Definite trip hazard."

While Stabbington's expression was part sympathy and part amusement at the overshare, Kennedy's face lit up with instant burning fury the moment he heard the name. "KAYLA?"

"I know, right? She's SUCH a bitch." Arke took the water that Gurdi handed to her and drank it, still chuckling to herself at random intervals.

Before Kennedy's blood pressure got too high, Stabbington put a hand on his shoulder and eased him to a chair. "It is fine, captain, we won; wait until the end of the story. Now relax, Arke is entirely booted, and we must enjoy this time while it lasts." The ogre sat on the floor next to the bed and Gurdi, noticing his bloodied shirt, handed him one of her post battle potions.

"Don't think I've had any of those," Arke's fingers tapped him on the head, and he batted them gently away with a warm smile.

"You have had more than enough. Start telling us what happened – at the beginning."

As retellings of battles went, this one was an absolute banger. The combination of the story matter and the extreme amount of magical drugs in Arke's system created a pure and perfect example of how to satirise mind-bending concepts and extreme violence along with a very interesting window into her internal monologue. As she finished her part of the tale at the moment where Stabbington-Krugg turned into a purple werewolf to take on the spear-wielding toothless witch, the audience were both enthralled and confused.

"Before you get out the silver bullets, please remember she is very, very high," Stabbington remarked with a chuckle.

"So did she actually feed Irash to the jaguar?" Kennedy queried, wondering what the truth behind that particular part of the psychedelic story was.

"Yes!" Arke pointed at him with a grin. "Absolutely did. He's in a magic box in a magic bag in a magic cat! And he'll fix my leg – once he gets out!"

"Is THAT why you wanted the cat litter?" Ruby's voice sounded in the doorway and the others turned in surprise. The Ornithol had arrived without them noticing and stood looking at Arke, her beak open in shock. "You fed that THING to my cat? Are you

TRYING to kill him?"

Stabbington covered his face with his hands as Arke's immediate reaction was to laugh until she cried, and Kennedy tried to work out if he was actually the one who had taken drugs, as the whole situation was so incredibly surreal.

While the demon was telling his brisk and well-received tale of revenge, Arke fell asleep, her hand resting on his head as it usually rested on her sword hilt. As Kennedy left, Stabbington informed him he intended to stay in the infirmary and Gurdi sat quietly, carefully grinding up herbs ready to make more heady concoctions to keep her patient both in bed and out of pain while they waited for the crystal jaguar's digestion to deliver.

XXX

ALTHOUGH HE WAS not enjoying his time in Krugg's body for obvious reasons, Stabbington was more than grateful to his super-sized host for giving him the ability to be more than just the voice of sympathy when Arke was struggling. Gurdi's powerful drugs always wore off overnight so just before dawn each morning he was ready to keep her company as she woke to the dual grind of pain and nausea. He watched over her, doing everything he could to relieve her discomfort as the minutes dragged on into agonising hours until the dwarf appeared with the next batch of happy haze. Since there was nothing more onboard to supplement what Arke was already taking, and Gurdi was still convinced that she should just amputate, neither the patient nor her companion wanted to give the healer any more reasons to worry, so they dealt with it together.

Stabbington had been with Arke through many

unpleasant, painful and awful experiences but while he was in Krugg's body he was able to help her in practical ways. It was true that she could have used his powers to cool down or warm up, but she could not hold her own hand or rub her own back while she was retching. Granted, the ogre was an exceptionally clumsy meat-suit, but Stabbington found that being able to give her even a small amount of physical comfort made a huge difference.

He was also incredibly relieved to see that whatever chasm had yawned between them had been bridged by their time together in the infirmary. He'd even managed to find the time and the words to apologise for his behaviour back in the corridor while Arke was sober enough to understand. She'd taken it well, only threatening medium levels of violence if he ever tried to bring his ogre lips near her again. What she took less well was his reluctant admittance that she had hit on the truth in angry accident. With them in separate bodies the contract would be on hold; there was no way that he could take her soul.

"So if I jumped off the ship and died? My soul would be free," she asked, eyes wide.

"You cannot get to the edge of the bed, let alone the ship. If you jumped off, you would be an incredible idiot, but technically yes, you are correct. Your soul is currently not mine; but not not mine either." Stabbington folded his arms and looked down at her with an inscrutable expression.

"Not not yours? Are you having a stroke?"

"How could I forget that you are already an idiot. No other demon can sign a contract with you while my contract, even if it is on hold, is there."

"Ah, all the hot demons in my area will be SO disappointed." Arke rolled her eyes expressively before looking hard at him. "So, if I died right now, you couldn't take my soul?"

"I have said this several times: no, I could not."

Then came the question he was hoping she wouldn't ask. "So why were you such a dick back there? I was so worried about Philip and yet you decided to pick a fight. Why?"

Stabbington looked down at his feet for a long moment before answering. "I have no excuse... other than that I had missed you so much I was not thinking straight."

She reached over to tap his cheek with a single finger. "I've missed you too." Her hand dropped to his shirt, pulling him closer so she could rest her head against his shoulder. After a moment of waiting in that position she added. "You could give me a hug."

"I was scared that you might hurt me again." With a blissfully satisfied smile, Stabbington slipped an arm around her shoulders, carefully pulling her closer.

"You're such a massive dick."

"Thank you."

"Shut up." Arke closed her eyes tiredly, resting against him for a good minute before she spoke again. "But how long does it take that bloody cat to take a dump?"

"And *there* it is. The moment – ruined."

✗✗✗

RUBY HAD NO idea that the jaguar had such an iron constitution when she had voluntarily placed herself on round-the-clock Kevan watch. She had thought maybe a day, two at tops, but soon realised that giant extraplanar cats seemed to suffer from extreme anxiety around their toilet habits. She started by hanging out in the storeroom with him, but the pair of them simply sat and stared silently at each other for hours. Then she drilled two eye holes in the door so she could be outside and still watch. That was no better, and the cat just sat looking at the not-creepy-at-all bird eyes watching his every move. Finally, their relationship suffered yet another blow when Ruby started to try and feed him prunes stuffed with bran. Her efforts, as well as her jaguar, remained fruitless.

With the absence of dried plums in its diet, it took until around three am on the fifth day for the jaguar to finally lose the battle to contain its bowel movements. Ruby's tired eyes had been fixed on the litter tray all night but when she walked in at eight with its least favourite dish of mince and prunes, she found the extremely cold, voluminous pile of excrement. That would have been cause for celebration had she not located it through the medium of her bare foot. The cat had apparently sneaked over to the door and offloaded his long-awaited gift there even as she'd watched the actual toileting area. At the exact moment that his prolific deposit squished unpleasantly between her toes, Kevan moved to the litter tray and flipped it over with one dismissive paw before sitting down with his back to her.

After some less than pleasant moments using her foot to isolate the bag from its surroundings, Ruby finally clutched her prize firmly in her talons. Unwilling to touch the offensive object, she decided to hop her way to sickbay, while trying to keep happy thoughts about her pet foremost in her head. It was tricky to do so, especially when the entire gross experience was unnecessarily prolonged after entering into a stand-off with Stabbington about who should touch the noxious item. Thankfully, Gurdi appeared after a few minutes, instantly ending the debate by casting a spell to clean both the bag and its bearer.

"Now it's up to you." The dwarf handed the now-pristine bag to Stabbington.

"Ah yes, of course, Arke said there were magical locks on the box inside." He sighed heavily. "I agreed to open them so the other guy can come back."

He'd looked so desolate that Ruby reached over and squeezed his arm gently. "It's got to be done."

"Has it?" Stabbington sighed again and eyed the bag as it sat in his huge hand.

"Fine." Gurdi nodded decisively and took it back. "My surgical kit is all ready. Time to get busy with the bone saw."

"What?" Stabbington's jaw dropped open and his eyes nearly bugged out of his head.

"I'm so sorry." The dwarf apologised with a sweet smile before continuing with a briskly businesslike tone. "There's not enough bone left to need a saw, I can probably do the job with some scissors and a cauterising iron."

The demon snatched the bag back from Gurdi without another word, turned and disappeared inside the infirmary, slamming the door behind him. Looking at Ruby with the smile of someone who felt very smug about her actions, the healer added a conspiratorial wink before heading into the galley for breakfast. The Ornithol stood uncertainly in the corridor, unsure if she should go in to give Stabbington some moral support or just wait for him to emerge again.

Over the last few days, when she wasn't on jaguar poo patrol, Ruby had been in the infirmary. She'd worked out that it was far less emotionally taxing to sit and watch Arke than sit elsewhere and worry about her. She was also Stabbington's substitute when, as he delicately termed it, Krugg's body needed maintenance. It hadn't escaped her notice that the more time she spent with a sober Stabbington, the more she liked him. As well as being funny, he was warm, friendly, extremely easy to talk to and never made her feel bad for how terrified she'd been of him back on the mountain.

Even if she hadn't warmed to his personality, his devotion to Arke would have been enough. One of Chromatia's teachings Ruby had always kept close to her heart was that a person may be judged on two things only: their deeds and those who are loyal to them. Everything about Stabbington told her that he was a good person, no matter what label he wore, and the Ornithol felt exactly the same about Arke. When she wasn't on a heady concoction of drugs, the Soulbound worked hard to be unapproachable, but unlike a lot of the crew, Ruby hadn't let that push her away, and continued in her quietly helpful manner. She'd lived all her life with nuns, some of whom would politely be called incredibly characterful women, so Arke's dark stares and sharp comments had never even dented Ruby's warmth towards her. They'd made a tremendous team when they fought aboard the Barsian cutters and ever since, the Ornithol had noticed Arke softening towards her. Or she hoped she had.

That hope was confirmed one morning by Arke's medically loosened tongue. Once Ruby stopped laughing at being called 'a ridiculously persistent purveyor of goodwill', 'a rainbow flavoured fluffy hug bird' and a 'spiky nosed kick ass weirdo', she realised that the Soulbound suddenly had tears running down her cheeks. Stabbington had also noticed and reacted quickly, leaning to whisper something in Arke's ear. However, Ruby's attention was drawn away from their moment as she noticed a cluster of snowdrops growing rather impossibly by Arke's bedside. Their roots seemed to be anchored in the cracks between the planks and their white flowers were oddly orange tinged. She was certain they hadn't been there before.

Brow furrowed with confusion as she tried to work out how or more importantly, why, flowers would suddenly grow and bloom in an instant, the Ornithol stayed sitting quietly until Stabbington's murmurings stopped and Arke drifted off to sleep. Ruby watched as the demon carefully eased the plant from its unnatural habitat before carrying it to a shelf where there was already a planter full of other blooms and herbs. She followed him curiously and watched his clumsy fingers making space for the snowdrops before settling them into the earth. When she finally caught his eye, he smiled back with quiet reassurance.

"As you have seen, Gurdi's concoction suppresses Arke's body but sets her mind free, so her emotions are as loose as her tongue. I will tell you why she was upset if you promise to keep it a secret."

Ruby nodded earnestly. "Is she OK?"

"She is Arke, so that question has no beginning and no end." He picked up a jug and watered the new addition to the planter with as much delicacy as an ogre could manage. "The tears were because you remind her of someone else, someone she loved like a sister. This is why she likes you. This, and the fact that you are a kick ass fluffy weirdo who refused to let her ignore you. Please, never change, she needs all the friends she can get."

⚔ ⚔ ⚔

IT WAS A good few hours before Arke woke, her head swimming as she struggled with the concept of reality while under the massive fluffy duvet of the potent herbs and magic. She was usually helped back to consciousness by Stabbington's voice, but he wasn't sitting in his usual spot. A moment after that realisation, Arke spotted the box sitting at her bedside and her hands went straight for it without hesitation.

"You're still alive!" The moment she lifted the lid, Irash's surprised voice sounded in her head, his tone quickly changing to a much more robust one as he recovered his composure. "I had complete faith in you, of course."

"Of course." She reached into the box, wrapping her fingers around the icy cold chalice and lifting it clear of the heavily-runed container.

Irash flooded back to her so quickly it hit like one of Ruby's ninja punches, and Arke winced with the sudden pressure in her head. He didn't even attempt to control her, but in an almost Stabbington-esque monologue, made an excessive commentary on her physical and mental state while she closed her eyes and wondered if he would ever shut up.

"Of course I will. But that box was VERY boring when I've been used to being out here, in the world, seeing things, going places... Arke, show me what happened after you put me in there."

"Maybe you could fix my leg first?" She'd tried to come off as nonchalant, but even to her own boggled hearing, she knew she sounded utterly suspicious.

"Yes, obviously, but what are you trying to hide from me?" Irash asked.

Arke knew that her head was far too fuzzy to really put up a fight against his curiosity. "I fed you to the jaguar."

There was a pause as her passenger waited for more information, but his arrival hadn't changed the fact that his host was absolutely wasted, and she could no longer stop herself sniggering. "In a box, in a bag, in a cat."

"Ah that's a shame. Is Ruby upset?" Irash was clearly in such a good mood that he attempted a little empathy. Normal Arke wasn't a great role model for that, but he did know the theory.

"Not really. She was a bit annoyed but it's not like we hurt her vile, spitting kitty, homicidal pet." Arke was still giggling to herself despite her best efforts to be serious.

"You... didn't?"

"No? Why would we? *Oh!* Of course we didn't kill it to get you out! We're not monsters!" Arke completely lost her composure and burst out laughing as various cartoon-like scenes of the crew chasing the big cat around with murderous intent flitted through her head.

"So someone gave it something to make it vomit?" Irash asked, his tone serious, when her laughter had died down a little.

"No! I mean that would be CRUEL when all we had to do was wait. And he won't even eat prunes. Or curry. Or drink milk. Did you know that milk is bad for cats? It upsets their stomachs. He wouldn't touch any of it! Ruby tried everything – milkshakes, porridge, bread soaked with milk, milky mince, milk sausages – and now we've completely run out. So all the coffee is black unless you put vanilla ice cream in it and that's just gross." Arke heaved in a breath after her rapid explanation, and then as images of the poor crystal jaguar being bombarded by milk flooded over her, had to put her hand over her mouth to smother the laughter, even though she absolutely knew that Irash, from his position inside her head, knew exactly how funny she found it all.

A long and very pregnant pause ensued as she fought to stifle her amusement and her passenger said a lot of nothing.

"But it's alright now. You're here – he must have dumped you out this morning!" Arke, much like the jaguar, couldn't hold it in any longer. She dissolved into utter merriment, repeating her pun amid torrents of helpless laughter.

※ ※ ※

IRASH THE DESTROYER, an indescribable creature from another plane, possessor of incredible power, and the previous object of worship for peoples who regularly sacrificed their own children in his name, could not hide from the truth. It was perfectly and inescapably clear that not only had Arke fed him to a mere beast, but also, and far more damningly, that no-one had even slaughtered it in order to save him from the ignominy of being ejected from it on a wave of excrement.

And after he let that reality settle in his mind while looking through her memories and healing her leg in a blast of icy white heat, he too started to laugh. He'd been bored for so long, even while he was being worshipped, even while he could just think about a thing and make it happen. Nothing had ever excited or engaged him, only anger and violence had ever even scratched through his ennui. Then he'd experienced life on this tiny little ship, with its frail crew of mortals who survived by good teamwork, pure luck, and sheer stubbornness. They were rough, irritating, and incredibly ignorant, but they stuck to their purpose with a tenacity that he couldn't help but admire. Despite their rocky beginnings, Arke had risked her life to save him without a second thought. The entire crew were still risking everything by just having him on board, even though they hadn't been threatened or forced to do so. No-one had ever done anything like that for him before, only sought to appease, control, or trick him.

Irash, who had never been, or wanted to be, part of anything in all the thousands of years he had existed, was suddenly aware that he had changed. He absolutely wanted to stay with this peculiar group of mortals. He wanted to find a body and live alongside them, adventure with them, fight next to them. He wanted to live with the risk of losing it all because he suddenly realised that that was the only way to really feel anything.

Back on the imp ship he'd considered becoming

mortal because it seemed to be the only way to be free of his pursuers. But now he was excited by the idea, ready to embrace life with all its risks and charms. So Irash the Destroyer laughed as he felt, actually and truly felt, pure amusement at the knowledge that he'd been saved from capture by being fed to and excreted from the vilest tempered ship's pet in history.

Chapter Twenty-Six
Keeping it Classy

DESPITE THE GLORIOUSLY sunny weather the *Warrior* sailed into as it neared the city of Theogenes, its captain still needed some serious stress relief. The entire voyage had been borderline catastrophic right from the start, and he felt that the Kayla incident meant it was spiralling even further out of his control. As soon as Arke had come down from her medical high, he'd changed the meandering course that kept them safely in cloud cover to one that took them straight to the coastal city and ordered the helm to bring the ship up to full speed, fervently hoping that once Irash was offloaded, things would go back to normal. He knew *Warrior* normal wasn't the same as everyone else's, but he also knew that the absence of uber-powerful ancient spirits and their time-controlling psychopath pursuers would allow him to actually relax.

One morning when they were a few days away from their destination, Kennedy marched out of his cabin to start the first of his daily exercises. He was growing more and more frustrated at his lack of progress back to fitness as all he was allowed to do was gentle stretches and slow-paced walks around the deck. It was no secret that he was desperate to get back into fighting shape despite his wounds which were still painfully red and puckered even after days of the best magical healing Gurdi could supply.

After his last circuit ended, Ellie, who was on duty, whistled to get his attention before beckoning him over and offering him a cup of coffee from her flask.

"Thanks." He sipped at it and looked at the wheel with a bit of a smile. "She been kind to you overnight?"

"Of course, flew straight as an arrow." Ellie patted the helm fondly. "How're you feeling today?"

"You know how it goes. Everything takes too long."

Silence sat between them for a moment, then both spoke at once, stopped and started again before Kennedy pointed decisively at her.

"You go first."

"I just wanted to say thank you, captain, for being OK about me and Sparkz – he told me you'd had a chat. I'm so glad you don't hate me. I know Arke wanted to drop me off the side when she found out I turned you down… she's very protective of you."

A wry expression slid across Kennedy's face. "Maybe; but you've got her all wrong – she's adorable..." He changed his voice into a decent approximation of Arke's. "Chuck the bodies over the side, they can't feel anything now… Stand still while I try and imagine you with a personality… You can leave or die, and you know what, I'm in a good mood, let's do both…"

"Shush! She'll hear you!" Ellie looked anxiously at the door of Arke's cabin.

"She doesn't need to listen. She – just – knows." He chuckled, amused at his first mate's squirming.

Satisfied that the Soulbound hadn't appeared, Ellie looked back down at the wheel, smoothing one finger along a spoke, cleaning off some imaginary dust. "She's not been the same with me ever since I upset you, and it's been *months*."

"I wasn't upset," Kennedy blurted, before shrugging

with a boyishly embarrassed expression. "Well, briefly… A bit… Yeah, so you could've basically been those sharks and I'd have been happier. Rejection sucks."

"I am truly sorry for hurting you, but you're like the big brother I always wanted. I just couldn't see you any other way."

Kennedy's eyes suddenly twinkled with mischief as he looked down at her. "So… wouldn't that make Sparkz your half-brother?"

Ellie burst out laughing and pointed a finger at him warningly. "Stop! I'm not going to even think about that!"

"Just messing with you." His smile faded into a more serious expression. "You be careful, OK? He might be my brother, but I've known you longer – my door is always open if you need to talk. However, when it comes to Arke, you're on your own."

He went to walk away but Ellie reached out a hand and rested it on his sleeve, stopping him for a moment. "Did she really kill them? Your parents?"

Kennedy nodded, his expression quietly resigned. "She had no choice."

"But what about 'there's always a better way'?"

"That *was* the better way." He put his hand to his neck, opening the pendant hanging there to reveal a portrait of his mother on one side and his father on the other. "I like to keep them close."

"No mistaking whose son you are! They look like lovely people." Ellie smiled warmly. "I'm sure they'd be proud of you."

With a quiet smile, Kennedy snapped the necklace shut and headed back to his cabin. As he opened the door he turned to look around, taking a long glance at the sunlight warming the ship, chasing away the brisk cold of the night. He closed his eyes for a moment, replaying the memories of his parents on that same deck when they were the captains of the *Warrior*, and sighed.

"I hope so," he murmured to himself.

Kennedy's stressed state of mind was no secret to anyone on board. They understood that he'd been embarrassed about the manner of his injuries and felt awful about the fact that he'd agreed to the job which had been a shitshow from start to finish. However, nobody blamed him for anything that had happened, so they were all careful to keep any interactions with him positive and light-hearted to try and make him feel even a little bit better. Their softly, softly tactics had been working, after a fashion, Kennedy's mood wasn't quite as morose as it had been and the recent go-ahead from Gurdi to step up his exercise to actual running had cheered him up even more.

And then milk-gate occurred.

He'd just finished a deeply unsatisfactory evening workout, where he'd failed yet again to run as many laps of the main deck as he wanted to, his injured leg stubbornly refusing to return to its pre-shark state. As the sun fell away, leaving a nip in the air, a thought stirred in him, a childlike yearning for the sweetest and most comforting cup of cocoa that could be made. But when he arrived in the galley and started to prepare his hug in a mug, he suddenly remembered they were completely out of milk. Not a single grain or drop of powdered, condensed, evaporated or frozen was left after they'd tried and failed to use it to purge the jaguar.

Porro's apologetic suggestion of ice cream was received with all the grace of a jilted lover. Kennedy had reached the end of his tether, eaten the postman and was ready for seconds. He strode back up the stairs, bellowing for all hands.

The crew loved their captain; they wouldn't hesitate to defend him with their last breath. But milk-gate had been followed with three days of constant drills, both day and night, until they reached the point where they were just about ready to tie Kennedy to a chair and set him on fire. Nonstop jangling alarms, bellowed orders, combat training, battle drills, emergency drills and drill drills took their toll, and in what quiet moments they had, the crew plotted. Thankfully, their final decision was that distraction, however risky, definitely came before mutiny in the dictionary. However, in what could have been a perfect storm of coincidences, their attempt to return their captain to his more usual headspace also happened to coincide with the Soulbound's decision to intervene.

⚔ ⚔ ⚔

As ARKE, LADEN with a large armful of bottles, headed over to Kennedy's cabin, she was perfectly aware that this wasn't exactly the most altruistic decision she had ever made. Her head was constantly aching from the combination of Irash's enthusiasm about his upcoming transition, the incessant bells and shouting from the drills, as well as the chemical residues still in her system after her stay in the infirmary. Plus, she was also deeply irritated (and upset if she were ever to be honest with herself) that Stabbington point-blank refused to spend any time with her while Irash was in residence. She needed a break and Kennedy's hyperactive stress fest was the perfect excuse to dig out every half-drunk and ancient bottle of alcohol she'd forgotten she owned.

"Knock knock." She pushed his door open and started placing the bottles on the chart table. "Stabbington didn't drink ALL the booze on board; some of these might even be older than you."

At first, she didn't pay Kennedy much attention. He was sitting on his bed reading when she walked in, but as she organised the bottles, she slowly became aware that he was looking incredibly guilty and had dropped whatever was in his hands quickly down onto his lap. There was a toe-curlingly awkward exchange of glances before she slowly started to back out.

"Did I interrupt something personal? Five minutes be enough to… finish?"

"What? No? Arke NO! I was not… No. Definitely not." Kennedy blushed and stood up quickly, gesturing to show he was absolutely not doing what she'd insinuated he was. "I'd have locked the door!"

"Well, there was that time with the…"

"Stop!" he interrupted quickly, going to the cupboard and grabbing two glasses. "I was a lot younger then." He walked over to the table and eyed the bottles with interest. "Some of them are more like syrup and half of them don't have labels."

"Happy days." Arke unscrewed one and wiped the crystals from its thread. "Smells like kirsch? Why do I even have this? I don't even like the stuff."

"Everyone has that one bottle at the back of the cupboard. Mix it with this?" He opened another bottle and sniffed it curiously. "Or do we go old school and just stick the lot in a bucket?"

"I was hoping you'd say that." She pulled a bundle of faded and battered cocktail umbrellas from her pocket. "Keeping it classy."

"Outstanding!" Kennedy's face lit up with amusement and he grabbed one, sticking it behind his ear as he went to grab the nearest bucket.

A good few glasses of Bucket Fuel later, Kennedy was looking an awful lot more relaxed and Arke had completely forgotten about her headache. They were sitting together, feet propped up on the table, the dubious-looking bucket on the floor between them. He was talking more nonsense than usual, and she'd companionably tuned him out, right up until he started to giggle like a schoolboy. She turned her head to look at him, one eyebrow raised in query, ignoring Irash who had been asking far too many questions about the nature of the pleasure obtained by poisoning your body.

"What's so funny?"

"Maddington Dare!" Kennedy sniggered, downing his drink, and dipping his glass in the bucket for a refill.

Arke just looked at him, both eyebrows now raised in silent query.

"I'm not supposed to tell you!" he protested.

"Well, Flip." She sipped her drink with a small smile. "You know that by the time those words come to your lips that it is, absolutely and completely, *way* too late to stop talking."

"You have to promise that you won't be angry with them."

She gestured for him to continue, and Kennedy being Kennedy dropped the lot without any further provocation. He explained that as she well knew, the crew were inveterate gossip whores and after the 'incident' between her and Stabbington outside the infirmary, they'd been obsessed by the possibilities of the love story they thought they'd happened upon. That was the moment that Arke dipped and downed two shots to deal with both Irash's hilarity and the realisation that her life was now a subject to be discussed over coffee and cake.

"Shall I go on?" Kennedy asked as she'd slammed her glass back down to the table.

"There's more?"

"A bit? While you two were in the infirmary together…"

"I was flat on my back!"

Kennedy snorted, barely able to contain his smile at her unintended innuendo. "They know."

"Seriously? They thought we were…" A memory washed over her, and she goggled at Kennedy before throwing another shot into her mouth. "Ellie kept coming in and offering us tea. Was she spying on us?" She shook her head with a burst of indignation. "Well, if she came looking for something, she sure as hell didn't find it."

"No, of course she didn't. But according to the crew's book, Larka and Maddington Dare were banging like a door in a storm when something similar happened to her."

"Their WHAT to the WHO NOW?"

Kennedy walked to his bed and picked up a rough manuscript, bound together with bootlaces. He explained that Gabbi and Ellie were co-authoring a rapidly growing novel based on the adventures of a power couple on a dashing delivery ship called the *Courier*. He'd overheard several odd conversations and had requests for paper that had only made sense once the book had been delivered for his perusal earlier in the evening. Ellie's rough hand had scrawled the first few pages, but after that, the penmanship had drastically improved, as had the quality of the writing. Gabbi was, when compared to the rest of *Warrior* crew, a literary revelation.

"Look, I know it's a dick move on their behalf." As she choked on her drink Kennedy quickly apologised for his choice of words. "But hear me out, they're going to do it anyway *and* it's great for morale."

"Give." She held out an expectant hand.

He clutched it to his chest with a pleading look. "Promise you won't set it on fire?"

"No. But I *definitely* will if you don't hand it over."

An anxious looking Kennedy slid the manuscript into her waiting hand and Arke settled it on the table before starting to read. Her eyes had barely skimmed the first line when she snorted with sudden laughter and looked up at him, shoulders shaking with mirth.

"Captain Overshare?"

"Oh, that's nothing; keep reading. And definitely keep drinking. I'm going to the little captain's room, so try not to throw anyone overboard until I get back."

"Hey, that's not fair, you know I always wait till they're dead."

Kennedy patted her on the head as he stood up. "Exactly."

Arke was still reading so barely even noticed when

Kennedy returned to the table, but she did down another shot before answering his tentative enquiry. Tapping a finger on the manuscript and asking him to sharpen up several pencils, she raised her eyes to meet his as she spoke.

"I love books. Good ones. And this… whatever this is, is a hate crime against literature. However, it has some promise and I think I can rescue it."

"But the errr… subject matter?" He handed her a pencil.

"Far less irritating than its grammatical or spelling errors."

She gestured for him to shush while she went to work, hissing through her teeth and making notes either on the lines or in the margins. A wide grin lit Kennedy's face and he budged his chair up next to hers, joining in with the edit while keeping their glasses full as they worked until both fell asleep where they sat, faces smooshed to the table.

As stress relief, it was a fantastic tonic. As editors, it was a great effort. As the next day went, they were utterly wrecked.

Gabbi was on morning watch when Arke stumbled out of the captain's cabin, the book in her hands. With a slow, deliberate tread, entirely indicative of her renewed state of inebriation as the bucket hadn't been quite empty when she'd woken up, she approached the petrified young man, her insobriety leaving her completely unaware of his state of pant-soiling terror.

"Breasts is spelt with an A," she remarked, slapping the manuscript into his chest with a thud. "And if their tongs entwined then they'd be cooking, not kissing.

Tongues! T-O-N-G-U-E-S! We've made a lot of corrections." She took a breath and smiled hazily at him. "Send it back when you've written more."

$$\text{✗ ✗ ✗}$$

TWO DAYS LATER, which was almost as long as it had taken Arke and Kennedy to fully overcome the after-effects of the Bucket of Doom, the *Warrior* reached Theogenes. The city was full of white-walled buildings that gleamed brightly in the morning sunshine, the picture-perfect scene only accentuated by the glowing turquoise expanse of ocean behind. As the *Warrior* drew slowly towards the air anchorage, the crew looked down with fond regard. Barely anyone disliked the southwestern bastion of the Barsian Empire, its cosmopolitan nature and perfect climate making the sprawling metropolis universally popular. The central hub was easily spotted from the air, its mathematical street plan, and huge public buildings absolutely unmistakable, all surrounded by lush green public gardens. Even though they knew they wouldn't be heading down for shore leave, the crew were more than happy with the prospect of relaxing on the deck in glorious weather.

It had taken that very drunk night for Kennedy to unwind, the reset from his dead-drunk stupor allowing him to wake up with a more positive mindset. He was now able to look forwards to getting on the ground, getting the job done and getting the ship resupplied so he could have that decadent mug of cocoa he'd been looking forwards to. In fact, he was serenely confident that it was all going to work out beautifully. However, his high hopes for the apparently simple task ahead suffered a body blow as a distinctly murdery looking

Arke appeared on deck in a set of Ruby's acolyte robes. She wouldn't even fool a blind man into believing she was a nun.

"Doesn't suit you, don't make it a habit." Sparkz clearly thought this was hysterically funny.

"You look – perfect!" Kennedy quickly turned on his charm as Ruby appeared behind her, also dressed in Chromatian robes.

He hadn't anticipated that he'd need to intervene to rescue the job before they'd even got off the ship, but knew he had to do something before Arke boiled over. He had to admit that he hardly blamed her as even he'd been taken by surprise at the sheer eye-popping colour of the rainbow people who emerged from the hatchway. He looked at the very unrainbow-like Arke, party in the robes, murder in the eyes; before reaching to pull up her cowl to shield the majority of her death glare from public view. "And the transformation is complete. Sister of mercy, say 'ahhhhhhh'." He held his hands up in a praying motion and Ruby chimed in quickly with a joyful trill of musical notes.

Arke just turned and walked to the gangplank where a taxi boat was just pulling up. "Let's get this done before I puke."

Sparkz fell in beside his brother as they followed the two 'nuns'. The possessed ogre joined them, hands in his pockets, his eyes on the ground. If the demon had found Arke's forced re-style amusing, he wasn't giving any hint of it away. Kennedy greeted him with a smile and a nod. He had every sympathy for Stabbington's aversion to his old host while Irash was still in residence, suspecting that if he were in that position, avoidance would probably be the most vanilla of his reactions. The demon's agreement to join the party had been slow to arrive, but Kennedy's trump card had been the entirely truthful explanation that the ogre's extra muscle was needed, given they weren't going to risk taking weapons down to the city. He hadn't voiced his ulterior motive, but secretly had every hope that positioning Stabbington close to Arke when her passenger left would allow his friends to reunite as quickly as possible.

He stepped aboard the taxi and sat down, eyes roving over the rest of his party in a final check. Sparkz was wearing a bulky backpack – he'd finally had time to finish his personal wingjet, jetwing, wings 'n' things, jet 'n' go... everyone had a different idea what it should be called. If things went wrong, he could help Ruby evacuate the others. But things were not going to go wrong. Kennedy was determined that this would be a simple trip and by the end of it, everything would be back as it should be.

Chapter Twenty-Seven
Moving Day

THEOGENES WAS A bustling city, and as Arke
walked with Rainbow Ruby through the streets
towards the hospital, she saw that the Ornithol
was thrilled with absolutely every sight. The white stone
houses, the tropical palm trees, the beautiful cascades of
flowers, the smell of the food; she wanted to look in
every shop window and bless every beggar. However,
Ruby's joy only made Arke, the fakest of fake nuns, even
more irritated. This was turning into a terrible day. Right
from the moment she'd got out of bed, it seemed as if
everything was conspiring to cause her the maximum
amount of deep, personal dissatisfaction. Firstly, they'd
found a family of mice nesting in the tea leaves. Granted,
the discovery had explained the unusual tang in her
morning drink that she'd been ignoring since she came
back to the ship, but Urzish's assertion that since she
wasn't already dead she should just keep drinking it had
not gone down well. Morning tea-less, she'd headed
below decks to don her disguise.

Per Kennedy's orders they were all going unarmoured
and unarmed; and though it was an anxiety-inducing
call, Arke knew it was the right one. Theogenes was a
city that prided itself on law and order, the city guard
patrolled everywhere, and they had very sharp eyes. The
shore party needed no unwanted attention and certainly
no interactions with the law. The plan was simple: get

the job done and get straight out. Despite knowing it made total sense, leaving all her body protection behind made Arke feel like she was heading out in her pyjamas.

Luckily for her bedtime chic, but unfortunately for her mood, Arke had been about to receive one hell of a dressing gown. Down in the main crew quarters she'd almost had to cover her eyes from the glare as Ruby handed her the set of Chromatian robes she'd tailored to her friend's smaller size. Pirates and religious orders were two very un-intersecting subsets and so Arke was caught completely by surprise by the horror that was proudly handed to her.

When she'd agreed to wear the robes, she'd had no idea that Chromatia's acolytes wore the most lurid rainbow-coloured gowns that had ever existed in the history of bad fashion choices. Arke had frozen in place as the nauseatingly neon garment was draped over her arm and Irash's intensely irritating laughter only paused briefly so he could tell her that blending in by standing out was so bold it had to work. Almost as bold as the terrible colours. His host's already grey tinged mood had descended fully into darkness at the precise moment she'd slid the offensively bright robe over her black shirt and trousers, her passenger still unhelpfully chuckling away in her head.

Walking through Theogenes dressed like a floating migraine while trying to keep the Ornithol moving in a straight and purposeful line was not improving her temper in the slightest. She knew the others were nearby; she'd already spotted Kennedy with Stabbington at his shoulder, stopping at every sweet-smelling stall to buy snacks, then strolling along smiling happily as he munched his way through some famous Theogenes pastries. On a normal day she'd have been eating too, for the myriad of flavours: apricot, almond, pistachio, strawberry, watermelon, orange, were all deliciously perfect. As she'd waited for Ruby to stop gawping at the busy marketplace, she'd caught a glimpse of Sparkz and noted that as usual, he was far less relaxed than the captain. The engineer's eyes were constantly scanning the crowds and he was carefully steering Kennedy and Stabbington away from any uniformed patrols that he noticed.

Eventually the two groups made it out of the crowded streets and into the open square in front of the Central Apothecarium. The hospital was surrounded by beautiful gardens covered in lush grass, with a chain of effortless fountains set among passionate displays of tropical flowers. Arke ignored it all. Her attention was fully and uncomfortably focused on the building itself. The place looked like it was consecrated to the god of WHITE and the god of CLEAN, with its immaculate white flagstones, sparkling white pillars, perfect white bricks, and blindingly white marble façade. She swallowed dryly and forced herself to concentrate on the practical, looking for anyone who might be paying them too much attention or who looked out of place. That wasn't easy, for all manner of people were constantly going in and out, visitors, sick and injured, rich and poor alike; everyone was clearly welcome in the pursuit of health. However, no-one stood out to her and despite a mounting sense of unease, Arke kept walking towards the wide, white steps. She knew the others were going to take stations outside to keep watch for any trouble; all she and Ruby had to do was get inside and find Irash a new body.

The closer the Rainbow sisters got to the eye-wateringly bright complex, the more unaccountably tense Arke became. The vast whiteness of it seemed to loom over her, and she felt her body react to her anxiety, fists clenching tightly while her breathing started to accelerate. The unutterable sense of dread seeped further into her as they climbed the steps, and by the time they approached the main doors, she had to force her reluctant legs to step over the threshold. Everything around her seemed to be throbbingly oppressive as she gritted her teeth and made herself follow Rainbow Ruby into the busy reception area.

The cavernous hall echoed under a high ceiling which was decorated with endless frescoes depicting the cycle of life, and it was all as painfully white as the exterior.

Arke wiped some errant drops of sweat from her face with a jerky hand. She knew this building should be cool inside and yet she felt nothing but heat from every direction. She had no choice but to tail Rainbow Ruby with her head down, trying not to look at the overwhelming whiteness that seemed to be the source of her increasing anxiety. The barrage of inexplicable panic was so alien to her that she had nothing to counter it with, and she could not understand why her body seemed to be reacting as if this entire building were a physical threat that she must run from.

"Blessings to you!" Rainbow Ruby had found an elderly sister who seemed to be directing visitors around the massive hospital.

"Bright blessings to you! It is not often we see Sisters of Chromatia in these parts."

Ruby seemed to slip into her old monastic language effortlessly, charming the older sister while Rainbow Arke stood to one side, hands clasped as if in prayer. She was desperately trying to concentrate on her friend, listening to every word in case she was needed. It definitely helped to think about something else and for a few moments she was able to push away the oppressive whiteness and the thundering heartbeat that was pulsing in her ears.

Painstakingly memorising the plan and being adorably wholesome when she wanted to be was the key to Rainbow Ruby's success – she quickly charmed the other sister with her innocence and desire to help those who had no hope. Within a couple of minutes, the two Sisters of Chromatia were invited to offer prayers and calming words to those in the Palliative Ward.

Once they left the main thoroughfares and turned down the narrower but still glisteningly white side corridors, Arke felt her mind and body begin to rebel again. With every step the sense of dread was almost uncontrollable within her, and even though she knew she was in a hospital, she had never felt less safe. Suffocating heat flooded her entire body, her breath caught in her throat, and she could feel her pulse bounding alarmingly through every vein, as their echoing footsteps sounded so loud it hurt. Arke felt as if she was being crushed and dragged backwards into a tiny pinprick of existence, the white walls pushing on her, the floor shimmering under her feet.

"ARKE! LISTEN TO ME!" Irash's urgent shouts

finally broke through to her strangled consciousness. "Listen to my voice and ONLY my voice. I am here, I am with you, you are not alone. Something about this place is triggering a traumatic memory and what you're feeling is a response to that. It isn't a real threat. You are safe. However, your orange magic is reacting to your distress, and you need to take back control before it overloads. Bring yourself into the now, force yourself if you have to. There are too many people here, too much damage you could do if you cannot contain your reaction to the past. Think about something else. Do that really irritating thing where you count backward in threes. One thousand, nine hundred and ninety-seven, nine hundred and ninety-four, now your turn... Keep going... It's OK."

To Arke's immense relief, once Irash's voice had pierced the wall of distress around her, the tide of her panic began to ebb. She had never enjoyed maths but as she clung to the logical progression that forced her brain to stop reacting and start thinking, she'd never been so grateful to it.

Turning a corner just ahead of Arke, Rainbow Ruby stopped in front of the Palliative Card sign and heaved a relieved sigh. Despite the best efforts of the builders who had made every corridor look exactly the same, they were finally at their destination. The Ornithol led the way through a pair of huge white doors under a huge white archway and into a beautiful courtyard setting, blessed with sudden sunlight that filtered through the entire ward from a glass dome situated high above. Here, everything was different, the sanitary requirements were relaxed, there were muted colours instead of blanched white and no masks or endless cycles of cleaning. A small grove of trees grew directly under the dome and the air was lively with the delicate scent of flowers, rich warm-coloured plants in pristine and perfect bloom.

Around the outside of the central square, under a portico, were the rows of patients who were not expected to leave this place on their own feet. While Rainbow Ruby blessed and was counter-blessed by the sisters who moved between the beds praying and giving comfort, Arke went straight to the central area, feeling her body begin to relax with every step away from the overwhelming whiteness. Sunlight washed over her as she approached the trees and without thinking she quickly wrapped her hands around the nearest one and pushed her forehead against the trunk, its solid familiarity utterly comforting.

"There, you and your strange feral magic are calmer. Wild needs wild, and this is as close as you'll get in here." Irash's voice exuded relief as his host's heartbeat finally dropped back down to a more normal level.

"Are you OK?" Rainbow Ruby hurried over, balancing a refreshment tray in her hands.

"Just blessing some trees. Let me do the carrying while you do the talking." Rainbow Arke was back in the game, keen to get Plan B done so she could escape the Apothecarium as quickly as possible. As she took the tray, a wry grin sprang to her lips, her half-smile hinting that the words that followed were closer to the truth. "Forgot that I don't like hospitals. Must be the smell of clean."

It was a slow job, making their way from bed to bed, giving tea to visitors, speaking to every single person they saw, with extra blessings and prayers for those who were on their own or close to their transition. Irash made sure to keep Rainbow Arke's mind busy, having her use his powers to assess the most unwell people in the ward. However, and deeply disappointingly, by the halfway point, he'd already dismissed most as too old and the rest as too unwilling or not quite what he was hoping for.

During their methodical progress around the ward, the Rainbow sisters' curiosity was piqued by two burly orderlies standing at a doorway in one corner of the courtyard, a huge figure bound in bandages visible on the bed inside. Rainbow Ruby was quick to offer them the brightest blessings and Rainbow Arke was interested enough in the unusual situation to break her silence, offering refreshments before asking the men about the poor soul inside the cubicle.

"That poor guy, he's a danger to himself. We have to keep him restrained, and that's no way to be treated in his condition." The taller orderly brushed the crumbs from his beard. "My oath forbids me from wishing anyone dead, but by the looks of him, it'd be a mercy."

The other dipped a biscuit into the mug of tea that Ruby handed him. "I agree – both him and the guy he came in with. The nurses were in a right state after treating them and I've never seen Father Brythe so pale. He said to me that they weren't alive, not really, but it was his duty to try and make sure they weren't in pain."

"What happened to them?" Rainbow Ruby asked, offering the men a second dip from the plate of cakes.

"No-one knows and they sure can't tell you. They were brought here after they got caught in fishing nets over to the east of the Straits. Gotta be some sort of magic involved." The orderly made a quick warding gesture before taking another cupcake.

"Where's the other one?" Arke asked, topping up their tea.

"Over there, all bandaged up. He just lies there, don't eat, don't drink, nothing. This guy's different." He jerked a thumb towards the room behind him. "He's tormented for sure."

The sisters backed away with blessings on blessings and continued their slow way around the rest of the ward. As Rainbow Arke approached the bed of the other heavily bandaged figure that the guard had indicated during their conversation, Irash erupted enthusiastically in her head.

"This one! This is the body I require. He is perfect in every way."

"You don't know anything about him!" She was confused, knowing that her passenger had been much more methodical in his previous investigations. Kneeling at the bedside, she placed the tray of refreshments to one side and linked her hands together as if in prayer.

He was certain, his excited anticipation unmistakeable. "This is the one."

Rainbow Ruby also moved closer and spoke in a low voice. "He's chosen?"

"Apparently. What does the chart say?"

The Ornithol positioned herself at the end of the bed, ostensibly calling her god to deliver blessings on the patient, but in reality letting her sharp vision decipher the scrawled writing on the chart. There was barely any information on the clipboard, so her fake prayer didn't need to be particularly long, and once she'd committed the brief details to memory, she walked around to the side of the bed to kneel beside Arke.

"Patient Name: Unknown. Condition: Terminal. Cause: Complete magical destruction. Sex: Male. Estimated age: Young adult. Ethnicity: Orc. Notes: Found at sea near Fullport."

It was definitely a good thing that it was only his host who could hear Irash's boomingly inappropriate sentiments as he grew more and more excited about the potential of the terribly injured young man lying in the bed. Having to reach out to so many people who were in the last hours of their lives had been stranger and so much harder than Arke had expected. The huge room was full of unfortunate souls, all treading their slow roads towards release from bodies which were reaching the end of their physical endurance. Over the years she had seen so much death in so many forms, but not in such melancholy concentration and never when she had the ability to dip her consciousness so near to it.

From a distance, the beds had seemed to contain only silent stillness, but once among their number, it was impossible to unhear the soft rattling breaths and mindless murmurs that rippled across the ward. At such close quarters to the patients, it was also obvious that the sweet smell of flowers from the courtyard was barely able to cover the earthy scents of the desperately ill. There was far more peace in these deaths than any Arke had ever seen, but as she'd visited each bed in turn, she'd become more and more convinced that this was not the way she wanted to leave this life.

On acknowledging that thought, Irash's good humour had made his pithy comment that she was much more likely to die alone in a gutter somewhere sound far more joyful than the subject matter would suggest, but his host didn't even react to his words. Hers was an existential crisis that she intended to solve later by introducing herself to the bottom of several bottles of alcohol. Her passenger's quick affirmation that he would happily join her in person if only she just got on with the job in hand was enough to spark Arke into movement. She placed a hand gently on the bandages over the silent body's chest, only to recoil instantly as her mind was filled with a flurry of jumbled images, unearthly sounds and dissonant whispers.

"He is perfect. Do not waste any more time."

Perfect was not a word Arke would have used about the immobile, mummy-like figure on the bed. The onslaught of garbled sensations that had flooded through her at a single touch had been deeply unexpected and equally as unsettling. From that brief exposure to what was left of his mind, she had the feeling that whatever had happened to the young orc had been so catastrophic that he was nothing but a shell populated by the ghost of who he used to be.

"I still need his permission." She squared her shoulders, steeling herself for what she knew would hit her the moment she reconnected. With a brief glance at Ruby, she placed her hand back on the bandaged chest, shutting her eyes as she used Irash's powers to try to communicate with whoever was still inside this tortured body.

Probing past the initial onrush of jarring visions, it was all Arke could do not to cry out as increasingly vivid images of agony, pain, anger and loss flung themselves into her mind. Her first assessment had been utterly correct, whoever this had been was enduring a suffering so terrible that they had lost all ability to communicate in any active sense of the word. She forced herself to concentrate on her own thoughts, pushing the flashing visions aside long enough to ask if they wished to move on, telling them their pain would end, that they would be at peace. She almost lost her connection with the young man at the sudden shock of having a single image flung into her mind in response to her questions. Unlike the other pictures she'd been bombarded by, this one was crystal clear. She instantly recognised herself, standing in her usual fashion, hand on Stabbington's hilt.

"You know me?" she asked, before the picture changed to one of Kennedy standing at the helm. "Who are you?"

Her attempts at communication brought her an image of the *Warrior* before the maze of jumbled voices and blurred visions slammed into her again, the dissonance swirling inside her head so jarringly that she could no longer maintain the communication.

"What happened?" Ruby threw an arm around Arke's shoulders as she reeled backwards from the bed and almost collapsed to the floor.

"I don't know." She leant on her friend for a long moment, every square inch of her head throbbing painfully.

Irash's voice cut through, his tone suddenly as respectful as she'd ever heard it. "What you saw must be more reason to see his suffering brought to an end."

He hadn't needed to say a single word, for Arke had already decided that if it had been her lying on the bed, so tormented and alone, she would have leapt at the chance to check out. As the pain in her head began to clear, she took a casual look around the ward to make sure that they were unobserved. Once she confirmed that no-one was paying them any attention, she reached under her clothes, opening her shirt and unstrapping the deeply uncomfortable chalice with a deep breath of pure relief.

"Are you ready?"

"This is a new adventure." Irash's voice boomed excitedly in her head. "I am ready to eat my own peanuts."

With a nod to Ruby, Arke watched as her friend carefully peeled a small section of the orc's dressings back, exposing what they expected to be skin but looked more like pure bone. The instructions from Irash had been simple, connect him with the body and step away, he would do the rest. As the Ornithol finished preparing the area, Arke slid the base of the chalice into the gap, pushing it slowly forwards until it could go no further.

"You really do need crayons."

Chapter Twenty-Eight
Destiny Takes the Wheel

IRASH HAD HELD his final comment until the last moment of Arke's contact and as she withdrew her hands, her vision blurred, his self-satisfied words echoing in her head. Then the nauseating dizziness of his sudden absence hit, the sensation of instant emptiness roaring through her like a tempest. This time Ruby was ready to hold her friend up as she struggled to restore her equilibrium, digging a thumb and forefinger into the bridge of her nose hard enough to leave an indent. Slowly regaining control of her senses, Arke opened her eyes, looking curiously at the body on the bed. The chalice had disappeared and the unmistakeable grey aura of Irash's power was slowly oozing out from the bandages as the body started to move. Little by little the limbs and digits began to flex as if the new owner was taking stock of his new home, assessing every finger and toe individually.

Initialisation clearly complete, Irash sat bolt upright in bed, puffs of smoky magic sparkling around him before the bandages completely melted away to reveal a starkly skeletal form. Even more shockingly, that very body was starting to remake all its organs and soft tissue layer by anatomically explicit layer. Ruby's eyes went wide, and she leapt to her feet, spreading her wings as if in fervent prayer to shield the living biology lesson from any prying eyes.

Arke quickly looked away. She was still feeling

417

nauseous so did not need to see reverse butchery in action, however grimly fascinating it might be.

"Surprise."

The voice that spoke was definitely familiar. The Rainbow sisters looked back at the body on the bed and reacted in a very similar way. Arke spat a mouthful of curses and even Ruby dropped a whispered F-bomb.

In front of them, re-fleshed and strangely radiant in his new skin, was Irash, wearing a very familiar young orc's body with a look of satisfied smugness that only a teenager basking in his own brilliance could pull off.

"Grimlet?"

"Don't you think this has the perfect ring of karma to it? A life lost, a life regained. Your friend has gone on to wherever he was bound, and I have fused successfully with this impressively sturdy body. Now, let us go, I have so many things I want to do."

As he went to get out of bed, Arke shook her head quickly. "CLOTHES!" she hissed, grabbing the sheet and holding it over his nakedness.

"Ah yes! *We* mortals and *our* clothes!"

While Irash conjured some clothes into being, Ruby and Arke became aware of a disturbance at the other side of the ward. The orderlies on the locked room were calling for help as the patient inside had broken free of his restraints and was banging bandaged fists on the door with such force his blows threatened to smash the entire thing off its hinges.

That distraction was all they needed, and with no further ado, the two Sisters of Chromatia walked the shiny-faced teenaged orc out of the hospital. As they crossed back through blinding white hallway after blinding white hallway, Irash kept a firm grip on Arke's arm while asking the most banal of questions and insisting she answer them. Ruby listened with a confused tilt to her head but said nothing, even if she did wonder why her friend was being subjected to the oddest maths test ever.

Finally, they strode clear of the huge reception hall and down the marble steps into the sunlight, the concourse in front of the hospital just as busy as it had been when they arrived. The interminable quiz ended with the first breath of fresh air, Irash now busy looking around him with his new eyes and trying to appear completely natural as he controlled his large feet while navigating the broad stairs.

"When can I take these things OFF!" Arke hissed and Ruby looked over to where her friend was tugging irritably at Chromatia's finest cloth.

"You don't like the robes?"

"She *really* doesn't like the robes," Irash added, grinning gleefully.

He proceeded to tell Ruby the exact phrases his previous host had used about them in her inner monologue while Arke tried to work out if she would get arrested if he 'accidentally' slammed his eyeball onto her finger. Knowing that it would be tricky to explain to the authorities that Irash was over sixteen by some few thousand years and therefore it was assault rather than abuse of a minor, she made a mental note to 'remind' him of her privacy later.

⚔ ⚔ ⚔

KENNEDY SPOTTED THEM first, his eyes almost bulging out of his head when he recognised Grimlet 2.0. After a

419

few surreal seconds of eye contact with his repurposed crew mate, he managed to recover enough to drag his gaze away and follow them at a little distance. Kennedy had wanted to get back to normal. Or at least the new normal, with Irash in a body. However, he wasn't so sure about the new old normal, now that body was Grimlet's. He shook his head, trying to clear the large number of disturbing thoughts that raced through it. The job was done, it was time to regroup and get back to the ship.

The shore party's rendezvous point had been set before they left the *Warrior* and as Kennedy walked through the gates of the chosen park, he saw Ruby and Arke back in their normal clothes, sitting on a bench watching Irash chase ducks across a shallow pond nearby.

"How did his body even get here?" Kennedy sat down next to Arke, nodding with appreciation as the orc's quick reactions nearly caught him one, but then frowning. "He knows he can't just eat it raw, right?"

"Soon find out." Arke shrugged. "I'm pretty sure if he took a bite, it'd be the first and last time. Probably." She took a deep breath and ran a hand through her hair, slicking it back against her head. "Anyway, apparently what was left of his body was picked up in a trawler's net near Fullport. Wasn't much left of his mind."

"In the Straits?" Kennedy furrowed his brow thoughtfully, before his expression cleared with fresh realisation. "We weren't far from the Grey River Valley during the battle. He must have fallen into the water and been washed out to sea."

Arke nodded and turned away, spotting Sparkz sauntering down the path towards them. Having already decided that whatever conclusions she might draw from her time connected to what had been left of Grimlet would stay unshared, she was working hard to dismiss the memories of the Apothecarium from her head. Everything had worked out for the best, the boy was at peace and Irash had a body, he was no longer a commodity so valuable that people would kill to possess him. And now she could get Stabbington back. A smile spread across her face and she looked away from the mighty duck hunter, eyes searching for the ogre's unmistakable bulk.

"Where's Stabbington?"

"Haven't seen him since we got to the hospital. He was watching the western side. Probably still there," Kennedy suggested. "Ruby, can you take a quick flight over? Tell him we're ready to leave."

By the time the Ornithol returned, all the ducks in the park had flown off and Irash was sitting with Kennedy and Sparkz, animatedly discussing what his first ever meal should be. Arke stood up as Ruby landed, eyes narrowing as she read her friend's body language.

"I couldn't find him anywhere around the hospital."

"He's not used to being his own navigator. I expect he got lost, it's easily done." Kennedy shrugged before standing up and stretching. "Let's split up and find him."

Sparkz started undoing his backpack. "He won't be difficult to spot, I'll head to the south and work back up. Meet up at the taverns on the quay for a beer when we've got him?"

"I'll take the north side of the Apothecarium." Ruby swept her arm around the direction she intended to take with a decisive nod.

"Beer sounds ideal. Arke, you take the west road

heading to the old port, and I'll check the market."
Kennedy pointed at the orc. "Irash, you're with me, I
have a lot of pastries in my pack to keep you going."

The party split up quickly, Sparkz taking to the air
with a grin, his *Jet-You-There* working perfectly, the
engine now equipped with a muffler to keep the noise
down to a medium roar. Ruby's far more classic flight
apparatus took her silently in the other direction while
Irash walked alongside Kennedy towards the bustling
market and Arke headed down the road towards the old
port.

⚔ ⚔ ⚔

As ARKE WALKED, the area became both less affluent as
well as quieter, the houses changing from pristine white
stone to aged wood, a good majority of them leaning
together like playing cards. She ventured into a few
musty taverns to check for any sign of the ogre but only
found some sour-faced locals who silenced their
conversations until she turned around and left again.
She barely paid them any heed as she dealt with the
strange sensation of having no alternate voice in her
head. Going from forty years of having a permanent
companion to silence was more disturbing to her than
any of the dark alleyways she walked down while looking
for Stabbington. All she wanted to do was find him and
re-sign the contract even if he had told her he had learnt
plenty of new songs while he'd been in the ogre's body.

Heading down the narrowing streets, she spotted a
water fountain just off to her left. It was a welcome sight
and she cast a thirsty glance over it, noting that it looked
well maintained – there was nothing dead near it nor
any signs of tampering. Desperately needing to rehydrate,

she ducked down, drinking the cool water with pleasure.

She was just straightening up when something hit her from behind and the world went black.

⚕ ⚕ ⚕

WHEN ARKE WOKE, her head was throbbing, and as she checked in with every part of her body, she realised she was tied very securely to a chair and gagged with fabric that tasted like paint thinner. She blinked and looked around as her vision cleared, seeing a group of men with their backs to her over on the other side of the room, and a large circle painted around her chair, the entirety of it covered in runes. She recognised a few of them from the box that Kayla had used to contain Irash, and realised that whoever these men were, they had put these sigils down to prevent her using magic. They clearly didn't know that right at that moment, the most dangerous thing about her was her hairstyle.

There was no point in doing nothing though, so Arke started rocking on her chair as quietly as she could, trying to tip it over so she could inch her way out of the circle or find something sharp on the floor to cut the ropes that held her. Unfortunately, while her movement had been subtle, the crash she made when she and the chair fell, was not.

"It's awake."

Rough hands grabbed her, quickly hauling her upright and dragging her back into the middle of the circle. That avenue of possibility was now firmly shut, and Arke knew she'd have to let this play out to find another angle. Knowing what they wanted would be a start, but none of them seemed to be interested in talking to her, at least not yet. She could hear movement behind her, but the back of the chair was too tall to see around. Listening hard, she made out that her captors seemed to be opening packets or boxes of some kind. She heard the unmistakable creaking of a lid being levered off a crate and people moving around. Occasionally one would ask another "This goes here?" or "Can you check that's right?" Whatever they were doing, this was their first go. It wasn't a comfort.

"You know what this is?" Finally, one of the men, presumably the leader, came over to stand in front of her, right on the edge of the circle. She could see he had something hidden behind his back as he pointed to the painted lines on the floor with his free hand. "Try some magic. Just to be *sure* you know."

She was absolutely not going to show them that she was running on empty, so shook her head slowly.

"And don't think of trying anything on me. Amulets against everything, fire, weather, ice, women..." He droned on for some time, showing her the multiple charms that were heavy around his neck. He clearly wasn't one to take chances. "FYI – You bust some of your magic out in this circle and it bounces back on you. So feel free to mess your day up even more."

Someone moved behind her and untied the gag. She said nothing, just tried to get rid of the vile taste in her mouth while never taking her eyes off the man in front of her.

"Ready for a little surprise?" He moved his hand around so she could see what he held in it.

The moment she saw what it was, Arke had to work exceptionally hard to hold onto her composure. In the man's hand was a glass sphere, and in that sphere was

Gorki's face. Real time.

"Hello there Arke! Boy oh boy have *we* been looking for *you!* I've been BESIDE myself with worry. Oh no, not worry, that's the wrong word. Anyway, when my people saw you wandering around their city, they made sure to let me know. You're very memorable, a blessing and a curse I suppose."

The halfling harbourmaster seemed to expect a response from her, but Arke simply looked at him impassively and he continued, his expression beyond smug, clearly having a great time now he was the one in charge.

"Well just look how things have turned out. Sitting there on your *chair*, I'm reminded of another day, another chair, another place; but you're not talking any more. Such a shame, I *loved* your smart mouth, especially when you made us look stupid. That gave me such a thrill, I know Kayla would LOVE to be here to talk to you but she's out and about… somewhere."

His eyes bored into her face, clearly trying to find out what she knew about his psychopathic assistant, but Arke said nothing. She was too busy thinking through options and possible outcomes. None of them were looking great at the moment, but she'd dealt with enough arrogant people to know that overconfidence sometimes led to a chance to get away.

"Anyway – a little birdie tells me that you have the company of someone powerful up there," Gorki tapped his temple meaningfully, "and that he's kicked out your demon. It's amazing what you can hear on the radio. We were RIVETED. By the way, thanks for that night where you put our transmitter gem under your oily-fingered friend's bed while he was knocking boots with one of the crew. Great joke, love it; I'll get to him another day. But for now, it's all about you and your malevolent entity. Let's talk Irash. HEY IRASH! NICE DAY! How does it feel not to be able to possess this particular mortal? Must be embarrassing as all heck!"

Arke was busy picturing the ways she could have killed the vile little man back in his office, when a pair of hands suddenly grabbed hold of her head, restraining her tightly. Then, without any warning whatsoever, someone else drove what felt like a piece of pipe into the back of her neck, starting to twist it like a screw, driving it further in.

"Oh go on, don't disappoint me, I had them take your gag out so I could hear you scream. That has to be terribly agonising, doesn't it?"

Even if Arke wanted to answer, she couldn't. All she could concentrate on was the unbelievable pain that was radiating from her skull to the soles of her feet. Every time they twisted it further in, her ears rang with a grinding hum and she could feel her nose starting to gush with blood. She had no idea what they were doing, and she didn't care. At the worst point she wasn't even sure if she was crying out or if the screaming was just in her head.

"Now it's time for the fun to start."

The pain had lessened but Arke knew beyond a doubt she was not having any fun. Her head was still held tightly but at least now no-one was trying to dig any further through her spine.

There was silence for what felt like an age but was probably only a couple of minutes. She finally recovered enough to open her eyes, only to see that Gorki's face had disappeared from the magic sphere though the connection still seemed to be active. Behind her she could sense the men waiting and heard them muttering something, but it was in a language she didn't understand.

"And how ARE we doing, ridding you of Irash?" Gorki reappeared, his expression expectant as he looked at his men.

They replied, still using words she couldn't translate, and his face suddenly clouded over, fury warping his features.

"Of COURSE he's in there! Where else is he? She's the only vessel they use for him!"

"Nothing's coming out, boss. Like nothing but blood."

The harbourmaster's glitteringly malevolent eyes turned to Arke, his tone no longer triumphant but staccato with a hint of desperation. "Still with us? Good, I have questions."

She blinked slowly, trying to muster her strength. "So do I. I have questions about how disappointed you are right now. Is it with yourself? Because we did what you couldn't? And then made you a laughing stock."

Her voice was hoarse but full of every bit of venom she could muster. She'd seen terrible things done by men with the same look in their eyes that Gorki had suddenly acquired and knew she needed to try and buy time, find the loophole, get him to make a mistake. She needed to rally every bit of Arke she could and use it.

"I can see you're confused, so take a few deep breaths, clear your mind. Well, FIND your mind first, or do you need sweet Kayla to find it for you? Shame you don't know where she is — maybe she had a little accident. Nothing to do with the *Warrior* of course. Nothing at all."

As the harbourmaster's expression darkened yet again, Arke let him have a moment for her words to sink in before she continued.

"Back to the tricky Irash question. Have you worked it out yet? Do you need a hint? How about this — did your badly trained monkeys actually think to search me for the chalice?"

There was an awkward shuffling behind her, and Gorki's voice exploded into what was almost a scream. "WHY NOT?"

"You said don't touch it, boss, so we... you know. Assumed cos you said it'd be there that it was."

"You need me to explain it with crayons? I — don't — have — it. It no longer exists. And nor — does — Irash."

Arke wondered if Gorki would actually pass out from the paroxysm of rage that flooded his face. Whatever they had stuck into her neck was suddenly yanked out and thrown to one side with a metallic clunk — thankfully it hurt a lot less leaving than it did arriving.

"He has not left this plane! I have agents, mages, people everywhere!"

"He's gone where you can't touch him." She had nothing to hide, and her words were calm, measured, and entirely honest.

The harbourmaster glared at Arke. Their gazes were drawn together in a long battle of wills as he desperately sought to uncover a lie. However, with the cold dawn of realisation, his expression altered again. His eyes still glittered dangerously but the anger had faded, pure, implacable hatred replacing it.

"I believe you," Gorki said with a slow and deliberate nod.

An arm shot around the Soulbound from behind, snaking around her neck, keeping her chin elevated and holding tight to her left shoulder. Her eyes widened in horror, and at the exact instant of her reaction she saw Gorki's lips twist in an ice bright smile. She'd lived long enough in the shadows to know exactly what was coming but was powerless to resist as with a sudden sharp shock, she felt a blade enter her ribcage on the left side. It was a deadly surgical strike, angled upward, razor sharp, performed by a master.

"Surprised you twice in a day. Life is good. Well, mine is, yours is just – short." Gorki's smile had widened as he was clearly delighting in watching her whole body shudder involuntarily in reaction to the mortal wound. "And I get to watch you die, get to watch as the life, that nasty, dangerous, twisted life of yours leaves your body. It's not quite as good as being there myself but it's a close second. How're you feeling there now? I told them not to kill you too quickly. Didn't want to miss a thing."

Arke's eyes had flickered shut and her head would have dropped forwards had the arm not remained, pinning her upright as she struggled to breathe from the shock of the blade which was twisted as it was withdrawn. This was not how she wanted to go out, tied up like an animal while her enemies gloated. She could feel the blood coursing hotly down her side, soaking through her clothes and dripping to the floor. She would not give him the satisfaction of seeing her last breath. She *would not*.

Heat blasted her body from within, her feral magic reacting, desperately shaking her, provoking her into thought. The only thing that mattered any more was stopping him getting what he wanted. She felt her power at work, giving her energy, doing what it could, reminding her she was not alone. Irash's words back at the hospital echoed in her head and her scar burnt in response, in encouragement, in affirmation. Arke knew what she had to do, there was just time for one last clutch, one last play, but she had to hurry. Her eyes snapped open and she glared defiantly at Gorki who waved a hand in sardonic greeting.

"Ah shame, I was hoping you'd be begging for your life right now. Or at least struggling with the pain. Was the knife too sharp? I told them to use a blunter one so it would hurt more; you can't get good help these days. Hey, whatever your name is, angle me down so I can see the bitch's blood on the floor in the dirt where it belongs."

The man holding the glass sphere obediently tilted it downwards and Arke could vaguely hear the halfling gloating.

"I'm not done yet." Her voice was barely even audible, but she needed to speak. The box of memories she was looking for would not open itself. She needed to rouse her strength with words. "I'm – not – done – yet!"

Her summons worked and Gorki's face was back, looking at her with a wicked smile, doubtless hoping she would give him more entertainment. Her body began to shudder again, but she paid it no heed as she spat her truth at him, her orange magic bubbling hotter with every word that she flung from her lips, with every memory that she forced herself to confront.

"Because when I look at you, you sadistic, creepy, sad excuse of a man, I remember who you remind me of. His name was Jennert, Knight of Thum and he thought he was powerful too. He thought he could do what he wanted. He was way better at this than you because he made me WANT to die to get away from him."

As she spoke, Arke was tearing open the box that contained her memories of that hated man and forcing herself to look at them. Natural magic rushed faster through her body, overcoming the encroaching cold as her heart pumped its own blood to the floor. She looked back at herself and what Jennert had done to her to control her, to use her and finally to try and destroy her. Pressure was building in her head, adrenalin spiking in every cell. It was not enough. She needed more. Arke looked harder, her mind reaching for the last piece. The box within the box. The black bound container she never even wanted to remember existed. She reached in and watched it all happen again, as powerless as she had been the first time. Emotions from those terrible moments overwhelmed her entirely, power bounding stronger than her weakening heartbeat. She could feel herself screaming and with a final lurch of volcanic heat, her untamed magic hit critical mass.

The roiling font of oblivion obliterated the circle of runes as it exploded outwards, the primal force in full flood as it reacted to Arke's tormented memories, blinking her out of her bonds, out of that room, out of their reach, in a blinding flash. It did not stop there, her indescribable pain magically translated into a whirlwind of pressure that tore through the bodies of the men who had tortured her. It melted their flesh from their bones and tore those bones into fragments in an eruption of incredible intensity, rolling through the house, turning timbers into splinters and setting everything ablaze in a fountain of furious destruction.

⚔ ⚔ ⚔

ON A PEACEFUL quay away from all the houses and taverns at the waterfront, Arke lay dying. Stoking her power into its cataclysmic reaction had been the ultimate clutch; she'd had no idea what would actually happen, but Irash's urgent reaction to her rising anxiety in the hospital had made her hope it might be explosive. He'd mentioned her opening boxes of memories then and she hadn't understood what he'd meant, but she had remembered.

She thanked her feral magic for her freedom. It had teleported her away from its eruption in the blink of an eye and given her the chance to bow out on her own terms. Maybe wild did go to wild and it didn't want to ebb away being taunted and laughed at, so chose this quiet place as near to nature as it could manage.

Her legs were numb to her knees and the cold was creeping up her body, making it difficult to concentrate or move. Blackness hovered at the edge of her vision and Arke knew that her time was measured in seconds. She felt strangely relieved, after the life she'd lived and all the ways it might have ended, this was almost a win. She wasn't withering away in a hospital or dying in a gutter. Gorki might have ordered the killing blow, but the orange magic had taken away his final triumph and that was more than enough. She struggled to lift her hand, wiping the blood off so she could look at the scar. Blinking slowly as she fought to focus, Arke realised it had suddenly grown and spread across her palm. New lines had scored into her skin creating the outline of a beautiful tree. Its roots were in the dark, but its head was in the light. And she was in the light, the sun shining brightly overhead even as she felt her life ebb away.

Her hand dropped back on her chest, then slid to the ground as Arke concentrated on the faces of the people she didn't want to leave. It was hard to let them go. She'd never been able to say goodbye and there was so much she'd wished she'd said. She heard a cockerel crow, the sound ringing clear to her ears over the noise of the waves lapping at the jetty. She vaguely knew that tears were running down her cheeks, but she lacked the strength to clear them.

With the last of her energy, Arke set herself free. She sent a message with everything she was, sent it out to the waves, to the wild, to the sun, to the moon. She sent the last beats of her heart, she sent all the love that she'd hidden for so long, she sent her truth, she sent her thanks. Where she was going, she needed none of it, but as the orange magic rippled her energy into the atmosphere, she felt sudden peace flood into her.

She was no longer lying alone on a deserted jetty in a dying port. She was sitting on the deck at night, looking up as he tried to make shapes from the patterns of the stars; she was curled up with him in the sunshine reading her favourite book, and oh so clearly she could hear them say her name in the most perfect chord she'd ever heard. She wasn't alone, she'd never been alone.

A sudden gust of wind ruffled her hair and Arke noticed something move above her. She just managed to angle her head enough to see the corpse of a long dead, hanged man swinging on his gibbet.

Chalice, Hanged Man, Death.

The cycle the tarot cards had predicted was complete, but she didn't even have the energy to care. The coldness reached her ribcage, and she heard every breath begin to rattle in her chest. Darkness claimed her vision and she felt herself falling down and down, all feelings and thoughts left behind as she sank into oblivion.

Arke's scar pulsed once, twice, and then faded to nothing.

Chapter Twenty-Nine
Engage the Clutch

THE FAR NORTH-WESTERN area of Theogenes was once affluent, with fortunes boosted by the magnificent seaport but as the sky trade rose to ascendancy, everything had changed. The harbour became run down and dirty, the ships which docked there grew drab and dangerous to sail in. The rot spread outwards, turning the bustling streets to empty ones and once beautiful homes into rundown shelters.

Ruby had been flying for a long time, scrutinising every road, yard and dead-end street for the missing ogre but had seen no sign of him. Just as she banked towards her last search zone, she noticed a rainbow glimmering in the sunshine over by the main quays, and being a child of Chromatia, she turned towards it, ready to offer her worship.

Then the rainbow moved. Her eyes widened and she flew towards it, wing beats increasing in speed and power as a strange anxiety gripped her. Suddenly, a giant orange explosion shattered the peace near to where the rainbow hovered, and Ruby's insides contracted with fear. She flew faster, throwing every ounce of energy she had into pure speed, desperately praying to Chromatia that it wasn't anything to do with her friends.

⚹ ⚹ ⚹

OVER TO THE east of the main port, Stabbington-Krugg was walking with Sparkz, the pair of them heading towards the new meet-up point. To Stabbington's chagrin, he'd been sitting under a tree in entirely the wrong area when Sparkz had finally found him.

"It is a very busy place, and I did not think there would be two parks so close," the demon had explained. "I am sorry."

"I'm not going to argue about spending more time with my wings," Sparkz had grinned. "Let's go catch up with the others."

"Is it... done?" Stabbington had asked.

"Oh yeah. Guess the body he's got?"

Having no interest in where Irash had gone, the demon had just shrugged.

The search had taken up almost all of Sparkz's fuel, so the pair were on foot, each lost in their own thoughts until the sound of an explosion from the harbour area stopped them dead and they traded worried glances.

"It's probably nothing to do with us." Sparkz frowned. "Surely there's plenty of reasons for things to go bang around here?"

Neither of them were convinced by that, and without any further discussion, they started hurrying towards the port.

They had barely gone a hundred feet before they heard Ruby's unmistakeable voice as the warm winds carried her anguished cry across the rooftops.

"Arke!"

At the first syllable of the terrible shout, Stabbington froze, fear flooding through him. As the second was fading he turned desperate eyes on Sparkz. "Fly me to her, I beg you. Hurry. Please."

"I've got hardly any fuel. We'd get nowhere. Too

heavy." Sparkz checked his tank again, clearly hoping somehow the dial had changed but there were still only dregs left.

The ogre grabbed his shoulder, looking at him intently. "Get – me – to – her."

There was a sudden clatter at his feet and Stabbington the sword lay on the pavement. Krugg, abruptly released from his possession, sat down with a thud, but Sparkz had no time to explain. He grabbed the rapier, breaking every vow he'd ever made about not touching possessed items, tucked it in his belt and rammed the jet pack to emergency power, running into take off as the engine engaged.

There wasn't time to fly high, so Sparkz hugged the rooftops in the most terrifying flight of his life. He took the direct route towards the smoke from the explosion, the engine randomly losing power and nearly smashing them into roofs and walls as the fuel dipped dangerously low.

⚔ ⚔ ⚔

THE ORNITHOL'S SHARP eyes followed the rainbow, not to the source of the explosion but a little distance away. She suddenly spotted her friend, lying perfectly still in a pool of blood and cried out her name with all the volume she could muster. The others would hear her, the others would come. Ruby flew and Ruby begged.

"Chromatia please save her. Save her. Save her!"

She had no breath for anything else. Even those few words burnt in her chest, but she knew she had no choice. She must pray, she must invoke divine intervention, for her keen sight had told her what she already feared.

Arke was dead.

Ruby slammed down on the quay and scrambled to her friend's body, cradling it in her arms, screaming to Chromatia to help.

There was no heartbeat; there was no breath. Arke was cold and Arke was gone. The Ornithol had no *Jumpstart* in her pack and even if she did, she knew by the size of the pool of blood that it would be useless.

Tears blurred her vision as she turned skyward to look for the rainbow, the symbol of her god and the only hope she had left. Grief twisted in her throat, destroying her ability to speak so she was unable to summon more than a broken and discordant shriek as she desperately clutched her friend's lifeless body to her chest.

Suddenly, the world seemed to stop, her own cries silenced for a single second as all around her was the sound of a sweet, melodic chime. She stopped crying, eyes wide in amazement. Glimmering with the brightest of colours, a new rainbow was falling from the sky, surrounding Arke in its heavenly light. This was no time for wailing. She knew she was witnessing the most incredible boon, the rarest of events, spoken of with the greatest reverence among the faithful; the very hand of Chromatia, a sight that only true believers could witness. Her god had listened and was trying to hold Arke to this life while help was found.

Ruby's voice returned with a rush, though it was hoarse with emotion, and she began to pray again. She threw every ounce of magic, belief and hope she had into trying to hold the rainbow in place, knowing it was the only chance she had to save her friend.

✕ ✕ ✕

Arke saw none of this as she sat on one of her chairs, in her cabin on the Warrior. She wasn't sure why she was there. Everything felt normal but also terribly strange at the same time.

The cabin door opened, and a tall man with a friendly smile walked in. There was something eminently likeable about him; he looked interesting, someone she felt she already knew. The fact that he was a little see through and barely three dimensional hardly registered with her at all.

"Well hello there." Sitting opposite her at the table, he picked up a file that she hadn't even noticed was there, a file with her name printed on the front. "Arke, isn't it? Love the name. So, let's see what we have to talk about today."

"Who are you?" she asked curiously.

"I have many names, some of them are even polite." He paused to smile, as if waiting for her to smile back. "I'm the Arbiter, my job is to try and find lost souls a place to go, even though it can be tough sometimes. Mostly, I can sort them out with some god or other who suits their style; I guess that makes me a matchmaker of sorts."

"Souls?"

"Oh yes. I'm afraid the only reason you are here is because your mortal body is no longer in service. It's a shock, I know. Take a few moments while I read all about you."

Arke blinked a few times as his words sank in. Of course she knew that. She'd died. The memory was fuzzy, like viewing the ground from the deck of the ship. The ship. The… Why couldn't she think of the name of the ship?

"It's OK." The Arbiter's voice was soothing, and he handed her a bucket that appeared in his hand from absolutely nowhere. "Being a soul you won't be able to hurl, but holding this will make you feel better about retching.

439

Not my first rodeo. Now, let's get you a placement and you'll feel a whole lot better. This in-between existence takes its toll, that's why we make sure you're somewhere familiar while you wait."

He finally opened the file with her name on it and frowned. It was empty. Almost comically he lifted it up, turned it upside down, shook it, blew on it and slapped it. It remained empty. He looked up, mouth dropping open before getting quickly to his feet.

"Ohhhhh! THAT Arke! Let me just get the boss."

Suddenly his semi-transparent body shimmered, transforming into a fully solid three dimensional one and his tone changed instantly from the scripted version of himself to a more natural way of speaking.

"Arke! Yes of course! Arke. Just sit there, I'll be right back."

The Arbiter virtually sprinted out of the room. Arke turned her head curiously as she felt the memories of her cabin slipping away. As they did the scenery changed, the illusion gradually dissipating. She looked around and saw no rooms or walls, just rows upon rows of people, talking with rows upon rows of semi-transparent Arbiter clones. As soon as one person disappeared into the ether, they were instantly replaced with another.

Looking around and then back down at the table in front of her, she blinked and sighed heavily. The sooner her memory finished fading the better. She wouldn't feel so empty once she'd forgotten they existed.

That melancholy was suddenly displaced by the sound of her name being spoken. Arke frowned and started to concentrate on the location of the voice. She was pretty good at tuning into conversations and blocking out other noises

— the skill had got her out of, as well as into, a lot of trouble in the past. She turned her head, tracking the source to a small group of people standing on a floating platform only a little way above the endless floor of souls. She tried to get up but found that she was unable to move from the chair. So she awkwardly but determinedly took it with her. They should have nailed it down if they didn't want people shuffling around on the furniture.

Arke could hear the entire discussion much more clearly once she positioned herself as close as she could to the platform. She'd been careful not to disturb the other souls but even when she'd almost bumped into one of the tables, there hadn't been any hint that the young woman dressed in rags with her hands clasped in her lap had seen her. Arke craned her neck, wishing she could see over the lip of the floating island but although she couldn't see any faces, she could make out their every word so listened intently to the deeply divided meeting.

"Did no-one know she was coming in? We need to pay more attention!"

"I'm holding the body open, but I can't do it for long."

"This is an excellent chance to make a decision. I vote we should stop this – she's too much of a wild card. We have the perfect moment to pull the plug and no-one the wiser."

"They've done better than YOUR last nominations already. The task is done and they ticked every box, you can't deny that."

"It wasn't done the way we foresaw it!"

"But it is done."

The Arbiter's voice calmly cut through the squabbling. "There is no point in blaming anyone. We need to decide."

Arke's frown only grew deeper as she listened to their

arguments. About her. It was none of their business, whoever they were.

Thus it came to pass that Arke disturbed an entire section of limbo by shouting at a cluster of judgemental strangers that they were being incredibly rude, and that if anyone deserved to make a choice, it was her, since it was her life and to be frank, they sucked at whatever jobs they happened to have because no-one had bothered to nail the bloody chairs down.

Five heads suddenly appeared over the edge of the platform, all looking directly at her. The Arbiter leant his arms on the railing, his warm brown eyes twinkling with what she thought looked a lot like amusement. He pointed at her with a wink and Arke found that she was now able to stand. Naturally, her first move was to climb on her chair and from that more elevated position got just as busy judging them as they were judging her.

"Arke. Are you SURE this is what you want to do?"

She nodded at the Arbiter, because she absolutely did. Firstly, she pointed to him and then the four others with an imperious finger. "Arbiter, Scowling Golf-Gear Guy, Cool Hair Woman, Dismissive Guy In The Really Smooth Suit and The Lady Who Is Trying To Be Stern But Keeps Smiling At Me. I don't know who you are or what you do here. But I want you to send me back to my body because I know I have more to do even if I can't remember what." She blinked as a sudden burst of memory hit her before squaring her shoulders and glaring at them all. "Plus I'm not going to any afterlife without Stabbington." She held up her palm, revealing the tree shaped scar on it. "And while we're having this conversation, you look like you should know something about this." The scar crackled with orange light, prompting her fading memory yet again. "Why do I have this feral, crazy, weird magic? Which isn't that feral, crazy or weird at all, by the way."

"It's not?" The tall woman with the multi-coloured hair looked at Arke in astonishment.

"She remembers him still! Oh, my darlings!" The stern but smiling lady clutched her hands together wistfully.

"Does she ever shut up?" The man in plus fours scowled and folded his arms.

The Arbiter appeared next to Arke, offering his hand to help her down from the chair. "Never saw that coming." His remark was punctuated with a rueful grin and flick of his eyes to the errant furniture. "I'll get them all nailed down tomorrow."

Out of sight, a new and commanding female voice silenced the others instantly. "Arbiter, wipe this memory, send her back with my blessing. We'll keep things on track better from now on – we have to. And Arke. Your magic is exactly as feral, crazy and weird as it needs to be, just – like – you."

The Arbiter winked and leant in. "Looks like you got the job."

⚔ ⚔ ⚔

DEEP IN THE covered marketplace, Irash had been waxing lyrical to Kennedy about the citrus buzz that tingled his lips after his first ever taste of orange juice when the unmistakeable sound of an explosion had suddenly silenced him.

"That…" Dropping to one knee, he pushed his palms onto the flagstones as the shockwave rumbled under their feet… "that's magic." He looked up, eyes wide. "It's Arke's."

Kennedy was gripped with anxiety so instant he was barely able to hear himself speak for the sudden thundering of blood in his ears. "Which way?"

Irash pointed to the right. "HURRY!"

That was all the information Kennedy needed. Accelerating to full sprint, he shoved his way through the crowds of shoppers with desperate determination. The distant sound of Ruby's anguished shout only spurred him to greater efforts. He had to get to Arke, and he didn't care who he needed to push, kick or punch to do so.

As he burst from the market and down onto the road that led toward the port, he knew he was going in the right direction as he began to battle his way through the people running in panic from the blast site.

Dashing down the narrowing streets towards the sea, he smelt the smoke before he saw it. His chest was a burning band of agony and every stride sent red hot daggers searing through his leg, but he forced himself to keep pushing. He couldn't slow down. He had to find her.

The only thing that stopped him was the site of the explosion. Fire raged in the buildings around it, but the epicentre was obvious. The house was only visible by its absence. There was nothing left, not a wall or a door, not a beam or a roof tile. Everything was debris, reduced to ash and the detritus of destruction.

Despite the sweat running down his face, the agonies of his muscles and the pounding of his heart, the instant he saw the devastation, Kennedy felt nothing. The numbness of desperate hope stilled the scene and chilled his mind to icy clarity: he'd heard Ruby's shout, but he couldn't see her here. She must be with Arke so Arke must not be in the rubble.

Shouting Ruby's name, he peered down every alleyway and darted into every open door. He found no trace of her until he dived down the nearest side street and emerged from the smoke onto a road overlooking the port. On any other occasion, his attention would be gathered by the few ships moored there, but at that moment, he saw only two things. One was a seven-foot tall Ornithol, and the other was the rainbow-wreathed body she held in her arms. Arke.

Kennedy sprinted towards them, his strides powered by something beyond himself. He had to get to Arke. He would not lose her. But more than that, he simply *could* not.

Gritting his teeth as he vaulted the barrels by the quay side, Kennedy forced his body far beyond its limits. He thundered down the planked walkway toward its end. He was nearly there, all that was left was just one sharp turn and a final sprint.

From behind him he heard the unmistakable sputtering backfire of Sparkz's jet pack, then silence.

"KENNEDY! GO LONG!"

He turned to see his brother, still airborne, gliding in to land by the barrels he'd leapt over not that many seconds ago. As Sparkz's feet hit the ground, he pulled a familiar rapier from his belt and in one massive over-extension, launched it through the air.

"Stabbington!" Kennedy shouted, the sudden renewal of fading hope flooding his body with one last burst of energy. Seeing the sword coming in fast and high, he leapt to catch it before skidding around the corner and accelerating again.

This was the final stretch.

He was close enough to see everything.

Close enough to see the rainbow around Arke ebbing away.

Not close enough to get the demon blade there in time.

"NOW! THROW HIM NOW!" Ruby bellowed, her voice cracking in desperation.

It was the longest throw of Kennedy's life, and he gave it absolutely everything he had. But just as he released the sword, he felt something in his shoulder tear, and to his horror, he saw the rapier veer off the path he intended. Stabbington was going to land in the water.

The rainbow around Arke was barely a glimmer.

Kennedy dropped to his knees as complete desolation rushed over him. He couldn't watch. It was all his fault.

⚔ ⚔ ⚔

SUDDENLY, A BURST of orange light wreathed the demon blade as it plunged helplessly towards the sea. Blazing with rippling shards of energy, the sword twisted back on course and flashed through the air towards Arke at an incredible rate.

Hitting the centre of the tortured wound in her neck, the rapier dissolved into a swirl of blue smoke which disappeared into the ragged crater, leaving the torrent of orange static to cascade over Arke's body. It rolled over her skin like an ethereal shockwave, the glow visible even through her clothes. Her wounds began to heal as bursts of energy flared like fireworks, creating new flesh, joining the old.

Ruby held her breath as magic flooded the body in

her arms and the incredible power of what was happening stood every one of her feathers on end.

A juddering convulsion shook Arke's frame, and the Ornithol clenched her beak so hard it hurt as she waited, desperate to feel what must come next.

Then there it was, a single shuddering heartbeat. A second followed the first, then another, their resonance growing, forcing every cell to answer their call. But they were slow, still too slow.

"Come on Arke! Come on!" Ruby held her friend at arm's length, the Soulbound's head lolling in a disturbingly dead manner. "YOU'RE NOT EVEN TRYING!"

With a giant effort, Arke's limp body heaved in a massive gulp of air, all of its muscles contracting as life pulsed violently through them. That sudden, explosive movement pushed her away from Ruby in the same moment that her head came up off her chest, her eyes shooting open, orange flames burning brightly in each. Arke took another huge breath and hurled a curse so loud she set a flock of sleeping gulls into panicked flight. Finally, staggering backwards as her weakened legs collapsed, she tumbled straight off the edge of the quay.

And so it was that Arke won her battle against death but lost against physics.

ⅩⅩⅩ

"YOU'RE SAFE, WE'RE ALL HERE. Try to lie still, you've lost a lot of blood."

As Kennedy spoke, Arke felt his gentle hand smooth wet hair back from her face. She blinked slowly as she tried to force her eyes to focus. She was pretty sure she was alive and that was probably good. Everyone else was

OK, that was definitely good. But her body felt entirely alien, it was barely responding to her, and she was so exhausted that she could hardly stay awake. That was not good.

"Can she talk yet?" Ruby's anxious voice sounded nearby and suddenly the Ornithol's blurry face loomed over her. "Arke? Are you alright?"

All her muscles ached, each breath was an effort and everything else was muddled and conflicting. Arke had no idea it was possible to feel so dead when she was clearly alive.

"Fine." Her voice was barely a whisper, the effort to speak almost too much.

"Ah you are more than fine, for I, the legendary Stabbington Bear, am with you once more! You know, of course, that I will never let you forget that poetic moment when I brought you back to life, you cursed some very bad words and fell in the water. It was sublime comedy!"

Arke felt sudden warmth flooding through her as Stabbington announced his return with perfect timing and inimitable style. With a smile not even her exhaustion could conceal, she summoned his blade. The demon sword flashed instantly into existence and settled perfectly into her palm as her fingers automatically tightened around the hilt.

"He's back," Kennedy beamed.

"Like he never left," Arke mumbled, shutting her eyes tiredly, the smile still on her lips.

"No, not like that. There will be new rules: you will always listen to me, and do as I say, and you will never threaten me with your cupboard or clean me with your dirty shirts…"

Stabbington's teasing ceased as she began drifting off to sleep, his voice now softly soothing.

"Rest now, my Arke. I am here, we are together. Everything is as it needs to be."

Somewhere close by and yet so far away, something stirred in the bright darkness and turned towards Theogenes.

Glossary

Aetheric – a concentrated, crystalline form of magic which can be harnessed as a power source. Aetheric crystals are made in Nidea so are both expensive and illegal in Barsia.

Barsian Empire – commonly referred to as Barsia; covering a large landmass, hugely influential until the Night of Terrors where it lost both its capital and its ruler, the Autarch. Now ruled by a High Council of nobles and religious leaders who are focussed only on survival through laws and taxes.

Bonelords – an ancient tribe living in the Greyspine Mountains, known only for their unusual armour and ferocious opposition to outsiders.

Bior – a race of metal constructs who gained sentience during the Night of Terrors. They are all uniform in basic appearance and similar in overall outlook, being loyal and inclined to serve.

Flotilla – a floating anchorage over the north central part of Nidea, below the Barsian border.

Fullport – a small coastal town on the Azure Straits, the hub for Barsia's southern fishery fleet.

Greyspine Mountains – the greatest mountain range in Barsia. Hellish in every way, inhabited by savage tribespeople. No-one in their right, left or central minds would go there.

High Haven – a unique floating city anchored over the Azure Straits on the border between Barsia and Nidea. Free in every way and fiercely protective of its independent status. No laws, no taxes, no guarantees.

Mage – a wielder of magic. Since the Night of Terrors, Barsia requires any mages to be sent to internment camps or officially licenced.

Nidean Empire – commonly referred to as Nidea, located to the south of Barsia. A loose collection of principalities, all united in their use of magic and their distrust of each other. Once a vassal state of Barsia, now fully independent, Nidea is only one charismatic ruler short of declaring war.

Night Of Terrors – the night when Great Barsia, the capital of the Barsian Empire, and everyone within a hundred miles were removed from existence by a huge magical explosion. The shockwave that surged outwards from the epicentre killed and created in equal measure. Two hundred years later, Barsia is still trying to recover, unsanctioned magic is now illegal and the area around Great Barsia still an irradiated swamp.

Levenbrandt – the Bastion City of northwest Barsia. A small and picturesque but ancient city isolated by geography, Levenbrandt's ruler is not considered powerful enough for a seat on the High Council.

Orbella – a truly ancient mountainside city, constantly vying with Tattenberg for capital status but always falling short due to its constrained size. This is a city of modern marvels, clean air and deep thinkers.

Orbiculum – a magical way to kick down doors between planes. Very much banned in Barsia.

Ornithol – a race of birdlike people who came into existence after the Night of Terrors. There are as many types of Ornithol as breeds of bird in Barsia. They all look like giant versions of their parent bird, with the addition of humanoid arms and legs.

Soleya – the religious capital of Barsia. Situated to the southeast of the Empire, Soleya houses the most temples and cathedrals of any city anywhere. Soleya is strongly ruled and deeply conservative.

Soulbound – selling your soul to a powerful entity in return for wealth, power or other gains makes you a Soulbound. The contracts are usually long, detailed and absolutely binding.

Tattenberg – the capital of Barsia since the Night of Terrors. Tattenberg is 'where work is life'. A hive of industry, its skies are always grey with smog, its innovative might and productive factories second to none.

Theogenes – situated to the southwest of Barsia. A beautiful coastal city, bathed in perpetual sunlight. The main city is perfectly designed and heavily regulated.

Tiax – a race of fox-like people. They range from nearly hairless and very humanoid to almost feral looking. Yes, the Night of Terrors again.

Vonti – a race of sentient snails with vaguely humanoid characteristics. Night of Terrors, you say? You'd be right. Almost unnaturally attuned to the natural world, they're slow and deliberate, in general, they have found Barsian life far too fast moving for their tastes.

Warrior – the best ship ever.

Coming Soon
Memory's Claws
The Barsian Job: Part 2

"WE SERVE THE Autarch."

Dust carpeted the Faithful as thickly as the Faithful carpeted the floor at the end of the cavernous chamber. Their woven words of worship were the only sounds that broke the endless years of silence. They were dead, yet death could not claim them while He commanded their obeisance. Their leathered tongues rasped the ceaseless chant while their withered eyes stared unblinking towards His infinite magnificence.

"We serve the Autarch."

His bright darkness burned far above the Faithful as He watched and waited. He who was suspended in the hollow between always and never, the haze between reality and possibility, caged in the absence of the end.

He would be free. His will would be done.

He had laced His web meticulously. He had baited His lines and cast them wide.

He would be ready.

"We serve the Autarch."

And then it came. The briefest flare of energy from the world outside. The most sublime of signals. A challenge. A promise. That sweet taste on His lips.

The Autarch shuddered with a surge of memory. Rivers

of static flowed from His bright darkness, crackling torrents of expectation that cascaded over the maelstrom of platforms suspended like stepping stones in the centre of the chamber.

"They are within Our grasp. Go now, learn more, prepare them. I await." His order resonated around His domain, yet He did not speak.

A grotesque creature slid out from behind His shattered throne. Finger-like tentacles clustered randomly on its obsidian skin, while arms that had once been legs hung limply at its sides, toes curling and uncurling in hesitant rhythm. Where a face should be, grey smoke shimmered over a shiny, featureless void. When it spoke, its voice was hollow, lipless words ripped from airless lungs. "I could send others and remain at your side, Your Majesty."

"YOU ALONE." The retort smashed explosively into the creature's consciousness, and it reeled, gibbering backwards in instant submission.

A spectral hand loomed above the prostrated servant, one slender finger pinning it to the stone platform. "They must not be harmed. Stay unseen, seed their dreams. And bring – them – here."

The creature flickered as grey energy wreathed its form, twisting and warping it beyond comprehension before it disappeared in a hiss of heavy magic.

The throne room boomed with anticipation. Years of preparation were coming to fruition. On the wall in the ante chamber, a lone clock began to tick once more.

"We serve the Autarch."

Acknowledgements

You CAN KEEP your literary muses, for I have the five Hamsters of the Apocalypse! My agents of chaos, love, and marmite on toast have never stopped encouraging me to embrace anarchy and weirdness at every possible opportunity. They're my test subjects, problem solvers, world enhancers, support crew and mic drop connoisseurs. Rory, Jamie, Mitch, Nick and Ian, I can never thank (blame) you enough. Now get back to the wheel, the electricity won't run unless you do.

Editing would probably get on my nerves, and to be fair, I probably get on my editor's nerves. However, every live wire needs an earth and Francesca Tyer has been just that for *Destiny's Boot*. To put it another way, if I was adamant that I wanted to swim the Channel, she would be in the support boat with snacks and a compass, shouting such gems as "France is this way!" "Where are you going?" "Was that a kraken?" "What do you mean, Atlantis?" I am incredibly grateful for her voice of reason, technical knowhow and exceptionally glad I couldn't see her eyes rolling as she read the first draft.

A special thank you to Nataly Zhuk whose incredible artwork graces the front cover as well as two illustrations inside the book. Hugely talented, meticulous and patient, I love working with her to bring my worse than mediocre designs into bright and brilliant images. My sketch for the cover was so bad I had to label it 'ship' 'mountains' 'sword' in case she thought she was drawing a narwhal flying towards some triangles and a stick. She was too kind to comment on my lack of artistic talent as she produced her masterpiece and now that's all done, we're plotting the cover for the second book in the series!

Other thanks go to my dedicated writing support dogs, Bruce and Dizzy. They show true devotion to their self-appointed positions – sprawling on the sofa – while I work at my desk, and make sure I take regular breaks by rushing outside to bork at delivery drivers, walkers and absolutely nothing at all.

Lastly, a big thank you to my publishers, my beta readers and all my wonderful friends who have been so excited and supportive right from the start.

www.fjmitchell.co.uk